HANGING 

I swam up out of the black depth of nonexistence, propelling myself mindlessly toward the light of day. I felt a tightness, a panicked thundering, the slickness of sweat. Light: I squinted painfully in the glare, reaching out wildly for stability as the earth swayed under my feet. My hand encountered only open air.

I hung suspended over a chasm. Far below me, a thundering cataract crashed and frothed within its steep, rocky ravine. Like a spider stretching its thread between two twigs, I crouched in a blanket attached to a rope that stretched between two pinnacles on either side of the gaping chasm. I looked wildly around myself, as if seeking someone from whom I could demand an explanation. What had happened? How had I come to be here? But no one else shared that precarious basket where Alasil had abandoned me in the midst of some personal adventure.

A faint sound brought my attention to the rope, and I noticed that, strand by strand, it was breaking.

THE
WATCHER'S
MASK

LAURIE J. MARKS

DAW BOOKS, INC.
DONALD A. WOLLHEIM, FOUNDER
375 Hudson Street, New York, NY 10014

ELIZABETH R. WOLLHEIM
SHEILA E. GILBERT
PUBLISHERS

First Printing, August 1992

1 2 3 4 5 6 7 8 9

DAW TRADEMARK REGISTERED
U.S. PAT. OFF. AND FOREIGN COUNTRIES
MARCA REGISTRADA,
HECHO EN U.S.A.

PRINTED IN THE U.S.A.

For my beloved
Deb

Chapter 1

In the river city of Akava, as the harvest moon grows round bellied in the sky, scarlet flowers suddenly bloom on the walls in the city. Every parent picks great armloads of these fragrant blossoms and makes them into garlands with which to bedeck their children on the feast day of Iska. They take their children by the hands and parade in the streets with them. Pipers and drummers dressed in harlequin patchwork, trailing clouds of holiday ribbons from their coats, lead the parade. Behind them march the children: from the five-year-old too young to let go of her mother's hand, to the young adolescent, who glances through his eyelashes to see if the girls are watching him.

The parade follows the twists and turns of the narrow, cobbled streets, and out onto the boardwalk which edges the bending shoreline of the river Iska. The last dock, which is known as Iska's dock, pierces deep into the river's current. Down this dock the pipers go, with parents and children following them. Then the parents take hold of their children and throw them into the river to drown.

This year, it had proven impossible for me to avoid Akava during the feast of Iska, though I did hope to leave town tomorrow, before the drowning of the children. An idiot burgher named Avari Paza had come calling at my rooms. Being pressed for time, I hurried him out into the streets with me.

The Race Day crowd parted before me like two hands unclasping. At either side of the narrow, cobbled road, brightly painted shopfronts with diamond-paned windows bore the weight of balconies jutting like a woman's heavy breasts from the buildings' flat torsos. Among decorations of garlands and bunting, servants banned from attending the pending footrace craned their necks, peering toward the waterfront where the race would soon be run. Excited book-makers worked the crowd, shouting their odds and waving yellow slips of paper. Vendors balancing heavy trays of breads and sweets on their heads danced gracefully among the street's obstacles, hoarsely sing-ing their wares.

The idiot burgher purchased for me a round loaf of bread, with a whole egg nestled in the crisp dough. It is impossible to eat while wearing a full mask, so I gave the bread to a passing child, who dropped it in the gutter as soon as he thought I wasn't looking.

I interrupted the man's nervous chatter to say coldly, "The practice of ritual drowning has always offended me."

"But we must feed the river god," protested Paza, looking nervously around himself as if he hoped that somehow no one would recognize him. "If we let Iska go hungry, then the river might flood its banks, or a boat might be overturned. To lose two or three small children instead . . . it is a small price to pay."

"The river still floods every year," I said. "Boats are still overturned every year."

"Think of how much worse it would be if we had not offered Iska the children!"

Well, the people of Akava are known far and wide to be fools. And how could they be anything else, when for hundreds of years every child with even the faintest spark of intelligence or creativity has drowned in Iska's embrace? Yet I persisted in my questioning of the burgher, more for sport than for knowledge. "Is there no one who protests the tradition? No one who considers it cruel?"

"Oh, madam, it is not cruel at all. The children spend all summer preparing for the event. When they safely reach the shore, all their relatives present them with gifts of toys and candy."

"And what gifts are given to the children who drown?"

"But it happens so rarely! And only to weaklings, who would always have been a burden to their families."

This complete lack of vision so infuriated me that I turned my blank, eyeless mask to face him. Through the veiled eyeholes I watched him bite his tongue.

There are two cardinal rules in dealing with the Separated Ones: first, never ask for help. And second, never argue. In the short time that we had been in each other's company, this man had broken both of these rules. That a man of such limited perception could have been a serious contender to be town mayor, even of Akava, the town of fools, strained the imagination. Of course, now that he had been seen publicly in my company, his political career was over.

He cowered in my shadow like a beaten dog as I led the way down the narrow street to the wide boardwalk, where the footrace would be run. On either side of the boardwalk people pressed, cursing and sweating as they jockeyed for a better view of the racecourse. Women in baggy trousers and knee-length tunics edged with broad bands of embroidery and men in their tighter breeches and gathered shirts pushed and shoved and shouted good-naturedly at each other.

Through the cracks in the boardwalk I could see, two bodylengths below, the flowing brown water of the hungry river. Pierced by docks and jetties, ridden by high-prowed boats with their sails tightly furled, the water spread like a giant ruffled blanket to the far shore.

The Iska River still smelled faintly of the high mountains, where, in a desert of snow, the crystalline springs which are its source first break through the frozen stone. In crashing cascades and spectacular waterfalls the river had bolted out of the high mountains. Here, in the middle plains, it flowed more civilly. Soon, it would crash down mountainsides once again, as it dropped at last to sea level, where it would break into a thousand streams like the veins in the back of a hand, to feed the dense jungle which grows in the fetid heat of the delta of Ipsenum.

Through the delta, across a hundred delicate bridges, the Emperor's steam engine belched and rumbled along the skirts of the ocean. Having completely encircled the island empire of Callia, the engine's journey would end at Ashami, the Emperor's city. There, too, my own journey would soon end, after half a year's wandering throughout the middle plains.

The long summer lay behind me, like a lengthy and pointless play which had finally exhausted itself into autumn's closing scenes. Soon I would go home to the comfort of my cluttered rooms and the echoing marble chambers of the library. Soon I would hear the caged nightingales singing throughout the night, and I could walk unmasked through the lush gardens of the Separated District, where it is always spring.

A man who did not move quickly enough out of my path flinched as my mirror flashed in his eyes when I nudged him aside. Like the burgher, he would spend a sleepless night tonight, wondering if he were cursed, or condemned to the mysterious death which often follows in the wake of a Separated One's visit.

The crowd began to roar with anticipation. The runners must have appeared at the broad red starting line painted across the boards. I did not turn my head to look. I approached some ramshackle, heavily decorated bleachers, which shook and trembled under the weight of the region's finest and most overdressed citizens. A full quarter of those on the bleachers suddenly decided they had other business to attend to and vacated their seats as I approached.

During the last twenty years that I have wandered the middle plains of Callia, I have become a master of manipulation. I wield influence and intimidation as skillfully as any master swordfighter wields her weapon. Only rarely do any of my kind resort to violence to achieve our goals. Yet people curse us and call us knackers behind our backs, as if death were our only business. I am accustomed to engendering such revulsion by my very presence. I rarely notice it anymore.

I chose a seat. Avari Paza sat next to me, responding with a miserable glare to the many startled glances that focused on him. "Madam," he began in a brave fury.

"Which one is this Agamin Oman?" I asked, as if I did not know him on sight, and it had only been by accident that we sat so close to him.

The burgher stammered, "To your right and up three tiers. The older man, dressed in scarlet—"

"Point him out for me."

"But, madam, surely he will then guess that . . ."

"Are you trying to teach me my business?"

The fact that I did not like the man seemed to have finally penetrated his awareness. He pointed an unsteady finger. With everyone in the bleachers overtly or covertly staring at myself and my escort, the gesture could hardly have been missed. The dour, preoccupied expression on Agamin Oman's face did not alter, though the slender, white-skinned lad at his side bleached white as a corpse. Beside me, the burgher, having identified himself before the entire town as one who does business with the Separated Ones, collapsed in upon himself, like a coat tossed into a corner.

Renewed shouts from the starting line told me that the first race of the Emperor's Concourse was about to begin. Hopeful runners from all across Callia journeyed here, dreaming of the fame and fortune which might be won by running the twelve races of the Concourse. The winner of the final race, run in the Ashami Arena before the Emperor himself, would be named a champion and return home a hero. But at each of the twelve races a substantial purse might be won, making a young runner's fortune.

Many times I had watched the Ashami Championship race, where, after months of competition, the runners' gloss of excitement had long since worn away. They ran the race with their heads, not their hearts; and experience rather than passion won the victory. Surely this first race of the Concourse would be much different.

From my vantage I could soon see the distant cluster
of leading runners, closely tracked by a second clot of
contenders. Behind them struggled a ragtag trail of
others. It was these, the most unlikely to win, who
would be weeded out during the Concourse so that by
the time of the Ashami race the field would be narrowed down to fewer than ten experienced runners.
Running among the packed spectators, the contenders
pushed and jostled each other, struggling for the lead.
One fell heavily, no doubt tripped from behind. Smelling blood, the crowd roared their approval. With each
step they took, the pack leaders changed position. Two
exchanged punches. A spray of spilled ale splashed
over them, and it looked about to become a free-for-
all.

Already, two-thirds of the race had been run, and
the runners could now see the finish line. They lowered their heads and truly began to run, arms pump-
ing, feet thundering on the boardwalk like drums. The
crowd screamed, but I had already lost interest. The
winner would be one of the town-sponsored runners,
like every year. I scanned the rest of the trailing pack
disinterestedly, already considering the plans I needed
to make for tonight's execution.

I could have been the only one who noticed her, as
she escaped from the trailing knot of second level contenders: A compact woman, barrel-chested and long-
legged, with beaded locks of hair trailing for an arm's
length behind her. She ran with her eyes half closed,
her face slack and loose, her palms open at her sides.
She seemed to float among the other runners, her bare
feet soundless on the polished wood, her powerful
thighs propelling her so lightly across the ground that
she might have been flying like a bird. Soft as a shadow,
she slipped into the first group. In a moment she
emerged from that group as well, as casually as an
eagle dives through a cloud, and pulled ahead of them.
Two strides, and three. The other frontrunners strained
behind her, like hounds chasing their prey, one of them
reaching out with his hand to try to grab at her trailing

hair. But she floated arrogantly across the blue line, the clear winner.

Immediately, the shouting crowd surrounded the woman, and I could no longer see her. That barrel-shaped torso suggested an origin in the high mountains. The unique styling of her hair should have identified her tribe, but the style was unfamiliar. Her running tunic, plain white with a green sash, had a certain anonymity in its very plainness. Puzzled, I turned to my crushed companion, who had scarcely lifted his head to watch the race.

"Who was that runner, the winner?"

He shrugged. "Some tribal girl."

"Which tribe?"

"How am I to know? I did not manage the race!"

I turned away from him in disgust, and collared an unfortunate townswoman, who had been pushed too close to me by an excited group of youngsters. "What was that runner's tribe?"

Her face pale with fear, she stammered, "Asakeiri."

"Asakeiri!" They have never run in the races before!"

"Yes, madam," she said, clearly not wishing to extend this unwelcome conversation.

"And her name?"

"It was . . ." she stumbled, clearly too frightened to think clearly. "Adline," she finally said desperately. "Adline Asakeiri."

The Asakeiri people had been thorns in the Emperor's side for thirty years, ever since they turned an authorized representative of the government out into the snow, where he should have perished. Since then, no amount of threats, armed intimidation, and all-out attack had succeeded in forcing the Asakeiri to allow outsiders to enter their land. The army had blockaded all the known pathways into their lands (a rugged and lonely watch it must have been for those soldiers, in so isolated and miserable a country), but the Asakeiri, as they did not depend upon outside trade for their survival, had not relented. Of course, the Emperor's army would not have hesitated to enter their communities and simply wipe them out, but the nomadic people had proven impossible to find.

So, for thirty years, while the rest of the isolated communities of Callia were physically united by the Emperor's road, bridge, and train builders; and were subverted and subjugated by the Separated Ones, the Asakeiri alone remained untouched, isolated by choice and decree, and unremittingly proud and independent in that isolation. To the other peoples who often found it easier to regret what was lost than to embrace what was gained, the Asakeiri had become a symbol of rebellion. But for an Asakeiri native to run the Concourse—that might be taken as an act of sedition.

I let my informer go before she fainted. Meanwhile, Paza, taking advantage of inattention, had slipped away into the crowd. I stood on the shaking bleachers, watching over the dispersing crowd, hearing the faint sound of music. I climbed down from the bleachers at last, and followed the boardwalk to the dockmaster's office, where I wrote a short dispatch to the Emperor's Secretary, Aman Abad, who is also the Commander of the Order of Separated Ones. The message would probably arrive only a day or two ahead of me, but it was essential that it be known quickly that an Asakeiri woman had won the Akava footrace. Of course, I had written the death warrant for a gifted and surprising athlete, which was a pity. But the Asakeiri people should have known better.

Having visited the street where Agamin Oman lived, and checked on my horses where they were stabled, I did not return to my rooms until nearly sunset.

I could not wait to get out of my cloak and mask. The chambermaid, hurrying with her taper to light the lamps for me, gave a squeak of surprise as a pale face appeared in the shadowed corner. "You may go. Give me the taper," I said. She was only too happy to leave the room. I finished lighting the lamps, revealing a young man who stood in the corner, with a velvet cap crushed in his nervous fingers. His skin was as white

as bleached linen, whiter, even, than when I first saw
him, where he stood beside Agamin Oman, as my idiot burgher pointed his condemnatory finger. Even in
Ashami, where outlander blood is not completely un-
common, skin so pale is a rare and startling sight.

"Did your father send you here?" I asked.

"My father?" The young man's clutching hand
broke the cap's jaunty feather as color flooded his face.

I opened the door and waited for the boy to go out.

"My *sponsor*," the boy said haughtily.

"Your sponsor, then. Did he send you?"

"No. And I did not tell him my plans."

I nodded noncommittally, though secretly it pleased
me to learn that Oman had not sent this helpless child,
like a tasty young pig to the canny jaws of a wolf. The
boy's eyes scanned my mask. He made his living by
anticipating desire, but with my features hidden, he
could not even begin to guess my thoughts. I tapped
my fingers on the knob of the open door, to give him
a clue. I could have ejected him more forcefully, but
sometimes it amuses me to pretend that there is a human being hidden behind my mask. Encouraged, perhaps, by the fact that I had not yet behaved like a
monster, the boy crushed the brim of his cap beyond
any hope of recovery and cried, "Why must you harm
him? He is a good man!"

With the heel of my polished boot I tapped the door
shut. The boy flinched at the sound of the latch catching, and fell back before me as I crossed the room to
lean over him. "It is a rare thing for a Separated One
to give advice, so listen carefully. Good people are
those who put their personal desires behind them and
set out to serve the needs of the land. But Agamin
Oman has set his face against the Emperor. Therefore,
he is pitting his own will against the will of the entire
land. Though he may indeed be a kind and honorable
man, he is not good; not at all. My advice to you,
little man . . ."

The lad had backed as far from me as he gracefully
could, and now he jumped only a little, like an unbro-

ken colt, as I patted his shoulder. "My advice is that you find yourself another patron. And, incidentally, that you learn the foolishness of trying to make a bargain with a Separated One."

The impetuous child grasped me by the sleeve as I turned away. "But lady, it is no *bargain* I am offering you."

"Oh, no? I thought you had come here hoping I would bed you in exchange for Oman's life?"

The boy had the grace to blush once again. No trollop he, but a boy truly in love with his man. Such a shame, really. I eased my sleeve out of his grip. "Sit down."

He sat in the overstuffed chair, the best the inn had to offer, with not even a smudge of dirt staining its upholstery. I poured a glass of wine at the sideboard and brought it to him, setting it onto the table beside him when I saw that his hands were shaking. "I am going into the next room. See that I am not disturbed. When the maid comes back to lay the fire, order a supper for both of us."

He set down the destroyed lump of cloth which had been his cap, and clasped his shaking hands in his lap. "Yes, madam."

I took one of the lamps into the bedroom, and firmly closed the heavy wooden door so that the boy would not be able to overhear me. I stripped off my cloak and hood and sat at the dressing table with a sigh. The sitting room had still retained some of the heat of the warm day, but in here it was cool, smelling faintly of dust, strewing herbs, and lamp oil. I had taken over the best room in the inn, which I did not doubt the innkeeper had hoped to rent out to a rich trader or shopkeeper for the feast of Iska.

Moving the lamp so it would better illuminate my face, I took off my mask. By autumn, when I have worn mask and robes for six months or more, I begin to feel a strange sense of expectation when I remove the mask each night, as if I will have a great insight, or something important will be revealed. But this night, as with all others, I saw only my familiar face:

Broad forehead, narrow cheeks, and thin, parsimonious lips, cold, intelligent eyes, smooth, richly colored skin, like fine black farm soil. Around this piecework face, my overgrown hair rose like a leafless thornbush, crushed but not subdued by the weight of the hood.

I am Jamil, but few know me by name. My greatest talent is a gift for taking small pieces of information and deriving from them the larger truth, or guessing on the basis of small events what shape the future will take. In twenty years, I have overturned fifteen governments. At home in Ashami, I am a scholar and a teacher, and Aman Abad frequently calls upon me to assist with the administration of his ever increasing black-robed army. On the road, I am a symbol, a ghost, a visitor more feared than death or plague. Within the Order of Separated Ones, I am one of the eldest, closer in age to forty than I am to thirty.

To all of us there comes a time of despair in our youth, when we realize how far we are indeed separated from the true heart of human experience. This despair I had experienced, survived, and forgotten. As I grew older, I experienced a new despair, which haunted me, like the ghost of a dead dog following at my heels, for most of a year. It was an existential despair, a kind of a silence within my souls, as I asked myself my identity and my purpose, and I could not articulate any answers. This despair, too, I have survived, though it is the same despair which has driven so many of my fellows to madness.

Now, by virtue, it seems, of simple survival, I had become a ranking member of the Order, second only to Aman Abad, who in turn answers only to the Emperor himself. Many times, Abad had offered to take me out of the field entirely, for he is growing old and looks to me as his successor, and wishes I would take more of his burdens upon my own shoulders. Perhaps, I thought, as I gazed at myself in the illuminated mirror, this would be the year I finally agreed.

For the second time today, someone had come to me, begging me for what they thought was their heart's desire. But I am no spirit in a bottle who can satisfy such complex hungers with the wave of a hand. When I say yes to them, I am always lying, and they always know that I am lying. Yet they come to me anyway. In their hopelessness, are they deceiving themselves into believing that, beneath my many masks, there is something other than emptiness where my heart should be?

Even for a woman with two souls and no heart, it can become a burden over the years, to have disappointed, betrayed, broken the hearts of, or destroyed so many people. So I have this weariness, that is all: as if I were a peddler too heavily burdened by the wares of my profession.

I lifted the silver mirror which still hung at my neck. "Alasil," I said. In a moment, a face appeared there: not my own face, which I could still see in the expensive glass mirror of the dressing table, but the face of my other soul, my other self. Though we look very like each other, the difference in our spirits so alters the cast of our features, that I doubt anyone could mistake one of us for the other.

Alasil is indeed my mirror self. If I am ice, then she is fire; if I am discipline, then she is action. She is a master poisoner, a deadly knife fighter, a passionate and occasionally indiscriminate lover. She tells long and complicated stories which can keep an audience spellbound for hours. She loves rich food, fine wine, and silk clothing. If I gave her free rein, she would spend every night in the brothels and dance halls, carousing until dawn.

"What dreams?" I said to her, as I always say. The long periods that she spends in oblivion are like sleep to her, full of such vivid dreams that she sometimes hates to awaken.

"I dreamed of a house full of staircases. There were many rooms, and all of their doors were open, except for one, which was locked. When I put my ear to that door, I heard a sighing, as if the sleeper within were about to awaken."

I do not understand Alasil's dreams, and she knows it. I think this is why I keep asking her to recount

them, and why she always obliges, smiling slyly to
herself. I allow her to keep many secrets from me; I
cannot afford to break her lively spirit.

"There is a boy for you in the sitting room, and
supper will arrive soon. You will have to wear the half-
mask while you are with him."

Alasil shrugged. Wearing a mask while seducing a
frightened boy whose patron she was about to assassinate would be a great sport to her. She also would
enjoy the rich supper that the boy would have ordered,
while I would have been satisfied with only some bread
and cheese and a glass of wine. I do not mind missing
her pleasures. When I give quarter to Alasil, I do not
simply sleep, as she does. I am extinguished. I welcome this lack of existence even more than she wel-
comes her dreams. It is so rarely that I get to rest.

I explained to Alasil what she needed to accomplish
this night. She would assassinate Agamin Oman
quickly and efficiently, and spend the rest of the night
exploring the Feast of Iska's offerings. The concerts,
parties, orgies, and street brawls would provide op-
portunities for every imaginable pleasure. After such
a night, Alasil would stay content for months to come.

"What clothes do you want to wear?" I asked her.
She chose the blood red silk with the black piping. I
washed away the day's sweat and changed clothes, as
the boy in the sitting room called diffidently, "Madam,
the supper has arrived."

I tied a wicked dagger to my belt, tucked in a pistol,
and slid a second knife and the blowpipe into my boot.
Tonight's assassination would be by poison, but I liked
Alasil to be prepared, should something go wrong. I
laid the half-mask atop the dressing table, so Alasil
would remember to put it on. Then I lifted the silver
mirror once again.

"It will be a fine night for you," I said. "I hope
you enjoy it to the fullest."

I felt that slipping begin, the chaotic overlay of my
selves, a familiar confusion of passions and silences
and unrevealed secrets, and then the oblivion welcomed me: the peace of emptiness, the absence of ex-

istence. A thousand times I have entered that oblivion, and a thousand times I have awakened in bed the next morning, as rested and refreshed as if after a good night's sleep. I had no clue, no flash of intuition, that this time something had gone terribly wrong. But, oh, it had.

Chapter 2

I swam up out of the black depth of nonexistence, propelling myself mindlessly toward the light of day. I felt a tightness, a panicked thundering, the slickness of sweat. Light: I squinted painfully in the glare, reaching out wildly for stability as the earth swayed under my feet. My hand encountered only open air.

I hung suspended over a chasm. Far below me, a thundering cataract crashed and frothed within its steep, rocky ravine. Like a spider stretching its thread between two twigs, I crouched in a basket attached to a rope that stretched between two pinnacles on either side of the gaping chasm. I looked wildly around myself, as if seeking someone from whom I could demand an explanation. What had happened? How had I come to be here? But no one else shared that precarious basket where Alasil had abandoned me in the midst of some personal adventure.

A faint sound brought my attention to the rope, and I noticed that, strand by strand, it was breaking.

I grasped hold of the rope and pulled on it to move myself toward the nearest edge of that rocky canyon, but the rope popped alarmingly as a dozen strands gave way at once under the added strain. For now, the basket hung over water—which might be deep and might be shallow, and was certainly full of rocks—but water, nonetheless. The farther I moved toward safety, the farther I moved myself away from the water, toward the boulders which clustered at the river's edge. Which did I want to choose: the chance that I would survive the fall if I landed in the water, or the chance that I would make it to the canyon's edge before the rope broke? A beggar's choice.

Thin as a child's wail in a cold night, a voice called from the far escarpment. There I could make out the scar of a treacherous pathway, and a rickety platform where I must have first entrusted my life into this mildewed basket hanging from its rotten rope. Huddled by the platform, a pallid shape crouched, as if dizzied by the precariousness and height of the perch. Once again he cupped his hands around his mouth and hollered, but the abyss swallowed up his words.

I put my own hands around my mouth and cried, uselessly, as there was nothing he could do about it, "The rope is breaking!"

The pale boy leaned forward, holding a hand behind his ear.

"The rope is breaking!" I cried once again.

Obviously misunderstanding me, he grasped the rope where it was tethered and gave it a tentative tug.

They are all fools in Akava, I thought hopelessly, as the last strands of the rope shattered like glass on stone.

The broken rope lashed wildly, like a coachman's whip. The boy's face, sullen with shock, white as a bone, froze in my vision, and then suddenly disappeared. My stomach pressed into my throat. The sharp mountain clarity of the canyon's cliffs seemed to blur and swoop wildly skyward. The wind snatched a cry out of my throat and flung it carelessly away. A thought crashed into my mind like stone through ice. "I am going to die." I fell, and I fell.

The basket shattered around me, and the water hit me like an avalanche of stones. I blacked out. In a spray of water, choking desperately for air, I regained consciousness. My head cracked against a rock, and I blacked out again. I regained consciousness underwater, with my leg caught in a crevice between stones, and the wild current battering my shoulders rhythmically against another jagged boulder. I floundered like a fish in a trap, and with a desperate jerk tore my leg free. The current threw me into the boulder, and I scrabbled madly for a handhold. Half-drowned, gasping with cold, I managed to get my head above water for a breath of air before the cataract tore me loose. The current flung me from stone to stone; here holding me under water until my vision disappeared in a black curtain, there sawing my body over sharp stones. I fought the river doggedly, though I was like a mouse in the paws of a tiger. I fought for one more breath of air.

It was only by chance that my flailing arm lodged into the crotch of a tree limb. I hung there, scarcely conscious, legs still trailing in the heartless grip of the mad river. Then I began to cough, and the air burned into my lungs. The river god had been cheated of his victim.

To drag myself out of the water and onto the rocky shore seemed an impossible task. I leaned my head wearily upon the soggy bark of the tree, and watched my blood leak away in delicate red trails. The rags of my clothing flapped like the scarlet wings of a bird. Maybe I will just let go and let the river have me, I thought. It seemed a sensible choice, given the overwhelming alternatives which had already begun to loom at the edges of my imagination.

I heard, far away, a voice shouting, and it gave me a little hope, enough to make me claw with numbed fingers for a better grip on the tree limb, and drag myself a finger's breadth or two farther out of the water. I rested again. The sun hung low in the sky, and shadow filled the canyon. A cold wind washed over my sodden body, and suddenly I began to shudder. Then the pain hit me.

It could not get worse than this, I thought after a while. I flung my hand as far as I could reach, grabbed hold of whatever solid thing I could find there, and jerked myself firmly out of the water.

* * *

I heard a voice. Urgently it called: "Ishamil!"

"Ishamil is lost," I said. "She is lost, she is drowned, she is lost."

"Ishamil!" the voice cried.

"Ishamil is lost," I said.

Blood trailed across the golden stone. Remotely, as if it had no relevance to myself, I examined this smeared trail, which marked my passage from the water's edge to the rocky nook which now gave me a modicum of protection from the wind. I did not clearly remember traversing the stone. The flames of sunset burned in the sky now. Here in the cleft of the canyon, darkness had long since gathered.

"Ishamil!" the voice cried again.

"Ishamil is lost!" I screamed irritably. Then I asked myself, Who is Ishamil?

I lifted my head painfully from the pillow of my arms. Everything hurt: my neck, my scalp, my face, and all the contents of my skull. Breathing deeply to try to avert another faint, I raised my head carefully so I could gaze at the cliff looming above me. A spray of pebbles and dislodged soil rebounded down the side of the canyon, evidence of another person's presence on the trail above.

"The rope is too short!" he cried.

I would have recognized that rope anywhere. Even if I were capable of climbing it, after being so battered by the river, how could I forget how that rotten cord had betrayed me? As for Agamin's boy, the canyon walls would already have defeated any of his attempts to scale them, if he had in fact made any attempt at all, which I doubted.

The frayed end of the rope disappeared out of my sight. Another spray of sand fell, striking me in the face. I leaned my throbbing head wearily into my arms once again, panting in the thin mountain air.

"Ishamil!" the boy cried again.

Why did he keep calling that name? He shouted some other words as well, but the wind blew them away. I cried angrily, "What! Say again!" But the boy did not reply, perhaps because the roar of the crazed river swallowed my voice. More pebbles fell, and a sharp shard of rock which narrowly missed my head.

Red and orange clouds streaked the sky, which had

begun to fade now from gold to lavender, as the blanket of night was tossed across the mountains. Like the walls of a magnificent hallway in a house built for giants, the canyon loomed over me, holding the sky, like a painted ceiling, balanced on its ridges.

With the advent of nightfall, the chill wind turned frigid. Clad only in the bloody rags of Alasil's now grimy silken festival clothes, I began once again to shudder with cold. Still, I gazed at the sky, riveted by its beauty. Within its lavender depth, stars emerged, like mislaid pieces of a fractured sun. Their cold light shone softly upon my battered face. They danced before my eyes, and slowly resolved themselves into familiar patterns: the Dancing Boy, the Hunter, the Winter Maid. Surely, the last time I saw that maid, she had not advanced so far up the sky! Could half a month have passed while I hung in oblivion?

Rocks and sand rained down onto my face again. A dark, shapeless lump came into my view, silhouetted against the fading sky.

The boy yelled something, and the bundle fell with a dull thud to the rocks, as the useless rope slithered after and landed, with a splash, in the river. Another rattle of stones, and the boy was gone.

Like the small creatures of the earth which hibernate through the winter, I had folded my battered and shivering body into its little stone cubicle, as if somehow the frigid cold could not affect me there. Now the cold and the pain had frozen me in position. The slightest motion would only bring back the unendurable agony of my injuries. But without a source of warmth, I would certainly die of exposure in the cold night. Galvanized by this thought, I set my teeth and forced myself to move.

A lifetime later, it seemed, I finally sat beside the bundle, wrestling with the knot in that cursed rope so that I could get at the blankets. They proved to be wrapped around one of my horse packs, the straps altered so that a person could carry it on her back. With numbed, bloody fingers I fumbled at the fasten-

ings. Within, crammed on top of the carefully folded
cloth of my dark travel clothes, were two loaves of
stale bread, a large packet which proved to contain
dried fruit, an empty water flask, a flask of wine, and
a roll of bandages. Feeling through the rest of the
pack's contents, I found my pistol and knives.

By the time I had cut off the rags of my clothing,
doused my wounds with the wine, dressed the worst
of them in sloppy bandages, and put on all the clothes
I could find, full night had long since fallen. Bringing
the blankets with me, I half crawled, half dragged myself to another place where the rocks offered some
shelter from the wind. Panting with pain and cold,
shivering uncontrollably, muttering incoherently in an
attempt to keep myself conscious, I wrapped myself
in blankets to wait out the night.

The pain grew worse as the cold gradually retreated
from my flesh. I forced myself to breathe deeply between waves of pain, hoping that this strategy would
conquer the sick dizziness which washed over me in
waves. I longed to dull my pain with the last of the
wine, pillow my battered head in one of the blankets,
and sleep through what remained of this miserable agony of a night. But I had heard that people who have
injured their heads should not sleep, lest death come
calling and steal them away.

The night grew ever colder, and still dawn tarried.
I had held off my demons as long as I could. Appalled
by my helplessness, I wept.

At last, daybreak. I felt my head with cautious fingers, finding an eye swollen shut, a bloody place where
my hair had been scraped away, a swollen knot atop
my head, another on my forehead, a sore and bloody
nose. I already knew that my right knee could not
support my weight. My fingers, with which I had
dragged myself to safety, now were stiff and swollen,
scarcely capable of undoing my trousers so I could
relieve myself. I did not yet feel as if I could eat, but
I did allow myself a sip of the wine, as a grim toast

to the invisible sunrise before whose hounds the stars
fled the sky.

Agamin's pale boy was gone, of course, busy saving
his own skin. I could expect no more help from him—
in truth, that he had done anything at all surprised me.
As for me, my choices were few and offered little room
for optimism. I could remain here, hoping for some
kind of rescue, or I could patch myself together enough
to walk, and try on my own to find a way to climb out
of the ravine. The likelihood of rescue, I had to admit,
was slim indeed. Though I did not know how I had
gotten to this place, I could assume that no one else
knew my whereabouts. It was almost winter, the time
that only madmen and fools try to travel. No, there
would be no casual passersby, especially in so remote
a place. If I were to be rescued, it was I who had to
do the rescuing.

I wrapped my knee in more bandages, found a piece
of wood to act as a crutch, and began to walk.

That first day, no obstacle was too small to impede
my progress. I sweated and cursed from the pain of
my knee, and once wept in frustration when a boulder
blocked my path, though it would have required little
enough for me to go around it, had I not been injured.
At high noon, the sun's rays warmed the chill canyon
for a few short hours. I sat down to rest in the sun,
and fell asleep on my bed of bare rock. I slept until
the cold awoke me. I could scarcely get to my feet,
much less hold my balance. I traveled no farther that
day.

One stick at a time, I gathered some wood. For a
little while, at least, I would have a fire. Then I lay in
a sheltered place, and studied the rock walls looming
above me. Throughout the day, pain had made clarity
of mind an impossibility. Now my agony subsided to
a less demanding undercurrent. I considered these
sheer cliffs, and the piles of shattered stone amid which
the river leapt or lurked. The determination and resolve of morning had evaporated all too quickly. I con-

sidered what my life was worth to me, and found the
price had been discounted.

I do not remember ever having been a young child.
In my earliest memory, I am already seated at the feet
of one of my teachers—Aman Abad, or one of the
others? I sit in a huddle of black-dressed, silent, at-
tentive children who have the eyes of old men and
women. Carlas is sitting beside me. He eventually became the closest thing to a friend that I have ever had.
Three years ago now, he died after drinking a cup of
wine which his alter-self, a master poisoner, had left
out for him.

In my early memory, the teacher—how odd that I
can't remember which one it is—calls us the Emper-
or's Children. We stare at him in bleak astonishment.
I see my own bewilderment in every child's face. He
reaches out to pat one girl on the shoulder, and she
begins to scream. She disappeared soon after, I think.
I do not even remember her name.

The Emperor's Children: Children with two souls;
born into the hands of madness; rescued from the people and parents who would have exposed, strangled,
starved, drowned, or otherwise rid themselves of us
once they realized what we were; and raised to serve
the Emperor. I think of that earliest memory of mine
as my first moment of sanity, the moment when I,
Jamil, was first able to separate myself from the insane
tangle in which I had somehow survived the first seven
or eight years of my life. No wonder I felt bewildered:
I was a newborn.

I remember the girl who screamed. To this day, I
myself can scarcely tolerate another's touch. I remember Carlas, and I wonder. It is a good thing that Alasil
cannot read my thoughts because I watched the stars
come out that evening and asked myself if she were
trying to murder me.

I had taken my silver mirror out of the bag and
hung it by its chain around my neck. Now I lifted it
to my mouth and breathed upon it, clouding its polish
with mist. I had still been a child when I first saw a

face other than my own in the mirror. Had the power of my will not exceeded hers, Alasil could have been my master, rather than I hers. Certainly, we had begun as equals: two lost souls who settled into the same home by chance. I had often wondered why she did not now resent being forced to live her life in these brief, intense hours, separated by lengthy periods of sleep. If it were me, I might choose instead not to live at all.

I polished the mirror on my shirt, and looked into it. Alasil gazed back at me, her expression of mild hostility swiftly giving way to one of curiosity. "What happened to you?"

"I fell. Into a ravine."

She raised an eyebrow. "It must have been a wild party. But where did you find a ravine in Akava?"

"I don't know where we are—certainly not in Akava. I hoped you could tell me."

"But why would I know?"

It is hard to talk with her, sometimes, when all I can see is her face. I suspect that her hands might give her away, if I could see them. But her face tells me nothing—like myself, she is never really without a mask. I said, "Well, tell me what happened in Akava."

"You tell me!" She glared out of the mirror. 'I ask little enough of you! You had promised me the festival! Why are you asking me now what happened, when I never even opened my eyes in Akava, except that one time, to speak with you through the mirror?"

"What game are you playing? You cannot lie to me without lying to yourself!"

Her voice grew very soft. "I have never lied to you."

Knowing that I could not afford to make a mistake, I had hesitated to speak with her at all. Now I knew I had miscalculated, but I could do nothing as Alasil turned her face away. I called her name, but she did not respond. I told her, "I was unconscious until the moment that the rope broke. Who else could have brought us here, if not you?" But she would not answer me. At last I said, desperately, "Our life is in peril. If I die, you die, too. You have to help me!"

"*I* was not injured in the fall. Let me bring us safely home."

We Separated Ones must learn to leap some extraordinary chasms of logic. Though Alasil and I inhabit the same body, we do not inhabit it in the same way. No, the injuries from my fall would not disappear if I gave the body to Alasil, but they would not affect her so profoundly, as she would not feel the pain which so disabled me.

Responding to my silence, she turned her face to me, wearing a sardonic smile. "You don't trust me, do you? In thirty years I have never failed you, and now you don't trust me, not even to save your life."

"It's not that I don't trust you."

"Then what, Jamil?"

"I gave the body to you in Akava, but now you say I never did give it to you. So, between the moment I offered it and the moment you grasped hold of it, something must have come between us . . . and taken over. I cannot risk having that happen again." I had said these words only to shield myself from her anger, but as I spoke I realized the value of my own logic.

Alasil pursed her mouth, eyes narrowed. "Sorcery."

"It must be."

"What enemy?"

"Agamin, perhaps. His boy was traveling with us."

"Agamin is no sorcerer! And there are no sorcerers in Akava that he could have hired."

"None that we *know* of. But it would be easy enough for a sorcerer to hide from us in that region of fools."

"That sorcerer is a fool, too, for bringing us here alive."

Alasil had made a good point. Why had the sorcerer not killed us at once? Because the temptation of having a Separated One to control was too great for the unknown sorcerer to resist? Or because there was more to this event than a mere hired assassination? What better way to reach the Emperor than through a Separated One?

I said to Alasil, ''There are too many question. But if it was a sorcerer—and Agamin—''

Alasil licked her lips. ''They will regret it,'' she said. ''They will certainly regret it.''

Chapter 3

I awoke to a windy, desolate dawn. The stone walls of the ravine shimmered with hoarfrost. Exhausted by pain and cold, I stumbled to the river's edge and dipped pieces of stale, dry bread into the running water to soften them enough so I could chew them with my sore mouth. When I had finished, I drank more water to fill the void that remained in my belly.

Daylight revealed only barren stone. In two days I had seen no sign of life, either plant or animal. Since I knew from the stars and the sun that the ravine ran northward, I had tentatively concluded that I traveled in the southern quarter of the uncharted mountain wilderness which constitutes over half the area of Callia. With every step I took, I traveled farther from the populated flatlands.

Walking, if my clumsy, stiff-legged movement could be called that, did not thaw the frost out of my bones that day. The cold wind cut through my wool clothing like fire through wax. With frozen lips I cursed my unknown enemies as I doggedly struggled upstream.

At my right, the river crashed and roared, pounding on the boulders which blocked its path. I followed dry channels that the spring floods of a thousand years had carved through the living rock. The water-worn gravel crunched under the sodden leather of my left boot and grated under the drag of my right.

I had warmed my shoes by my little fire the night before, but the small amount of wood I had been able to gather had burned itself out long before the sodden leather could dry. My numbed feet never thawed, not even after the sunlight, which first appeared on the western rim of the ravine, had finally begun to shine on me. Then the black wool of my cloak felt warm to the touch, but the wind still drove through the weave, piercing through shirt and undershirt all the way to my skin, as though I wore nothing at all. At least, I thought wryly, I would not repeat yesterday's mistake of falling asleep in the warmth, thereby sacrificing my entire afternoon's progress.

That afternoon, the river slipped up to embrace the harsh side of the cliff, making it impossible for me to continue my journey without crossing the water. To keep my clothing dry, I bared my skin to the bitter wind and carried my belongings on my head, using my makeshift crutch to brace myself against the current. Even though the river had quieted within its banks, sparing me any further battering, it was a miserable crossing.

Some time after the shadows had crept across the water and begun to climb the other side of the ravine, I first became aware of the voices. The sound rose and fell with the wind: sometimes a hollow cry, sometimes a faint sigh, as the wind vibrated across the sharp edges of the rock. I heard a rushing sound as well, so that I feared I was about to encounter another waterfall, even though the river continued in its usual docility.

At last I noticed the pine needles crackling under my feet. Galvanized by the hope that a change in the vegetation would signal a change in the terrain as well, I hitched myself more eagerly up my rough path. Soon I could see the tops of the pine trees scalloping the canyon's rim. Patches of soil appeared between the stones. Squirrels lived here, in tunnels they had dug among the rocks. Skeletal pine cones littered the ground, their scales scattered, their seeds consumed.

The rim of my canyon had grown no closer to me that day, and once again I saw the sun set behind it. Only half a loaf of bread remained in the horse pack I carried, and a few swallows of wine. The scabs of

my wounds had cracked open in the dry cold and begun to bleed again, but I had no unguent with which
to treat them. I lay exposed beneath the darkening sky,
as the stars came out, keeping watch on the death that
haunted my shadows so patiently, like a wolf waiting
for its injured prey to drop to its knees.

The next day I ate the last of my bread, which had
become as hard as gravel and as dry as sawdust. The
trees began to spill over the edge of the ravine, clinging here and there among the stones overhead, like the
foreguard of an army breaching a defended wall. Here,
too, a few young saplings grew at the water's edge,
more innocent victims for next year's spring flood. The
escarpments of the ravine began to soften, and the river
continued to flow quietly in its bed. My knee still could
scarcely bear my weight, but at least the agonizing
headaches had ceased to plague me, and the ache of
my bruises had begun to fade. The terrain impeded
my progress far less than usual, and it was with a
modicum of cheer that I stumped along beside the quiet
river, watching for wild ducks in the hopes of bagging
one with my pistol.

A clatter of stone, a startled huff of breath, and five
gray deer leapt away from the riverbank, spraying water from their hooves. They froze, wide-eyed, craning
their heads to stare at me. Then, in a rattle of hooves
upon stone, they were gone, springing easily among
the boulders as they leapt up a well-worn path over the
edge of the ravine.

I sat at the edge of the river to fill both my flasks
with water. With my pack and blankets slung across
my back, I leaned my weight into the battered stick
which served me as a crutch, and climbed the path the
deer had shown me. So I finally escaped the ravine
prison where for two days the death wolf had stalked
me, and I laughed in triumph as I stood at last on the
edge of the chasm.

My laughter died soon enough, as I viewed the land
into which I had now entered. A rugged mountainside,
thickly forested and choked with thorny bracken, sloped

upward to my left and downward to my right. Peering through the thick trees, I could catch a glimpse of the mountain peaks rising above me, lavender giants crouched among the clouds. But of the land below I could see nothing which might give me a clue to where I stood in relation to the rest of the world.

Half the day had already passed. My stomach hurt with hunger, and my head had begun to ache again. I found a fallen log on which to sit as I considered what to do, but my blurred vision did not clear readily.

I had never doubted that I would make my way home safely once I escaped the ravine, but now I realized that this belief had been only a way of holding despair at bay. When I fell into the ravine, I had still been wearing my festival silks, a fact which I construed to mean that I had not traveled too far from Akava. But if I had been in the control of a sorcerer, then why assume that my clothing would be changed at all, no matter how much time had passed? I could have worn the same clothes for days, or weeks. The stars themselves, the Winter Maid and the rest of the constellations, offered evidence of an autumn more advanced toward winter than I had reason to expect. How far into the wilderness had I traveled?

And to where, I asked myself, had I and Agamin's boy been traveling? With only four loaves of bread remaining between us, assuming the boy had given me half, surely we must have been drawing close to our destination when disaster occurred. Since then, I had crossed the river. If I traveled down the edge of the ravine, I would encounter the path which had been my destination when I first climbed into that accursed basket. Where would that path lead me? To the home of the sorcerer, perhaps? A dangerous place to go begging a meal, I supposed, but on the other hand I was well-armed and had no reason to fear this or any other sorcerer. Magic takes time and forethought, and I would give the sorcerer the opportunity for neither.

I had another reason, besides my hunger, for wanting to seek out this sorcerer: not the need for revenge, as I know better than to risk my life for so hollow a purpose, but the need to be able to prove, when I came once again to my own city and my own Order, that it had not been madness which ailed me. If, at the same time, I uncovered a plot against the Emperor, so much the better. So I stood up from my seat on the log and was able to convince myself that the wave of dizziness which washed over me was only a reaction to my unaccustomed hunger. I began walking back the way I had come, keeping the ravine to my right as a guide to keep me from getting lost as I forced my way through the bracken.

I camped that night on the edge of the forest where it gave way to rocky, barren mountainside. Though I had made myself a bed of pine boughs behind stones which sheltered me from the wind, I could not seem to force the chill from my bones. I slept badly, and awoke, shuddering, before daybreak. I have never dreamed while I sleep, that I can remember. But I had been thinking in my sleep: fragmented, obsessive, fevered thoughts. The shattered remains of those thoughts haunted me in daylight: the conviction that someone was stalking me, which kept me frantically checking my tracks, and the voices once again, the lost voices of children, screaming on the wind.

I had forgotten my hunger, but thirst tormented me. I drank water heedlessly, and by sundown I had emptied both my flasks. Once again, I slept badly and awoke to a dark dawn, with stormclouds pouring over the ridges and the wind cold with the breath of winter. I fled before the storm, careless in my panic as I crossed rocky ground which could so easily have reinjured my healing leg. I knew that I could not be far from the path I sought. Soon, the thundering of the river in its chasm told me that I had once again drawn near the rapids which came so close to killing me. So much effort, I thought hopelessly, and in five days' travel I had only come back to where I started.

I nearly missed the path, which was little more than a scuffed track across the stone. The stormclouds had spread their cloaks across the wan face of the sun, and a vicious wind began to blow. I fled the storm as quickly as possible, running when I could, cracking my stick onto stone so sharply that it finally broke and I flung it angrily away. The first spatter of rain fell tauntingly. Ahead of me, I could see a shadow of trees. By the time I had entered their shelter, it had begun to rain in earnest.

For a while I huddled against the trunk of a tree, my lungs burning, my head swimming. I ceased to pant at last, but my dizziness persisted. Using the trunk of the tree as a brace, I stood up, easing my weight gently onto my bad leg. For now, the trees caught most of the rain in their dense canopy, but I could not expect their shelter to last forever.

The path had ducked with me under the trees. I continued to follow it, walking as quickly as I dared. Though it was not even midday, I could scarcely see in the gloom. The carpet of pine needles all but obscured the path. I followed it by a kind of sixth sense, never hesitating even at the most obscure of turns.

My sense of urgency only increased as the rainy afternoon passed. Of course, I desperately needed to find shelter in which to spend the night. But that same sense which guided me on the path also spoke to me of something which drew closer with every step I took, something which was not to be feared, but eagerly anticipated.

Perhaps it was the sorcerer's house. The thought of a sound roof and a warm fire cheered me considerably. I paused to check my weapons. The pistols would not work in this damp, of course. Knives were more reliable. I hid them in my clothing where I could easily reach them.

Thunder cracked, and water poured out of the sky. Under the canopy of the trees, however, all was eerily still. Rain dripped from the saturated boughs, to disappear into the thick pine needle carpet without a sound. The wind shook the tops of the trees, but here below scarcely a twig moved.

I tripped over something in the gloom and fell, cursing, onto my bad knee. When I had recovered somewhat from the pain, I felt around for the thing which had tripped me. It was a stone; a pile of stones, actually, a low, curving wall which the accumulation of pine needles had hidden from sight. Peering into the darkness, I realized that the wall formed a complete circle, into the center of which I had fallen.

Thinking it might be a sorcerer's trap, I crawled hastily over the obstacle, out of the circle. As I did so, I set down my hand on something sharp. Feeling through the pine needles, I found a shard of pottery. Light as a leaf, it lay in my hand, curved gracefully, like a piece of eggshell. The inner side was colored amber from the pitch that had been used to seal the clay. On the outside, partly obscured by mold, were delicate tracings of a pattern drawn in faded yellow and red. Perhaps that jagged line represented the mountains, and the curved line the river.

I raised my head and wiped the rain out of my eyes. I had fallen in the middle of a glade, where a few interloper saplings had recently taken root. Through the mist of rain, I saw several humped shapes; piles of debris they seemed at first, but as I walked closer I saw that they were ruined stick and mud huts, built on circular foundations such as that over which I had tripped. Long abandoned, they had begun to crumble back into the soil again.

At one of the more intact huts, I scraped away the debris of many years from its low doorway, and peered in. I could see little in the gloom. A hole gaping through the rounded roof let in some muted light. The leather flap which had once kept the draft from coming through the door crumbled to dust under my touch. A squeaking mouse scuttled through the debris of mud and twigs that covered the floor.

I peered into several other huts. In each one, a hole gaped through the roof. The walls had begun to disintegrate into rotten debris. Stores of stovewood, still shielded by the deteriorated remains of crude roofs, had avalanched into half-rotted piles. Ten or fifteen structures crouched in the gloom, loosely gathered around a clear central yard. Even under the accumulation of the pine needles, I could feel the hard-packed soil of this yard, where for a time the life of the little village must have focused. Here the babies, watched over by their grandparents, had crawled. The basket maker had sat among her reeds, the weavers had hung their looms, the shepherds had carried a goat up from the meadow below and dealt out the butchered meat.

"Where did they go?" I asked myself confusedly. For a moment, I felt as bewildered as a child coming home to a vacant house.

I continued my search through the village until I found one hut which seemed to have survived the passing time better than the others. No hole gaped in its roof, and relatively little debris littered its floor. Upon the stone hearth in the center of the shelter, the cold sticks from a long extinguished fire lay. I dug through a nearby woodpile and brought armloads of half rotten firewood into the shelter. Perhaps I had nothing to eat, but for once I would be warm.

The dusk of the storm gave way to the dusk of coming night. I went out one last time, to locate the village water source before full dark had fallen. I found it nearby, a frigid little stream running in a bed of polished stones, with a small waterfall where a waterpot could be set to fill. I put my mouth to the stream to drink, though its icy water made my teeth ache. I filled my flasks and returned to the village.

I stood at the edge of the village, listening to the raindrops fall into the trees above me and wondering what could have happened to the people who once lived here. Leaning against a tree trunk, I found the answer to my question as my hand brushed across a crossbow bolt growing out of its bark.

I returned to my little shelter and built a fire. The cheer of the flames seduced me, and I added more wood until a veritable blaze brightened the interior of the rude shelter. I placed my wet clothing by the fire, turning it several times while it dried. At last, groggy from the unaccustomed warmth and comfort, I lay down to sleep.

I awoke suddenly, knowing I was in danger. But it was too late.

Chapter 4

For them to subdue me, in my condition, did not take very long. Afterward, as I lay bound hand and foot, shivering in reaction to the sudden assault, my two captors built up the fire, set a pot of water in the flames, put some pinches of tea into a couple of dented tin cups, mixed water with flour to make flatcakes, and set some moldy sausages to grill over the flames.

They had not hurt me much more than they had to. I stared at the wall, where the light of the renewed fire outlined in sharp relief the swirling patterns embedded in the dried mud. Here and there, fingerprints indented the mud: small fingerprints, the marks of a child's hand. How old would the child be now, I wondered? My age, or even older? As I considered this question, the panicked thundering of my heart slowed gradually.

Before the Separated Ones had completely established their reputation for ruthlessness and inevitable revenge, I had survived my share of sudden assaults, and even remembered those wild free-for-alls with a kind of glee. Through experience, I had learned what factors decide who will win and who will lose in hand-to-hand combat, and I always won because I always rested well, ate well, gathered reliable information, considered my options in advance of the crisis, and armed myself with the most effective weapons. So I taught my students: Just as we engineer our victories, we engineer our defeats. Never had the verity of this lesson been more neatly demonstrated.

I could hear the rain falling now, a hiss and a sigh and a nearly silent rhythm, like the tap of gloved fin-

gers upon the upholstered arm of the chair. I heard
harness chains jingle as a horse tethered outside shook
its head. Within the hut, the man, having gone through
my clothing and blankets, fumbled at the stiff buckles
of my horse pack. The woman squatted beside the fire,
her sodden clothing beginning to steam in the heat,
staring at me. I could make no sense of her expression:
Either she felt and thought nothing at all, or her ability
to mask her thoughts rivaled my own.

She had uncovered her head, revealing a greasy tangle
of graying hair, tied carelessly back with a leather
thong. Her flesh sagged wearily from her bones, but I
had reason to know that she posessed a vigor and energy which belied her appearance. To take her blankness of expression to mean a blankness of mind as well
would also probably be a mistake. She wore leather
breeches over heavy wool trousers, three ragged shirts
of various lengths, and a cloak of such thickly woven
cloth that it could have been an old horse blanket. The
water dripping from her clothing had formed a muddy
circle around the perimeter of her body.

The man grunted, producing out of my pack the
knives which I had so carefully wrapped in oilcloth to
keep them from rusting in the damp. Then he found
the pistols, also carefully wrapped, and my small store
of powder and gunshot. He turned to look at me curiously, but the woman, who had glanced at him briefly
to see what he was doing, did not alter her expression.

"The cakes will burn," she said harshly.

The man hastened to give the woman my knives and
pistols, and then turn the flatcakes. She examined my
weapons without much apparent interest, and set them
aside. I winced as my weapons became soaked in her
proximity.

"The powder," I said, "It's too close to the fire."

"Shut up," the woman barked harshly. But the man
hastily took the powder canister and set it far back
from the flames. He returned to his perusal of my belongings and once again grunted with surprise as he
produced my silver mirror on its filigree chain.

"Separated One," he said, the first words I had
heard him speak.

"Don't be an idiot!" the woman spat. She spoke a
northern dialect, but she seemed to be well accustomed to the cold and damp climate of the mountains.
I doubted she had been home in a long time.

The man next discovered the half-mask. "Lookit
this."

The woman turned her head again, irritably. "Trash!"
But she held out her hand for the man to give her the
mask. She examined its construction, the silk lining,
the straps to hold it in place. Then she lifted it to her
own face. "Now *I* am a Separated One."

The man, however, looked at me nervously.

The woman handed him the mask again. "Keep it.
And the mirror. We'll get a good price for it."

"The Emperor's dogs will hunt you down and kill
you," I said softly. If killing a Separated One was the
worst crime, to impersonate one ran a close second.

In a spray of water the woman leapt to her feet and
strode to my side. She stank of wool and horses and
unbathed flesh and greasy meat. Her heavy boots had
mud on them as thick as my hand. "Did you say something?"

I pondered whether I wanted those boots to kick my
belly, or my breasts, or my kidneys, but I did not pon-
der long. I have long studied the art of intimidation,
but never from this position. I said politely, "Why,
no. I said nothing."

The woman gave a nasal grunt and settled herself
once again by the fire. "There's nothing worse than a
thief."

Behind her, the man discovered my pouch of coins
and shook it, snickering. The woman instantly
snatched the pouch out of the man's hand. "Nothing
worse," she continued, talking half to herself as she
opened the pouch and poured its contents into her
hand: gold and silver and a little copper. "Nothing
worse than a thief. Where did you get this money?"

"From the Emperor's coffers."

She hawked and spat into the flames. "Did you hear that, Moy? She says she got it from the Emperor."

"Ya, ya," said the man.

"She's a Separated One, Moy. She lives in that walled city where no one but her kind can walk. She can do anything she wants, go anywhere, talk to anyone."

"Ya, ya," said the man again, looking at me worriedly.

"Now answer my question, Moy, answer me well. If she is a Separated One, then what is she doing here, half naked in a mud hut?"

Moy looked thoughtful.

"Not a thing to eat. Thin as a bone. Looks like she was at the losing end of a bad fight, eh? Lookit that shiner. Nah, she's a thief all right. And there's nothing worse than a thief."

"Nothing worse," agreed Moy. He took my empty horse pack and shook it upside-down: a few crumbs of bread, a powdering of dust. "That's all she got."

I said, "There's more money where that came from, if you help me."

"Hah! You hear that, Moy? You hear that?" The woman tipped her head back and roared with laughter. But even her laughter did not tell me what I needed to know. Had I awakened her greed, and was this laughter merely a decoy? Or was she genuinely amused at what she perceived to be the empty promises of a desperate prisoner? In the complex, meandering mazes of human relations, I have often seemed to myself to be the only one who knew what I wanted and how I could achieve it. But the frustration and hunger and anger and physical pain of my predicament had eroded away even this basic talent. With my body doubly imprisoned by injuries and bonds, my wits were my only weapons. If these, too, abandoned me—

I slammed shut the door on that vagrant thought. I could not afford to doubt myself!

Flames flared as fat dripped from the charring sausages. In a miasma of ripe smells, of stinking sweat, dirty wool, rotten leather, and old food, the man

poured boiling water into the metal cups, heedless of
the ashes now floating in the water. With the sizzling
flatbread protecting his hands from the smoking fat,
he plucked the sausages from the sticks and passed
half to the woman. She sat in a cloud of steam now,
her fragrance increasing as the water evaporated from
her clothing. Without a word of thanks, she began to
eat.

At the rich, greasy scent of the food, I shut my eyes
in disgust, my stomach churning. All my old injuries
had flared into renewed pain after the strain of fleeing
the storm, and now I had new bruises to torment me.
With my hands and feet bound, I could not achieve a
position that even resembled comfort. I lay in abject
misery, forcing myself to consider, however desperately, how I might escape or subvert or overcome my
trail-hardened, mountain-wise captors. But I could not
think of even one resource left with which I might
challenge their supremacy.

I escaped in the only way I could. I slept.

I awoke to a strangely silent dawn, the sound of the
renewed fire crackling and hissing in the wet wood,
and the sharp agony as the man reached down to shake
me sharply by the shoulder. He spoke, his voice muffled and far away, and took away the blanket which
one of them had tossed over me as I slept. Half my
body felt completely numb, as if I had halfway died
while I slept. Despite the fire, it was cold as a tomb
in that hut. The man's breath condensed into a white
cloud around his face.

"Get up now," he said.

"Leave me alone."

"Hit her," said the woman, from very far away.

The man struck me, a stinging slap across my face.
It was not much of a blow, really, but it shocked
through my being like an earthquake, toppling mountains, flattening hilltops, opening a great fissure of terror within my spirit. The man struck me again. I
writhed like a trapped animal, struggling against my
bonds, panting with terror. My words sobbed out of

my throat: "I can't get up. I can't—" I struggled into something between a sitting and reclining position, and the man seemed to suddenly remember that I was bound hand and foot and could hardly be expected to stand up under my own power. He gestured to the woman, as if to point out this fact to her.

She grinned across the hut at me. Her missing teeth made her smile seem sinister. One of my pistols, newly cleaned and loaded, lay at her hand. She had pulled my trousers on up to her thighs, but I have always favored a close fit, and she struggled to make them stretch around her wider hips.

Certainly, my wits were slow indeed for it to have taken me so long to realize who this woman had to be. Why should she care that her prisoner was a Separated One, if she had succeeded in taking not only my body prisoner but my very souls? Why should she be impressed by the coins in my traveling purse, when she was motivated by a far more ambitious vision of wealth and power? No, this encounter was no accident. This woman was the sorceress I sought.

"What do you want of me?" I asked hoarsely.

She threw my shirt at me, and my overshirt, and peeled off my trousers and threw them at me as well. "Get dressed."

I did as I was told. The man unbound my hands so I could put on my shirts. The thongs had cut deep red lines into my wrists, and my fingers had swollen so badly during the night that I could not do the fastenings of my clothing, and the man had to do it for me. Having once again bound my hands, this time in front of me, he untied the thongs of my ankles so he could dress me in my trousers, my socks, and my boots. He dragged me to my feet and propped me against the mud wall. Even with this support I could scarcely stand, but the woman kept a sharp eye on me as she finished getting dressed.

The man packed up the last of the goods and brought them outside. I heard the murmur of his voice and the jingle of a harness, but the sounds seemed far, far away.

The woman stamped her feet into her boots, leaving chunks of hardened mud scattered on the floor. She picked up one of my pistols and stuck it into her waistband, then plucked her heavy cloak from where it hung over the fire. Bits of charred cloth floated away in the updraft of the fire.

The man reentered the hut, with tiny droplets of water sparkling in his beard. The brim of his battered, shapeless hat drooped wearily over his deep set eyes. His eyebrows, as stiff as horsehair, were bleached white by the sun. His skin looked like crumpled leather. He glanced at the woman, who had tied back her greasy hair and now fastened her cloak with an incongruously delicate jeweled pin, and then at me, where I still leaned against the wall, my chin digging into my chest under pressure from the slope of the ceiling.

"Could I have a drink of water?" I rasped.

The woman ignored me. "Let's go, then."

Pushed forward by the man, I stumbled out the door of the hut. A heavy mist had settled over the forest in the wake of the night's storm, so thick that I could not see much farther than I could reach. The sodden carpet of pine needles gave way like sponge under my feet. Far away, as if I listened to a sound coming from another world, water dripped. The packhorse tethered nearby jumped nervously as we drew near, panicky because of the fog. The man soothed the horse, clucking softly as he tied a rope to my bound hands and then attached its other end to the horse's harness. It lowered its head to lip a few last grains of oats from the ground.

"We won't get lost in the mist?" said the man.

"Haven't I traveled this way a hundred times?" The woman strode forward, kicking casually at me as she passed. The man took the lead rein of the horse, and so the four of us began to walk through the mist, the woman leading, and the three of us following her like a line of shackled prisoners. At the end of the procession, I wove drunkenly on knees that constantly gave

way under my weight, so that I was always on the
verge of pitching face forward into the loam.

My gait steadied after a while, and the mist began
to clear, though my vision did not. The trees thinned,
and we trudged along a ridge which overlooked a forested valley far below. Beyond that valley, another
cloud-shrouded mountain swelled, and another, beyond which I could not see. In the valley I could see
glimpses of a dark river winding among the trees. Perhaps it was the same river I had been following for the
last nine days, the river I presumed to be the Iska.
Perhaps it was some other river entirely.

At mid-afternoon, we stopped to rest and let the
horse graze in a meadow of frost-yellow grass. The
man unfastened my trousers so I could relieve myself.
My need had become so great that I did not care that
he and the woman watched in brutal amusement as I
urinated. They gave me a mouthful of parched corn
and a strip of dried meat, but my mouth had become
so dry that I could scarcely eat. At last, the man held
the flask they had stolen from me to my mouth, so I
could have a few sips of water. "Where are we going?" I asked.

"Over the mountains," the woman said.

"But why?"

"Because they always need workers in the diamond
mines, my dear. They'll pay a good sum for you, I'm
certain." She cackled. I wished I could believe that
no worse fate than the mines—which offered only certain, brutal death—awaited me.

I had to escape. My bindings were of leather. If I
could somehow wet them, they might stretch enough
that I could free my hands. We passed only one stream
that afternoon, where the horse was allowed to drink.
I had been stumbling on my feet all day, and my fall
did not arouse their suspicions. But I did not land with
my hands in the water, and so I got for my trouble
only more bruises and another punishing slap from the
sorceress' leman.

That night they tried to feed me, but I could not eat.
I refused to drink as well, so that I could avoid as

much as possible the humiliation of making water in front of my captors. "She's fading," commented Moy, as if I could not hear.

"Nonsense," said the sorceress. "She's got the mountains in her bones. She's got the dragon in her blood. Just look at that face."

"She don't look so good to me. Some price we'll get for her."

"You're a fool, Moy."

The two of them lay down together after they had eaten, and the man serviced the woman there on that bare mountainside, under the cool regard of the shimmering stars. Had there been more business and less pleasure in their encounter, to be forced to witness it might have been less disgusting. But for these two scrapings from the moldy pot of humanity to take such pleasure in each other seemed truly squalid. I finally fell mercifully asleep, but their love talk still mumbled obscenely through my thoughts as I slept.

I awoke the next morning before dawn, to the sound of Moy quietly stirring a pot on the coals of the fire. It was cold as death. The chill hand of winter reached through my blankets to finger my bones, but I felt completely indifferent to my own misery. Moy came over with the pot and spooned unsalted gruel into my mouth. I gagged on the food but had become too weak to fight him. I cursed him later, as I stumbled down the trail on my tether once again, vomiting my guts out as I walked.

I remember little of that day. We climbed a steep and precarious trail, and I remember watching stones fall into a deep ravine that dropped away, only a step away from my stumbling and unsteady feet. I remember the cold, which retreated not at all before the assault of the watery sunlight. All day long the frost crunched underfoot. Steam rose from the horse's thick winter fur. I remember the burning in my chest, too, as if a fire blasted there, searing away my flesh in its heat. I remember the first time I fell, and the child's whimper I uttered when my bad knee hit bare rock. And I remember the sorceress watching me—

watching, and waiting. Waiting for my heart to break or my will to give way? Watching for the first signs that I had decided to shift control to my alter-self? I was more than ready to do it! Oh, they would have had their hands full if I had been able to set Alasil loose on them. But surely the sorceress knew that I could not shift selves without the mirror to aid me. How could she have worked such damage upon me, lacking this most basic piece of information? Yet she continued to watch me, and in my confusion I wondered if she knew something I did not. I began talking to Alasil under my breath, on the chance that she could in fact hear me. Later I must have begun speaking out loud. Out of a confusion of nightmarish memory, this one last piece stands out clearly: the sound of the evil sorceress screaming at me to shut up.

"Wake up." Under Moy's hand my bones rattled in the bag of my skin. Suddenly he snatched his hand away from my shoulder. "Gah! She's fouled herself!"

Faintly I heard the sorcerer he served begin to berate him. "It's snow weather, you damn fool! Let's go!"

I heard Moy's heavy breathing. He touched me again, less certainly. He touched my forehead; his fingers felt cold as winter's heart. "She's on fire," he said. There was a dull shock in his voice. "She ain't well, Clar."

"Nonsense!" The sorceress' heavy boots crunched across frosty gravel. Even in my stupor I flinched away from that sound, but my eyelids felt like stone and I could not open them. I felt the woman's regard like an indifferent touch. "She's a dragon woman. She lives to trick fools like you. Get her on her feet."

The man reluctantly tried to lift me. My disconnected bones hung in his grip like a bag of sticks. He dropped me at last, none too gently, onto my bed of stones. Silently, both of them studied me where I lay.

"If it's the plague—" the man began again.

"Dragon woman," the sorceress insisted. "Thinks to best us with her tricks." She considered once again.

My ears had all but gone deaf, but my mental acuity had become so sharp that I could almost hear her thinking. They could not carry me with them on these narrow mountain trails, nor could their horse bear one more burden. With a snowstorm brewing, they could not delay. They would have to let themselves be cheated of their prize. The woman hawked and spat. "Huh. Wouldn't have gotten much for her anyway. Thinks to trick us, eh?" She laughed harshly. "Fine. Let her lie. Let the snow bury her."

"Eh," Moy began, as if to object.

"Go, Moy!"

I heard the man scuffle about their campsite, gathering up the last of their belongings and loading the packhorse. Slowly, realization penetrated to the dying embers of my consciousness. They were going to abandon me on the mountainside, helpless, with my hands still tied. I moaned an outraged objection, and heard Moy pause in his work. I could not hear the woman—had she gone away from the camp to relieve herself?

All in a moment, the man rushed upon me, hacking with a dull knife at the leather bindings on my hands. "Now don't you move a muscle," he gasped. "Not a sound, or we're both dead. You hear me, girl? Not a sound!"

Then he was gone, and I heard the crisp sound of the sorceress' boots and a mutter of ill-tempered curses against the weather. "Snow, Moy! Let's go!"

"Straps stiff in the cold," Moy said distantly. "Ready now? Hup, baby." The horse, who loved him as if he were security itself, started up the stony path, and they were gone.

I burned in my body's fire and listened, disbelieving, to the silence.

Chapter 5

My common sense had been so completely obliterated by my illness that I actually felt triumphant at having forced my captors to release me. Dismay crept upon me more slowly, as the stormclouds gathered and I began to ask myself what to do now with this worthless victory. I understood that to remain where I was meant certain death. But the fabric of my reason had been worn through by great gaps of fevered delirium; instead of seeking shelter where I could conserve what little life force endured in my tortured flesh, I devoted the remaining shreds of my energy to a mindless journey up the mountainside.

I could not walk. I could scarcely crawl. The cold wind froze the grimace of pain onto my face and the tears onto my cheeks. My sweat-sodden clothing stiffened into rigid armor. My swollen hands slapped the bare ground like bloated fish washing in on the tide. The path, such as it was, abandoned me entirely. I dragged myself across bare stone.

"You will not defeat me," I declared in a raw whisper, obstinately defying all the forces of nature which had conspired against me. I stumbled and fell and crawled and crept onward, like a mechanical toy whose spring has not yet wound down. But I knew that my own defiance made a fool of me. I had been defeated when that rope which held me suspended over the ravine first began to fray. All that had followed afterward had been only death throes.

I imagined the bafflement of my peers as they realized that this was the year that Jamil would not come home. Abad would cry treachery, but who would ever suspect that his brave Jamil could be overcome by a ragged, heavy-booted, foul-mouthed sorceress? They would never find the culprit; they would never find me; they would never know.

Deliriously, I lectured my fellows. You think you know everything (I said). You walk, you talk, and execute your dreams. You serve your god—oh, yes, you do—just as I did. And then out of the silence comes a hand, the wild hand of the stars, and it stirs your life like a pot on the stove and you must face your own death. You ask yourself who you are, what your life has meant, and you have no answers.

Oh, no—you have no answers, because you have not truly been alive at all.

I lay on the barren stone, sobbing with exhaustion, as the manic voice railed on in my head, repeating this crazed lecture over and over. But I regretted it when at last the maddened babble fell suddenly quiet and I could hear the silence.

It was the ageless silence of the mountains. My ears rang with it, my heart screamed with terror before it. It was the silence of a hunter about to spring, the silence of a seer about to ask the most unspeakable of questions. I wept uncontrollably, clutching at the raw stone with my useless hands.

Something nipped at my flesh with teeth like flames. My maddened grief evaporated, and I dragged open my weighted eyelids. Another snowflake landed on my fevered skin, and the cold pierced my flesh like fangs. I dragged myself onto my knees and elbows and stared, gape-mouthed, at the sky. I had never seen anything like these white flakes, floating like goosedown from the gray sky. The faintest breath of wind set them dancing and swirling. "The first snow," a child's voice whispered in my ear. "Quick, make a wish!"

I stared at the falling snow, dizzied by their hypnotic dance. "I wish . . . I wish I could go home."

I lowered my gaze at last. The snow had powdered my frozen clothes like sugar on a sweet maker's finest confection. I licked it with my tongue, and it burned. I realized my danger then, and I began to crawl on

knees and elbows. Soon I crept through a blowing
powder of snow. The sodden elbows of my overshirt
wore through, and those of my undershirt as well. The
cold crept from my numbed, raw arms into the center
of my being, where my heart beat wearily and the
bellows of my chest huffed hopelessly at the thin air.
The gray stones turned white. Snow iced my body and
fell in soft clots from my jerkily moving limbs. I lipped
the snow thirstily and shivered at its fire.

Just for a moment, I had to rest. The snow gave me
the softest bed available in these inhospitable mountains. How easy to sleep. But not just yet. I gazed,
open-eyed, at the traitorous beauty of the falling snow.
How smoothly it covered this rugged ground, soften-
ing the harsh edges of the stone, taming the steep slope
of the mountain's cold breast. But here—something had
pock-marked the lovely coverlet. I promised myself
I could sleep, as soon as I had guessed what those
marks might be. Narrow, neat hooves—too small for
a deerprint. Had a herd of goats passed this way? Wise
creatures, they . . . could I follow them to shelter?

My limbs had frozen in their sprawl, and I had become too weak to crack them loose from their gentle
prison of snow. Like a wild creature caught in quick-
sand, I floundered mindlessly, and in my panic managed to crawl halfway to my feet before I collapsed
again onto my elbows and knees. One arm's length at
a time, I continued through the snow, following the
disappearing shadows of those dips in the snow, listening with my aching ears for the telltale voices of
the does calling on their spindly goatlings to stay near.

But I heard only the terrible silence, and soon I became incapable of distinguishing those delicate footprints any longer, as the housekeeper snow filled them
up and made them vanish away. It did not matter
really; this bed was comfortable enough. I shut my
eyes at last.

My bones clattered in my skin as I shivered in the
brutal cold, but then, slowly, I began to feel warm.
My instincts rebelled against this incongruity though
I did not clearly know what it meant. But all the fight

had been battered out of me. I had given up and would struggle no longer. With relief I exited my frozen husk and looked about myself curiously. The falling snow kissed my bodiless being as I walked slowly up the mountainside, making no footprints in the perfect white carpet. It was all over; there were no more questions left to ask. How strange now that I walked alone, with no executioner's shadow at my side. What had become of Alasil? Was I finally free of the burden of my other self, alone at last?

I had dreamed of this freedom. But I felt only unutterably sad that Alasil would leave like this and never even give me a chance to see her or to know her. In our forced companionship there had never been room for friendship, as friendship implies choice. But I had gotten used to her, and I had grown to depend upon her one fine quality, her loyalty. Clearly, that loyalty did not extend beyond the grave.

I had wept so much lately, in rage and helplessness, in disbelief and weakness and pain. But never did I weep in grief. Now I wanted to, but I had become a being of snow and my tears would only have been shards of ice. I walked aimlessly up the slope of the mountain. Far away, I heard the bleating of goats, and I smiled humorlessly to myself. I had found them much too late. Then I heard another sound, the barking of a dog, muffled by the floating feathers of the snow. A wolf, perhaps?

Far behind me, as if from another, lost world, a child wailed. It was a hopeless, exhausted sound. It tore at my snow spirit with claws of despair. I turned, searching wildly for the source of the sound, but I could see only the snow, falling more thickly now, so that the very shape of the mountains was obscured and I could not distinguish between land and sky. Once again I heard the weary cry of a child, lost in the storm. I looked down at my insubstantial body and saw that it had been rent through by the sound of that voice, like a knife stabbing through paper. I opened my mouth to beg the child to sleep and be at peace, but I had no voice, only a breath of wind that set the snowflakes to swirling around me.

The dog barked again, and now I saw it, a gray being of cloud and ice, rushing forward through the storm. Two people with staves in their hands strode in the animal's wake. Behind them, a mule picked its way daintily through the snow, bearing on its back a person wrapped in furs, gazing with old eyes at the storm. She had seen many storms before this one, certainly, but still there was a kind of delight in her face as she watched the flakes fall, as if the beauty of it had never palled for her.

Then she turned her head, and she saw me. I was only snow swirling in this first storm of winter, a wandering wind with the marks of a child's pain rent through my belly. But she saw me. And she beckoned imperiously. I saw now, just beyond her, another spirit like myself, faint as starshine on water, following her through the snow. It was Alasil. The woman beckoned again, and of their own will my spirit feet began to follow across the perfect snow.

Side by side, Alasil and I walked. We did not speak to each other. But once, Alasil looked at me, curiously, as if to ask me who I was. Then she shook her spirit head slowly and looked into the storm. The woman on the mule did not turn her head. She knew that we followed, obedient as children, in the footsteps of her mount.

Ahead of us, the dog began to bark excitedly, and the two foot travelers began to run. They called back to the old woman on the mule, but she said nothing, her face impassive. The dog helped them dig, in a flurry of flying powder. I could not see clearly what they had found, encased in a coffin of soft white. Was it the lost child? But no, they lifted her, a battered bag of sticks, wrapped in bloody rags, out of her white chrysalis, and I recognized her. It was myself.

They beat the snow out of my frozen clothes. They breathed on my face to melt the ice that had frozen my eyelids shut. Then they lifted me to the mule's back, and the old woman, with surprising strength, took me in her arms and wrapped me in furs.

"What do they want with a corpse?" I said to Alasil. But she only gave me a sardonic, pitying glance and looked away again.

A long, steep way they bore me, over mountain crags where snow spilled, into the heart of a high, proud forest, and out again into a land of shattered black stone powdered with white. The snow continued to fall, and the mule waded patiently through drifts that reached as high as its hocks. The two people on foot, who were featureless and shapeless in their jackets and trousers of greased goatskin, strode steadily through the snow, tireless masters of the harsh terrain which had so quickly defeated me. The obscuring snowfall did not bewilder them; unhesitatingly they followed a pathless route, walking like people who knew their land well.

Behind them followed the patient mule with its double burden, and Alasil and I trailed behind, compelled to follow, forbidden, by the beckoning gesture of the woman's hand, to desert each other. Through the broken stones and the drifting snow we followed, as the day's gray light faded toward darkness. Before us rose a white cloud, shimmering faintly in the early twilight. More heavily now, the snow continued to fall. We walked into the cloud, and suddenly the path we followed dove steeply downward.

Though my spirit self could not feel it, I knew that we had come to a warmer place, for the snow melted when it touched the ground. We passed a skin tent, stretched in the gloom like a blanket drying on a line. The steam grew thick. The foot travelers paused, standing in soft mud, and began taking off their clothing. A woman and a man were gradually revealed under the complex layers of their clothing, their smooth brown skin still kissed by the summer sun. They spoke to each other in a language I could not understand, and held up their arms to the woman on the mule. She let her burden, myself, slide from the mule's back and into their arms. They laid me down on the mud and stripped off my clothing which, having thawed during the journey, now hung from my starved frame in lank rags.

Their hair hung in long, twisted locks to their waists. Their beads dragged in the mud as they worked over me. They pulled the length of rawhide from where it had become embedded in the swollen flesh of my wrist. They used a slim little blade to cut the fine wool of my shirts, and the gray, grimy linen of my underclothing. My body had scarcely begun to heal from the battering it had received in the river. I heard them exclaiming softly over the clots of blood dried in my hair.

They lifted me in their arms and carried me forward. I followed myself, profoundly curious, but Alasil hung back, nearly invisible now in the mist. She moved like a cat. I had always suspected that she might, but I had never known for certain, until now.

The old woman said something as she dismounted, holding her armload of furs and blankets carefully out of the mud. The two who carried me replied respectfully. They crouched and set me down in what I realized now was shallow water, practically invisible behind the steam. But they held my hands and my feet above the water, and so they remained for a long time, soaking me in the bubbling water of the hot spring, keeping close watch upon my face that it not go under water. I stood and watched them, standing neither in nor on the water which I felt only as a kind of a caress. How gently they treated this husk of a woman, this stranger.

After a while the old woman, also naked now, came out to them. They took turns watching over me and warming themselves in deeper water. The melted snow rained upon them. I watched the long locks of their hair trailing behind them through the water.

The man left the water and built a fire under the shelter of the skin tent. I spotted him from time to time, dressed now in lightweight underclothing, as he boned and sliced smoked fish and put it in a pot to cook. I sensed Alasil pacing restlessly through the snowy darkness, then suddenly she was gone. The old woman pressed my swollen hand against her cheek, and then dipped it into the steaming water. The other woman did the same with my feet. Gracefully, they moved in a slow ritual of warming: dipping and lifting my flaccid limbs, unconsciously keeping rhythm with each other.

I began to feel very strange. Light-headed. Sleepy. Heavy. Suddenly my awareness slipped, shifted, as it does when one stands suddenly after sitting for a long time. I jerked, startled, and water entered my mouth. I choked, and then I stared in disbelief at the two women, old and young, who gazed at me solemnly with the long beaded locks of their hair trailing into the water. The old woman's eyes narrowed, the lines in her face deepening with cautious suspicion. I felt their hands gripping my ankles and wrists. I lay, weak as a newborn calf, in their arms. Every nerve in my being ached in outraged shock at having been dragged back like this from the point of death. All my old wounds and bruises and cracked bones throbbed. It was no warm welcome home.

I turned my head, as if seeking to see the silent spirit standing there, with those gaping rents ripped through her being where the child's cry had hurt her. But, of course, she was gone.

Chapter 6

I believed, beyond any doubt, that the sorceress Clar had manipulated, tricked, and trapped me. But it never occurred to me that my rescue could have been something other than a fortuitous accident. I had recently been reclaimed from the dead; perhaps I may be forgiven for only appreciating the irony of my rescue, and giving little consideration to the unlikely and alarming coincidence of it. Many different peoples live in the mountains, but I had been rescued by Asakeiri.

Had Moy and Clar not taken my mask and mirror, my rescuers would certainly have recognized me for an enemy, and either left me to die or killed me outright. But, as with most tribes, the Asakeiri observe certain laws of hospitality which absolutely require them to give succor to strangers.

And I, though terribly weak from my ordeal, half starved, and with my intelligence clouded by fever; despite these things, I still retained enough presence of mind to secure one guarantee for my continuing survival. When they set a bowl of salty fish stew beside me, I put the bowl to my lips and drank. And when they gave me a piece of flatbread, still hot from the baking stone, I put a piece in my mouth and ate it. Salt and bread: In every tribal culture, to be offered one or the other meant that I had been offered all the protection and resources of the tribe.

The loneliness, and aimlessness, and the strange vulnerability of death had galvanized me to ensure that I would not die again. So it became easy for me to overlook the fact that this matter of taking on tribal obligations goes both ways. Yes, they offered me the

food, but it was I who ate it, of my own free will.
And yes, that heedless decision would haunt me.

The mule, blowing clouds of steam from red nostrils, breasted a mountain ridge. The old woman,
Ata'al, allowed him to stop and rest. I lay in her arms,
heavy and nerveless as a bag of flour, wrapped from
head to foot in a fur robe. In a fevered stupor I had
traveled since daybreak with my three rescuers and the
herd of goats that now accompanied them. As we
paused, the goats who had been allowing the mule to
do the hard work of breaking through the snow,
crowded up behind us. The two young people glided
on skis along the edges of the herd, chirping sooth-
ingly to the goats. The scarlet-tongued dog brought up
the rear.

Clouds of steam masking their faces, the young people paused beside the mule. The two of them were of
the same height, and their sharply angled faces had
become indistinguishable behind the disguise of the
fur hoods. One, the man Orlil or the woman Talesan,
pointed down the gradual slope. My eyes automati-
cally followed the direction of the pointed finger. A
wide expanse of snow lay before us, broken here and
there by the humped shape of a snow-capped haystack.
All across this vast meadow, livestock browsed in the
snow, scraping it away with their hooves to uncover
the vegetation underneath. At each of the haystacks,
several small, brightly dressed figures shouted threats
and lofted snowballs to keep the goats away from the
hay.

Beyond the meadow rose a concave cliff of black
stone, stark and startling against the dazzling snow.
There, huddled within the shelter of the palm of the
cliff's hand, surrounded by stockfences, stood a village of stone and timber and many steep staircases,
with one home piled atop the next like a child's building blocks, so that the entire town crawled halfway up
the side of the cliff.

We only know the Asakeiri as nomads, a dispersed
and disorganized people who, in small family groups,

follow their flocks from meadow to meadow, or grow
crops in their ancient, terraced gardens. How they survive the mountain winter, with no shelter but a goatskin tent or a hut of sticks and mud, had never been
determined. That they might be builders, or that their
thousand or more tribespeople returned home to a city
every winter, had never occurred to anyone.

Busy people hurried up and down the staircases and
passageways of the village. From this distance, I could
not clearly see what they were doing. The sharp cracking sound of an ax splitting wood carried across the
snowy field, and I smelled the faint scent of woodsmoke. One of the children guarding the haystacks
yelled shrilly. We had been spotted.

I felt too weak even to lift my head from Ata'al's
shoulder. As weariness overwhelmed the brief flare of
my curiosity and wonder, I once again allowed my
eyes to fall shut. I felt as if a giant fist had closed
around my chest. I could scarcely breathe, but to cough
was agonizing. Earlier in the day, I had been able to
convince myself that I had only picked up a fever,
which would disperse quickly once my natural vitality
had recovered itself. But now, with my bones aching
and my lungs burning, I could not keep up the pre-
tense. I knew I was developing pneumonia.

Ata'al clucked to her mule, and we started forward
again. With a flare of terror, I felt my last grasping
clutch on consciousness begin to slip. I could not hold
on any longer. I simply could not hold on.

* * *

An unlocked door, hanging ajar, banging in the
wind. I am standing in the hallway of cold stone, a
gauzy phantasm. For days beyond memory I have
wandered this maze of barren corridors, but always
I have come back to this open door. And, always, a
sense of doom and horror draws me helplessly to
the doorway, where I must look through.

But, this time, I do not pause to look. In a des-

perate, courageous rush, I cross the threshold . . .
and I am falling. . . .

* * *

The yowling of a cat woke me. Disoriented, I stared
into the gloom. A single, smoldering flame cast its
orange glow across the small room, picking out the
rough cut timbers of the low ceiling but leaving the
spaces between them in darkness. Woven hangings
covered the stone walls; the flame picked out the bright
simplicity of their geometric designs. Straw mats and
rugs covered the floor. Across the one low doorway
hung a leather curtain to cut the draft. The cat who
had awakened me slipped out again through this door.

Strangely, there did not seem to be any furniture. I
tried to sit up. The bed, little more than a wooden
box, crackled softly as I moved, and I smelled the
sweet scent of the dried grass and herbs which formed
my mattress. I lay atop a soft woolen blanket, and a
robe of fur covered me. Goatskin, I guessed, and remembered suddenly where I was.

Asakeiri Home. Pneumonia. But the fist compress-
ing my chest had eased its grip, my fever had receded,
and, although my muscles felt flaccid and weak, I actually felt far stronger than I had been when I arrived.
With some effort, I managed to sit up and get a better
look at the room. The lamp sat on a simple, low table.
Except for a pair of three-legged stools, there was no
other furniture. The Asakeiri may have been builders,
but they did not seem to be carpenters.

I lay back in my bed. Relief coursed through my
body: I had been well cared for. I was not a prisoner.
I was going to live.

By the creaking of the floorboards overhead and the
faint murmur of voices, I knew that morning had
come. No dawn lightened the gloom; there were no
windows. I did not feel strong enough to get up,
though my stomach grumbled hungrily. I lay in my
warm nest of hay and wool, trying to reconstruct what

had happened while I lay ill, and how much time had passed.

Of my actual arrival at Asakeiri Home, I remembered nothing. Of my illness I also remembered nothing. Or rather—what memories I retained were tricky, slippery things: shattered pieces of dreams, strange and meaningless without their contexts. I remembered wandering the barren corridors of a maze. I remembered ships, spreading their white wings and flying into the arms of the sun. I remembered a vicious battle, where warriors staggered, ankle-deep in sticky blood. I remembered the uncovered face of a child buried in snow, her eyelids frozen shut by ice. I remembered jungles, and peddlers, and people dressed in black with gaping holes in their chests where their hearts had been cut out. And I remembered that unlocked door, hanging ajar, banging from time to time in the wind.

I heard a murmur of conversation and saw a glow of advancing light. With a gesture she must have been using her entire life, Ata'al swept aside the leather curtain and confidently entered the room. But she paused there in the doorway, with Talesan at her heels.

The lamp in her hand illuminated her face. Age and sun and the harsh mountain winds had wizened her features into an extraordinary sculpture. Lines marked her skin like woodgrain. Every time she had smiled or laughed or squinted into the sun, it had marked her face. Every time she frowned, or fretted, or wept, that, too, had marked her face. Now her entire life was written there, an annotated frame for her sharp, glittering eyes.

At last, she said, "You are awake?" But in her voice and on her face were written the intonations of another, unasked question.

"How long have I been here?" My voice was a hoarse caw.

She turned her face away sharply and spoke to Talesan, a low murmur not meant for my ears. The younger woman clutched her burdens more tightly to her chest, glancing at me and hastily glancing away again. Ata'al strode into the room and began refilling the lamps with a pitcher of oil. "Several days. You don't remember?"

"No. Have I been quite ill?"

"You have been ill."

Ata'al lit the lamps, and an orange, smoldering glow suffused the room.

"How many days?" I asked.

Ata'al looked at Talesan, who said, "Eight days between first snow and second."

"Then—ten days since we found her."

I sat up, astonished. "What is the phase of the moon?"

"First full moon of winter."

The moon had also been full for the festival of Iska. Twenty-eight days had passed, but I could not remember more than half of them.

Talesan set down her burdens on the table and floor: several bowls, a teapot, and a bundle of what appeared to be clothing. She poured some tea into a bowl and set it aside to cool. Ata'al knelt beside the bed to press her ear to my chest. Then she got to her feet with a grunt, and gestured for Talesan to give me the tea.

"What is your name?"

"Jamil."

Talesan's hand trembled, spilling a little of the tea. "The tea will build your strength," she said, but her voice also trembled.

I drank the tea and consumed a bowl full of hot cereal. There was no spoon, so I used my fingers. The two women left and returned with a basket full of dried beanpods and a narrow-mouthed pot in which to put the shelled beans. If I was well enough to talk, it seemed, I was well enough to work.

They left me alone again. Figures carved in stone lined a ledge in the wall: a squatting female with an infant emerging from her womb, a coiled dragon, a pot-bellied person grinning with good cheer. They had to be wellness totems, I realized. I lay in the town hospital.

I had heard of the aching, exhaustingly cold winters

of the high country. The warmth of the room, which actually made my blanket of furs unnecessary, surprised me; especially considering the lack of a hearth and a fire.

I wore simple wool clothing, such as I had seen the Asakeiri wear underneath their furred outergear. Clean rags wrapped my feet. In my hair, a lock had been twisted at the nape of my neck. A single bead had been slipped onto it, and secured with a strip of cloth. As I fingered the bead, a memory teased at me: *"A blue bead, the Sky Woman's color, to mark the end of your soul's wandering."* I grasped at the memory, but it had all the substance of a handful of mist.

I tottered on my own two feet to use a low basin for its designated purpose, and returned, exhausted, to my herb-scented bed. As I recovered from my efforts, I felt at the flesh of my limbs, trying to assess how emaciated I had become and how long it might take me to rebuild my strength. What I felt under the layer of soft wool surprised and unnerved me.

Some time later, as I sat shelling beans, Ata'al returned. This time, she spoke outside the curtain and awaited my reply before she entered. She squatted on a stool and clasped her bony hands across her trousered knees. She had recently been outside. Some snow still clung to her clothing, melting rapidly in the warmth of the room. I became restless under the focus of her considering gaze. The old woman looked at me as if she knew me. She looked at me as if she knew everything I had done.

"I will not be a burden on your people for long," I said. "As soon as I am able to travel. . . ."

"Jamil, winter has arrived in the mountains. It is a long journey to the nearest road, and even farther to the nearest town."

"But I am in much better condition than I ever imagined I could be. I find it hard to believe that I have been so ill."

"The dragon's back is a harsh land."

In the silence that followed, I heard, faintly, the sound of water splashing into a basin. The old woman sighed, and I heard the soft, clicking sounds of her beaded locks rattling together. "I am troubled about you."

I split a dry pod and dropped its yellow beans into the pot. The old woman's attitude had begun to irritate me. Like most people who go out of their way to help another, she now assumed she held a kind of power over me. Perhaps, according to the laws of the Asakeiri culture, I now owed her an extraordinary debt. I would have to give her my firstborn child, perhaps, or swear to serve her all my days. I popped the beans into the pot, wondering how deep the snow would lie by the time I had recuperated enough to be able to travel.

Ata'al spoke, the rhythmic intonations of her words chanting into the gloom. "I climbed alone to the mountaintop. There I took the dragon's breath into my own lungs. I felt the fire of the dragon's heart begin to burn in my own body. I raised my eyes to the Sky Woman's face, and I waited. But no answer came to me."

Once again, her beads rattled. She looked into my face. Her eyes had a blind look, her pupils dilated from the effects of breathing the toxic volcanic fumes. "To whom can a wise woman turn when she cannot see into her own heart? To another wise woman?"

"Not to me, then," I said with a laugh.

"No?" The old woman leaned forward. "Do you think you can make me believe you are a fool, Jamil? I see you more clearly than you ever saw yourself."

I forced my hands to lie flat at my sides. Perhaps she was an old woman, but I was weak as a babe. She could easily have killed me.

"What have I brought into our village?" she said. "What have I saved from death—not once, but twice? What have I eaten bread with, and treated as gently as if she were my own child?"

"I am a Separated One."

Her level gaze told me that she had already guessed my secret. And how could she not know? She had summoned my ghost and the ghost of Alasil, then bidden us to remain nearby so we could return to the

frozen husk we had been so ready to abandon. She
knew I had two souls. She must have known what I
was before they ever found my body in the snow.

"Tell me what I should do," she said softly.

It seemed to be my doom, to go from one unexpected event to another and never have the opportunity
to make a plan. What could I tell the woman: That I
posed no hazard to her people, when she and I both
knew that I did? I was too weak and ill to speak wisely,
and instead I said angrily, "Thirty years ago, when
your people first defied the Emperor, you might have
thought of this!"

"Is it not the Emperor who should have considered
that the trust of the Asakeiri might one day be of value
to him? He stole a child from us."

"The Emperor does not steal children!"

"Where did you yourself come from, Jamil?"

It was maddening, to be in a position where I had
to explain the Emperor's actions to this primitive
woman. I controlled my temper, since my life was at
risk here, and said politely, "Yes, the many-souled
children are taken from their parents. Certainly you
know that they would be killed as soon as their . . .
difference . . . becomes apparent. The Emperor has
been rescuing the children to save their lives."

The old woman gazed at me out of those disturbing
eyes: so deep, so lively, so piercingly intelligent. "Is
that what you believe?" she finally said. Her fingers
spread across her knees: knobbed joints, skin like stiff
paper, fingernails blunted by hard work. "Then tell
me, servant-of-the-Emperor. If the Asakeiri people kill
our many-souled children when they are still young,
then why am I alive, and an old woman? Explain that
to me."

Illness had dulled my wits, I suppose. "What do
you mean?"

"It is no secret. I have three souls, and so I am the
village wisewoman, and no important decision is ever
made without first consulting me."

"Is that so," I said distantly. Why would the woman
attempt to impress me with such a blatant untruth?

Were a many-souled person to survive childhood by some accident, the endless contention between their selves as they each struggled for dominance would drive them mad. And Ata'al clearly had all her wits about her. Did Ata'al truly think to deceive me with this simple assertion? And why? Had she, too, recognized that there might be value in holding a Separated One hostage? Or did she actually think that she could win my sympathy and my collusion on behalf of the Asakeiri?

Certainly, it could be in any tribe's interest to have the Emperor's ear. To encounter such political sophistication among a remote and isolated people was certainly surprising. But this I could turn to my advantage.

I said, ''Well, maybe the truth is not always so simple as our teachers make it out to be.'' Better not to sound too enthusiastic too quickly.

Ata'al abruptly stood up, grunting with effort. ''I will send someone with some food for you. And more beans.''

I smiled secretly to myself. She would not feed me if she intended to kill me. She meant to manipulate me, then. Well, two could play this game of deceit.

She left me alone once again. She left me alone, with the pieces of a tremendous mystery lying scattered around me, like a child's puzzle dropped carelessly to the floor. And I was such a smug bastard that I didn't even bother to examine the pieces, much less to consider the various ways they might fit together. To those who think they know everything, there are no mysteries.

Chapter 7

I told them I wanted to bathe. They took me, Ata'al supporting me at one side and Talesan at the other, down the narrow, dark corridors at the heart of Asakeiri Home. The living rock felt cool and hard through the rag wrappings of my feet. Ancient overhead beams bore the weight of the town on their backs. Low doorways gave access to small storerooms, filled with bins of potatoes and jars of grain, racks of dried meat and neat stacks of corn dried in the husk. Cats with thin, ascetic faces and hoarse, yowling voices walked through the shadows, waging their timeless war against rats and mice. After the warmth of my room, this region of storerooms and bare stone seemed very cold, and I shivered in my light clothing.

The corridor ended at a doorway, this one closed by an actual wooden door with metal hinges. It gave access to a narrow, dark dressing room, where Talesan set her lamp on a ledge to give a yellow, smoky illumination. We undressed and left our clothing here. A cloud of hot steam rushed out as Talesan opened the second door, revealing a deep room, dimly lit by narrow windows slit through the high walls. Steam floated like mist through the gloom. Slippery mosses, thriving in the warm half darkness, covered the stone. At the center of this room, water boiled in a stone basin like soup in a cauldron, spilling clouds of steam to trail slowly upward, toward the black chimney which rose where I might have expected the ceiling to be.

Around this central pool ranged several smaller pools. In one, women bathed small children. In another, a pair of men pounded sodden laundry with washing stones. Artificial waterways, lined and bridged by tile, carried the runoff away and into a chuckling stream which dove underneath the walls of the town to begin its journey toward the sea.

The moisture that settled on my lips tasted strongly of salt and minerals. "Dragon's water?"

"Heated by the dragon's heart," confirmed Ata'al.

The Asakeiri are not the only people who believe our land to actually be the back of a dragon asleep in the ocean. For the Asakeiri, this belief seemed to be the lodgepole supporting their entire vision of the universe. They did not worship or placate this dragon as a god. Rather, the dragon seemed to function for them as a constant reminder of the precariousness of existence in this harsh land.

The Asakeiri lived from season to season, with only the summer rains, the health of their flocks, and the rarity of volcanic eruptions standing between themselves and extinction. I expected such a people to be both resourceful and profoundly conservative, two factors which might sometimes work together like partners, and at other times might tug away pieces of the community, like wolves fighting over a kill. A strong, stable, and visionary leader who could form partnerships and enforce harmony would be essential to the survival of the community. Ata'al seemed too old for the role, but as I had not yet met the rest of the community, I could not objectively judge her effectiveness. If her position were even slightly unstable, I could probably find myself some allies and hatch a plot or two, so long as I was here.

Thirty years of stubborn resistance on the part of a tribal people could probably be attributed to the influence of one strong personality. If that one person were to topple, then the entire people would give way.

I had walked into the pool without knowing it, and looked with some surprise at the hot water lapping at my knees. Behind me, Talesan and Ata'al laid some fibrous pads and a soap pot at the edge of the pool. The water smelled richly of sulfur and dissolved stone. I knelt and slowly eased myself into its hot embrace.

The two women sat and chatted in the shallows. Ata'al's breasts sagged into the water. Ten children, she had suckled. Telesan took a fibrous pad and washed Ata'al's back. Her high, pointed breasts and narrow, childish hips marked her as a newcomer to womanhood, too young yet to lay with the equally young man who courted her so patiently.

In her lifetime, Ata'al had trained many other healers but had outlived all of them. Talesan, her most recent apprentice, demonstrated a particular facility for midwifery, but she had less patience for the slow tedium of long illnesses. In another ten years, Ata'al judged, she would have learned enough patience that she would be a very good healer. Ata'al planned to live that long, so the knowledge she had acquired throughout her lifetime would not die with her.

All this Ata'al had told me, as I lay recuperating from my illness and she sat sewing by the light of the lamps.

"Does Talesan have the second sight, like you do?" I asked.

"No, she will never be a wisewoman," said Ata'al. "She has only one soul."

"What are the names of your souls?"

Ata'al gazed at me thoughtfully. "I have three souls. But I have only one self, and my name is Ata'al."

I had lounged in the hot water long enough. What a luxury it was! I washed myself briskly with one of the pads, and we returned to the changing room, where we dried ourselves with cloths. I had taken the blue bead out of my hair when I first undressed. Now Ata'al put it back again, unasked, securing it with the scrap of cloth that I had laid aside.

Her insistence made me impatient. "What is the bead for?"

"It is your life bead." Without needing to look, she touched her own chipped and cracked blue bead, where

it pressed against her scalp, clasping a lock of gray hair. More beads crowded up against it: beads of wood and glass and stone, round and oval, carved and polished and glazed in every color known to humankind. I touched one, deep red glass with a black heart. "And this one?"

"By this bead I remember the loss of my eldest daughter."

"And this?" A wooden bead, painted green.

"The year of the great harvest. All of the old people have a bead like this."

"And this?" Another red bead, this one the color of fire.

Ata'al's faded eyes gazed inward. "I remember one summer night in the high meadows—" Smiling, she took the lock of hair out of my grip. "A very good night."

Talesan giggled like a child, and shook her head to make her beads rattle. "How do you remember, without beads?" she asked me.

I shrugged. "What is there to remember?"

"Why, births and deaths, your first menses, your first—" Talesan glanced at Ata'al and giggled again.

"Your husbands and lovers and friends," said Ata'al. "Your journeys and your harvests, your victories and your defeats."

So much to remember, I thought. And I felt, faintly, the prickling of jealousy on the skin of my spirit. Nothing belongs to me which does not also belong to the Emperor, and that includes all the events of my life. "Well, it's a good thing my hair is so short," I said. I meant it as a joke, but nobody smiled.

I had always heard that recovery from pneumonia is a slow, painstaking process. But my strength returned rapidly, and only a few days passed before I became restless in the muffled darkness and solitude of the sickroom. Without telling either of my caretakers, I decided to go exploring. I put on a plain, sleeveless goatskin smock similar to the one Talesan usually wore over her woolens, and a pair of fur-lined slippers. My

knees still wobbled under my weight, but I leaned my hand on the wall for support and shuffled out the door and into the corridor.

The storerooms which occupied this lowest level of the town I had already seen. I followed another gloomy corridor, past more storerooms, most of these filled with the neat architecture of woodstacks, until it ended in a double door. Pale light and icy wind blew through the cracks in its ancient wood. Through this door, the supplies must have been brought in throughout the summer, but now it was barred against the pressure of the snow. I backtracked to a narrow staircase, whose ancient, uneven stone still bore the gouges of the stonecutter's tools. After climbing a few steps, I doubted I could make it to the top. It took all my strength to mount my heavy body up those steps, and when I felt faint or dizzy, there was no banister to which I could cling. But the pale light glimmering overhead and the faint sound of voices gave me inspiration. Eventually I sat, gasping, on the top step.

I had come into a large, gloomy hall, barren except for a few rugs and a long table. The only light entered through miserly windows, tightly covered by semi-transparent greased hide. Bats hibernated in the rafters, undisturbed by the shrieks and laughter of the children who played hunt and sneak at the far end, near the cold fireplace. I watched them stalk and chase each other, but they were too absorbed in their game to notice me.

By now, I had wandered far from the hot spring which warmed the inner rooms of the town. Winter's iron chill had penetrated here. When I sat still too long, the cold soaked into my bones from the icy stone, and I began to shiver. Resolute, I resumed my exploration, crossing the pillared hall and entering a corridor which at last brought me to the busy living areas of the village. In the warm, windowless interior of the village, the people slept and ate in their small family groups. But it was in the cold outer rooms, where leather curtains could be drawn to let in the

light, that most of the population of the village spent the short winter days.

Here, following the sound of their chattering voices and the din of their tools, I found the Asakeiri hard at work. Crowded into many large, smoky rooms, where cookfires blazed in open hearths, they made and repaired tools, spun thread and wove cloth, prepared food and made clothing, nursed and watched over the children, and courted each other. All but unnoticed, I walked from room to room. In one, all the occupants argued irritably with each other. In the next, they worked together in silent harmony. In the next, a storyteller finished her tale amid raucous laughter.

At last, I found an empty stool by a fire and sat to rest and warm the chill out of my bones. In this room, an old man crafted a pair of snow boots, hovered over by a young girl who watched every move of his hands. A weaver squatting at a small floor loom threw and caught her shuttle. Three spinners perched on high stools dropped their spindles toward the floor, and then recovered them with a tug on the thread. A woman on a low stool by the fire rocked dreamily back and forth as her fur-wrapped infant nuzzled her breast. At a chopping block, a man cut fresh meat into chunks and dumped it into a large stewpot. Nearby, a very slender adolescent talked to himself, gesturing wildly in the empty air. A broken bowl full of interesting, brightly-colored odds and ends lay at his feet.

Children came and went. Everyone in the room chattered energetically as they worked, except for the woman nursing the infant who seemed to be in her own world. Below the sound of their chatter murmured another sound, the rhythmic clicking of hairbeads. Even the mad boy with the broken bowl had beads in his hair, as well as several small silver bells that must have cost a fortune in trade. Bells, I thought, so his keepers could track him by the sound, like a willful goat who is always wandering off.

I went to the window where the hide curtain had been pulled aside to let the fresh, frigid air wash into the workroom. I saw a woman with a twig broom, sweeping snow from a narrow flight of steps. Two men, a father and son perhaps, climbed rapidly up from below, their arms full of bloody hides. Far below, in the stock pens, the trampled snow was blotched with scarlet as the butchers grimly culled the flocks. Squinting in the glare of sunlight, I tried to guess how deep the snow lay now. Deep enough, I decided, and bound only to get deeper while I convalesced here.

Even though I had realized that I could make my stranded state into a wonderful opportunity, I still hoped to escape. I could not remain here, waiting for the wheel of the stars to turn slowly from winter to spring. I had unfinished business to attend to: I could not allow the Akava fools and the sorceress they had hired to think that they had gotten away with murder. I could not risk the loss of my position and responsibilities in Ashami.

The mountains stretched as far as I could see: jagged peaks clothed in the gray foliage of pines, with an overcloak of blinding white. One of the mountains bled steam and smoke into the air: dragon's breath. If I left Asakeiri Home, the stars would point the way homeward. But the stars could not teach me how to avoid avalanches, ravines, snow bridges, or the hot flow of magma from the dragon's heart. They could not show me how to survive without shelter, what to eat, or how to find a safe path to follow.

I fretted at the window as the frigid air tickled my flesh with icy fingers and behind me the spinners broke into a giggling, raucous song. Below, the goats struggled through the snow, watched over by a crew of goatherds on skis. The goatherds' bulky furs made them seem misshapen and awkward, but they glided across the snow like a sailboat glides through the water. Watching them, I had my first inkling of an idea of how I might get home.

Ata'al found me huddled by the fire, holding a skein of scarlet wool as a young boy wound it onto a weav-

er's shuttle. Throughout the afternoon, I had wandered
from group to group, and room to room, asking what
I could do to help with the work. I had chopped potatoes and onions, I had used a beautiful obsidian knife
to slice thin strips of goat meat for salting and drying,
and I had carded wool for the spinners.

To try to win the trust of the people without first
giving them plenty of evidence that I deserved that
trust would have been impossible. I had decided to
start by proving two things to them: first, that I did
not take the gift of survival for granted, and second,
that I would earn my keep. Many times in my lifetime, I had been in the position of needing to win
someone's trust. I did it well; well enough that I was
often called upon to teach the skill to the young nov-
ices. But, in this case, I worked under two major
disadvantages.

First, my target population knew I was a Separated
One. Most people think that the Separated Ones use
masks to disguise our identities. The truth is that my
bare face is my best disguise. Without my mask, no
one knows who I am, and it is this anonymity which
makes my most covert work possible. With the Asakeiri, I had lost this advantage.

Second, I had to win the trust of not one person,
or a dozen, but an entire community. We had thought
the Asakeiri people to be relatively autonomous from
each other, but I now knew that just the opposite had
to be true. Like bees in a hive, each individual's
work benefited the entire community. All knew their
own value and exercised a modicum of power. I
could successfully escape the mountains and find my
way home again only if all the experience, knowledge, and survival skill of the Asakeiri people was
at my disposal. Therefore, I had to win the trust of
everyone.

So Ata'al found me, hard at work, and stood
watching, grim-faced, with a steaming pottery cup
in her hand. She wore her indoor clothing: wool
smock, a goatskin vest that fell to her knees, loose
trousers tucked into the tops of her soft boots. Her

hair swung like a beaded curtain as she squatted beside me, holding out the cup. I smelled the familiar
sharp scent of herbs, and carefully hooked my skein
of wool over my knees so it would not get tangled as
I drank.

"You should not let yourself become tired," Ata'al
said.

"Yes, mother," I replied, addressing her as I had
heard others do. "But I do not want the people to
regret having given me shelter."

The boy said proudly, "I am teaching her."

"She has much to learn."

Ata'al took the empty cup from me, and without
another word turned and walked away.

In the night I awoke from a dead sleep. One lamp
smoldered on the low table, and the carved figures on
the ledge danced in its light, casting their long, quivering shadows across the wall. The fresh scent of the
bed herbs, roused by the heat of my body and the
motion of my restless turning, filled my nostrils. I sat
up in the bed, wrestling for a few moments with the
tangled bed fur. Something had awakened me.

Then I felt it: a faint vibration in the bedrock, like
the tremor of a bird's heartbeat. I crawled hastily out
of my bed, and gave a cry: "The dragon! The dragon
stirs!" My hoarse voice, sharp with urgency, penetrated to the room overhead, where I immediately
heard an answer. "The dragon!" a man shouted. I
dragged the furs from my bed and fled through the
darkness, as the earth began to tremble under my feet.
Behind me, one of the stone figurines fell with a crash
to the floor. If the entire village collapsed, with me at
its heart—

I ran down the black corridor. The earth rocked.
The timbers groaned as if the town were a ship in
heavy seas. In my panic, I ran at full speed into a wall.
The shock and the sharp pain shook my wits into order. Moving more slowly, riding the bucking floor like
a wild horse, I headed for the stairs. As I climbed, I

heard the faint cries of frightened children and a throbbing, rhythmic beating of drums.

By the time I reached the crowded hallways of the
living quarters, the violent shaking had begun to ease.
The Asakeiri people calmly made their way down the
hall, hushing their children and singing softly. I alone
gasped for breath and trembled with weakness in reaction to my wild flight. As I drew closer to the workrooms, where firelight flickered, the sobs of the
children and my own gasps had quieted. I could hear
now the sweet ringing of finger cymbals, and the
breathy tootling of a flute. "Sleep," the people sang.
"Sleep, dragon: sleep."

Shivering in the harsh night cold, we huddled together around the hearthfires. My eyes burned with
smoke. The voices surrounded me, hypnotically
soothing. Someone opened the windows, so the sounds
of our voices would carry out into the harsh cold of
the night.

> Warm as blood, the water holds you
> Sleep, dragon, sleep.
> Through the night the moon views you
> Sleep, dragon, sleep.
> In the arms of the earth, in the gaze of the sky
> Fire burning in your dreams as the days go by
> Sleep, dragon, sleep.

The floorboards trembled, and again fell still.
Through the window, I saw the cold light of the stars
glimmering on the snow. Far away, on the ridge of a
remote mountain, the smoldering fire of the dragon's
flowing blood glowed in the darkness. "Sleep," the
people sang. "Sleep, dragon, sleep."

Children dozed off in their parents' arms. Lovers
swayed against each other, clutching blankets around
themselves to stave off the cold. Sweetly, hypnotically,
the people sang to the night, sang to the restless earth
on which they had built their village, sang to the hot
blood boiling up out of cracks in the mountains, sang
to the black, crouching stone curled in the ocean upon

which their world was built. "Be still," they sang.
"Be still and do not wake. A thousand thousand years
have passed while you slept, and now your back has
become our world. We graze our flocks along your
backbone, we heat our houses with your breath. Do
not awaken and rise up from your sleep, for you are
our world now. You are our home."

Some of the parents took their children back to bed,
but others remained, singing, until they swayed upon
their feet in exhaustion. They sang a confusion of
words now, each one singing his or her own song:
sweetly, softly, beseechingly coaxing the dragon back
to sleep.

I sang, too. At first, I sang because I did not want
to return to my bed at the heart of the stone and
timber village. I sang because I did not want to die,
buried in stone. I sang in a hoarse whisper, and my
words dripped like water on a hillside, carving a
channel that flowed to a river and from there flowed
into the sea.

"Oh, do not wake," I sang. "Oh, do not make me
remember. Oh, do not make me pay my debts. Let me
sleep; let me sleep, let me sleep."

When morning dawned, we sat on the floor, red-
eyed with sleeplessness and hoarse from long singing, passing cups of hot tea from hand to hand and
staring blearily into the flames of the new-built
fires.

Ata'al came into the room with snow on her boots
and snow in her hair. The sky had clouded over, a
new storm brewing. I wondered where Ata'al had
been. The people gazed at her wearily, and there was
a kind of hopeless exhaustion in their faces, the exhaustion of one nightmare survived and a thousand
more yet to be faced.

Someone said, "Every time, the dragon raises his
head a little higher and shakes himself a little harder."

"Yes," said Ata'al.

"How long can our voices be enough?"

"Not much longer," said Ata'al. She looked directly into my eyes then, and I wondered what she

meant by it: that cool, measuring glance, filled with lurking accusation. Had I done something to awaken the dragon? After this weird night, I might believe anything.

"Adline," someone said then. "Adline, run your race well."

Chapter 8

After two days, the snow ceased to fall again, and a crew of young, vigorous tribespeople went out to dig pathways from the goatsheds to the haystacks. Unlike sheep, the goats would not venture into deep snow, as if they knew how easily they could be trapped in a drift and die. Instead, they waited impatiently for their keepers to dig a path for them, noisily bawling their hunger and irritably refusing to stand still to be milked.

After snowfall, everyone had a job to do. I, too, had set myself a task, a secret task that only I needed to know. I climbed down the outer staircase, the snow crunching and compacting under my weight, edging past the snow-sweepers with their stiff twig brooms. I smelled like the Asakeiri now, of goatskin and damp wool and woodsmoke and the earthy perfume of the dragon's water. But, after I had reached the churned, icy snow of the stockpens, I realized that anyone could tell I was an outlander by how awkwardly I walked in the snow.

The people digging in the snow wore woven shirts and trousers of greased leather. Their shovels were large and flat, and they scooped up great mounds of snow with each swing of their arms. They dug all the way down to the ground, exposing a crushed layer of dead grass, the sight of which excited the goats into a competitive frenzy.

I worked my way into the midst of a struggling herd, and quickly realized that I had chosen the hard route to my destination. I pounded on the goats with my fists, trying to get them to move aside, but their thick

winter wool absorbed my blows and they scarcely
seemed to notice my presence. They stood on my toes
with sharp-edged hooves. When I leaned my weight
into a goat's shoulder to shove her out of the way, I
might as well have been pushing at a boulder.

Yelling and cursing and punching my way through
the herd, I finally reached its leading edge, where a
man flung great shovelfuls of snow into the air, and
the goats ripped at the exposed brown grass, jerking
their heads up with every bite. Their placid, innocent
faces made me want to laugh. For all their stubborn-
ness, I found them to be likable creatures, with strong-
willed, complex, eccentric personalities, rather like
cats.

The man looked up from his digging, startled for a
moment by my presence. Many of the thousand or so
souls who inhabited Asakeiri Home had not yet gotten
accustomed to the sight of me. I was not the only
outsider in the village. Some members of the lowland
tribes, close racial cousins to the Asakeiri, had mated
with Asakeiri and come to live here in the high mountains. But I was the only stranger. I am used to being
a stranger; it suits me. I leaned against the wall of
snow, out of breath from my struggle with the goats,
and said to the man, ''How can I help?''

I had picked him out days before, as I looked out
the window of a workroom high in the village. That
had been after the earthquake, before the most recent
snowstorm. He knelt in the snow beside a small child
dressed in scarlet, and attached the bindings of a miniature pair of skis to the child's feet, then waded along
beside the child, holding her hand as she took her first
gliding steps across the snow. Ever since then, I had
been watching him.

Only a few people lived alone in the community.
Ata'al was one of them, and there were a few others
who, for whatever reason, did not choose to live within
the chaotic circle of a family. This man lived alone but
did not overtly associate himself with the men who
prefer the company of men. He was a welcome guest
at various family cookfires. He was popular among the

children but seemed to have none of his own. I could only conclude that he was single or widowed. In a community so small, it might sometimes prove a challenge to find a suitable mate.

"Keep the goats out of my way," he said, and kept digging.

Fortunately, the passageway he dug was narrow enough that I needed only to confront one or two goats at a time. I punched them in their noses, which they did not like at all, and they learned to keep their distance from me. I let him catch me watching him, from time to time. "I'm afraid I don't know much about goats," I finally said, apologetically.

He paused to rest, out of breath. We had progressed a good distance, and our goal, a snow-covered haystack with a cave eaten into the hay, was now in sight. He said, "Goats are as stubborn as people. They seem foolish, but I have never seen one fall, no matter how precarious the path they follow. They have their likes and dislikes, and nothing you can do will make them change their minds. They always know the weather; in the summer, they take shelter before even one drop of rain falls from the sky."

"I want to know how to make them behave."

"Well!" Steam puffed out of his mouth as he laughed. "No one knows that! One winter, when the thaw came late, we ran out of hay, and the goats came right up the steps of the village and climbed in through the windows, looking for food."

"Shall I bring you some water?"

"We're almost there now." He resumed his shoveling. When we had reached the haystack, he cleared an area around it so the goats could reach the hay, and then came wading through the deep snow to give me a hand out of the pathway, where I still blocked the goats' passage. The snow came up to my knees, and I stumbled. He gave a friendly grin. "Walk in my footsteps." He was not much taller than I, but he took short steps to make it easier for me. His solicitousness made me a little angry, even though I was still weak and needed the help.

"You make skis," I said, when we had reached the trampled slush of the stockpen. We stamped our feet to knock off the worst of the snow, and I pulled down my hood so he could see as much of me as possible. I am not much of a seductress, actually; that is usually Alasil's business. But he gazed at me, long and thoughtfully.

"Yes," he said at last, "I do make skis, in the winter. Do you want a pair?"

"It looks like fun."

"It can be, going downhill. Mostly, it's work."

"It's hard to have to spend so much time indoors."

He nodded. "Take care, winter madness can make you foolish. I will make you some skis, then."

He said it so suddenly that it surprised me. No bargaining, no manipulation, nothing. "I don't have anything to trade," I began.

"What trade? You are Asakeiri. Mine is yours."

He tramped off, to help with the butchering of a kid which had taken sick in the cold. I watched from a distance. He soothed the frightened goatling with gentle hands, so that it scarcely noticed when the knife went in. I caught myself wondering a strange thing: How one could be so gentle and so heartless at the same time. It must hurt, I thought, hurt deeply. How much easier to simply pluck out one's heart and throw it away.

Ata'al came out to scold me for staying so long out of doors. I took her by the arm. "I had to finish what I had begun," I said apologetically. "I am going inside now, and sit by the fire and drink tea all afternoon."

I looked again at the man. He held the kid's body now, and he had blood on his hands. He laughed at something someone had said, but his eyes were sad.

"A good man, my son," said Ata'al pointedly.

"He is your son? I thought you only had the three."

"He is my daughter's man, and so he is my son. He comes from the Clay People, the pot makers. But he is good with wood. The trees know him."

I thought I had determined the man's kinship status

better than this! As far as I knew, I had met all of Ata'al's daughters and sons and their mates and their many children. Completely confused, I said, "Which daughter?"

"Adline won a race with the Clay People and chose Corlin as her prize."

"Adline is your daughter?" This astonishing coincidence set all the alarm bells ringing in my mind, and I said nothing more as I frantically tried to reel in the unraveling threads of my thought. But every thread led me to that unlocked door, hanging ajar, banging in the wind. Beyond that door, I could not go. I pounded my frozen fingers on my jacket to warm them, using the vigorous activity to conceal my dismay.

We climbed the stairs together. Every last trace of snow had been swept from them, lest it later turn to ice and cause someone to slip. The Asakeiri are careful about such things. "I saw Adline run the first race in the Emperor's Concourse," I said at last. "She won it beautifully."

"She has the heart of an eagle," Ata'al said solemnly, as if these words were an important revelation. They made no sense to me.

"The Emperor won't tolerate her competition in the races, you know."

Ata'al paused on the stairs and turned to me. Her eyes frightened me: dragon's eyes, black and hard as obsidian. "The Emperor is a little boy," she said scornfully. "He wants what he wants, and will do anything to get it. Do you know how we Asakeiri deal with little boys? We stand back and let them make fools of themselves. The land of the dragon's backbone does not tolerate fools. So, they learn. They learn that they have a choice to make; they can work for everyone's good, or they can die."

The morning after the earthquake, I had moved in with Talesan's family. The actual move had been simple enough, since I could carry all my worldly goods in one hand. Talesan helped me clean the hospital room for its next occupant, then we took a bag of

straw out of storage and took it upstairs to make my
new bed. Her family had offered me a small cubbyhole
of a room, which they called an aunt's cupboard. It
was warm enough, and isolated somewhat from the
noisy chaos of the younger members of the family. I
did not complain.

I shared the suite of rooms with twelve people: Talesan's parents, whom I called brother and sister; Talesan herself and her two younger siblings; a maternal
aunt and uncle, their three children, the eldest of whom
was not three years old; a very old man, whose relationship to the rest of them I could not determine; and
an adolescent boy, a cousin of some sort, who apparently was moving restlessly from family to family,
driven by the mysterious forces which make some
young people so intolerably unsettled.

The aunt and uncle were preoccupied with their
children most of the time. Talesan's duties as apprentice healer kept her busy, and her two younger siblings
were often outside, caring for the family flock. Both
of Talesan's parents, Moris and Selin, were skilled
craftspeople, and spent their days in the workrooms.
The old man, though disabled by a joint disease, did
all the cooking. The first time I tasted one of his stews,
I realized why he was treated with such respect. I
swear, I have not eaten any better food in the Emperor's palace.

Anyone who sat down in that place would immediately have a baby put into their lap, so I could not
entirely avoid childcare. I also helped with the house-
keeping, but usually tried to join a community work
crew to keep myself occupied and to keep my partic-
ipation in the community as public as possible. When
there was a roof to be patched, a wall to be repaired,
corn or beans to be shelled, meat to be preserved, or
wood to be carried, members of the community
quickly learned to come looking for me, because I was
usually at loose ends and made it a policy never to
turn down a job, no matter how cold, wet, or disgusting it turned out to be.

Moris, Ata'al's eldest son, was not much younger

than I. For the purposes of argument, all the members of the Asakeiri tribe had assigned me to Ata'al's family; therefore Moris treated me like an older sister. I played the role as well as I could, considering that I had never had the chance to learn my lines.

Two days after the snowfall had ended, the old man made a stew of goat meat and chunks of orange squash, onions, and potatoes. He had made bread, too, out of corn and barley ground together on a grinding stone, and mixed with the bread starter that they kept in a covered pot near the fire. The starter was as ancient as the people who ate the bread, having been kept alive from generation to generation, passed from parent to child, and nurtured as carefully as the Asakeiri nurtured all of their charges: their goats, their children, their gardens. I doubt that a more responsible and serious people ever walked the face of the earth. Not a crumb fell to the earth in their households; nothing went to waste.

Hungry after the day's work, the family gathered in the warm central room, waiting for the old man to bring in the stewpot. Corlin suddenly appeared with a bowl of parched salted corn, which was passed around, each of us taking a handful until the bowl was empty. He sat with Moris and Selin, and they discussed the milk fever that some of the does in their family flock had developed. They were dosing the goats with one of Ata'al's herbal concoctions, but so far the cure hadn't taken. It worried them; they didn't want to have to kill any of their prime stock so early in the season. At least one of the afflicted goats belonged to Adline, which explained Corlin's concern. In her absence, he was expected to care for her herd. But, as a relative newcomer, he must have often needed to depend upon the advice of others.

When the stew and bread was served, he came to sit beside me. "You are looking well, Ata'al-daughter."

The other members of the family turned their faces politely away, just as they did when Orlil came calling for Talesan.

"My strength returns too slowly," I said.

"Well, you are impatient, like all of your kin." He tore a piece of bread and gave half to me, smiling a little. I accepted the bread uncertainly. To offer to share one's food so intimately usually means only one thing, no matter what land one is in. "Come out tomorrow, if the sun shines, and I will teach you how to ski," he said.

Later, I found Ata'al in the herbary, frowning over the pot in which she carefully brewed one of her potions. A child of the village had fallen seriously ill, and I had not seen much of the old healer lately. I squatted on a stool, and waited for her to acknowledge me. She mixed several more ingredients into her brew and stirred it carefully, then poked at the coals of the little fire to make it flame. "Jamil," she finally said.

"You have made me your daughter, but I am still a stranger in this land. I am confused, and wish you would give me an answer to my question."

"Well," she said neutrally, and sat down on her own stool. She looked tired; the battle for the child's life was not going well.

"If my sister's husband wants to sleep with me, is that wrong?"

"Well, what does your sister have to say about it?"

"I have never even met Adline."

"Oh, it is Corlin. Of course your sister would be grateful if you kept him company in her absence. Corlin longs for a child."

I did not know how to respond to this. Ata'al got up to check her potion and sat back down again, looking at me questioningly.

"I don't really want to sleep with him. It's just that— I didn't want to do the wrong thing."

Ata'al sat back a little on her stool. My ignorance seemed to amuse her. But, in my city, to sleep with another person's husband or wife would be intolerable. "Well, then," she said. "You are single, and an adult. If another person is single and of a proper age, and not too closely related, then you may sleep with him or her. Or if that person is mated, and their mate is willing, then it would not be wrong. However, if your sister is barren, then it would be considered your proper duty to give her a child.''

''But she isn't really my sister.'' I had to remind myself from time to time that this whole business of my being Ata'al's daughter was just a convenient fiction. Completely immersed in the community as I had become, it would be too easy to get trapped into the Asakeiri way of seeing things and never be able to extricate myself.

Ata'al shrugged, and stood up again to stir her brew. I didn't tell her that there would be no child in any case; the Emperor's doctors had seen to that.

I truly did not want to sleep with Corlin. All Separated Ones have at least one self who dislikes sex in any form; in my case it was me. If it did turn out that I had to allow him to seduce me, in order to get what I wanted, Corlin would probably notice that I took little pleasure in it. I should have picked a less sensitive man, I think.

''Tell me about Adline,'' I said to him the next day, as he helped me out of the snowdrift into which I had sprawled.

''It's just like walking with your feet sliding across the floor,'' he said patiently, not for the first time.

''When feet grow as long as my arm, maybe.''

In many stops and starts we had crossed half the field together, following in the tracks of an earlier traveler. Now we had turned back and were working our way toward the village again, making far better progress than we had at first.

Corlin said, ''The Clay People do not travel like the Asakeiri. We stay near our clay mines and kilns, and people from all over the mountains come to trade for pots. Three springs in a row, Adline came to visit us, alone. The first time, she must have been younger than Talesan. She just wanted to see the world, she said. She said she was tired of goats, and of goat things. We taught her how to run a potter's wheel. She learned quickly, and then she wouldn't go near the potter's

shed any more. The wheel made her dizzy, she said,
but I think she got bored, once she knew the secret of
it. That is the way she is—restless, willful. The next
spring, we went out walking one night, to the hot
springs, and did what young people do there at night.
I pleased her, I guess. She told me she would come
back for me. I really didn't believe she would, but she
did.

"The Clay People don't like it when the Asakeiri
take one of their own to live up here in the high places.
They make them pay a dowry first. She ran a race for
me, instead of paying the dowry, and it made them
angry when she won against our fastest runner.

"There were some who thought she was arrogant. I
loved her restlessness, and her hard wit, and her stub-
bornness. Maybe I balanced her out: a pound of flour
to her pound of gold. I was happy to go with her, and
we did not tire of each other."

He added, "You look like her."

"I'm not really her sister," I reminded him. He
spoke of Adline in the past tense, as if he did not
expect to ever see her again. This bothered me, even
though no one had more reason than I to know that
she was dead.

"No, you're not her sister," he said, after a long
moment.

"Do the Asakeiri ever take long trips in the winter?"

"Sometimes, to trade. Salt is what we need, and
anything made of iron. The Emperor's guards are easier to slip by, in the winter. But it's hard to come home
again; skiing uphill, with all that cast iron on your
back."

"There's a trade town nearby, with a forge?"

"Not so nearby. Eight days, if the weather is good,
and your pack is not too heavy. They'll trade anything
for dragon's glass."

"What town is that? Do they have a road?"

I suppose I sounded too eager. Corlin leaned on his
ski pole and looked at me. His eyes were like goat's
eyes, in their mildness and placidity hiding their deep

wisdom and occasional fits of temper. "You belong to
the Emperor. Am I teaching you how to ski so you
can go home and send the dogs out after us?"

I said, as if affronted, "After the Asakeiri saved my
life? I have my honor."

"I had not heard that the Separated Ones have any
honor." Corlin's pole sank too deeply into the snow,
and he plucked it out again. He gazed off toward the
clutter of buildings huddled in the shelter of the cliff.
The village looked as if it had been there forever.

Corlin said, half to himself, "What does it matter?
Emperor or not, the dragon will still throw him into
the sea."

"Only if the dragon throws everyone else into the
sea too, including the Asakeiri people."

"There is only so much that singing can do! There
comes a time—" As if he wanted to flee my presence,
Corlin started away toward the village. Then he
seemed to remember that I could not effectively follow
him, and he stopped to wait for me.

"Why is Adline running the Emperor's Concourse?" I asked, as I caught up to him.

"Ask Ata'al," Corlin said coldly.

I did not reply. How could I tell him, without ad-
mitting it to myself, that Ata'al frightened me?

Chapter 9

I found Ata'al in the herbary, a narrow, dark room, crowded from floor to ceiling with sturdy wooden shelves. There the ingredients for Ata'al's simples crowded in a mysterious clutter of unlabeled jars, bottles, and paper-wrapped boxes sealed with the mark of a well-known herb trader. Dried herbs hanging from the beam formed the illusion of a forest canopy: a jungle of flowers and twigs, leaves and seedpods, mostly unidentifiable to my untrained eye.

Ata'al had been twitching down bits of this and that when I came in, and now she stood at the worktable, which stretched from one end of the room to the other, grinding the herbs in a mortar. The sharp, sweet, dusty scents made my nose itch. I rubbed it irritably. "Why is Adline running the Emperor's Concourse?" I said. In the days that had passed since my talk with Corlin, the mystery of it nagged at me, persistent as a dog yapping and scrabbling at the rabbit's burrow. The Askaeiri people had demonstrated themselves to be neither ignorant, nor foolish, nor fanatically devoted to a great political cause. Therefore, I could no longer explain away Adline's competition as a simple slap in the face to a despised ruler.

Ata'al said, "Adline loves to run and to win. Since childhood, she dreamed of running the Emperor's Concourse. Why should she not do it if she chooses?"

The night of the earthquake, I heard someone say, 'Adline, run well.' What did they mean by that?"

"They have no reason to wish her to lose."

"But that comment implied to me that her running had something to do with the dragon."

"The dragon has always been restless, Jamil. Life goes on." Ata'al's mortar and pestle crackled and ground rhythmically. She gazed into space as she worked, grinding by feel alone.

Clearly, this matter was a closely guarded secret, and the direct approach would get me no answers. "How is the sick child?" I asked politely.

Ata'al's mouth thinned. "The child died. Did you not hear the wailing?"

"I'm sorry," I said, still polite. "Would you keep me here at Asakeiri Home against my will?"

"I have lost three children, and outlived two husbands. I know how to grieve. Do you think I could not endure the pain of losing you?"

"I am not a child, to play games with you. Am I a prisoner here, or am I free to go?"

Ata'al gave an ironic smile. "You are free to go . . . if you want to leave more than you want to live."

"Well, that comment is a trifle misleading, don't you think? Corlin told me that people often take long journeys in winter, to trade for salt and iron. So I know it is possible to survive such a journey."

"Yes, there are a few people among the Asakeiri who have the dragon's luck, and sometimes make such a journey, and survive."

"If one came with me as a guide, their luck would travel with me as well."

"It would take a great deal of good luck to counter your bad. Are you asking me if you are free to find yourself a guide? Surely you know that you may do as you like."

"I can seek a guide until my voice is gone, but no one will agree to accompany me without your say-so!"

Ata'al rubbed her fingers through the herbs, testing the fineness of the grind. She said at last, "Without my say-so? When I was young, I dreamed I might one day have such power. . . ." She dismissed her childish dreams with a snort and sat down abruptly on a stool, brushing powdered herbs from her fingertips. "Listen to me: You have a hard lesson to learn. You have always made your own opportunity, forming it like a clay pot out of whatever materials came to your hand. But that will not work for you now. You must wait patiently, and when the time is right, your opportunity will come to you.''

"You call this advice? Just don't expect me to thank you for it.'' In a foul temper, I left the herbary, and went stamping angrily throughout the village. But everyone ignored me; they, at least, had work to do.

Lugging a basket full of tools and materials for repairing the roof, I climbed the long stairway that mounted the height of the village. The stairway dove between outcropping walls, and emerged onto flat rooftops burdened with slumping piles of snow. The feet of a thousand generations had worn the treads, hollowing their centers and smoothing their edges. In the cracks and crannies, packed snow had been polished to ice. I climbed cautiously, my vision clouded by my own condensed breath, knee joints aching, calves cramping, clawing with one mittened hand for something to grip hold of. The children scrambled up these stairs as if they ran across flat ground, but the lingering effects of pneumonia made me feel like an old woman.

The sickly, wan face of the sun lifted weakly above its coverlet of clouds and cast a weary glare of light across the snowy world. Dazzled, I crouched on the steps, squinting against the light.

Goats cavorted in the meadow below, oblivious to the bitter wind. Beyond the meadow, the gray forest merged into the snow, smearing and running like paint dragged carelessly across wet paper. The mountainside sloped gradually out of my sight, giving way to a view of the forested ground below. Beyond, yet more mountains, snow-gilded, blue and lavender now as the brief light faded once again. I glanced up. The sun had buried its face once again in the clouds.

I could see my destination: a rooftop where several people used shovels to lightly cast aside the snow which covered its leaky beams. Between myself and my goal, a slender figure blocked the way, legs splayed, buttocks firmly planted on the steps. She wore no furred outer tunic, but only a goatskin vest, unfastened to the cold. Her wool undergarment was brightly, lovingly embroidered with a swirling net of flowering vines. She glared at me sullenly as I approached. The wind had scoured her cheeks to an angry red.

"Aren't you cold?" I asked.

She neither replied, nor moved aside to give me passage. I bedded my basket into the snow beside the stairway and sat on the step below the one she blocked with her left foot. Solemnly, I pretended to study the view. No intruder could approach the village unseen, I realized, except at night. Even then, the village dogs, who sleep in warm dens in the snow, would warn of the unfriendly approach. I turned to look upward, at the highest point of the village, where within a stone watchtower, someone paced, eyes shaded with one hand from the light glaring through the clouds.

"Do you always have a watchman?" I asked.

"You must be going somewhere," she said sullenly.

"I was, but now you're in my way."

Her boots grated on stone as she moved to let me pass. But I, still pretending to be riveted by the view, leaned back on one elbow. "I'll just catch my breath. You're Vicci, aren't you?"

I knew who she was. Since I first left my sickbed, I had been seeking her, the fraying thread in the fabric of the community. She had not been hard to identify. Without ever asking a question, I had been able to learn her entire history; for everyone talked about her, their attention riveted upon her as if upon an open sore. An only child, her mother dead, the father who had cosseted and indulged her had not returned from a hunting trip this summer. Now her obstinacy and short, violent temper were driving her caretaker aunts mad. I had been witness to more than one of her screaming tantrums, as she crashed through a workroom, trailed by a yammering, pink-face aunt. She was the sort who created misery wherever she went, and then complained endlessly that no one liked her.

I gestured toward the sweeping vista. "That's quite a view. You have looked at it your whole life, haven't you? Gods, this is a dull little town! Do you ever get any visitors here? Traveling players, peddlers, storytellers?"

The girl snorted.

"I suppose the army would turn back any travelers."

"Why would anyone want to come here, anyway?"

"Well, certainly, there's more interesting places in the world."

The wind picked up. I shuddered, pulling my hood more firmly over my ears. Vicci's young hands, laid so languidly upon her knees, had turned gray and corpselike in the cold. Her knees gave a tremor, which she defiantly suppressed. She must have come out here in a rage, leaving her furs to scour at the tender hearts of her aunts. Perhaps the aunts wove distractedly at their looms now, whispering to each other fretfully about illness and frostbite and the sudden death that can come from the cold breath of the wind. But they had not yet come out in search of her, and, by the sullen, dull glare of her gaze, I saw that Vicci held this failure against them, just as she would have held it against them had they come after her.

"More interesting places," I repeated, pretending to be in a daydream. "Did you know that the Emperor's train now loops completely around Callia? A road runs beside it, the crossroads marked by shrines and sacred trees, and fruit trees growing wild from the pits that people spit out on the way home from market. The train goes from Aslates to Freeport to Antin, and then down the long grade to Forbes, where an entire town has been built in the branches of the binale trees. From there to the coast, where the waves crash on jagged black stone, and into a strange desert, three days out of Ashami, where once a lush forest stood. The dragon's blood flowed there in my lifetime—I went to see it, rolling like a river into the sea. Now the whole region is covered with bare stone, where not a green thing grows nor water flows.

"The train crosses this region faster than any horse can run—and suddenly dives into a dense forest. It stops at a place called Tanavon, where they take on spices and rare wood, and crates of exotic fruits. Passengers get out and buy rare flowers to pin on their shoulders, and to drink tabal, a drink made of fermented fruit juice. Tabal is renowned the world over. Once you have tasted it, its flavor haunts you the rest of your life. Some people ride the train every year just so they can drink tabal in Tanavon. But the train delivers a fresh supply to the Emperor's door, every thirty days."

Here, sitting on this worn, ancient stairway, being brutally caressed by the bitter wind, the luxurious forest of Tanavon seemed to belong to another's lifetime. Of course, being on the northwestern coast, the summers there are unbearable: sweltering and disease plagued. But I doubted Vicci cared to hear about the rich stink of the place, or the mosquitoes the size of duck's eggs. I glanced up at her. Her eyes had glazed, and she no longer bothered to hide her shivering from me.

"Did you ride the train the whole distance?" she asked dreamily.

I felt vaguely surprised that she even knew what a train was. No, despite their enforced isolation, news still reached the Asakeiri. "I have ridden it many times, from Ashami to Ikabeck and back to Ashami once again. Anyone can ride who has the coin."

I did not tell her that most people ride in the crowded coaches, a tedious, uncomfortable, noisy, and smelly journey, in space shared with old and young, human and animal, all sleeping and eating and shitting in horrible intimacy. Not many could afford to travel as I did, in a private chamber, attended by anxious stewards, my meals served with silver and fine porcelain, even my windows washed clean of cinders and soot at every stop, so I could view the countryside unhindered.

"Won't you tell me some more?" she said.

So I told her of the nineteen bell towers of Acapo,

the gem-studded costumes of the gypsy dancers who whirl the day away during the festival of Ativo, the grim desert of the north, framing the beautiful oasis of Ikabek, the black-skinned Ika people themselves, each one as silent and narrow-eyed as an assassin. I told her of the rolling hills of Saurus Plains, and the people who wander them on the backs of half-wild horses. I told her of the Simmerman Fair, the food, the dramas, the exhibits, the games, the trials, and all the goods of the world to be had for a price. Vicci shivered violently, her lips purple from the cold, gazing vacantly at the visions I had conjured for her.

I stood up stiffly and reached for my basket. "Well, I have loitered long enough. Best go in before you freeze."

She blinked and frowned, rudely awakened. "What about Ashami, the Emperor's City? What is it like?"

Oh, I had hooked her right well. "Shall I tell you about the Shadrich Orgy? Well, some other time, maybe." I gestured toward the cleared roof. "They are waiting for me."

"Let them wait."

"You forget, I am a guest here. I must not make people wait. We will speak again."

A girl so obstinate and prideful as she would not easily be seduced. A full day passed before she sought me out, and then under pretext. I had just come in from another lesson at skiing, given reluctantly by Corlin. In a cluttered entryway among clots of tracked-in snow, I sat greasing my bindings so they would not stiffen. Vicci came in, pretending to look for something. She feigned indifference when she saw me. "Oh, it's you."

"Hey, Vicci. It was a fine talk we had the other day. I hate to speak ill of the Asakeiri, but not many seem to care about more than the goats and the weather."

Willingly, she let me flatter her. For all her ill temper and willfulness, she was as innocent as any fish in a pond. No, she never even felt it, so gently did I reel her in.

* * *

That night, Ata'al came to my family's quarters, after we had finished supper and washed the children's faces. She ignored the fuss of greeting that met her entrance, and beckoned me firmly aside.

"Leave Vicci alone."

"I'm not allowed to talk to a lonely child?"

"Not when your words worsen her illness."

In my experience, people like Vicci tend to cut the very bindings which keep them afloat, and then curse those who would save them from drowning. To learn that anyone besides Vicci's ineffectual aunts still cared for her welfare astounded me. But I bowed my head submissively, even while I fumed at Ata'al's unexpected interference. I said, "Of course, lady, you are in charge here. I did not mean to offend anyone."

After she left, I helped put the children to bed and went early to my own bed, the only place in the entire village where I could be alone. I lay with my fists clenched, forcing myself not to move, so that no one would know by the crackling of my hay bed that I still lay awake.

In these warm interior rooms of the village, the only daylight filtered faintly down the halls from the remote windows of the work rooms. Within this perpetual twilight, the residents made their way by feel. After sunset, a few smoky lamps smoldered in high niches, well out of the children's reach. But these would be quickly extinguished as soon as the evening meal had been eaten, for the fat that burned in them was a precious commodity, and though the Asakeiri used beeswax for other things, they had never discovered the secret of making candles. As the lamps were snuffed out, darkness took up residence, the undisputed ruler of every winter night.

As the gloom thickened to impenetrability, the intense fetor of the village became even more vivid. These were a cleaner people than many I had encountered, yet the piercing scents of urine and excrement dominated the lesser smells of burned fat, woodsmoke, and the harsh, vinegar stink of sweat. Though the old man carried a burning wand of herbs through the domicile each morning, swirling the sweet smoke in climbing spirals as he chanted a cleansing song, this effort did little to improve the smell of the place. The village had been built by a people more concerned with warmth than with ventilation, and I had to admit that I, too, would choose the one over the other.

My rage at Ata'al settled into dull resentment; and still I lay awake, as the rustles and murmurs of a thousand people settled slowly into silence. When I felt I could lie there no longer, I eased back my bedrobe and got up, my straw mattress crackling and popping noisily in the silence. I used the chamberpot, and then pressed with my hands upon the mattress, to make it seem to anyone who heard me that I had gotten back into bed again.

I stood very still then, waiting. Darkness cloaked the rooms, thick and heavy and fragrant. Even the bare, polished boards under my feet felt warm with the dragon's fire. How precarious these people's lives, I thought, to be warmed by the same fire which could burn them, to love and depend upon the thing they most fear: the dragon's back, the dragon's breath, the hot, destroying magma of the dragon's blood.

I slipped my feet cautiously across the floor, and edged along the wall to avoid creaking boards. The wood felt uneven under my feet, rough-split boards, laid down raw and unfinished, and polished only with a sticky coating of melted wax. I crossed without even a whisper of sound, negotiating by touch the clutter of pots and cloths and crude boxes with which the floor was littered. When I had slipped out into the hallway, I did not fret so much about silence, though the tension which constricted my chest did not ease until I had left the living quarters completely behind me.

In the workroom, I paused to take a deep breath. The exterior shutters had been closed in the face of the bitter wind, but its chill breath still seeped in through the cracks. Coals glowed within the round stone hearths, but the terrible cold overwhelmed their gentle breath. Shivering in my camibockers, I picked my way among the stools, equipment, cooking pots, and baskets of supplies which crouched in the shadows. The window shutters rattled. A bitter night, this, cold enough to freeze any hapless wanderers dead in their tracks, as occasionally happens to heroes of Asakeiri folklore. Remembering my own near death by freezing, I shuddered and hurried on.

I felt death stalking me, breathing at my neck like a lover long denied. Under pretext of my secret errand, I fled that fell touch, along a corridor and down a flight of stairs which dropped like a well from darkness above to a lightless void below. Here in the great hall, I wished I had brought a light with me. Darkness overlay darkness, like a series of closed window curtains. My feet numbed by the intense cold, I could not feel the floor across which I stumbled. I could see nothing. The width of the hall expanded and constricted trickily. I walked forever, it seemed, and then suddenly I had crashed face first into a wall. A moment later, sheer luck saved me from falling down the flight of stairs which gaped, invisible, under my feet.

The impenetrable darkness palled my spirits. I felt my way awkwardly down the stairs, walking on numb blocks of wood where my feet should have been. The vast, ancient weight of the village lay over me. I sang, my voice a rough whisper: *Sleep, dragon, sleep.*

I descended slowly to the lowest level of the village, out of unbroken darkness into a pit as black as tar. I felt for the edge of each step with my fingers, for my feet had lost all sensation. By the time I reached the bottom of the stairs, I had become completely disoriented. I walked into one wall before I realized where the corridor ran, and then I chose the wrong direction, realizing it only after I had reached the barred double doors which led outside. I found my way back again, shivering violently, for I was much too lightly dressed to be wandering these frozen corridors.

"Sleep, dragon, sleep," I sang in a whisper, haunted by my memory of the recent earthquake. At last, I reached the door to the hot spring. In the dressing room beyond, a friendly lamp burned. I stripped hastily, too cold to care if the room beyond were already occupied or not. I opened the door, and took a deep breath of startled wonder.

The mosses glowed with phosphorescence. They encircled the pools with rings of eerie fire, green and white and blue. I looked up, and saw a few stars shining through the narrow vents. Had their gentle light called forth this brilliance from the humble, slimy plants that so proliferated in this mineral-rich place? I walked among the glowing plants cautiously, but the soles of my feet left glowing footprints in the black walkway. Ahead of me I saw a different light, the distinctive smoldering orange of a fat-burning lamp.

Vicci floated, up to her neck in the bubbling water. A bowl of parched corn and dried fruit sat within reach of her languid hand. Farther from the edge of the pool sat a bowl of snow, glimmering strangely in the light of the plants. Without opening her eyes, Vicci reached for some corn. Her movements were stiff and stylized; perhaps she imagined herself to be a high court noble. I took the little bottle out of my pocket and jammed it into the snow.

"I thought you said some friends would come."

Vicci opened her eyes and made a face. "Oh, Markel and Tan are such cowards. Their parents told them that if they had anything to do with you they'd get their butts skinned. Did you bring some shel?" Her gaze focused on the bottle in the snow, and she grinned. Then her grin faded. "Not so big a bottle."

I had wondered if the bottle contained too much liquor for four drinkers, and now I only had two. "The old man only takes a little at a time, for the pain of his joints. He would notice if I tapped too much out of his bottle."

"Old crow," said Vicci, referring, no doubt, to Ata'al, whose dictatorship extended over all the products of her herb room distillery. Shel, distilled out of a stinking mix of grain and rotten potatoes, was distributed only to people like the old man, as a sleeping aid. As far as I could determine, the Asakeiri did not even drink in celebration of holidays.

I waded into the pool, flinching as the hot water caressed my numb feet. But the pain was endurable, and I let myself into the hot water with a sigh. "Why did you leave a lamp in the dressing room?"

"Anyone who happens to come will leave us alone. Think we're having sex."

Vicci reached for the bottle, but I stopped her. "The bottle's not cold enough yet, is it? . . . Did anyone tell you not to have anything to do with me?"

"The old crow herself! Who needs an emperor when we have her? Somebody should sneak up to her some night and cut off her life and hide it. Bury it in donkey dung, maybe, or give it to the dragon."

It took me a few moments to realize that the girl was talking about Ata'al's hair. "What would happen if she lost her life beads?" This complication had never occurred to me.

"She'd die, surely. Good riddance."

I allowed myself a small smile. Surely someone as clever as I could figure out how to steal the beads out of an old woman's hair.

"Tell me about Ashami."

So I told her about the city: its walls and minarets and painted frescoes and lush gardens, its entertainments and orgies and petty disputes, its abundance and waste and self-indulgent eccentricity. She sighed with wonder and begged me to tell her more. I offered her the bottle of shel then, and she took a swig, grimacing slightly as it bit the back of her throat. I took a swallow, too. Foul stuff it turned out to be, tasting even worse than it smelled. If we had not chilled it first, it certainly would have been a nauseating cordial.

"Now you tell me," I said, when I had settled more comfortably into the warmth of the pool with the warmth of the shel spreading through my belly. "Tell me about the dragon."

To my surprise, her face grew solemn and even a little frightened. "The dragon? Bad luck to talk about him."

"Just tell me what everybody already knows. Why do you sing when the dragon gets restless?"

"To sing him back to sleep, of course."

I offered her another swallow from the shel bottle. Then I surreptitiously spilled some, so there would be less of it to drink. "There must be a story. Tell it to me." The shel was beginning to work; even in the faint light of the phosphorescence, I could see a flush creeping across the girl's cheeks.

Vicci spoke in a sleepy, sing-song rhythm, unconsciously imitating the stylized words of the village storyteller. "He was a great, ancient dragon. He had flown across the face of the world a thousand times. He had killed and loved and stolen whatever he wanted from whoever had it. But now he had an old heart, and when he looked upon the world from high above, where he flew upon the Sky Mother's breath, he felt tired and weary. His fire no longer burned hot in his breast, and the world no longer interested him. 'I will sleep,' he thought, 'and when I have slept for a thousand years, I will be young once again.'

"So the dragon landed in the ocean and he sank deep into the water, until at last his feet touched bottom, and only the ridged scales of his back and his nostrils remained above the surface of the ocean. And he slept for a thousand years.

"As he slept, plants grew on his back, and trees. Birds came and lived in the trees, and soon many other creatures had made their home upon the dragon's back. At last, a great canoe, adrift in the storm, washed ashore, and the first people arrived. A wisewoman who traveled among them immediately realized that this was no island, but the back of a sleeping dragon. 'We cannot remain here!' she cried, 'for what if the dragon should awaken?'

"But also among them was a woman whose voice was as sweet as birdsong and as soft as the spring wind. 'Whenever the dragon begins to awaken, I will sing him to sleep,' she said. So she took her husband and her children, and traveled with them to a place high on the dragon's back, where the earth settling upon the standing scales had formed the great mountain range. Every time the dragon stirred, she sang

sweetly and softly, and the dragon fell back asleep
again.

"Now the rest of the people scattered across the
land, and soon they forgot all about the woman singing
in the mountains. But she never forgot, and her children's children never forgot. Her name was Asakeiri,
and to this day the Asakeiri people sing to the dragon
to soothe him back to sleep."

She finished with a sleepy smile, and reached again
for the cold shel bottle. I plucked it out of the snow
slightly ahead of her grasping fingers, and made a show
of slowly uncorking the bottle. "The dragon has been
more restless than usual lately, hasn't he?"

"Hush!" she said in some alarm. "When he stirs—"
she shuddered, eyeing the great blocks of stone in the
ceiling overhead.

I idly slopped the contents of the bottle out onto the
glowing mosses, as if to see how they would react to
the alcohol. "They say he's more restless because of
the Emperor," said the girl, anxiously eyeing the bottle I played with so casually. "For a thousand thousand years we have lived in peace, but now the
Emperor's hand has caused turmoil in the land. Fire
calls to fire; the dragon is stirring and will awaken.
And though we sing until our throats are sore, the day
will come that our lullabies are no longer enough. The
dragon will rise, and throw everyone into the sea."

Despite the heat of the water, Vicci shivered. I let
her have the bottle, and she gulped the liquor as if it
were mere water. She drank like a veteran; hopefully
her aunts would not pay any particular attention to her
drunkenness, it being a thing which happened often.

I pretended to empty the bottle into my mouth, and
then dumped the rest of its contents onto the stones.
Vicci, her eyes closed, did not notice. "The Emper-
or's doom," she murmured. "The Emperor's heart
calls the dragon. Everyone will die. Everyone."

"There must be something you can do."

"Nothing *we* can do," Vicci said. She sat up a little
in the pool and rubbed her eyes. "The Emperor, yes.
Pluck out his heart and give it to the dragon."

Certainly the Emperor's Concourse was a direct route to an appearance with the Emperor; and if Adline won— "Gods," I whispered, remembering the runners I had seen, bedecked with champions' ribbons, climbing the stairs to the Emperor's Box to receive the highest honor of all. If Adline were an assassin. . . .

She would never make it that far . . . unless she had the dragon's luck.

Soon, the moon would be full again. In a little over two months, the last race of the Concourse would be run in Ashami. If I left this very night, I would be fortunate to reach home in a month's time. If I whiled away another month in this gods-forsaken village . . . I would arrive too late. Was it an accident that Ata'al, with her tales of harsh winters and the need to protect my health, kept delaying my departure? Cursing eloquently, I rose to my feet in the shallow pool.

"What is it?" asked Vicci groggily.

I emptied the bowl of snow into the water, and took the bottle, which might be recognized as belonging to my household if it were left here. "My menses started," I lied, pressing my hand to my belly where I would have cramps, if I menstruated like most women. "I need to get some rags. Are you going back now?"

"Not yet."

"What if you fall asleep?"

"My aunts know where to find me," she said with a shrug. "All wrinkled up like a dried plum. Who cares? Is that bottle empty?"

I shook it to demonstrate its emptiness, and she sighed. "You're not going to tell me more about the city?"

"Not tonight," I said.

Thinking about it now, I wonder why I felt such haste. What could I do in the middle of the night, unless I meant to simply take my life into my own hands and risk the journey alone? Did I still feel death stalking me? Death, in the weight of the stones looming overhead; death, in the growing tension that filled the darkness, like a stretched string about to snap; death, in the faint throbbing of the dragon's heart.

I sat warming my feet on the hearthstones of a workroom, thawing the numbness out of my flesh so I could once again feel my way across the creaking floorboards that lay between myself and my bed, when the earthquake began.

Chapter 10

In a nightmare hailstorm of shattered beams and broken blocks of stone, the watchtowers fell first. Then, the unsupported inner walls of the highest and most isolated living quarters collapsed into the hollow chimney which heated them. The walls, shaken loose from their foundations, collapsed into rubble. The beams which they had supported on their backs fell like trees in an ancient forest, bringing down the ceilings with them. From the top downward, and from the warm, hollow heart outward, the village dissolved.

The noise is what I remember: the crash and the thunder, the screaming of timbers, the explosion of the heartrock shattering into dust. The earth itself churned and roared. Passengers upon a stormy sea, we were shipwrecked.

And then—silence: the whisper of dust and ground stone sifting from gaping cracks ripped through the walls of the village; the faint screaming, sobbing, shouting and wailing of the people. I slowly uncurled from the position into which I had fallen, with my knees clutched to my chest and my face hidden in my arms. I thought I felt the earth beginning to tremble anew, and I gave a cry of fear. But this earthquake was caused by my own heartbeat, pounding so hard that my entire body trembled.

I lay amid a wrack of shattered pots, in a tangle of spun wool, spilled beans, and scattered tools. I dragged myself to my knees and crouched, stunned, in the wreckage. In the darkness, faint light flickered. Perhaps the coals of a fire, shaken free from the restraints of the hearth, had begun to flame. Incurious,

I watched the flickering light, until it proved to be a disembodied lampflame, bobbing and jerking spasmodically in the hallway.

I got unsteadily to my feet, the pottery shattering under my shifting weight. If I were to survive, I needed shoes and warm clothing. After that . . . an unimaginable night: a frantic, dangerous hunt for survivors, a desperate struggle to salvage what could be salvaged. For it was not just the heartless cold of one winter night that lay ahead of us. No, a hundred such nights lay before us, before spring finally dawned. I rubbed my clammy hands upon my gritty face. First, I needed shoes.

I found a lamp still in its niche, and lit it with a flaring piece of kindling. So, pathetically armed against the monstrous disaster, I plunged into the overwhelming darkness.

I found my family intact, their ceiling sagging but not yet collapsed, frantically packing together every blanket, fur, and bit of clothing that they could salvage. As they worked, they sang breathlessly their futile lullaby to the dragon. They scarcely noticed me as I pulled on my fur outerwear and my boots; perhaps they assumed that I had decided to take my chances alone against the mountains. But they looked up in surprise as I plucked the hysterical toddler out of Talesan's arms, and set him aside like useless baggage. "Are you dressed warmly? Good." I pulled Talesan to her feet.

The young healer trembled in my grasp. I suppose she wanted only to huddle here in the darkness, pretending to herself that, just because the dragon had fallen still again, the nightmare was now over. I grimly dragged her out the door. A dying woman lay in the hallway, surrounded by wailing kinfolk. They scrabbled at Talesan, begging her to help them, but I pulled her away from them, and continued down the hall. I heard Talesan begin to sob in the darkness behind me.

"This is no night for kindheartedness," I said. "What happens tonight will decide whether any of us at all will survive the winter. We need to save the people we can, and abandon the people we can't, and save the food supply, and ration the fuel, and get everyone sheltered against the cold. There's only one person who can make all this happen effectively: Ata'al. Finding her is the most important thing we can do.''

In the devastated workroom, Talesan writhed free of my grasp and faced me, her dirt-smeared face gray and grim in the faint copper light of my lamp. In that moment, I wished that I truly were her aunt, Asakeiri born and raised, so that I could compel her by right of kinship alone to follow my instructions. But Talesan, taking a deep breath, looked around herself. "We'll be wanting another lamp."

"Where would Ata'al be? I have never seen her rooms."

"Up one level, at the end of the hall." Crunching through the broken pottery, Talesan felt first one niche and then another, before at last finding an unbroken lamp. I lit it for her, listening to the sound of her scrubbing at her tears and pulling her beaded locks out of her face. When I took hold of her again, this time it was by the hand.

Obstacles of fallen stone, tilting lintels, and crumbling walls blocked our way. We mounted the mounds of debris, setting down and then retrieving our fragile little lamps as we climbed, dodged, and edged our way down the winding maze of what had once been a wide hallway. I cursed as I struggled in the darkness: cursed the dragon, the night, the useless little lamps, the mountains, the winter, the very stones with which the village had been built. Through broken doorways and across the debris of fallen walls, Talesan passed her lampflame, lighting the lamps held out to her. Before us, the hallway lay in darkness, but behind us, a dozen small lights illuminated the devastation. The sagging walls groaned. We passed a wall with only the doorway still standing, and heard within a mindless screaming. Talesan's hand, slick with sweat, clenched mine convulsively.

"The stairs!"

I raised my lamp. The narrow stairway, choked with rubble, rose into a devastation of shattered wood. Halfway up, a man used a broken piece of wood to lever aside a block of stone which had trapped another man by the leg. I felt Talesan lean away from me, and grasped her sleeve, to prevent her from going to help. "Ata'al," I reminded her.

Wordless, she lifted her lamp to give some illumination upon the top of the stairway. The shattered wood which blocked it had once formed the ceiling of the next level. Our dim light could not even begin to illuminate the disaster, but, clearly, any attempt to penetrate through the debris would be a hopeless effort.

"Maybe from the outside."

We went back the way we had come. The lamps we had lit on the way in now illuminated grisly tragedies of death and injury. Talesan's calm began to erode away again. We had not seen many able-bodied people at all. Muttering my litany of curses, I dragged the young healer back to the workroom again, and from there to a shattered exit, where a door hung ajar in its crushed doorframe.

The bitter breath of the frosty night sighed through the gaping door. We could not open it any farther, and had to squeeze through a gap no winder than a hand's breadth. Snow, shaken loose from the rooftops, clotted the landing, reflecting in faint silver the light of the remote, frozen stars. We set our burning lamps in the snow, to mark the entrance for any wandering survivor who came this way, and began, grimly, to climb the debris-clogged stairs.

At the outer edges of the next higher level of the village, many of the walls remained standing, and we even saw a few people, digging frantically in the ruins. But as we scaled the unsteady mountains of debris, the pattern of the village's collapse became apparent to me, despite the darkness. The deeper we penetrated toward the center, the greater the degree of collapse. Though Talesan should have been more familiar with

the layout of the village, I led the way through the
maze of devastation, showing her the way down what
used to be the main hallway, now almost indistinguishable amid the debris. I pointed to a mountain of rubble. "The stairway emerged here."

"How could you know?" asked Talesan, struggling
miserably behind me. "How do you know these
things? You must be a witch."

"Careful!" I grasped her arm as she began sliding
into a gaping hole. "Which way to your grandmother's
rooms?"

Talesan pointed uncertainly. We climbed across
more debris, feeling it shift and slide unsteadily beneath our weight. A dislodged roofbeam rolled slowly
down a sloping mound above us. Overhead, the stars,
remote and cold as the gods themselves, watched us
struggle. It was the ruin of our lives that we contended
with, a ruin so complete and all-encompassing that we
had not even begun to grasp it.

"Gods," I breathed, awestruck, as we mounted a
sloping pile and found ourselves at the edge of a chasm
partially filled with debris. Beams still spanned the
great chimney, like broken bones protruding from
shattered flesh. At the thought of the hot spring below,
now buried in shattered rock, I felt dizzy and had to
turn away. Stalking death had not grasped hold of me
that night, but oh how close she had come!

Talesan, sitting on a ruined bedroom wall, began to
sob once again. "Her room, it was here, at the edge—"

"Was it?" I looked around myself, like a dog sniff-
ing for a scent. Where had the walls stood? Here, and
here. I tracked out the edges of the hallway, seeking
the pattern. Here the wall had fallen, here the great
weight of the towers collapsing overhead had broken
the beam, and here—here the power of an obstinate
will had prevented a single wall from falling. I lifted
a block of stone and flung it aside, as if it were a piece
of fruit. "Help me."

"Did you hear something?"

"No, but she is here. I can smell her."

Had she asked me what I meant by that, I could not

have begun to explain it to her. But Talesan helped me
lift a piece of fallen beam, setting a great mound of
debris sliding into the chasm below. I heard someone
coughing in the dust. I reached a hand down into the
darkness, and felt another hand grasp hold of it.

We dragged her out summarily, Talesan and I, rak-
ing her across splinter and stone, standing on no cer-
emony. At last, she stood atop the wreck of her home,
facing down the gaping emptiness of sky above, and
the bitter breath of the mocking wind. As cold and
calm as I, she gazed around herself at the collapsed
village. "So it has happened."

"You expected this?"

The starlight etched her face with silver. I felt her
eyes upon me. By effecting this miracle of finding and
rescuing her, had I fulfilled some fate she intended for
me? In that moment, I could have believed anything.
All the threads being spun in the known world might
have been wrapped around her finger.

The wind howled down the face of the cliff, snuffing
out lives like candles with its harsh, heartless breath.
"Come now," Ata'al said reasonably. "There's work
to be done."

* * *

I stood, isolated, ankle-deep in snow which had entered the hallways through the gaping wound of the
roof. It lay in soft, pale drifts, as light as down shaken
from the dusty heart of an old comforter. It spilled into
the storeroom doors, their arches racked sideways,
their riches long since emptied into more secure quarters. A blanket, pinched between two blocks of rough-
cut stone, lay across the debris, shimmering with frost.
A woman's body, stiff and contorted and flattened by
the weight of the stones which had crushed her, lay
awkwardly covered by rags of clothing and tattered
wall hangings, whatever could be found to disguise the
horrid sight. The wood could not be spared for cre-
mation; the dead would all have to wait, preserved by
the cold, until spring.

Before me, a painstakingly devised entrance gaped amid the shambles of tumbled walls, shattered furniture, and splintered roof beams. Rope rasped against stones, as, in this charnel-house of shattered granite, the explorers who had disappeared into this hole felt their way through the labyrinth of their destroyed lives.

Throughout the long first night and into the day which followed, I had engaged in combat. My rag-tag army followed me, armed with shovels and stout levers and their own strong hands. Following the signals of a sense I could neither name nor describe, I found the people who still lived, trapped in secret pockets between one stone and the next. We snatched them from the grasp of our enemy Death, some forty people in all. And then, I could find them no more.

So Ata'al, having named me the enemy of Death, now gave me the cup of death and sent me to walk the aisles of the hospital set up in the great hall. The Executioner rose up, a ghost within me, and it was she who carried the cup, she who tilted it at the swollen lips of those whose bodies could not heal. I gave my cup of shadows to all who asked: a man, who begged it for his mate who lay in screaming agony. A man who begged it for himself, his back broken, his lover dead. A woman who begged it for her child, who still breathed despite a crushed skull.

I did it because I had no heart. I did it because no one else could do it. Ten people died by my hand that night, and ten more since the day had dawned.

Now, I stood ankle-deep in the snow, and watched the rope snake across rock as the explorers penetrated deeper and deeper into the labyrinth. Vicci's aunts, having drawn as far from me as they could, sat wearily on a piece of stone which had once formed someone's bedroom wall. I could see the traces of paint on it, the remains of a mural of flowers which someone had painted to help remember the coming spring. Snow caked the two women's knees, for the milking shed was now a morgue; and the goats had to be milked in the field.

Vicci's friends, Markel and Tan, also waited nearby,

restless and somber, their eyes like burned out coals.
Yet one of them sang as she waited: a low, melancholy
murmur of sound. They wore the bright clothing of
youth, incongruous and disrespectful in this place. But
they were young, and watched the rope with hopeful
eyes. The aunts turned their faces away, and twisted
the beaded locks of their long hair between their fingers.

"A bitter harvest," a voice said beside me. "Oh,
the Asakeiri will long remember this day."

"At least there will be someone to remember it."

Ata'al rubbed her bloodstained hands upon a cloth.
"How can you be so certain?"

"I see the pattern. The Asakeiri will survive."

"Only until you awaken the dragon once again."

My weariness lay upon my frame so heavily that
even my anger would not be roused. "Until *I* awaken
the dragon? How can an earthquake be my fault?"

"Not your fault," said Ata'al heavily. "Not you
more than any of the hundreds of other servants of
your heedless master."

Her skin was as gray as the sky which glared dully
through the ragged gaps in the ceiling. Her eyes had
no color in them, as if they had been bleached by acid.

"Let me go home," I said softly.

"Yes," Ata'al said. "Yes, it is time."

The aunts turned their faces as if they had heard
something: a cry? But it was just one of the explorers
coming out of the darkness, a slender, wiry girl who
had showed a talent for understanding the forces of the
piled stones. Behind her came another, a young man
clenching two corners of a blanket in his fists. The
silent form hung heavy within the water-soaked blanket as the three begrimed explorers hauled it between
the stones. The aunts hurried forward, moaning.

The explorers laid their burden onto the ground and
turned back the blanket. Naked, bloated, her skin
bleached almost white by the long immersion, Vicci
lay within the blanket's folds. One hand lay across her
small breasts. Her legs were crushed.

Vicci stood nearby in a soft drift of snow. She wore

the clothing I had last seen her wear: leather and wool, softly falling from thin shoulders to narrow waist where an embroidered belt gathered them up. Her hair swung around her face, life beads glinting. But her booted feet made no impression in the snow. I looked at her in dull puzzlement. Seeming to sense my regard, she turned to examine me. Her features blurred. Already, she was beginning to forget.

I whispered, "You always wanted to see the world. Why have you remained in this village, now that you have no limits? You could go anywhere you wanted to, now."

But she stared blankly at me, as if she were blind. Prideful youth, how certain she had been of what she wanted! How little she had considered what she could lose! Her aunts crouched over her lifeless form, crying out their grief. She watched them bleakly. Yes, they had lost her. And she had lost them. She put her hand to her face as if to wipe at an invisible tear. But her hand went right through her insubstantial flesh, destroying what remained of her vague features.

"That one will haunt us," said Ata'al. "She never joyed in life. Neither will she joy in death."

I awakened then, like a child startled out of sleep, asking myself what games the witch played with me now, making me think I could see the spirits of the dead.

* * *

In the hall where the injured had been gathered together, I walked with my cup, but no one asked me for a sip of its contents now. Those who could walk, though it be with the help of crutches, gathered near the blazing fire, where they sipped from bowls of rich broth and told each other, over and over, what had happened to them and how they had survived. With each word they rewove the bindings which held their spirits to the mortal world.

Friends and family cared for those who had not recovered enough to care for themselves. Ata'al and Talesan, both of whom seemed much older now, made their rounds wearily from pallet to pallet, dispensing medicines and checking bandages. Many of the survivors had been crippled by falling stone, and would never follow the herds across the mountains again. More than one of these, depressed and hopeless even as their injuries began to heal, asked me to let them drink from my cup. Fickle, I refused them, and would not explain that it was because I feared the haunting of their ghosts.

Elsewhere, a woman, newly widowed and deprived of her children, went mad and wandered the shattered hallways of the village, interfering with the work of those who labored to clear away the debris and make the village livable again, crying out that all was lost and the dragon would inevitably rise. I heard her voice crying in the deep of night. No one could quiet her.

But who was not a little mad in those days? I went without sleep until my eyes burned and I walked like a drunkard. When at last I lay down and closed my eyes, nightmares strangled my rest. The night was filled with the shouts and sobs of people trapped in their dark dreams. But, even awake by daylight, the smallest vibration of the floor could leave any one of us paralyzed with panic. Everyone had lost a friend, a lover, a parent, or a child. Many of the dead were still buried in the rubble, with my unproven declaration of their death the only word to give a modicum of peace to the survivors. No, no one wondered why the woman screamed throughout the night. "The dragon wakes! Oh, he wakes!" Everyone understood why she screamed.

Everyone with any strength in body took their turn at clearing the debris and rebuilding or shoring up the sagging walls. One day Ata'al brought three of those wrestlers of granite to me where I loaded stones into a rickety cart. All three of them were covered with gray stone dust, and wore ragged gloves on their bruised hands. The woman pursed her mouth a little as she looked at me, as if preparing for battle. The other two, one an older man, and one scarcely more than a boy, murmured among themselves as Ata'al introduced them. "Insa, Tord, and Alalin. They have the dragon's luck."

Insa gave a wolf's grin, with all her teeth showing. The other two gazed at me, expressionless, as if I were just a box of trade goods to be transported. These were the three who would take me home.

In my Executioner guise, I slowly walked the crumbling hallways of the ancient village. It was early afternoon, and the snow had begun to fall. It rimed the edges of the leather curtains that had been drawn over the windows. It dusted the stone floor, fading slowly into a sheen of damp where the faint warmth of the fires reached it. It melted in the rifts and cracks of the roof and dripped from the ceilings: slow, persistent drops. Children went about with rags in their hands, swabbing the floors and wringing their cloths out into pots. Old men and women rolled up the rugs to keep them dry, and gazed wearily at the leaking stone.

A dull, rhythmic pounding echoed down the hallway, where a man swung a huge mallet against a cut tree trunk, slowly forcing it into place to support a broken and sagging beam. In the corner, the mad boy huddled, gray-faced, uttering a yelp each time the mallet hit home. I found his broken pot of treasures and laid it at his feet, but he only stared blankly, his eyes dilated, yelping rhythmically and shivering as if he were chilled to the marrow. His parents were dead, I had heard, and there was talk of killing the boy, for mercy's sake.

I left the crowded day quarters behind. As I penetrated deeper into the tilting village, the winter cold grasped hold of my flesh. The chimney which captured the steady warmth of the hot spring had been completely destroyed, and the heat was now trapped beneath the rubble. Persistent as ants repairing their damaged nest, the Asakeiri cleared the debris, one stone at a time. They had already begun cutting the timbers with which to temporarily rebuild the roof. I had passed the builders earlier, where they sat around a little model of stones and twigs, trying to decide how to lay their beams across the gap. The old man of my own household sat among them.

In what had been the heart of the village, the living quarters closest to the warm chimney, the debris still had not been cleared. I clambered over piles of rock, and edged around the splintered spear of a roof beam. Sky gaped suddenly, fresh snow floating, a swirling column of faint light in the gloom.

I thought I saw a child playing in the falling snow. But it was only a trick, the shifting of light across gloom, the hypnotic motion of the snow.

I continued, deeper into the echoing silence, past rooms where broken potsherds scattered the floor, and the clothing and personal possessions of a dead man lay in a pile, waiting for the spring burning. A poor spirit, that, forced to enter the mysteries of death empty-handed.

I heard a sigh and turned my head sharply, but nothing was there.

At last I came to the end, where the wall had begun to crumble into the warm central chimney, only to be stopped by the debris piled on the other side. Only a few stones had actually fallen, and I peered cautiously through. Overhead, the snow fell silently from a darkening sky. There was no wind to speed the slow descent of the pale flakes. They settled on the raw stone below. The workers had partially uncovered another body, and now winter's frozen feathers slowly covered it again, obscuring the wrenched, unnatural pose in which the person had died. A child, her eyelids packed shut by snow. I rubbed my eyes: no, a grown man.

In partial shelter, several Asakeiri dressed in their outdoor furs continued to lift blocks of granite onto makeshift carts that shuddered under their weight. It seemed a chore that could never be finished, like trying to sweep the seashore clear of sand. Or trying to still the restless earth with a lullaby. I sang the old song now, as I turned away from the broken wall, not a lullaby, but a plea: Sleep, dragon, sleep.

A sigh in the darkness. "Who's there?" I asked

sharply. No answer, but a strange shifting in the shadows. I walked firmly over, and nothing was there.

Another sigh, a soundless movement of air, as if the village itself were weeping. Then I saw her, a faint, insubstantial glimmering of deeper darkness. "Vicci," I said. She had no face, but melancholy seeped out of her bodiless being like water from a broken jar.

"Vicci, you are dead."

A silent voice, like the pressure of air upon the ears: *No!*

"Your body is out in the milking shed. Go look if you don't believe me."

Not dead. Not. . . .

The silent voice faded to a mere shivering of my inner ear. I stared into the darkness; stared and saw nothing but the twisting shape of madness.

"I see her, too," Ata'al said with a shrug. "But she is dead. All that remains are her emotions and her memories. It is not she who haunts us, but she who is haunted. She cannot leave the village in search of her next life, because she refused to live the life she had. She is trapped here."

"What will you do about it?"

"Minda's child will soon be born. Perhaps I can work a beckoning magic, to encourage Vicci to accept that child as a new home. Then she can finish what she never had the wisdom to begin."

Someone seeking Ata'al's advice peered into the herb room where, with Talesan's help, she carefully heated a fresh supply of poppy juice over the brazier's glowing coals. Seeing her already occupied, the person left again, perhaps to wait in the hallway outside. Talesan whisked the curtain aside from the window, so as to allow more of the smoke from the brazier to escape. Cold air washed into the stuffy room, along with a few stray flakes of snow.

I said, "Don't the Asakeiri believe that when a child quickens, it is the sign that their new soul has found them?"

"Of course."

"Then Minda's child would have two souls, if Vicci chose to inhabit it."

Ata'al raised her eyebrows. "And you think that would be a bad thing? I say it is not good for the village to have only one wisewoman."

"What if Minda's child is a boy?"

Ata'al seemed unperturbed. "Then he will still be a wisewoman because he will have a woman's soul."

"You would do that to a child—on purpose?"

Ata'al gazed at me, her face all but expressionless. Then she finally said, in a voice made husky by the smoke perhaps, "You believe that the entry of your soul into your own body was merely an accident? How have you managed to live on such a diet of lies?"

"Of course it was an accident. Why would anyone purposefully condemn their child to madness?"

"Perhaps because they were young and arrogant, and believed that they could successfully raise a wise child to adulthood."

Something in the tone of Ata'al's voice distressed me. I rose to leave, saying stiffly, "How are the plans for my journey progressing?"

"Fine, fine. In a day or two, you will be rid of us."

In the hallway, I gestured the waiting man inside, and then stalked away, as stiff and offended as any of the Emperor's elegant courtiers. It was much later that it occurred to me how strange and convoluted this conversation had been. Ata'al had many secrets, and I would do well to stay on my guard.

The predictable cycle of village life had been completely disrupted by the earthquake. With many people missing, and many of the others occupied in more urgent work than the preparation of food, everyone ate from common pots, and did not ask whose family had cooked the meal. Having dallied away part of the afternoon while the snow fell, I worked late with the stone carriers, and stumbled with weariness when at last our lanterns could no longer illuminate the dark, crumbling passageways down which we wrestled our heavy handcarts. Those dark tunnels weighed upon my spirits, and I was always glad to climb up into the light and noise of the occupied work rooms.

But tonight everyone seemed quieter than usual. Since the earthquake, there had been more grim stoicism than mirth in that devastated place, but the quietness was a new and alien ingredient in the stew of the community. Ill at ease, I started for a stewpot, only to find myself inexplicably turned aside. Unwilling to argue, I went into the next room, where a woman briskly stirred the dregs of another pot. "Tell me it is not burned," I said wearily.

"Oh, no," she said, and brought up her wooden ladle, full of chunked potatoes and reconstituted goat meat and scarlet carrots the like of which I have seen nowhere else in the country. She filled my bowl to the brim. I took bread from the basket—scorched, of course, for the quake had damaged the bake-oven as well—and sat on the floor with my back against the wall.

The Asakeiri people flowed around me, life beads swirling in the smoke. A group of children gazed at me solemnly, and then dispersed, scattered by a sternly waved hand. I sipped from my bowl, picking out the pieces of vegetable and meat with my fingers, using the bread as a napkin. The stew had a spice in it that I had not tasted before: sharp, but not unpleasant.

The smoke from the coals of the cookfire swirled and eddied against the gloom. The people began to settle; squatting on their heels in the corners, sitting on stools with babies in their arms. Talesan came in, wearing her bloodstained leather apron.

The woman at the pot fetched my empty bowl and brought me another serving. The curtains had been closed against the falling snow, and the air seemed thick with smoke and the rich fetor of unwashed bodies. I ate, dreaming of the fountains and baths and scrubbed stone of Ashami.

Gray smoke swirled through the room. A baby began to cry and fell silent as its mother offered it her breast. Vicci's ghost stood in the doorway, staring bleakly into the crowded room. I swabbed out my bowl with the last of my bread. Ata'al came into the room, and everyone seemed to speak at once, but I could not understand what they were saying. The woman at the stewpot took the bowl out of my hands. She spoke to me, but I could not understand her words. Gently, she pressed against my shoulder, and I lay down on the floor. From somewhere, a blanket appeared and covered me.

I fell instantly asleep.

* * *

I shook off the blanket and rose to my feet. I reached eagerly for the bead in my hair, checking to make certain that it was still there. "She is stronger than I," I said apologetically to Ata'al.

"In some ways," she said gently. She put one hand on each of my cheeks, and bent forward to softly kiss my mouth.

"Mama," I protested. "Don't let her take me away."

She took me by the hand. "Come. We have work to do."

Chapter 11

Oh, I dreamed that night. I dreamed long and vividly. Familiar faces populated the territory of my sleep; the faces of the living, and one or two of the dead. Within the cracked walls and amid the uncleared debris of the great hall, they gathered, a hollow-eyed and weary people, limping on injured limbs, faces dusted with powdered granite. I walked among them, laughing like a child, calling everyone by name. They reached out with their rock-torn hands, softly patting my face or my shoulder. Every one of them wanted to touch me.

Ata'al lifted a wooden tray above her head, turning slowly so everyone could see. Herbs and ribbons trimmed the tray. In its center stood a tiny, frail figure of straw and thread, bedecked with glittering chips of obsidian. "Behold!" cried Ata'al. "Behold the dragon!"

As if in amazement or fear, everyone cried out.

* * *

I awoke late, muddy-mouthed and groggy, as if Alasil had been on one of her binges while I slept. Despite the blanket wrapped around me by the woman who had served stew the night before, I shivered with cold. Sunlight shone through the cracks in the shutters—surely it was not mid-morning already! I got up, stiffly and dizzily, to throw some wood onto the fire. Was I becoming ill once again? Another bout of pneumonia, and I would be lucky to ever leave these cursed mountains at all.

The village lay in utter silence. The mats and rugs and makeshift mattresses of the sleeping people crowded the workroom floor so closely that I could scarcely take a step without injuring someone. The sleepers lay still as death; deeply, peacefully asleep. No nightmares stalked through here, no dreams of the dragon rising. How had the memories of that recent horror been exorcised?

Faintly, I heard the wail of an infant, quickly hushed. I picked my way among the sprawled bodies to the window, where I held aside the leather and looked out. Sometime during the night, the snow had ceased to fall. Pure and stark, the unmarred snow spread across the meadow, a soft, unwrinkled blanket, glazed with sunlight. In the stockpen below, the goats milled, bawling irritably, in quite a temper over having been neither milked nor fed.

I fetched a snowbroom and went outside to begin clearing the steps. Snow flew in a cloud before the brisk beating of the broom's stiff twigs. I heard the faint sound of another infant crying, somewhere in the village. In the pens below, the goats' voices rose to a roar of complaint as they caught sight of me, sweeping busily. A curtain twitched aside, and after a while an old woman came out, grumbling, leaning heavily on her broom as if it were a cane. We swept together, the only sound the whisk and clatter of the twigs. A handful of children, briskly herded out of doors by a grumpy mother with an infant at the breast, attacked the snow with more vigor but less resolve. Their work dissolved into shrieking play, despite a shrilly yelling older girl's efforts to keep them in order.

The old woman and I continued to sweep in silence until we had reached the bottom of the stairs. I went back up to fetch my skis and several painted milk pots, strung together on a rope, which I delivered to the old woman. She solemnly strode through the deep snow, bearing the pots slung over her shoulder, and climbed the fence into the goat pen, where she was mobbed by the desperate does, swinging their aching udders.

I tucked my mittens into my belt and struggled with the stiff ski bindings until long after my hands had gone numb. At last, I slung a snowshovel across my back and skied across the snow toward the nearest haystack. If there was any chore I hated worse than sweeping snow, it was digging snow. In a bad temper, I plowed away at the snow which had filled in the previously dug tracks, flinging my shovelfuls in angry flurries over my head.

The sun had climbed a hand's length higher when I encountered a digger coming from the other direction, with a press of hysterical goats behind him. We cleared the last block of snow and scrambled out of the way as the goats charged the haystack. Out of breath and knee-deep in snow, I flung my shovel aside and sat down. The snow sank under me, to form a comfortable, albeit cold, chair. "What a party you must have had last night. The day half over, and scarcely a body stirring yet."

Corlin, as it happened to be, seemed none too pleased at having run into me like this. He leaned on his shovel and watched the goats struggle in their pathway, and said nothing at all. His breath huffed out of his parted lips in vaporous clouds, which lingered and dissolved even as his next breath renewed them again.

I had seen little of Corlin since the earthquake. For a while, Ata'al had feared that he was among the missing, but he eventually turned up, slightly injured, in the lower levels of the village, where he had been shoring up the sagging walls all night long. Like all the Asakeiri, he looked exhausted, but the dull, blank expression of shock had disappeared from his red-rimmed eyes.

"You didn't have to drug me," I said.

"Sure."

No, I didn't blame him for disbelieving me. That I would have quietly gone to sleep last night, knowing

that I was missing an event in which every last member
of the community participated, was clearly unlikely.

His hands tapped on the shovel handle: blunt, work
hardened hands, with rough, callused skin and fingernails broken at the quick, fingers red with cold. His
mittens hung at his belt, like mine. Mittens didn't give
a sure enough grip for snow shoveling.

"Good weather for traveling. Good snow." He
rubbed his foot across the surface, and it slid like a
wet finger across glass.

"We're leaving soon? Today?" Gods, not when I
felt like this!

"Tomorrow, is what I heard. The weather will
hold." He rubbed his hands on the wet leather of his
britches, using the friction to warm his numbed flesh.
"You'll give my love greeting if you see her, will
you?"

"Of course I will." The shattered village loomed
over us, a hulking pile of crumbling stone. The
cold had begun to seep too deeply into my clothing, and I rose up stiffly and set off to retrieve my
skis.

Even Ata'al had slept late, though I found her now,
working her way down the length of the hospital like
fury. Talesan rushed about behind her, lugging basins
of hot water and bowls of potions. "Don't stand
there," the old woman commanded. "Bring the folks
their stirabout, them that can feed themselves. Quickly
now; it's late."

I hurried at her beck, rushing back and forth from
the cookfire to the sickroom, filling bowl after bowl
of corn mush, topping it with milk still warm from the
goat, and scattering a handful of dried fruit on top,
for Ata'al would have my head if I did not see to it
that the sick folk got their fruit. By the time I had
finished delivering the meals, it was time to start clearing, for most of the friends and relatives, usually so
dutiful in caring for the injured, had not yet rousted
out of their beds. I grumped along, snatching a mouthful of parched corn when I had the chance, all the food

I had eaten that day. Last, I fed the few who could not feed themselves. When I looked up, afternoon had set in, the kinfolk had at last begun to appear, Talesan bathed a woman with a rag dipped into a basin, and Ata'al was gone.

Talesan told me to check in the herbary, but the old woman was not there, for once, nor could I find her in any of the workrooms where astonishing numbers of people sat about, talking or gambling with colored stones, scarcely a one of them doing any work. She had not gone down among the fallen stones of the village heart. At last I checked outside, and one of the late-rising snow sweepers told me that she had set off by ski. My informant kindly pointed out the track to me, and I strapped on my skis and set out to follow, wondering, as I set my skis into the neat parallel depressions which marked Ata'al's passage, why everyone was behaving so civilly toward me.

Winter's silence overlaid the stark mountains. Among trees burdened with snow I slid along the lonely track, mulling over the day's many mysteries and fretting to myself over what event I had missed as I slept my drugged sleep. I had only skied before on the flat surface of the meadow, and the upward slope along which Ata'al had traveled proved more of a challenge. But the trail rewarded me occasionally with a downward slope. Then I could slip across the surface of the snow without effort, though I teetered dangerously, always on the edge of falling.

I fell only twice or thrice on this journey. Ata'al's tracks ended at a jagged tooth of stone piercing up out of the snow, where her skis, upended, marked the narrow, frosty footpath that she must have followed. I removed my own skis and stumbled through the snow, as awkward as a bird whose wings have been cut off, until I reached more solid ground where I could stamp the snow from my boots as I planted my skis and poles to await my return.

On this grim rockface the wind had scoured, scrubbing away the snow and leaving the stone glittering with hoarfrost. The path slipped underfoot and I

climbed cautiously, grabbing at whatever came to hand
to steady myself, and regretting the fact that no matter
where this path led me, I would have to climb down
once again. But where the old woman had climbed,
certainly I also could make my way, and I persisted
stubbornly.

I topped the narrow path at last, and paused there,
astonished. I had entered a wide plateau which led, in
a jumble of broken stone, to yet another sheer slope.
Here the snow lay in thready patches, and water ran
in narrow brooklets, as if spring thaw had broken
through into this small corner of winter's domain.
Cracks, rimed with a harsh yellow mineral, gaped
open, bottomless. As I stepped over one, I stepped
through a draught of warmth, and caught a whiff of
the gasses emitting from the earth's hot heart. My
throat closed, and I hurried away, choking and hacking to get my lungs to open up again.

Ata'al's footprints were easy to follow. Through mud
and snow she had walked, and I placed my feet into
her footprints, step by step. The warmth of the earth
seeped through my boots, though a cold wind had also
picked up, and I paused to pull up the hood to cover
my ears.

I found her outer gear neatly piled in a dry spot:
britches and tunic, hood and boots. I also shucked my
boots and furs. Dressed only in my camibockers, my
bare feet pressing into warm mud, I slipped into a
deep warm crack in the mountainside, and found myself in a strange, hazardous place, where gases rolled
among grotesque, melted piles of rock mineral, and
light filtered hazily from a thin crack of sky. I laid my
hand onto a ledge, and yelped with surprise as something gashed open my finger. I picked up a shining
sliver of obsidian in my bloody fingers, and set it down
again.

The foul gases choked me. I pressed on dizzily,
holding cautiously onto the stone for balance, blinking
in the dim light. Suddenly the stones opened up like
cupped hands parting, and I hesitated, blinking muz-

zily in the glare. Ata'al took my hand. "Take care; to
fall is death here."

"I see that," I said thickly. She took me to a secure
ledge where I sat gladly, putting my hand to my throbbing head. Dragon's breath warmed the little hollow.
My extremities ached with the sudden thaw. I shivered
once, a shudder that vibrated into my bones. My ribs
were damp with sweat, and I stank.

Beside me, Ata'al sat at ease, knees askew, features
relaxed, her dilated pupils black as a night sky.

"This is your vision place," I said, and fumbled for
words to apologize for disturbing her here. But she
silenced me with a gesture, laying a hand onto my
arm.

"This is your last day with the Asakeiri people. How
shall you remember us, Jamil-my-daughter?"

What indeed would I remember? My frustration at
being trapped here for so long, or my anger at my
inability to take control of this place and people and
bend them to my will? A long time it would be, before
I forgave them for their strength, for the ease with
which they gave me everything I needed—except for
their fear or their trust.

I said, "I will remember that you called me daughter, but you never called me friend."

Ata'al glanced at me, her black eyes glittering, the
corner of her thin mouth lifting in a sardonic smile.
"Has anyone ever called you friend? Only a fool loves
a wolf."

"I have not been a killer here!"

"True. But not for lack of trying. Do you say you
never thought to disrupt our traditions, unseat the
elders, or turn the families against each other? Did
you never seek out the weak ones and try to enslave
them to your will? Did you never dream at night of
cutting off an old woman's hair and feeding it to the
dragon?"

Vapors coiled up out of the rift. Far below, I thought
I could see a glimmer of light: red blood flowing. I
coughed painfully, and asked myself what kind of fool
would breathe poisonous gas beside her enemy. But

Ata'al had roused my curiosity now. "You never tried to stop me," I said.

"You never came close to succeeding."

"But why let me continue?"

"Because you interest me, Jamil. Because watching you has taught me something that I needed to know."

"Well, then you must tell me," I said lightly, though I felt in that moment the sickening feeling which my own victims must feel when they realize much too late how heartlessly I have used them.

But Ata'al only smiled, gazing into the chasm that gaped below us, bony, gnarled hands clasped across her wool-covered knees. And, in truth, I did not need for her to answer my question. What better way to learn about the purpose and techniques of the Emperor's operatives than to set one loose, unmasked and without the usual supports, and make a study of what she does?

Perhaps the vapors we breathed disabled my rage. I said, "You are a clever woman, Ata'al." And I meant my words sincerely. "But the knowledge goes both ways, does it not? Surely I have learned as much about the Asakeiri as you have learned about the Emperor."

"Such as?"

"The Asakeiri are a strange people. You are isolated. Every day, you must fight for your lives. Yet when you sing to the dragon, it is not just for yourselves that you sing. Isn't it an amazing arrogance, that you think yourselves responsible for the survival of the world? Even I am not so self-important."

"Better, perhaps, to bear too much responsibility than too little." Ata'al studied the gulf of darkness below, her fingers playing against her knees. "Yes, it is arrogance, but it is not self-deception. We did have the power; the old ones will tell you—" Ata'al paused, and gave a sardonic laugh. "Well, I am an old one now. It is my grandmother I am thinking of, who once sang a star down from the sky and held it in the palm of her hand. Once, in her youth, the dragon began to awaken. As he struggled beneath the weight of the land, his blood began to flow and the smoke of his fires blotted out the sun. Ashes and cinders fell like snow from the sky. The crops withered; the goats fell ill; and the people sang. Forty days and forty nights they sang without pause, and on the forty-first day they awakened to a clear sky.

"But we do not have that kind of power now. Perhaps it has been taken from us, or perhaps we have given it up. Perhaps we are more like our Vicci than we care to know." Ata'al sighed. "You understand, Jamil. Power comes from wanting one thing, from wanting it with all our heart, without fear or self-doubt. But to want more than one thing, or to want two things which contradict each other, or to question ourselves endlessly as to why we want it . . . this diffusion of desire takes away our power and shrinks our hearts. This is how your Emperor has weakened us: not by breaking our spirits with violence, but by polluting our children's dreams with questions."

I glanced at Ata'al, but she did not seem angry with me. Her hands still lay quietly across her knees. Weather, laughter, and sorrow had quilted the skin of her face into a beautiful artwork. She smiled a little now, sardonically. "Yes, it is arrogance," she said again. "And we do not have too much of it, but rather too little."

For a long time we sat in silence. The fumes rising from the deep crack in the dragon's skin made me feel dizzy and ill. My headache increased to a vile, nauseated throbbing, but I would not stand up to leave.

"That was a strong drug we slipped into your stew last night," said Ata'al. "I hope it did not affect you too badly when you awoke."

"It was a cruel trick," I said, without much feeling.

"Did it give you any dreams?"

"Dreams!" I laughed a little at the absurdity of what I had imagined while I slept. "I dreamed of fires and singing. I dreamed that the earth dragon had become a small and insignificant thing, a dragon of straw, and we set it upon a stone and sang to it." I laughed again, dizzily. "And I dreamed that we danced together, you and I, and you kissed me and told me not to weep. Surely whatever I missed could not be half so strange."

Ata'al touched my hand. It did not seem a peculiar gesture at that moment, though it seemed very strange indeed, when I remembered it later. She said to me, her voice very soft, "You are a fool, daughter mine. You would do great things, were you not such a fool."

The next morning, at dawn, I stood in a frigid hallway, using a piece of bread to scoop stirabout into my mouth, as Insa, in a foul temper, packed and repacked the burdens we would carry on our backs. At last, one of the men stopped her, gesturing toward the blaze of light that marked the sunrise. We all hefted our packs experimentally, I contemplated drearily the effect that this heavy burden would have upon my already unsteady balance. I was none too eager to begin so early a day which would seem long no matter what its length.

Ata'al came then, with Talesan at her left hand. "You remember what herbs to get," she said to one of the men, and he dutifully recited a memorized list. Then she turned to me, and gave me a small box, made of stiffened, waxed leather, laced together with rawhide. It felt light as a handful of dried grass.

"What's this?"

"It is a token for Adline, to remind her of the mountains. You are returning to Ashami, are you not? You will see her there, when the time comes for the last race."

I held my tongue, and secured the small box in my pack. I could always dispose of it later, once I had safely made my escape from the Asakeiri.

"Out the door, then," said Insa impatiently, as if it had been we rather than she who fussed so persistently with the baggage. I lifted the pack to one shoulder, tucked my skis and ski poles under my arm, lifted a hand in brief farewell to Ata'al and Talesan, and walked out the door for the last time. I was glad to be leaving that desperate village, with its crumbling walls and frantic clinging to doomed traditions. Only in retrospect would I feel a kind of lonely sorrow, knowing that I would never walk that way again.

Chapter 12

The rhythm, lost and found and lost again. Falling, picking myself up, falling once again. The blur of snow-edged mountain and snow-laden tree, passing me by. I paused often to look behind myself, trying to memorize the way we had come. But I knew by the end of the first day that I could never lead the Emperor's army back to Asakeiri Home. The mountains closed protectively behind us, and soon they all looked the same to me.

Falling, picking myself up, falling once again, I traveled at the end of the line, following Tord, whose strength and weight most effectively broke through and compacted the snow. I traveled last, so that my frequent falls would not impede anyone.

In a grove of frost-edged trees, amid drifts that rippled like swells near the ocean's shore, we paused in a wind-cleared area, where hungry deer had eaten the grass to the ground. We sat in a circle, our skis and ski poles standing like a stockade around us, sharing food from the packs: Parched corn and dried fruit, dried meat charily distributed, for the salt. Insa gave me a little pot of grease, with which I rubbed the dry, stretched skin of my face, not for vanity but for protection against the wind. By mid-afternoon, the wind howled among the trees, spraying us with dislodged snow, numbing us with a vicious cold that drove deep to the bone.

We continued on in the face of that howling monster. Tord humped through the drifts, obstinate as a buffalo. Insa, muttering behind him, advised him on which path to take. Alalin watched for danger: snow bridges and avalanches and all the rest of it. He squinted in the swirling snow, wiping it frequently out of his eyes with the back of his mitten. Cold ached in my limbs, in my blood, in the pores of my skin. Stifflipped, I could not speak. Yet we struggled on, as the short day dipped swiftly nightward.

White upon white, overshadowed with the palest of gray, with the pale sky above, the colorless world shivered around us, the wind howling and moaning, our skis hissing across the rippled snow. My backpack felt like a boulder strapped upon my back. I skied by raw will, graceless and struggling as a creature dying in the snow. Gray shadows striped the blinding snow, and I realized that the sun would soon be setting.

I heard Insa's voice. "Up ahead, I think I see it." But I saw only another grove of trees, robed in snow, pierced with black stones like the broken stubs of spears. I tangled my skis with Alalin's. He had halted, and I could not pause my own automatic motions soon enough. Tord had already slipped out of his skis and gone blundering through the drifts, holding one mitten in his teeth. I flinched as he plunged his bare hand into the crackling snow. He floundered, arm deep in the snow, then grunted and withdrew his hand, grasped around the handle of a battered old snow shovel. The skin of his hand shone bright red against the white. Spraying snow behind him like a badger, he began to dig.

When he stood thigh-deep in a hole, Insa squeezed in beside him and started working with her hands. Soon she had revealed a twig wall, portion of a hut buried beneath the snow. Alalin, muttering something, finally managed to work his skis free from their entanglement with mine. "Do we need to gather wood?" I asked.

"Should be wood in there. Traveler's code. Dragon's Teeth!" Grumbling, he wrestled free of his backpack. "It's cold, though."

Swearing, I struggled after Insa through the entry tunnel. By the time I had dragged myself through, she had already begun knapping stone against knife, sending little sparks flying through the pitch darkness. The smell of the hut was familiar: the scent of earth and mud and ancient, rotting wood. I leaned my back against a curved mud wall and watched, as a spark, skillfully captured by Insa in a handful of tinder, glowed and suddenly flamed under her puffing breath.

The little flame revealed no surprises: a round twig and mud hut, set upon a circular foundation of stone, with a goodly pile of wood against one wall, and a rude hearth full of ashes and the charred bones of bird. I heard the faint sound of Alalin taking his turn with the shovel. Snow showered us suddenly, and pink-tinged faint light filtered through the smoke hole at the top of the hut. Immediately, the wind began whistling across the smoke hole, like a musician playing upon a flute. Insa's little fire flared in fresh tinder as she shook it out of the palm of her hand and onto the wood she had laid upon the hearth.

"I saw other shelters like this, in a wood near a canyon, where the river runs—"

"You came through ghost wood, did you?"

"A battle was fought there, years ago?"

Insa snorted. "Is that what you call a battle? A slaughter, I call it."

"What happened?"

"Used to be, at the Spring Moon, young folks and their families went down, and people from other villages—the Clay People, the Hamitari, and others from even farther away—gathered for feasting and dancing. It was to find mates for the young people who came from other tribes. But this time, it was the Emperor's dogs who came. Fifteen or twenty families had gone down with their herds. Most of them never came home again."

"But why?"

Sorting through the contents of her pack, pulling out packets of meat and grain, Insa shrugged. "The Emperor says he is a god. Gods do what they like and do not explain."

"There must have been something."

"Well. Story has it that a stranger lived with the Asakeiri for a season, and when he left he tried to take a child with him. He had eaten our bread and then broke the law—so the Asakeiri took from him the food we had given, the clothes from his back, declaring him out-clan. Maybe he didn't make it out of the mountains; I don't know. It's the Asakeiri way, to let the dragon take his own."

I had heard this tale before; amazing how different things look when viewed from another direction. "The Emperor always gets what he wants," I said. "Better to give it to him than to fight him for it."

"Well, I hear he did get the child. But he got our hatred, too. I was just a babe at the time, but my mother's brother was killed, and his wife, and their three children. I promised my mother I would always remember. Is that what the god-man wanted?"

By the time Tord had struggled his bulk through the tight entrance, the fire crackled busily, snow that Alalin brought in melted in the stewpot, and I had fallen over sideways, asleep. Insa had to wake me up to eat.

* * *

The seventh morning of our journey, after my sixth night in a mud shelter, I crawled out to find Alalin standing knee-deep in snow near our stockade of skis, gazing fixedly at the last trail of smoke from our doused fire. It hugged the ground as if pressed down by an invisible hand. The sky, which had been clear for most of our journey, was now filled with flakes of clouds, still pink from the recent sunrise. "Snow coming," Alalin said.

By afternoon, the stormclouds had blotted out the sun; a relief for my eyes which ached from squinting into the glare of the snow, but no relief for my mind.

"How long before snowfall?"

Alalin shouted back to me. "Too soon, I guess."

As quickly as tireless Tord could break the way, we had journeyed, mostly downhill now, following a blazed trail through thick woodlands that showed here and there the mark of a woodcutter's ax. Our last shelter had been built of stone, with a framed roof and a fireplace with a chimney. A trapper's shelter, my companions told me, used by long-standing permission. Despite our hurry, we took great care to replenish the woodbox before we left.

I could smell civilization. I could taste it. I could see it, marked in every tree. And the clouds loomed, black and ominous, and when I took in my breath I could smell the snow coming.

Despite the contents of Insa's greasepot, my lips had cracked and the skin of my cheeks had chapped raw. I had developed painful, weeping sores on my hands: chilblains, Insa called them. I moved in agony and slept at night as if I were dead, too weary to eat except that my companions would not let me lie down until I had swallowed enough food to satisfy them. The smell of my own body made me gag.

The trees spread apart before us. Our trail had become a road. I thought I smelled woodsmoke, only a whiff of it. I looked up and saw the snowflakes, floating like talcum powder against the black foliage of the pines. The smoke of our breaths clouded around us; with the clear road before us Tord had been able to pick up the pace. We slipped across the snow like sailboats across the water, dipping and gliding, swinging and sliding. The forest opened up; the road flattened; and suddenly we were in a valley, and a split-wood fence zigzagged along beside us, edging a fine field of unbroken snow where only a rabbit had left its double rows of tracks. I saw smoke, and in a little while we passed a farmstead. "Ongin's Farm," said Alalin over his shoulder. The snow began to fall in earnest.

Snowflakes flew into my face and melted there. They clung in the fur edging of my hood, shimmering in the gray light. I could not keep the pace and fell behind, then nearly rammed into Alalin when they slowed down to wait for me. "How far?" I gasped.

"Have to keep moving or we'll freeze up."

"Aric's Farm," said Alalin. A while later: "Brittlecrick." Then he sighed. "River's End." I ran into him again, but he had braced himself for it.

The steep roofs of the village humped through the

snow, close crowded between the drifts as if to keep each other warm. Stables and outbuildings crowded up behind them. Graceful swells of snow skirted the walled gardens. Smoke trailed from a dozen stone chimneys, each of which wore a cap of slate to keep the snow from drifting in. Narrow pathways had been shoveled out between buildings, but here in the narrow road, other ski tracks crossed our way.

Gray and white were the colors of this town: slate gray of stone and pale gray of shadow, white of snow. Gray cliffs hung overhead, with a frozen waterfall draped over one edge. I smelled cold snow and sweet woodsmoke. Someone peered out of an attic window at us; a curious child, perhaps. Faintly, I heard the sound of a restless horse, confined for winter, stamping his feet against the wall of the stable.

I could not see far through the falling snow, but I could see River's End on a map in my memory, with a road winding away from it like a piece of lace ripped loose from a petticoat. The road home.

My voice had eroded to a hoarse caw from panting frosty air. "Where now?" I croaked.

Alalin and Tord both waved mittened hands to crack icicles loose from their beards. Insa pointed with her ski pole at a building, larger than most, with a big front porch swept clean of snow. Smoke belched invitingly from several chimneys. Woodsheds leaned against its walls, and a full sized barn loomed behind. It was the inn, I guessed, or at least the rooming house, a busy and prosperous one, at that, for so small a town. I pondered, and realized that a fur-trade town would have few permanent residents, but many who came and went; moving from the mountains to town and back to the mountains once again. Would it have a tavern where I could sip a glass of brandy beside a roaring fire?

Ah, but I had nary a copper to pay for it.

We beat the snow from our gear and headed for the welcoming porch. Tord went up first, planting his skis in the snow and stamping the snow from his boots as he climbed the steps. We handed him our packs. Mine felt as if it had welded to my back, but it was too heavy for me to lift. Insa caught it as it dropped snow-ward, and passed it on.

The door opened suddenly. "I thought I heard stamping on my porch. Come in, then! Tord, you old bulldog!"

But I could not move. I stood ankle-deep in the snow, staring up at the man in the doorway. A brown-haired man, portly, wearing a shawl over his big, gathered shirt and loose wool trousers, with a curly beard to his waist. But it was not his appearance which left me so bewildered. He spoke the common tongue; one of four that I speak fluently: Common, Rasdil, Onditli, and Iadic.

"Ay, Mister Lefanu, some weather you greet us with," said Tord, speaking Asakeiri.

"Eh? The weather, you say? Pretty bad, pretty bad." Then the innkeeper spoke in the Asakeiri language, with an execrable accent, "Welcome and enter."

"Welcome and enter," I repeated to myself in Asakeiri. Then I said it in Common: "Welcome and enter."

When Ata'al first reclaimed my wandering spirit from the snow, I had been unable to understand one word she or the others said. When I awoke from my illness, I spoke the language fluently.

Insa held out her hand, to help me mount the steps. I must have looked at her strangely, for she drew back her hand and stalked away. I climbed after her, dizzied by the mystery: Mystery upon mystery. How had I learned the language, and why had I not realized until now that I had learned it? What had happened to me?

Painted wood paneled the stone walls within. Along the beams, in ornate letters bedecked with stylized flowers, was painted the traditional innkeeper's motto: "Food, warmth, rest, and good cheer. Welcome once, welcome twice, and welcome once again." We stripped off our furs in the hallway and gave them to a bustling woman who flinched visibly from the stink.

"You'll be wanting a bath?" said the innkeeper delicately.

He led us down the hallway and through the controlled chaos of a huge, hot kitchen, with meat and birds roasting on a turned spit, and pies coming out of the oven, and a cook, dough to her elbows, shouting orders at her hustling crew. It was strange, to see a woman cooking again. Among the Asakeiri, it is a craft of the men.

Greenery garlanded the shuttered windows, and painted medallions to fend off bad luck. Sawdust sprinkled the stone floor. The innkeeper hollered over the racket, and two children came rushing from somewhere, to duck out the door into the bathhouse ahead of us. By the time we entered, they had already begun ferrying buckets of water from the huge cauldron to the tubs. Any water they spilled disappeared in the gaps between the floor slats. I could smell damp earth. Several lanterns hung from the ceiling for light. We gave the innkeeper our packs.

"Draw straws," said Alalin. One of the children produced some straws out of a pocket and offered them to us to pick. I drew the second longest, but there were two tubs. Alalin sat on a stool to undo his boots, and the children swiftly drew the curtain, dividing the room in half to give at least the illusion of privacy. I smelled the sharp perfume of scented bath salts, and stripped.

I had not bathed or washed my clothing since the earthquake, twenty days or more of vigorous exertion. Even my hair stank.

"We usually eat well here," said Insa, from the stool where she sat watching me soak in the water. Remembering that she waited for her turn in the tub, I sat up and reached for the soap.

"How do you pay?"

"Trade."

Water swirled around my knees, brown already, still steaming. I dipped my head under the water and soaped my hair. Feeling a lump under my finger, I pulled loose a life bead . . . and then another. *A blue bead, to mark the end of your soul's wandering. And a bead of black obsidian, to remember that the mountains will always be your home.*

Blindly, I put the beads into Insa's hands. "Your hair is short yet," she said. "I'll bind these back in for you, when you're done."

"My thanks." I scrubbed my fingers against my scalp, groaning. I got soap in my eyes. "Do you remember when they first brought me to Asakeiri Home?"

"Oh, sure," said Insa cautiously. Without her heavy furs she seemed thin and insubstantial, though I knew from experience that she was tough as bone. Sweat had stained her camibockers. Mine lay in a limp heap on the floor; I could smell them from the tub.

"I don't remember it."

"Well, they say you were terribly ill."

"You didn't see me?"

"I can't say that I did."

"But they brought me up the outer stairs, didn't they?"

"I can't say," she said again.

I ducked under the water to rinse my hair. As I came up again, I caught a glimpse of the expression on Insa's face: half love and half fear, hastily masked into cool indifference. Yes, she knew something, and she would die before she told me.

The bathhouse door opened, and the children came in, bearing towels and clean clothing. I got out of the tub, and they brought fresh water as I dried myself. I heard a murmur of voices and sudden laughter from the men on the other side of the curtain. I dressed, and watched Insa bathe. She was an angular, muscular woman, with sharp hipbones and a broad chest. She pretended she did not notice that I watched her.

In the crowded tavern, the stone walls had not been paneled over, and the blazing firelight cast their rough surfaces into a relief of light of shadow. More quaint sayings decorated the beams overhead, and the wooden floor complained under the weight of many customers: a rough-dressed lot, most of them, in leather and wool,

with uncut, tangled hair. Many of them had the dark
skin and features of the mountain races, but I saw people of lighter skin as well, and even one head with a
trace of gold in the hair. This woman, with a scarred
face and her sleeves rolled up to her elbows, dealt
ivory wafers upon a game board.

Though my three companions had dried their hair
with towels, water still dripped from their long locks
of hair. Our entrance was hailed loudly, and several
people, better dressed than the others, rushed forward
to beg us to share their tables. Tord pushed his way
through the rough scuffle which ensued; Insa had already picked out a table, and beckoned him over. He
set three heavy bags onto the tabletop. Insa opened
one, and spilled out a mound of raw obsidian: large
pieces and small, catching the light strangely because
of their deep, black color. Was that what we had carried in our packs, which had made them so ungodly
heavy? She held one piece up to the light, which turned
it a deep, translucent blue. "Who will buy?"

The well-dressed traders, for that they seemed to
be, sat down at her table and began to bargain in earnest. The other residents of the tavern, engrossed in
food, drink, and talk, did not even turn their heads. A
man began to play an accordian loudly in the corner.

I took Alalin by the elbow and drew him over to the
bar. Bottles lined the shelf behind, but Alalin called
for ale. I hesitated, but others would be paying the
bill, so I asked for a brandy. The barkeep glanced at
me strangely then, as if noticing for the first time that
I was not an Asakeiri woman. I touched my fingers
self-consciously to the two beads, firmly tied once
again into my overgrown hair.

A woman came up and slapped Alalin on the shoulder, so I took my brandy over to the fireplace and
found a chair there, where I could put my feet up onto
the hearth. My boots had been taken away along with
my rancid clothing. I wore borrowed clothes: a loose
sack of a tunic, over sagging trousers and thick socks.
The barkeep set a plate of crispbread onto the hearth

near me, and a pot of white farmer's cheese, smooth as cream.

My muscles, loosened by the warm water of the bath, let me sink into the comfort of the chair. I sipped my brandy, and took a crunchy mouthful of bread and cheese. Oh, gods of earth and sky, it was good.

Her bargaining done, Insa sat in the chair next to me, holding up her tankard in a triumphant toast.

I took a small sip of the brandy and let it burn on my tongue. Comfort and relief all but smothered my dismay. Mystery within mystery, secret within secret, a hallway of locked doors. I shuddered sharply, and set my glass down upon the hearth. "How did I learn to speak the Asakeiri language?"

Insa shrugged, open-palmed. "In your own country you are a scholar. That means you are clever?"

"I am not that clever."

She shrugged again, and filled her mouth with crispbread. "The Asakeiri do not have food like this."

"How did the obsidian bead get into my hair?"

"I hear that Ata'al put it in while you slept. She knew you would not accept it—"

I looked into her face, and knew that she lied.

Insa took the bag of money from her lap and weighed it in her hand. Then she tossed it to me, the coins clinking pleasantly as they landed in my hand. "I bargained like a fiend because Ata'al said to give it to you. Your passage home."

Chapter 13

The rhythmic, musical jangling of bells awoke me from the luxury of a sound sleep. Insa slept beside me, one hand fisted around a rope of hair. From across the room, I heard the rumble of Tord's snore. The closed shutters kept the room gloomy, but thin shreds of light in the cracks of the shutters told me that day had dawned. Faintly, from the street below, I heard the sound of someone loudly singing off key.

I got out of bed and opened the sash and shutters, cracking through the crusted snow which blocked the sill. The snowfall had petered out in the night, and now the clouds were breaking up overhead, like ice in a lake, letting the weakling sun shine through. With daybreak, the village had come alive: bundled, busy figures dotted the snow, clearing the walkways, skiing down the street, or chatting, knee-deep in the middle of the road. Immediately below my window, a steaming horse with a red sleigh behind stood at the front porch of the inn. A shaggy, broad-shouldered figure levered a heavy bag out of the sleigh and slung it over a shoulder. An early morning delivery? Thoughtful, I closed the window and shutters once again.

Downstairs, the sleigh driver sat in the warm, abandoned tavern, her shaggy bearskin coat steaming by the fire. She chatted with the innkeeper as she sipped from a steaming, fragrant cup. "Is that chocolate?" I asked from the doorway, amazed. Apparently, the trappers who frequented this inn, having no household to support and no real need to plan for the future, could rather casually dispose of their incomes. Even in the coastal cities, chocolate was an expensive luxury. The innkeeper beckoned me over, bellowing for someone to bring me a cup.

"You slept well, eh?" he said. "Best beds in the central mountains." He introduced me to the sleigh driver, Newel, an older woman than I. Her broad, muscular shoulders came from managing the horses, I guessed. I asked her if she had traveled from one of the outlying farms.

"I make a three-day run from here to Calinton and back again. I should've arrived yesterday, but I got trapped in the storm."

"Calinton is below the snow line, isn't it?"

"Not quite, but another day's journey will take you out of the mountains, for sure."

My chocolate arrived. I sipped it delicately: it was as good as any they served in the Emperor's palace, strong and sweet and bitter. "Do you take passengers?"

"More often than not."

The innkeeper gave me a sharp, curious look. "It's rare that the Asakeiri travel far. I don't suppose you're off to see your Adline run before the Emperor?"

That I might need an explanation for taking a journey at so unpropitious a time of year had not occurred to me. Nor had I expected to be mistaken for an Asakeiri woman. But I answered quickly, "Of course I am. It will give her luck, to run before friends."

"Well, that's a whole new matter. Adline is practically one of our own." The driver examined me closely, my borrowed clothes and spare, hardened frame. "I don't expect you've got much money to travel by."

"Not much," I admitted. Insa's clever bargaining had only garnered a modest sum; I would have to spend it sparingly. I already regretted the chocolate.

"Well, since I'm going that way anyway, you can come along for the ride. Keep me company, like. It's a lonely stretch in winter."

"I don't know what kind of company I'd be," I said cautiously.

"You speak Common; what more could I ask? It's a deal, then?"

"How can I argue?" The girl brought a tray of sweetbread, hot and steaming from the oven. Newel dug in with gusto. At supper the night before, I had eaten as much as I could swallow, but this morning I matched her, bite for bite. Sugar-cured bacon followed the bread, and a bowl of good porridge with cream.

I said, "In your travels, you must hear all the news. Tell me how it goes with Adline."

"You hadn't heard yet? She won the Akava race."

"I'd heard that. What about Imato and Sholay?"

"She won those, too, handily. And in Green, they say she came in a whole furlong ahead of the next runner. She won Musong and River Break and Town-fall. In short, she's won them all. Woodwing would have been yesterday; I haven't heard about that race yet. But I expect she won. They say that there's never been another person on earth who could run so fast." Newell laughed, rich and deep. "Ah, what a day it will be for the people, when she takes the champion's ribbon from the Emperor's own hand!"

Because everyone assumed my alliances to be with the Asakeiri, I laughed, too. That people were secretly saying such things about Adline didn't surprise me, of course; it was what I had thought all along would happen.

"She's a hero, she is; coast to coast everyone acclaims her."

"Ay, she's a fine runner."

"A brave one, too."

When I asked the innkeeper to total up the bill for myself and my companions, he held out his empty hands in a gesture I had certainly not seen often. "Never mind the money. Insa says the earthquake just about leveled your town? A terrible thing; terrible. We'll pull together a crew, after spring planting, and help with the rebuilding. Tell them to send us a guide; and we'll come."

At this evidence of how badly the Emperor's ban and blockade of the Asakeiri people had eroded, I had to hold myself rigidly in check. "It's a hellish long journey," I pointed out.

"A fellow can't spend his whole life in one place now, can he?" He slapped my shoulder kindly, and went off to holler at the inn workers some more.

In our shared room on the second floor, Insa had just come back from a trip to the outhouse. Tord still snored in the corner, and Alalin, having gone off with his woman friend the night before, had not yet reappeared.

Our camibockers, washed cleaner than I would have thought possible, and our outergear, which now smelled only of woodsmoke and lanolin, lay in a neat pile upon my bed. The innworkers had worked miracles.

"I'm leaving with the sleigh," I told Insa.

She drew her knees up to her chest, as if she crouched on the bare floor of a mud shelter, and not on the neatly made bed of a high class inn. "Are you, then. Well, you'll take your skis with you, and leave them along the way for Adline? She'll need to get herself home, somehow."

Without a word, I began changing into my own transformed clothing. It was not that I wanted her to care about my comings and goings, but Insa's indifference surprised me. And I felt haunted again by the mysteries I had not been able to resolve. I felt as if I had walked onto a stage between acts, ignorant of what had happened before or what would happen after. How could I be expected to make a speech about the meaning of the play?

By high noon, with a fresh draft horse in the traces, the sleigh laden with labeled boxes and tagged bags and bundles of green-cured furs, Newel was ready to leave. I had little enough to add to her load: my own skin-and-bone self, my skis and poles, and a practically empty pack. Insa and the men stood solemnly on the porch as I mounted the driver's seat beside Newel and set my feet onto the foot warmer, freshly filled with hot water, and pulled the fur robe up to my chin. The cook came rushing out then, with a cloth-covered basket to tuck between us. Newel hupped to her horse and we were off, bells jangling.

I looked back before we left the village. The three Asakeiri people still stood without moving, their hair curtaining from their heads, beads glinting in the light reflecting from the snow. The thread reeled out between us, stretching unbearably tight. Then, suddenly it snapped, and I felt a sharp, brief pain in my belly. The three turned and walked back into the inn. I turned my face away.

The white, shining road stretched before us, edged by a fence on one side, and the slender poles of tree trunks on the other. The powerful horse trotted steadily through the deep snow, ears swiveling at the jingling of the bells. As we rounded a curve, a river came into sight, gray and clotted with ice. The river plunged into a canyon, and our road took a sharp turn. The stark vista which spread below us was breathtaking and nerve-wracking: white and gray, an unmarred forest, with the river winding through, shimmering silver in the faint sunlight. The road wound down the side of the cliff, like a twisted white ribbon.

Newel, the reins held slack in her gloved hands, abruptly began to sing. "Oh, Wester went a hunting and she caught herself a man—Sing Hiya, Sing Hiya, Sing Waddle-e-doddle-e-doo."

She was still singing three days later, as we jangled into Canlinton. A vocal companion she had proved to be; accustomed to making her own noise in the silence and solitude of the winter, and showing no self-consciousness about the harsh tunelessness of her voice. Though the constant racket tempted me to gag her, I was hardly in a position to ask her to be silent.

Two of the three nights we had stayed in inns, of not even half the quality as the one in River's End. One night we stayed in a farmhouse, which the enterprising farmers had turned into a winter hostel. In the summer, Newel told me, the larger numbers of trav elers just camped in the field, and ate breakfast in the big kitchen in the morning. Why did so many people visit the lonely places of the high mountains? For the scenery, Newel said, and the hunting. Some took the harsh trek up Mount Shino, so they could tell their friends they had looked into the mouth of a volcano.

In reaction to my stay with the Asakeiri I had become a gourmand; or perhaps merely a glutton. I reveled in any food which did not contain primarily potatoes and goat meat, and I ate more than I necessarily needed to keep alive. But, having been informed by the garrulous Newel that I traveled to watch Adline run the Ashami Race, innkeeper and farmer alike refused to accept payment for what I ate, or for the bed I slept in. Consistently encountering such mistaken generosity unnerved me after a while. Surely there would be an accounting. But the bill never came due, and I made the whole trip, from River's End to Calinton, without spending a single copper.

"There's something I've been wanting to ask you," said Newel, interrupting her own song as the rooftops of Calinton came into sight around a curve. A small enough town it seemed to be, with the usual shops and tradehouses fronting the main road, and a few modest clusters of townhouses. We had been passing outlying farmsteads for most of the day already. Because of the short growing season, the farmers did not seem to be overly prosperous. That is the way of farming: If your family is fed, and you own a good horse or cow, then you are a success.

It was a cold day; even colder than most. My morning footwarmer had long since cooled, and I huddled miserably within my furs. To see smoke trailing from the stone chimneys of the modest town cheered me. "What do you want to know?" I asked Newel.

"Eh; it's just curiosity—you'll tell me if I offend? With your short hair and all, and your ability to speak Common, you aren't—forgive my saying so—like the Asakeiri. If I didn't know better, I'd say you've done a lot of traveling; certainly, you know your way around a town. It's curious, that's all."

I had assumed, of course, that anyone could see that I was not a native Asakeiri woman. But the first impression that was given by the native clothing I wore, combined with the confirmation of my garrulous driver, had so far proved convincing enough to everyone we encountered that they never asked another question. Now I pondered what to say to Newel, who had done more than her part to smooth my way these last three days. How to tell her now that I was not Asakeiri at all?

But she helped me once again. "The way I figure it, you're more like kin: maybe your mother or your father was Asakeiri, but you ain't never lived much in Asakeiri Home. But you feel it in your blood, like. And from time to time you return, yes?"

"Actually, this was the first time."

"Well, then; but I'm right otherwise."

"Oh, yes. I'm sorry, I would have explained it to you—but I thought you already understood."

"And now you're going to see Adline run—family obligation, like."

"Yes, that's correct."

"Well!" Newel beamed, pleased at her own cleverness. "Now tell me somewhat else, if you don't mind answering. How is she gonna get away from the Emperor's Knackers?"

"What makes you think the Emperor would consider one native woman to be a threat to him?"

"Oh, come now, what about the Asakeiri War? For an Asakeiri woman to mount the steps and take her prize from the Emperor's own hand— Everyone in the country knows what an offense it would be. Oh . . ." She eyed me knowingly. "You're going to get her out safely, aren't you. A sophisticated woman like you; you must know the ways—"

I said, "If I were, it would certainly put my plans at risk for us to be talking like this."

"That's right. You'll pardon me—my mouth has always been bigger than my brain."

Smiling as smugly as any farmer after a good market day, Newel drove us the rest of the way into Calinton.

No doubt she saw herself as having had a small part
in an event which would be remembered through history. She would tell all her friends about it, adjuring
each of them to secrecy. And then, when word filtered
to the backwoods that Adline was dead. . . . Well,
Newel would imagine another story; a dolorous trag-
edy, perhaps, and sing about it as she drove her endless rounds from Calinton to River's End and back to
Calinton again.

She had deliveries to make in Calinton, and would
stay the night with her daughter on the outskirts of
town. She dropped me off on the boardwalk near the
inn, and bade me farewell and good luck. Hailing familiar faces from her high perch, she jangled off down
the hard-packed snow of the narrow road. I stood on
the boardwalk, with my near-empty pack on my shoulder and my skis tucked under my arm. A half dozen
townsfolk, out on business despite the sharp afternoon
wind, examined me curiously. The town had a play-
house, shuttered for the winter, of course, which in-
dicated to me that lowland holiday-makers often made
the trek this deep into the mountains in the summer-
time. Probably, a nearby lake provided boating and
fishing, and holiday cabins around its edges were shuttered now and buried under snow.

The Marquis Chavren, governor of this region, kept
a country home here, close to his income-producing
properties, sawmills primarily, and within easy riding
distance of good hunting. I had heard that his hunting
lodge was a sight to behold; of course none of my kind
had or would ever be invited.

In the inn's receiving area, a pretty woman sat behind a high counter, doing the accounts. A young man
sat negligently in an armchair, a dog-eared broadsheet
in his lap, gazing out the lavender-tinted windowpanes
with an expression of cold anger and unutterable bore-
dom. As I entered, he turned the full force of his stare
upon me, curled a lip, and looked away once again.

"A room for the night," I said to the woman behind
the desk. "And when does a coach leave for the lowlands?"

Startled, no doubt, by my linguistic fluency, the young woman stared at me. Quite the ruffian I must have looked, with my coarse, bestained and begrimed clothing, my uncut hair, and my features made harsh by illness, hard work, and starvation. "Why, there are no coaches in the winter, of course. You'd have to hire a sledge from one of the local farmers."

"No coach? Does the whole commerce of the town shut down with the first snowfall?"

Quite flustered now, the young woman rattled things on the countertop: a pen and an inkwell, a few pieces of local stone, with false gold glittering in the aggregate. "Well, no, of course not, but—" She noticed the skis in my hand then. "Most folks find their own way to get around," she finished pointedly.

"Would you recommend that a stranger to these parts travel alone on foot?"

"There have been known to be bandits."

Irritated, I leaned the skis upon the wall. "How much would a hired sledge cost?"

She named a sum, far more than I could afford to pay for a single day's journey. "I'll take the bandits," I said. I signed for my room, and asked my way to a dry-goods store. There I spent a good quarter of the money in my posession, outfitting myself with food, a small lantern, a pair of heavy wool trousers and an overshirt, smallclothes, and a pistol.

I changed clothes in my room in the inn, and went next door to the tavern, where, with sunset approaching, business had begun to pick up. The customers were mostly big, hulking, ham-handed people, with faces burnt red by the cold wind, long-haired or bearded, built like bulls. Lumberjacks, I guessed. A dour lot they were, crouched over their fried fish and ale. I slipped in among them as well as I could, ordering what they ate, along with a single cup of ale, though the mountain cold left me longing once again for brandy. The meal proved to be good mountain trout and salty fried potatoes; with portions to suit a hungry clientele.

I was picking at my leftovers and pondering ordering another cup of ale, when the sullen young man from the inn foyer pulled up a chair at my table. I examined him so grimly that he seemed to reconsider approaching me, but said, with a stiff and artificial air of philanthropic friendliness, "I have a business proposition."

"Buy me a drink," I suggested.

To my surprise, the man blushed fiercely. "I regret that my finances are in arrears."

"Then what can you possibly have to offer me?"

"If I may sit down—"

"Sit."

The barman came around, but I waved him away. The man, ill at ease, shifted his chair irritably. He wore breeches of glove leather, and a knee-length coat tailored to make him seem bigger than he actually was. His pistols, awkwardly hidden under his coat, flashed in the faint light: polished brass. I knew his type; I saw them every day in Ashami, boys and girls raised in privilege but unsuited to manage real power, all arrogance, but nothing underneath. Of course, his kind scorned mine.

". . . debt of honor," he was saying. "But I can get money in Lomit Crossing, to pay for hiring the sledge. If you would just pay up front and let me ride that far. I'm a good shot with a pistol," he finished lamely.

"What did you bet on?"

"I don't see what that has to—"

"Indulge me. Was it the footraces? The Woodwing?"

"Well, yes."

"Did you choose Adline to win, or to lose?"

"To lose," he said defensively.

"Then you are a fool." I was stunned to learn that Adline had won once again, but I hid it well.

"Actually, I bet her to win. But my friend bet she would scratch, and she did. My friend stripped me clean, then left me here."

"Some friend! Surely the Marquis' steward would front you the money."

If possible, the boy became even more embarrassed at this suggestion. "They've all shut down and moved south for the winter, except for a housekeeper."

"And Adline scratched in the Woodwind? Any word what happened?"

"Rumor is she's ill. About the sledge—"

"It's a deal." I offered my hand to shake his. No young blood would voluntarily embarrass himself like this, so I knew he had to be telling the truth. "But if you don't pay, I'll take it out of your hide."

The young man paled. "Oh, I'm good for it."

Bandit fodder, I thought grimly, and wondered what I was getting myself into.

Chapter 14

Hay littered the bed of the hired sledge, the joints of which had begun to come loose from hard use. The horse also looked to be well into middle age. I berated the farmer for hiring out damaged goods, until he dropped his price. I doubted that I would find better, since no one in his right mind would hire out his best horse or sledge, to be abused, lost, or otherwise jeopardized. Sick and tired of the mountains and the people who live there, I paid the farmer and mounted to the driver's seat to wait with little patience for my passenger. He appeared eventually, booted and jacketed, with his hair slicked back into a neat ponytail.

"Your ears will freeze."

"I have a hat." He patted the pocket of his jacket.

"You don't have any baggage?"

The young man shrugged. His creditor truly had stripped him clean. "Well, it'll be easier on the horse."

He sat down beside me and looked around, noting with approval the basket of food, and the hay and grain for the horse. "But where are the laprobes?"

"The farmer didn't bring any. We supply our own, he said. It'll be a cold trip."

"Gods help us if we get stranded somewhere."

I agreed. It went against my careful nature to travel without proper supplies or precautions, but I saw no help for it. I had loaded my pistol and stuck it in my boot, and put the powder and shot within easy reach. In my other boot I carried my obsidian knife. Such modest insurance did not greatly ease my mind. I

clucked to the horse, who pretended he did not hear
me until I slapped his rump with the reins.

"It's going to be a long journey," predicted the
young man dolefully.

"I don't know your name, by the way."

"Vail."

"Jamil."

"I've heard that name before, somewhere."

The horse pulled us unenthusiastically out of town.
The road was nearly flat here, and few conveyances
had passed this way since the last snowfall.

My fellow traveler persisted, despite my silence.
"You're not famous, are you?"

"Not that I know of."

He lapsed into dissatisfied silence, crossing his arms
across his chest and sinking his chin into the collar of
his coat in a vain attempt to keep warm.

We passed a miserable morning, the day only growing colder as the shadows shortened and the steep road
took us through forest and stone and across a rickety
bridge. A gray, half-frozen river flowed sluggishly below, edged by the jagged white of crushed ice. I have
crossed bridges like this a thousand times. Without
them, Callia would still be a country of fragments, a
hundred isolated peoples who travel only at risk of
their lives. Bridges gave the Emperor an Empire. One
would think that they could be built more sturdily.

"Haven't you ever crossed a bridge before?" said
Vail.

I gave him the grimmest of glances, but he actually
seemed to have asked the question out of curiosity
rather than out of a desire to torment me. "I nearly
died, falling into a ravine a few months ago," I said.
"Care to see the scars?"

"Sounds like you've had a run of bad luck," he said
lightly.

I whacked the horse with the switch. He jumped
with surprise and trotted a few steps before settling
into a laborious walk once again. "I've had better
years."

"What is it you do, if I may ask?"

"Tradewagon guard."

"With just a pistol?"

"You have no manners, boy." I whacked the horse again, considering seriously the option of throwing my companion out of the wagon. I would probably never see my travel money again anyway; and he probably couldn't shoot to save his life. My passenger said nothing. A sidelong glance revealed him to be rather pale. What a shock the boy had experienced, after living his life wrapped in an impenetrable armor of self-importance, only to realize one day that it was all an illusion, as easily taken away as a full purse. Without his money, his servants, and his family name (which he dared not use lest he bring shame upon it) he was just another penniless traveler wishing he had spent a little more time at target practice.

We traveled in silence after that.

At midday we stopped to rest the horse in its traces, and to share a loaf of bread, some sharp cheese, a couple of wizened apples, and some sweet nutcakes out of the basket. We had no way of knowing how much farther it was to Lomit Crossing. The milestones, if they existed at all, were covered by snow, and we had passed no crossroad. Vail got out of the wagon and ploughed about, knee-deep in the pristine snow. The air down here was thicker; it felt strange to have to work so little to get a good breath of air. How were the Asakeiri managing, I wondered? How many more ghosts haunted the ruins of their ancient town?

"Someone passed this way since the last storm," Vail said, pointing to a slim ski trail along the edge of the road.

I shrugged. We could not be the only people in the world with somewhere to go. He climbed in beside me and spent no little time brushing the snow from his boots. Soon enough, he would have a servant to polish them.

The thick forest had been gradually giving way to scrub and jagged stone, a terrain which reminded me of that in which I had first become stranded. With the

trees thinning, I found I could get a clear view of the
mountains behind us, lined like gigantic scales along
the humped back of the dragon. Blue and gray in the
weary light of the sun, furred by forest and limned
with snow, each mountain looked like the next: remote
and unassailable, a fortress of age and stone. Yet one
mountain, no different from the others, held my gaze.
I stared at it as if I could see to its very heart.

The horse jingled to a halt, head hanging. The sting
of my switch across his rump only made him quiver.
Exasperated, I jumped out of the sledge and walked
up to his head to have a chat. The horse's eyes rolled
as I approached. His withers were dark with sweat,
and he quivered again as I laid my hand upon his side.
"What is it?" yelled Vail, his voice piercingly loud in
the crisp, echoing silence.

"I don't know. I'm going to check his hooves."

Crouching in the snow now, I lifted the horse's
hooves one by one, cleaning the balled snow out of
them with my obsidian knife. The horse scarcely tol-
erated my attention; every time I touched him he
seemed on the verge of bolting. He had a deep dimple
in the muscle of his right foreleg. Thoughtful, I studied the terrain from below his belly. Then I came up
to Vail, who rattled his fingernails impatiently on the
wagonboard. "What do you know," I murmured.

"What?"

"The farmer who hired out his horse to us is in
cahoots with the local bandits. The horse has been
shot here before; that's why he won't go on. Don't
look at it directly; it'll rouse their suspicions; but
they're going to ambush us from that ridge up there,
where the road cuts between those stones."

I leaned casually against the side of the sledge, fool-
ing aimlessly with one of the sleighbells. "Little do
they know that we're both flat broke."

"Hell," said Vail.

'How good are you with those pistols?"

"Good enough."

"This is no time for bragging."

"Well, I'm no sharpshooter."

"Can you hit that person hiding behind the rocks halfway up the ridge? He seems to think he can hit us, once we get a little closer."

Vail considered. "Not bloody likely. Not only that, but I don't know anyone who could."

"As soon as the shooting starts, the horse is going to bolt. We both want to be in the sledge when that happens, or we'll find ourselves making the rest of the trip on foot. Why don't you stand up, put your hat on the wagonboard and take out your pistols and hide them under it—careful not to let them flash in the sun. Get one of those nutcakes out of the food basket."

I could see the idiot asking himself how he could know that this wasn't just a ruse to get him to disarm himself. He couldn't know, of course. The night before in Calinton he had made his decision to trust me, and he was stuck with it. Maybe he'd think a little more next time.

Vail stood up, stretched, and reached casually into the food basket. I climbed into the sledge at his side, giving him more cover in which to take care of his business. I sat down and tied the reins firmly; they'd do me no good now, but I'd sure be wanting them later. Then I leaned back in the seat, putting both my feet up on the front board, and accepted a nutcake from Vail. His glance flickered to the pistol in my right hand. "Won't that be a waste of a good shot? We'll only get three."

My new pistol was black and plain, without a bit of brass or ivory anywhere. When I braced it on my knee and sighted it, its color blended right into the charcoal gray of my trousers. The watchers up in the rocks wouldn't even notice it. I took my time: I had never even shot this pistol before, and, as Vail had pointed out, no one could hit the target. Partway up the rocky slope, in the shade of a boulder, a figure in nondescript gray stood motionless, all but invisible. As I squeezed the trigger, I realized I had felt this way before, like a bloodhound hot on a scent that only I could smell. Forty people I had saved from the shattered stones of Asakeiri Home.

The pistol kicked against my knee, with a sharp report that left my ears singing. The horse, with a wild bellow of terror, bolted. I shoved my pistol back into my boot, grabbed the other two pistols, and did what any other sensible person would do. I dropped to the floor and jammed myself as far under the wagonboard as I could fit. I shared the cramped space with Vail, who was laughing breathlessly. "I'd swear you hit him!"

"I did. Bloody hell!" The bandits, taken by surprise, opened fire too early, inspiring our terrified horse to a greater magnitude of panic. The sledge careened into a snowdrift, on the edge of overturning. The horse blundered frantically. More shots were fired. The horse screamed again and jerked us back into the center of the road. The snow proved too much of an impediment for a full-fledged stampede, but the horse carried us quite briskly between the overhanging rocks, scraping the sledge heedlessly among the debris. Then we were past, and there were no more shots, just the enraged bellowing of some stranger upslope, who had used up his ammunition too early and knew he wouldn't finish reloading before we were out of range.

"Are you all right?" asked Vail as we crawled out from under the wagonboard. His face was flushed with excitement; I guessed he'd never been gunshot or he wouldn't be having so much fun. I got a good grip on the reins and began hauling away at them, but it proved a waste of time.

"This horse sure has done this before," I said wryly. "Better get ready to duck again."

"What for?"

I pointed ahead. A lone figure had stepped out into the road, with three others lounging casually among the rocks. Apparently they hadn't realized yet that the two of us had escaped the ambush unscathed. I pulled Vail down and sighted one of his pistols around the edge of the wagon, right along the withers of the panting horse. The horse saw friends now: these were not the people who shot at him; these were the ones who would bring him to a nice stable and give him a bucket of grain. His pace slowed to an eager trot.

I squeezed the trigger. The figure in the road dove for cover as the horse squealed again, leaping into another panicked gallop. I caught a glimpse of a couple of wind-reddened faces, rifles in hand, watching us careen past with their mouths open, but I didn't waste a bullet on them.

"Gods," gasped Vail. I glanced at him, thinking he might have been shot, but he was just out of breath from laughing.

Somewhat before nightfall, the horse limped soberly across the bridge at Lomit Crossing. The river had tamed and broadened enough to carry a barge full of cut lumber which slipped past under us, the bargewoman's fire filling our nostrils briefly with the good smell of woodsmoke. Vail's hilarity had lapsed into abject misery, and he glanced down at the river without much interest. The cold had only grown more profound as we slowly traversed the last stretch of road, peering in the dimming light of the rapidly approaching sunset. The snow had grown so thin that the horse had to struggle to drag the sledge across it; if it got much thinner we would have to get out and walk. Then Lomit Crossing came into sight, and Vail gave a sigh, dreaming, no doubt, of a warm fire and clean clothing.

"Hell of a day," he said.

"Now where do I take you?"

His fingernails tapped on the wagonboard, making me wonder once again how likely I was to ever see my money again. "Up at Asram Al's," he finally said, pointing down the main street. The shops were shut up like strongboxes, with their shutters padlocked and the upstairs curtains drawn. I heard faintly an incongruous sound, the voice of a caged nightingale singing in someone's drawing room. A bent figure scuttled ahead of us, bowed under a burden of bundled twigs.

The horse plodded heavily forward, head bowed wearily, and turned of his own accord into the gate of a stockyard at the edge of town. I rang the bell vig-

orously, grabbed my gear, and climbed stiffly down
from the wagonboard. After what we had been
through, I had seriously considered stealing the horse,
but the truth is that I didn't ever want to set eyes on
the stupid beast again. We left the horse standing in the
stableyard, and never looked back.

The walks had been shoveled free of snow. Vail
tramped along beside me, deep in thought. "Is it
friends you have here, or are you just looking for a
moneylender?" I asked him.

"We were supposed to meet the main party here by
yesterday morning," said Vail. "My mother's chamberlain is among them." He looked glum.

"Winter hunting?" I guessed. Competition among
the bloods to display the most spectacular pelt has become intense in recent years. Other mountain travelers
claim to be invigorated by exposure to the frigid con-
ditions of winter. I think that they are bored of the
endless summer of the coast, and come into the mountains to experience the seasons once again. However,
I have noticed that they are always overwhelmingly
happy to return home again.

As if the weather were not bad enough, the nobles
complain often about the mountain people, who are
boorish and ill acquainted with the requisite courte-
sies. The people of this region have not forgotten that
once they reigned sovereign in this place, lords of the
fish runs and the timber harvest, kings of the low-
roofed burrows in which they waited out the winter.
The independence still in their hearts is offensive to
most noblefolk, who are always relieved to return to
their own little kingdoms, where their servants are at
least well trained.

Music wafted from behind the shuttered windows
and closed door of Asram Al's, a public house marked
by an ornately carved wooden sign, in which a naked
man was depicted riding upon the back of a deer, with
the vines and flowers of a lush forest winding around
him. Vail opened the door and peered in cautiously,
then hastily shut the door again. "Maybe we'll find a
moneylender."

Dusk was setting in, and the wind had begun to pick up. I had grown accustomed to the cold during my stay with the Asakeiri, but I had also learned when it was time to get indoors. I grabbed Vail by the arm, opened the door, and dragged him, protesting, into the public house. "Remember what I told you about taking it out of your hide," I muttered. "That was only a day ago; surely you haven't forgotten."

Vail stared at me coldly, as if he had never seen me before.

We stood in the flickering light of a lampflame mantled in red glass. A large painting hung on one wall, badly done in the classical style, with several dramatically posed, larger than life human figures, naked except for a few fortuitously placed veils. Greatcoats and fur-lined cloaks hung from hooks along the wall. Their owners, in gaiters and breeches and rustic wool, sat steaming in the heat, toasting each other with glasses of brandy. A fire roared in the fireplace, and the snow on my boots instantly began to melt. There must have been twenty-five or thirty people, each dressed as woodsmen and hunters, except that their bodies smelled of sachets and perfumes, and none of their clothing had even a speck of dirt on it.

The laughter and chatter fell gradually silent as a bulky figure rose and came forward, to examine Vail thoroughly. Ignoring this scrutiny, Vail took off his coat and slung it over a hook, and signaled to the barman for a drink. Yes, he had entered back into his own world.

"If I may ask my lord where he has been," began the fat man.

"I took a side trip."

"It is most unfortunate that I was forced to send your mother a message yesterday, informing her that you had disappeared—"

"Yes, that is unfortunate."

The man stood like a blockade between Vail and the barman, who stood uncertainly with the crystal tumbler in his hand. Perhaps this was only the chamberlain, but he had been given the power of the purse strings, and he knew how to use it. Vail said, "Perhaps I will send her a message tomorrow." The chamberlain did not move. "Tonight. Say," he gestured to the barman. "Do you have a pen?"

"And how will you send the message?" inquired the chamberlain, still not moving.

Vail jerked his head vaguely in my direction, too well-bred to point. I said quietly, "Guess again."

"I'll pay you well."

"I'm not your lackey," I muttered. "I have business to attend to."

"Well, then," said Vail, pretending to be oblivious to the mocking gazes of his friends. "I'm sure someone will be found to carry a message."

"I think," said the chamberlain ponderously, "that you had best bring the message yourself."

Vail opened his mouth to protest but seemed to realize that it would accomplish nothing except make him look even more foolish. "Of course, what a fine idea," he said solemnly. The chamberlain, satisfied at last, stepped out of his way. Like a moth drawn to a flame, Vail stepped forward, toward the blazing fire, the huzzahs of his friends, and the globe of brandy. But I gripped him once again by the sleeve.

"My lord is so honorable about paying his debts," I reminded him.

He paled slightly, recognizing the implied threat in my choice of wording. I suspected that he did not want the chamberlain to know about the gambling debt which had left him stranded and empty-pursed. He said to the chamberlain, "Pay her if you please. And, by the way, there is a matter of some bandits that needs to be taken care of."

Vail was grinning to himself as he accepted the glass from the barman and headed for the youthful woman in a rakish hat who leaned back with her boots on the table, laughing at him. The chamberlain watched him, frowning, his poise threatened by the knowledge that his charge's life had been at risk. "Tell me what happened," he said to me.

''I'll just take my money, sir. I'm sure the boy won't be able to keep from bragging about it for long.''

One by one, the chamberlain handed me coins in the hallway, as if I were trying to cheat him. I was glad enough to get out of that place.

Chapter 15

One last long day of foot travel freed me of the mountains. They loomed behind me now like childhood memories: simplified, drably colored shapes, with no hint of danger, no suggestion of the harsh death which had nearly claimed me there. I left my skis and my furs in a toolshed; they would mystify some farmer, come spring. My pack I filled with modest supplies, food that could be eaten out of hand: biscuits and jerky and dried vegetables as crisp as candy. Now in the flatlands of Norther Rift, I walked in the frozen mud of the rutted road, enjoying my solitude.

Winter had harrowed the flatlands, stripping the trees and baring the walled fields, etching the earth with spikes of hoarfrost. The flatland farmers had brought their sheep into the fold and shooed their chickens into the barn, and had set a few late eggs to incubate in stinking piles of fresh cow manure. They had shuttered their windows and barred their doors, and I knew better than to try to get them to open them to a stranger.

These were a sullen people, farmers of a heavy, rocky soil, flooded by rain in the wintertime, but subject to intolerable drought, come summer. To protect their pieces of land, they fought the elements and the wolves, the thieves and each other, unenthusiastically but obstinately. They had faces like stones in a wall, the faces of people who do not take long to make up their minds but take forever to change them. Long isolated by mountains to the north, the Rift on the south and east, and the ocean at the west, they wanted nothing to do with anyone whose people had not lived on that very land for time beyond memory. I stayed on the road, and drank from running streams, for I knew that they killed trespassers.

The towns were a strange contrast. Built by people who had moved in from elsewhere, taxed and controlled by the local gentry, these poor settlements were crammed with activity and color. In every town I passed, it always seemed to be market day. Sullen farmers knelt on bright blankets, surrounded by turnips and carrots and other winter vegetables. Vendors bellowed their nonsense cries, challenging each other to ever increasing volume. Dancers, stripped down to mere veils despite the cold, danced sinuously to the sound of bells and drums and briskly strummed instruments. Magicians hawked their spells and potions: magic rings and charms and aphrodisiacs, all the desires of your heart for a price. Horses and cows and sheep crowded the thoroughfare, lowing and moaning and bleating shrilly as their fate was decided: an open palm for a sale, a fist for no deal.

They welcomed travelers here, like snakes welcome a careless mouse. Men and women alike called me into the open bars, with their little knives, as sharp as razors, hidden in their sleeves. I prefered the honest hostility of the country to this vicious openheartedness. If I was going to be robbed, I would rather the thief did not shake my hand as he did it. Indeed, I took to calling these places thieftowns, and I watched my back trail when I left. I would not sleep in their inns. I bought myself some good blankets and slept among cold rocks with my pistol at hand.

I have not often heard anyone say this, but I was glad to reach the Rift, even though I knew I would have to find a way across it.

Two, maybe three times in my life I have stood at the edge of the Rift. The first time, I was drawn by curiosity. The other times, I came back to verify my own memories.

It is not a place for the timid. Its steep, stark black walls drop straight down into what seems the center of the earth, as if the very firmament has shattered and separated. Wind and rain have worn smooth the jagged edges of this open wound. Along its rim, trees cluster, teetering, roots exposed where they grip the eroding edge. Farther down, if you dare to look, is only bare rock. At the height of summer, the sun shines into the rift for only a few hours each day, and even the hardiest of plants cannot seem to survive such dearth. I stood at its edge, gazing at the far rim. It was farther away than I remembered.

Those who fall or are thrown over the edge of the Rift are never seen again. It is a favorite place for murders and suicides. But many an adventurer has climbed down into its sunless depth. A black, cold river runs at its bottom, nourishing a rich delta to the west, where some of the finest farmland of the country is to be found. But the farmers there have built a high wall which they guard day and night against the army of outlaws who make their homes in the dark, barren places of the Rift. Once a year, the Emperor's Guard makes a foray up the entire length of the dark canyon, but the outlaws always reappear again, having fled along secret paths to hide in places known only to them. Rifters, they are called.

I crouched at the edge of the Rift, feeling its great depth gaping before me like a question I dared not ask. If I followed its ragged edge westward, eventually I would reach navigable ground: a road and a series of bridges which would take me to sea level, and a town where I could wait for the train to come. If I followed the Rift eastward, it would eventually peter out to a mere ravine, where I could cross on one of the Emperor's bridges, for a fee. But both of these choices took too much time. And both of them would force me to bypass Akava.

Oh, yes. Akava.

I began walking westward along the rim. By day's end, I had found a path, scarcely more than a scuffed trail among the rocks. I sat awake that night, painstakingly sewing my coins into the hem of my shirt as I listened to the wind moan in the enormous canyon.

The Rifters are few in number; with a little luck I could climb into the canyon and out again, and never even be seen.

I rose early to begin my climb. The far walls, dim and distant in the pallid morning light, drew closer as my descent progressed. It was noon before the sun finally touched me, lying like a warm blanket across my chilled shoulders. I pressed my numb fingers to the side of a black boulder so that its small heat could warm them. The rim loomed above me now, ragged with distant trees. The sight reminded me too vividly of the way this desperate journey of mine had begun, as I dragged my battered body step by step up the ravine that imprisoned me, searching for a path out. Asakeiri medicine had healed me, but the long journey was wearing me down again. I spread my body out onto the warm stones, and rested, precariously perched.

The sun, that false lover, kissed me and then abandoned me. Black clouds had begun rolling across the sky. I sat up, jamming my arms into the straps of my pack. I did not think it was cold enough for snow, but rain would be just as bad. I climbed like a madwoman, inspired by impending doom. But it is not like me to lose awareness of my larger surroundings, even with danger treading so close upon my heels. So I paused after a while, my attention caught by a small stone that went bouncing down the sheer rock face along which I spidered. I watched it fall, asking myself another of those dismaying questions. I looked up, and saw the faintest of motions, a shadow among shadows.

For hours I had been discounting my sensation of being followed as anxious imagining. Now I cursed silently and kept climbing. One shadow I could handle. But trying to climb rain-slippery rocks would probably kill me. I continued my dash for safety, as the walls closed in on me like a clenching fist, and the curtain of clouds closed over the sky, and suddenly the black river appeared below. The grim gulf turned dim and gray. The wind began to moan among the stones.

Slipping, sliding on loose stones, ripping the skin from my hands, bruising my knees on rock, I climbed for my life.

They let me reach the riverbed before they stepped out from behind the fallen rocks. Oh, I had not let myself imagine that a welcome awaited me, but I was not greatly surprised by the four gray people, each of them thin as a bone, with ragged clothes and ragged hair and polished guns in their hands. One looked ready to explode with pregnancy, but the hand with which she held her rifle seemed steady enough. To shoot would only take away my bargaining room. Without being asked, I laid my pistol quietly onto the stony ground.

The fifth climbed down from the path above: a slender girl, all bone and hair, dressed only in the remains of a blanket, roped at the waist. She carried three knives that I could see, and a gentleman's ivory handled pistol. She clapped her hands at the sight of my nearly new clothing. I stood very still, feeling my life slip between my fingers like water. I had little enough, but it looked like a windfall to them. If they just let me go alive, albeit empty-handed and stark naked, that might be all I could hope for.

I backed a few steps away from my pistol, and the slender girl who moved like shadow came up from behind me to snag it. Dancing sideways in her grave delight, she jabbed a finger vigorously toward the sky. No, a rainfall could not be pleasant in this narrow ravine. Her companions gestured with their weapons, and I began to walk.

The river ran wide, and deep, and black as night under the stormy sky. I looked up at the looming walls of the huge canyon until my neck ached. The girl scrambled ahead of us, fey and elvin in the uncertain light, with her hair trailing like smoke. Behind me, the four adults kept their weapons trained on me. The pregnant woman walked carefully but gracefully among the stones. Her arms and legs were thin as sticks. She stared at me, her gaze steady and unblinking as a snake about to strike. Her hunger pondered me: fingering the contents of my backpack, poking my bones to see how fat I was, as if she were a cook planning how to prepare a fine roast.

The girl twisted between boulders ahead of me. I followed as slowly as I dared, frantically counting over my options: to fight, to bargain, to flee. If I fled they would catch me, if I fought they would kill me . . . and what did I have to bargain with that they could not simply take away at their leisure, once I was dead? They would not believe me to be a Separated One— and if they did, they would know better than to believe any promises I made them. I stumbled along behind the Rifter girl, worried not so much by my predicament as by the fact that I could not think of a way out of it.

A raven swooped past overhead, uttering a cry like the sound of bones rattling. The storm wind hurled it toward the steep, stony walls of the canyon. In a flutter of ragged feathers it landed among stones and sheltered among the shadows. A few icy cold drops of rain spattered upon the rocks.

The girl began to run, dodging in and out of shadows and among rocks. I began to run also. My body felt heavy and each step jarred my bones. My escort also began to run, guns still in hand. Maybe one of them would fall and kill themselves. Maybe their gunpowder would get wet.

The girl ran straight at the wall of the canyon, so it seemed she would collide directly with the stones. Then she was gone, like a candle flame snuffed out. I followed her more slowly, wanting to know what I was getting myself into. But one of my followers prodded me sharply, and I picked up the pace.

In the uncertain light, I did not see the opening until I had all but stepped through it. The Rifters had walled in a natural overhang, and the resulting shelter was all but invisible. Within, only the flames of a small cookfire illuminated the gloom. A few stones provided seats. A pile of rags lay in a shadowed corner. In another, the flotsam of their lives lay in scattered disorder: ropes and buckets, shoes and pieces of armor, weapons, baskets, backpacks, and trash. A cookpot sat near the fire, but I saw no sign of food.

The girl appeared out of the shadows. Prodded from behind, I stepped forward toward the center of the shelter. The rain had begun to fall in earnest, making fierce, sharp sounds as it splattered onto bare stone. My captors came in behind me, shaking themselves like dogs and muttering among themselves. I thought I heard the rhythm and accent of the Common tongue. I set my backpack onto the floor and said, as if I were a welcome guest rather than a prisoner, "I have some tea; maybe we could all drink a cup."

The four Rifters stared at me grimly, their faces flat as clay. The pregnant woman sat down heavily on one of the stones, and laid her rifle across her knees. The other three kept their weapons trained on me. "Lie down on the ground," one of them said.

Unable to choose between resistance and compliance, I did both, arguing even as I lay down on my stomach so the girl could bind my hands together. "I have nothing against you—I'm willing to share what I have. Why not reconsider?"

I grunted then, as the girl pulled the rope tight and my sockets popped. "Maybe we could even make a trade," I continued desperately. "I certainly could use some help getting out of the Rift again, and there must be some things you need that I could get for you—"

The girl poked a dirty rag into my mouth, silencing me. She pulled my boots off my feet and bound them. Only then did the others relax, adding fuel and putting the pot onto the fire, shrugging off their damp clothing. One of them brought my backpack to the pregnant woman, who began to go through it. Disabled now, with nothing I could do to affect my fate, my fear took over and I trembled like a wild animal at every touch as the girl searched me. "She's got money in her shirt hem," she said with satisfaction.

I wondered vaguely what they did with money in this gods-forsaken place. I supposed that any trader who dared do business with them could charge whatever he liked.

Her hand slipped between my legs and up my rump, a rough and impersonal touch that made me think once again of the hungry look in the pregnant woman's eyes. When I took someone prisoner, was this how I seemed to them, a butcher assessing the value of a piece of meat? My heart shivered within my chest, seeming to writhe rather than beat.

The girl's hand pressed between my shoulder blades, and up to my neck. There, her hand paused, fingers moving, and I heard the faint click of the two beads still tangled in my unkempt hair. She sat back suddenly on her heels, staring at me, her eyes angry and baffled.

One of the men spoke sharply.

"She has beads in her hair," the girl said sullenly.

The pregnant woman got to her feet and came to my side. From my point of view, her head peered absurdly around the edge of a great belly. She studied me, frowning, as baffled as the girl. Her hunger was still there, but it had been challenged by something else; something even I could not identify. Whatever the thought or emotion, it seemed alien to the woman. The men trailed over as well; reluctantly, it seemed.

Asakeiri. They thought I was Asakeiri.

I struggled frantically with the rag in my mouth, trying to push it out with my tongue. The girl suddenly grabbed a tail end of the rag, and jerked it out. "I am Adline Asakeiri's sister," I said. "I'm on my way to help her escape from Ashami after she wins the Concourse."

"Only two beads," the girl said. "And you talk Common."

The older people stood back, letting her ask the questions. I saw her intellect, burning bright as a flame, her energy not yet dissipated by the desperate life. The others had bands across their foreheads, hiding the thieves' brands burnt into their flesh. But she had no mark on her face; she must have been born within the Rift. How did she know so much about the world? That same trader, perhaps, a gossipy traveler, willing to indulge a lively child's curiosity.

"I was born out-clan," I said. "I never lived with my people until this year—but my mother taught me the tongue." I spoke a few words in Asakeiri, though I doubted it would make much impact. To my surprise, all of them moved back a step.

The third woman, who had never spoken a word, now said very quietly, "She looks like Adline."

"You met her?"

"Adline came into the Rift by the same path you took, on her way to Akava. We captured her, just like you. And then she told us."

The girl dropped abruptly to her knees and began undoing the ropes.

One of the men said to me, *"You* could have told us."

"We should have known," the other woman said again. "She looks just like her."

I held my tongue, lest I say something which would betray my lie. The girl finished freeing me, and the others gave me a hand up. They did not apologize; like myself they seemed baffled enough by the sudden shift in the roles we had thought we were destined to play. "About that tea," I said, to smooth over the awkwardness. I took my pack, which had only been partially unpacked, and pulled out the tea tin.

They each had their own tin cup, carried tucked into their clothing or tied to their belt by a cord. Once the tea was made, they used these to scoop a serving out of the common pot. I had my own cup as well. I sat on one of the stones, with the girl sitting close by. I often felt her gaze upon my face. She questioned me closely about the Asakeiri, still suspicious, but my answers seemed to match what Adline had been able to tell them, despite the barrier of language which must have separated them. Finally, the girl turned her head, and showed me, hidden deep in her own hair, an obsidian bead.

"Adline gave you a part of her life?" This was an Asakeiri tradition I had never encountered.

"Because I saved her life," the girl said. "With my curiosity."

"Tisha asks everyone questions," explained the pregnant woman.

"Even the people you are about to—" I hesitated delicately.

"Who else is there?"

"What did Adline tell you, that made you spare her life?"

They looked at me as if this were the question of a madwoman. "That she was going to run in the Concourse."

"You would spare the life of anyone who was going to run in the Concourse?"

"Of an Asakeiri! Oh, to see the Emperor's face."

The quiet woman turned to me anxiously. "Do you know what is wrong with her? She has been ill, they say. She has missed two races now."

"Well, you know, she only has to win one race in order to run before the Emperor. Most winners run every race for the sake of the purse."

My listeners nodded, crouched over their tin cups full of steaming tea. Beyond the ragged blanket which blocked the worst of the draft from the entry, I heard the sound of the rain falling vigorously. The light continued to dim: afternoon retreating before an early twilight.

"But if often happens that the people who win most often then lose the final race before the Emperor. They wear themselves out with all the races that go before. But Adline doesn't really want the winners' purses. Now that she has won enough to pay her expenses, she is pretending to be sick so she can conserve her energy for the last race, the race she most wants to win."

"I thought so!" declared Tisha. She leapt to her feet. "I told you so!"

The others, clearly accustomed to their youngest member's active and excitable personality, ignored her. They emptied out the pot of tea, refilled it with water from a bucket, and set it back onto the fire. Since it appeared that we were going to have only water for dinner if I didn't do something, I offered up all my supplies to the common pot: the last of my cornmeal, the jerky, the dried vegetables and fruits. We put it all into the same pot and let it stew, forming a thick mush. The result was a strange soup, but we ate it all, and licked the pot clean afterward.

I slept on stone that night, and the next day the Rifters showed me where to climb out of the canyon.

Chapter 16

Approaching Akava from the north, the first thing a traveler sees is the Althi Tower, a slender, copper-roofed spire which houses nine cast iron bells. The day Adline won the Akava footrace, those bells had rung. I remembered their sound reverberating throughout the city, vibrating in the very stones of the streets. The blooming flowers of autumn had shriveled now, and the cold winds of winter had stripped bare of their leaves the trees in the orchards at the outskirts of the city. In one of these orchards, I paused to rest, stripping off my boots to dip my feet into the cold water of a stony brook.

I had been on the road for nineteen days. As I traveled, the mountains had crouched slowly behind the horizon, so that now I could see only their highest peaks, hazy and purple in the distance. I gazed at them now, considering once again the mysterious circumstances which had brought me so far from the road I had intended to follow. In the company of the youth from Akava, I had traveled northward for fifteen days or longer, and I remembered not one moment of that journey. It had been early autumn when I left; now it was winter. An entire season of my life had been sacrificed to that one strange, inexplicable occurrence.

After today, I would know for certain what had happened, and why. And the man who was responsible would be dead.

I pulled my feet out of the water one at a time, to examine their blistered soles. Well, they could bear my weight for one more day. With my tin cup I scooped up some water from the brook and drank as

I waited for my feet to dry. The water had a musty taste. I shaved a few curls of cheese onto a dry biscuit and washed it down with more water. On the far side of the orchard, a man climbed down his ladder, moved it, and climbed back up again. The rhythmic snicking of his pruning shears came to my ears from time to time, depending upon the vagaries of the wind. I could hear an occasional sound from the river, as well: the shout of a pilot, the hollow lowing of a ship's horn.

I fingered my pouch, asking myself whether I could afford to pay ship's passage and rail fare, and still have enough money left over to allow me something to eat. It was ridiculous, for a Separated One to be in such financial straits. But without my mirror I could not prove my status. And without my mask, I had to keep my identity a secret. I could not commandeer what I needed; I could not even send a message to Abad letting him know of my predicament. It is the mystery which gives the Separated Ones our power, the mystery and the myth. If it became known that a Separated One had run into luck as sour as mine, that myth would be damaged. The people might begin to suspect that the thing behind the mask was not so awful as they had come to believe.

No, I had to reach Ashami on my own, though I arrived half-starved and walking on my own two feet.

I pulled on my socks and boots, slung my pack onto my aching shoulders, and limped into the city of Akava.

I was traveling in my own territory now, and had been for some days. But every town and farm, every turn of the road, which should have been familiar and unremarkable, had taken on for me the appearance of unfamiliarity. Though I knew my way, I reacted to each sight as if this were my first visit. I puzzled over things which I had long since accepted. As I came into Akava and passed by the carved monument which shows stylized children swimming gracefully among stylized waves, I paused, taken aback. A forlorn memory offering lay at the foot of this frieze, tucked into a corner by the wind: a shriveled flower, a few strands of hair, a ragged strip of cloth. It looked like a piece of trash, but I stood a long time, unable to go on. A child had drowned, pushed into the water by the same parent who now missed him. A drowned child, a child lost in the snow, eyes crusted shut—

I shook myself, but the image stayed with me: parted white lips, skin like bleached sand, nostrils caked with ice, eyes blocked by snow . . . *Jamil the Watcher, the Keeper of the Keys—why don't you unlock the door?*

I forced myself past the carving and squatted for a time on the curb, trembling. What had happened to me? *What had happened to me?*

I recklessly spent a coin at a shabby beerstall and stood there in the cold wind as the ragged awning cloth flapped in the dirt and the stallkeeper talked in the corner with a dirty harlot. The ale was not too sour and the meat pie better than it could have been. My trembling stopped after a while. I was not eating enough, I thought, looking down at my bony frame. I was just hungry and tired. Seven days' journey to Ash-ami; seven short days. All I had to do was take care of a small matter of business, and I would be on my way.

I picked up my pack and set out in search of the home of Agamin Oman.

In every city, individual streets have a character of their own. In some streets, housekeepers and servants abound, hurrying from place to place with heavy shopping baskets over their arms. Others are deserted, and only carriages or delivery wagons pass that way. I had always been free to walk where I chose, but now, as I started up the road where Agamin Oman lived with his boy, a constable turned me away. I had to go far out of my way, down a dark side street, where a few crumpled figures lay corpselike among the trash. At last, an alley gave me access to a boulevard beyond the vigilance of the constable, and I hurried up the street, too conspicuous in my plain clothes and dirty boots. I had planned to spend some time loitering about the outside of Oman's house, watching for my chance to spirit his boy away. Now I knew I would have to find a dark corner in which to hide if I hoped to remain for long.

Most of the houses on this road had small gardens in front, leafless and winter-gray now, though I remembered their brilliant flowers of summer. Alleys gave access to the mews behind, where carriage houses and horse stables clustered. Here, bored horses hung their heads out the windows, studying me with mild surprise as I made my reconnaissance. Perhaps I could hide in the mews behind Oman's house, I thought, as I hurried up the street, hoping that no curious servant watched me too closely. But as I neared Oman's house, I realized that matters would not be so simple as I had expected. His house was gone.

His neighbors had done what they could to clean up the mess, but some of the debris remained: charred bits of wood, smoke stains on the neighboring walls, the stump of a burned tree. I could still smell the faint, charred scent of fire. Not much time had passed since the house burned down; a month at most. Even the stables behind had burned, and the neighboring buildings had sustained some damage as well, damage being repaired even as I watched, by a crew of craftsmen.

Hearing a step behind me, I turned casually. It was a gardener, her knees mucky from planting bulbs in the mud. She reached out a hand to grasp my elbow, saying firmly, "Move along now, or I'll have to call the constable."

"I wanted to see where the old place used to stand. I was born there, you know. I could scarcely believe my ears when I heard—" I paused, hoping the woman would fill in the gaps in my knowledge.

She glared at me, her face unreadable as a blank piece of paper. "We don't talk about it around here. Move on."

I moved on, giving another constable the slip and making my way back to the part of town where I could be invisible. There I found a dirty pub where I spent another precious coin on ale and tried to get the bartender to talk to me about the fire. When he pushed me summarily out the door, I guessed that what had happened to Agamin Oman was no accident. If so, then no one in his right mind would talk about it freely, especially to a stranger. How could I get the information I needed?

The dull day had darkened to twilight. Though I had traveled far from the killing cold of the high mountains, a bitter wind blew down the narrow streets of the city. Cloaked and hooded people scuttled before that wind like ravens before a storm, ducking into the shelter of one or another narrow doorway. In the apartments above, lamplight flickered, children whimpered, dishes clattered. I smelled the smoke of a hundred stoves where supper was being prepared. Melancholy, I walked slowly down the road. The Separated Ones do not have much of a lifespan, as a rule. Is it the loneliness which is killing us?

A thief waited for me, huddled in a narrow alleyway that seemed perfectly designed for such as he. I strode right up to him, and pointed my pistol into his face. "I am looking for someone. A burgher, Agamin Oman's rival to be mayor."

Flabbergasted, the thief stared into the barrel of the pistol. "Avari Paza?" he stammered. "The one who sold his soul to the Separated Ones?"

"Paza, that's the name. What happened to him?"

"Who wants to know?"

I waggled the pistol in his face. "Are you a friend of his, to die for him?"

"Never even met the man," said the thief hastily. "Last I hear, he was a pub-sot at the Pilot House down by the docks. Those out of towners, they don't care who they drink with." He took a cautious step backward, checking to see if I would let him go.

"Down by the docks?" I repeated, watching the thief's hands. He would go for the blade hidden in his shirt if I pushed him too far. "North side, or south?"

"South, by Rheamer's Point." He backed away another cautious step, and I waved him away. Though I watched him go, still he disappeared like smoke into the darkness of the back alley. I eased down the hammer on my pistol and tucked it gently into my belt where I could reach it easily. Perhaps the onset of winter had caused more Akavans than usual to turn to crime. I kept my eyes open as I made my way to the docks.

The cold wind blew right through the thick weave of my clothing. The weight of my backpack and blankets made my shoulders throb wearily as I jogged down the cobbled street. A carriage clattered by, lamps lit, voices murmuring behind its shuttered windows. The coachman huddled within a thick greatcoat, his cheeks ruddy from the wind. On the other side of town, the bells of Althi Tower rang the seventh hour. A clutter of street kids scuttled past, carrying a stolen loaf of bread and string of sausages.

I slowed my pace when I reached the boardwalk, for I didn't want my footsteps announcing my approach like the pounding of a drum ahead of me. My breath rasped in my throat, rubbed raw by the cold air. Gods, I was tired.

Winter rains had swollen the river. Its black surface lay only a foot's length below the boardwalk. I smelled the faint mineral scent of the water, and suddenly, it brought back to me the damp, dark, warm heart of Asakeiri Home. A woman, bending gracefully to wash out her underclothes on the rocks. The mosses, glowing in the darkness.

A couple of sailors strolled past. "They say it's poison," one of them said, and I knew at once that they were talking about Adline.

"The Emperor's Knackers," the other began, then swallowed his words hastily as his companion nudged him, calling my presence to his notice. They both continued down the boardwalk in silence.

Nestled between two warehouses, the light of the Pilot House spilled across the boardwalk and shattered onto the water below. A steamship had recently come to port here, and its passengers, eager for a change from ship's fare, hurried down the dock and crowded into the entry. There were not half as many as there would have been in summer, and it was mainly traders and businessfolk, with only a few casual travelers among them: a woman with a pinched, strained face, an old man escorting two young girls, who clung to each other hesitantly as he urged them into the public house.

Rather than struggle with the crowd, I contented myself with peering through the window. Its panes of glass were thick, wavy, square, and full of bubbles: old glass, from the days when even cheap imported glass had better quality than what we could manufacture in the north. The view within was distorted, like looking through water. Unsteadily lit by hanging oil lamps, the publican and his helpers danced through the dense crowd, balancing plates of fish and mugs of ale on trays held over their heads. A fire burned briskly on the hearth at one end. The chimney did not draft properly, and an insubstantial haze of smoke muted the colors within. The pilots gathered at one table, laughing drunkenly, incongruous in the somber black uniform of their guild. The traders occupied their tables as if they were disputed territory, sharing their space with allies and glaring like disgruntled dogs at their rivals. Intermixed with them, the casual travelers were the only ones who seemed to be enjoying their meals.

Had my thief been lying to me? No, Paza was there all right, hunched in a corner like a deflated bladder balloon, dressed in ragged finery and laughing too eagerly at a joke that had been told in his general vicinity. His pathos was too much for me. I checked the building to make sure he could not slip out by the back way, then found a dark corner where I could watch the front door, sheltered from the wind. I made myself as comfortable as I could; it looked to be a long night.

The travelers, stuffed with fish and fruit pie, went back to their berths. The traders straggled out after them, one by one, and then the pilots. Most of them could scarcely walk; good thing the river was not particularly treacherous this time of year. The wind flayed my face. My aching feet went numb, and my back began to throb dully. I tried to decide where I would sleep that night, since I had missed my chance to sleep on board a ship as I had planned. To sleep here on the docks would be suicide. The Althi bells had rung the hour three times since I first began to wait there, before finally the publican put Paza out onto the street.

"It's an outrage!" cried Paza. But his voice was thin and weary, and the river and the wind ate it up hungrily. "An outrage," he protested, as the publican shut and barred the door. He pounded his fist upon the wood, moving slowly and wearily, like a child's wind-up toy running down. "You must serve me. Do you know who I am?" Abruptly, he gave up and turned away, still muttering to himself, "Outrage, it's an outrage. Treat me like scum, will they? I'll show them how to treat a burgher. Outrage, I say."

He began to walk briskly down the boardwalk but tripped on his own feet and nearly fell. The wind carried the sound of his uninterrupted litany to me as he stood, swaying, as if the near fall had depleted every last modicum of energy from his body, and he were about to collapse. But he turned and continued, weaving a little, down the walk. "Outrage," he muttered. "A despicable . . . shame upon the city . . . outrage!"

I walked behind him, slinking through the darkness like a street cat shadowing the ash man. Paza paused a couple of times to look behind himself with the exaggerated movements of a drunk trying to appear sober. Perhaps he had been waylaid here before. Certainly, he would be easy prey, despite his caricature of alertness. All I had to do to keep him from seeing me was to stand still in the darkness. He muttered on, a complaining whine as irritating as the sound of water dripping from a leaking ceiling: "The day will come. Just you wait! You'll be sorry you ever. . . ."

He led me along the waterfront, past padlocked warehouses, a narrow alley where a watchman swung his lantern, another public house, where a boy paused in shuttering the windows to listen to the sound of the bells beginning to ring one more time. Paza now seemed to be listing everything which anyone had ever done wrong to him, shouting and sobbing like a madman as he unsteadily strolled the unlit walk.

He paused again, to carefully check behind himself for danger. Once again, he did not see me, standing in my gray clothes against the weathered boards of an old ship's chandlery. He ducked aside and disappeared into a narrow walkway between dilapidated buildings, and I ran forward in time to see the flicker of his heels as he turned down another narrow way, a rabbit in its warren. I lengthened my stride, but by the time I had reached the turn, he was gone.

Drunk as he was, he could not have gone far. I trod as softly as I could down the dank, packed dirt of the alley, avoiding by smell the scattered piles of garbage and sewage. With the looming walls of the warehouses blocking out what little light had come from the stars, darkness filled the alley like fog collecting in a ravine. I walked cautiously, listening for the telltale sound of Paza's complaining voice. Paza, my idiot burgher, stone cold sober you couldn't give me the slip.

The alley opened up onto a broad boulevard, its shopfronts locked up like strongboxes, the windows dark where the citizens slept their virtuous sleep. There was a prickling at my back. I turned sharply, saw nothing in the dark alley, but began retracing my steps. I knew he was there, just as I had known that the highway robbers up in the mountains had been there. I took a few steps, paused, and took a few more steps. My skin itched. I turned, laying my hand upon the wall of the building, stroking down the surface of its rough bricks until I touched the foundation and reached abruptly into empty air. One of the foundation stones had been pulled out, leaving a knee-high gap. I knelt on the damp earth, and heard faintly the mutter of my burgher, settling himself down to sleep with the rats.

I hid my pack in the shadows and crawled in after him.

It stank in that place of urine and vomit and dirty

old clothing, a fetor worse than in any animal's den. My passage opened up into a subfloor region, too low to be a basement, though I found I could walk crouched over. Paza's sighing and muttering led me straight to his bedroom, but I could have found it by the carrion smell of the furs beginning to rot in the damp. Unlike Agamin Oman, his own personal disaster must have come upon him slowly, slowly enough for him to rescue his wardrobe. No doubt he would have survived for a time on income from the sale of his valuables, convinced all the while that it was just a matter of time before his fortunes turned once again. Now the jewels were all gone, and he slept like a slug in the mud.

The faintest of light slipped in through the cracks, revealing the faint outline of the man, huddled in his rotting bed of furs, holding his breath in the hope that I would not find him. I squatted down in the muck. "Avari Paza," I said.

"I don't have anything left," he protested.

"I'm not a thief. Don't you remember my voice, Paza?"

"I can't say that I. . . ." His voice trailed off. There is nothing to remember about the Separated Ones. We do not say our names; our faces, our builds, and even our height are obscured by the mask and robes. All the people have to go by are our voices. They tend to remember them.

To my surprise, Paza sat up in his bed and began to laugh hysterically, "You're dead! You're dead!"

I waited. After a while, his mad laughter trailed into hiccoughs. "You're dead," he said again, whining now.

"Perhaps I am, but it will do you no good."

"Well, what do you want from me that you haven't already taken? You ruined me, did you know that? They took my fortune and kicked me out onto the street. Thieves, all of them!"

I said, "I want you to tell me a story. Tell me what happened to Agamin Oman."

I heard the sound of him licking his lips. "Well, you should know," he finally said cautiously.

"Just tell me. What do you care what happens?"

"What do you mean, what do I care? I have everything . . . it's just a matter of time. . . ." His slurred voice trailed away. He had gotten too accustomed to talking to himself. Soon, the voices of others would seem like only the buzzing of flies to him, and the only voice he could hear would be the sound of the ranting in his own head.

"What happened to Agamin Oman?" I said again, gently. I eased the obsidian knife out of my boot, but I hoped I would not have to use it to convince him to talk. I was tired and wanted only to get out of that place.

"You never came for him. They say he had prepared to die—closed out his accounts, sent his family out of town. But you never came for him. The only thing is, that pretty boy of his—he had disappeared. Days passed, and Oman walked the streets of the city, gray as a ghost, and no one would speak with him. After all, you had marked him, and he was as good as dead. But they say it was the loss of the boy that broke him."

I heard more jealousy than relish in Paza's voice. "What was the boy's name?" I asked absently.

"Duhan. Duhan Fannig."

When the silence stretched out too long, I scraped the edge of my knife with my fingernail, making it ring faintly in the silence.

"Near two months later, the boy returned. I'd been turned out of my house by then—the bastards!"

"It's Oman's story I want to hear."

"Well, I'm telling it, aren't I? Like I said, the boy returned, telling some wild tale about how you'd told him to go with you on a journey—that you'd actually crossed the Rift and climbed into the mountains, but you'd had a bad fall into a ravine. Duhan went for help, he said, but when he returned, you were gone. So the people who'd come to help wanted to hold him prisoner—just in case the Separated Ones came around looking for blood. But the boy gave them the slip and came back home again.''

"How did you hear this story?''

"Why, it was told in the streets—everyone knew. Duhan had told everyone, like a perfect fool, before Oman found him and suggested that maybe it wasn't such a good idea to talk so openly. But your friends came that night—took Oman and Duhan away, burned Oman's house. The two of them had killed a Separated One, they said, and so they had to pay.''

I should have known that Aman Abad would beat me to the revenge. I could have spared myself a lot of trouble, and taken the rail route to Ashami. Agamin Oman and Duhan Fannig both were dead, of course: painfully dead, dead under the skilled hands of one of the torturers, dead long after they had first begun begging, pleading, and dreaming of death. If Oman'd had any sense, he would have killed himself and the boy the very night the boy came home. Perhaps they had planned to escape to the Rift. In any case, I would never know what either of them had said while under the knife, until I reached home.

"They announced it in the town square,'' continued Paza, "That Abad had hired assassins to kill you, and the boy had played his part in it. I never would have thought Abad had it in him, or that boy, either. But they said the assassins had confessed and they had your body—''

Paza had sat up as he talked, and I heard the sound of his hands fiddling with the edge of the fur cloak which covered him. But now his hands fell silent. "And I hoped that you'd died real slowly.''

"Like you're doing now?''

I heard a faint sound, the hiss of a knife being drawn. I reached toward the sound and took the blade from the fool's clammy hand. He screamed as I took it, a shriek of raw, maddened rage. Then, just as abruptly, he fell silent again, the passive silence of a game bird waiting to be slaughtered.

I had no stomach for killing the old fool; he would be dead soon enough anyway. I began backing away, keeping my face toward him in case he had any more crazed impulses.

"You're dead anyway," he whispered.

I pretended not to hear him, but his words slid like a garrotte across my throat.

"You're dead anyway," he said again. "They made a mistake. They killed Oman and Duhan for killing you, only you're not dead. Maybe Duhan was telling the truth. Maybe he did try to save your life, rather than kill you. It doesn't matter, does it?"

His voice followed me across the dank subfloor and out the passageway as I dragged myself out into the mercifully fresh air.

"They'll have to kill you. The Separated Ones are never wrong. They'll have to kill you, so that no one knows they made a mistake."

Out in the narrow alley, I put Paza's knife into my pack. My entire body throbbed with weariness. I swung the pack onto my shoulders, flinching from the pain. I would hail a watchman on the passenger ship, I decided, and convince him to let me aboard. I started off down the alley toward the boulevard which would take me back to the docks.

Chapter 17

At Iska Terminus, the river bells out into a swollen mere, where the docks splay like fingers grasping at the circling boats. Here the pilots earn their keep, for every year the deadly current carries a ship or two over the edge of the great escarpment which marks the edge of the central plateau. There, in a series of spectacular waterfalls, the Iska leaps from the highland plateau to the lowland delta, where its powerful stream shatters into a dozen smaller rivers which each find their own way to the sea. No ship could survive such a wild ride, so all cargo travels overland down the Vine to be loaded onto freight cars at the train station.

As my ship lay at anchor the night before, I had been able to watch the stevedores on shore, working by lantern light to empty the ships and load the mule wagons for the next phase of the journey. All night they sang, cursed, and sweated on the docks, half naked in the chill wind. I occasionally got a whiff of the various scents with which their flesh is perfumed: salt and dirt and mule dung and the tar with which they daub their ponytails.

Until I was ready to sleep, I watched the casual grace with which they approached their enormous and unending task, and the mules brayed in my dreams. At dawn, when with a hoot of its whistle my boat pulled up to the dock, I watched the elephants arrive, walking in a line, each one swaying like a ship at sea. The elephants have always fascinated me: with their sure-footedness, their incredible power, and above all their peaceful acceptance of the domination of their short tempered, demanding handlers. Why did they not turn against their masters, when the goading of the hook could not have been much worse for them than the stinging of a fly?

After spending five days on the deck of a noisy paddleboat, whose smokestacks filled the air with a haze of smoke, ashes and cinders had penetrated deep into the weave of my clothing. My skin felt gritty, and my hair, none too clean to begin with, was permeated with dirt. Weak-kneed, I crossed unsteadily on the gangplank from the ship to the dock. Except for an occasional morsel of food shared with me by my fellow passengers in steerage, I had gone hungry during most of the trip. As I stepped onto the steadier surface of the dock, the smell of spiced meats being broiled over a fire reached my nostrils, all but paralyzing me with desire. But I had to walk past the vendors with their sizzling meats, hot breads, and exotic fruits. I found a nearby store where I renewed my supply of hardtack and cheese, and purchased a couple of limes as well, since being around sailors had reminded me of what scurvy can do.

Here at the edge of the descent to Ashami-Sha, the jungle heat swells up from below. I have heard that the contention between the warm jungle air and the cold air washing down from the frigid mountains causes the violent winter storms for which Iska Terminus is famous. I have never experienced one of these storms, for I had passed this way a hundred times, but never in winter. I asked the storekeeper if it was safe to travel the Vine on foot in this season. The man shrugged. "No safer than any other way. Just watch out for the muleteers. They'll push you right off the road and over the cliff, and never even notice you."

Dry bread and hard cheese is no substitute for spiced meat. I decided to take a side street, so I would not have to pass the vendors again.

Terminus is a solid little town, built mainly of stone, with cobbled roads so that the wagons will be able to pass year round. Half of its shops cater to travelers, and the other half to the local laborers. A street away from the main road, grim, gray-faced row houses stared blankly out at the street as I hurried past, to emerge once again onto the road which parallels the river.

South of the docks, a team of elephants waded into the river to remove trussed bundles of cut lumber from a barge, and then load it onto waiting wagons. As soon as a wagon was full, its driver shouted to the team of ten mules and they started off down the road. On foot, quieting my stomach for a time with a piece of hard tack, I followed one of the lumber wagons out of town. My blisters had mostly healed during my five days of rest, but I felt the lack of food in my very bones. Each step jarred through my entire body; my muscles felt limp as rags. All I had to do, I told myself, was take a half day's journey downhill and then wait for the next train at the station. Of course, the next passenger train might not arrive for days, in which case I would have to continue on foot to Ashami. But I chose not to think about this reality.

By mid-morning, I had reached the Vine. This extraordinary road climbs like a twisted ribbon right up the nearly vertical side of a cliff as steep and massive as the Rift itself. Twenty years before my birth, Jude of Tarsil, a foreign engineer imported by the then suzerain of Ashami-Sha, had spent an entire day climbing up and down the narrow, treacherous path which was then the only link between the rich plateau farmlands and the sophisticated culture of Ashami-Sha. At last she announced that it was possible to build a road. Thus, an empire was born—or perhaps, I should say, engineered.

Having paid my toll, I found myself near the rim of a gigantic plate of land which stretched out behind me. Before me, a wintry sky blended into the misty gray of the ocean. There was no horizon, only a gulf of gray and blue, and a bank of storm clouds with their bottoms pressed flat, like mounds of whipped cream resting on a plate of glass. Another lumber wagon rumbled past, hurried by trotting mules toward what seemed the edge of the earth. A sharp turn, and in a moment they were gone, seeming to plunge heedlessly over the edge of that incredible cliff. It was not until

I myself stood at the very edge of the escarpment that I could see the road, dropping steeply down before me, and the mules, swinging wide to take the wagon around the first sharp bend. I hung my water flask at my waist, took another piece of hard tack out of my pack, and started down at a brisk trot.

I could not maintain that pace for long. The cobblestones bruised my feet, and my lungs ached. Soon I had slowed to a walk, and from that to a trudge. When I heard a wagon coming, I pressed wearily up against the cliffside and waited for it to pass, watching the wagonwheels roll past my toes. At the point of every turn in the road, a few large stones had been gathered, resting places for foot travelers making the weary climb uphill. I sat at every one of these, resting my head between my knees, and remembering ironically how firmly I advised my students to never go too long without eating. I suppose it never occurred to me that sometimes one has no choice.

At every other turn, the road brought me close to the extraordinary Iska cataract which plunged in a frothing torrent from stone to stone, plummeting hundreds of feet to crash in a cold cloud of spray among rocks once again. Its roar grew in my ears and receded again as I twisted my way down the steep road. The jungle below gradually emerged from behind the clouds, impossibly green and lush after the wintry dearth of color to which I had become accustomed. At this distance it looked like a strange and exotic emerald carpet with tiny streams of water running through the pile.

I began to sweat in my heavy woolen shirt and finally took it off and tucked it into my pack. The jungle grew closer. I could see the train tracks now, cutting through the jungle at cross-angles to the waterways. I watched a miniature wagon below make its way down the road to the station—slowly, it seemed from my vantage point.

I rounded the next curve. Now I could see one of the gracefully arched bridges, with its struts crisscrossing each other like the strands in a spider's web. The rooftops of the town of Iska Station appeared between the umbrellas of the overhanging trees. I trudged on, weary and dizzy, sucking on a lime, until the fronds of the trees suddenly rose up and cut off the view.

Here at the bottom of the Vine, a few makeshift shops catered to the needs of travelers too anxious to wait until they reached Iska Station. I must have passed these little shells of wood a hundred times, and always the same people shouted from their doorways: an ale-wife, with a row of rickety stools in the shelter of a palm frond roof, an old man who sat with his children and grandchildren, making and selling straw hats, and an Exchanger, with her collection of used clothing flapping in the breeze. The hatmaker and his kin were gone, of course, since no one would need a straw hat at this time of year, but the alewife did a brisk business, serving pie and beer to three muleteers, whose empty wagons and thirty braying mules stood in a row just off the road.

I walked over to the Exchanger and happily traded my wool shirt and trousers and one of my blankets for a long tunic of lightweight linen, leggings, a loaf of bread and some dried fruit, a little pot of butter, and a pair of sandals that she threw in because my Asakeiri snow boots looked so incongruous with my new outfit. I left the boots on, though, for my foot journey might be far from over.

"How long until the next train comes through?"

The Exchanger, busy inspecting my discarded clothing for vermin, replied, "Sometime today, by my reckon. I havna heard it whistle in yet. Do no' panic if ye do—it'll stay a' the station for a goodly time."

Scarcely able to believe my luck, I hurried down the last stretch of road to Iska Station, where a number of travelers sat on the ground in the shade, surrounded by boxes and bundles, children, and a few caged chickens. On a side track, a couple of elephants and a number of laborers worked steadily, sweating heavily in the sun, with the freight wagons lined up waiting for their turn to be unloaded. The string of freight cars was a long one; I could see why it might be a while before the train left the station.

I was paying my fare, when, at the faint sound of a tuneless whistle, the waiting passengers leapt to their feet and began peering through the dense foliage, hoping for a sight of the smoke of the approaching engine. But I had changed my shoes and devoured half my loaf of bread before the train finally came into sight, the chugging, chattering engine nearly obscured by steam and black smoke. My mouth was full, or I would probably have joined in the cheer.

The sun had set before the train left the station. In the coach car, on a seat that was little more than a wooden bench, with a chicken in a cage under my feet and three howling babies within an arm's length of me, I rode through the jungle of the Ipsenum Delta, able only to see a few blurry stars through the smoky glass of the small window. I dozed intermittently through the night, one shoulder leaning against the vibrating, jerking wall of the car, the other compacted by the weight of three other sleepers, each leaning on the other like trees knocked over in a typhoon. I saw the first light of dawn glimmer across the trees, and then suddenly the huddle of foliage dropped back, and we chugged out into the open arms of the Ashami Peninsula, as the sun rose over the burnished surface of the sea. The train pulled onto a side track to take on more fuel and water, and all the passengers trooped out to take their turn at the outhouse, and purchase cups of steaming tea from an enterprising family that had set up shop there. It was noon before the train chattered and rattled into Ashami, the Emperor's City, the jewel of the south coast.

As the rackety train entered Ashami, passing first the usual ramshackle encampment pressed against the outer walls of the city, I thought of Vicci and the romantic vision of the city with which I had infected her. She had been about the same age as the Rifter girl, hadn't she? The image of that girl outlaw, sucking

her victims for information about the outside world,
like a bat sucking blood, haunted me strangely. And
Duhan, Agamin's boy, hadn't been more than a year
or two older than those two. My journey had been
haunted by lost children.

The surge of activity as the train slowed and approached the station inspired the three babies to start
howling once again. I grabbed my pack by habit. It
was all but empty now, and I could have just as easily
left it behind as I had left my battered boots at Iska
Station. The press of passengers pushed me out the
door. On the crowded platform, a flash of black caught
my attention: A Separated One, accompanied by a
bulky, cloaked figure, with the crowd parting before
and closing behind them. Something about the sight
disturbed me, but the press of people prevented me
from following.

I have lived my entire life in Ashami. Yet, for just
a moment, as I made my way through the station to
the busy street, I saw the city as a newcomer must see
it: a city of ivory and ebony, its streets crowded by
people dressed in a thousand bright colors; a city
where the flowers always bloom and the daily rains
help the sweepers keep the streets clean of filth; a city
of polished wood and scrubbed stone, of silk banners
and the feathery fronds of palm trees, of curved rooflines and slender spires piercing skyward. A beautiful
city, meticulously managed, exotic as the rare flowers
which bloom in every crack of stone, a city like a false
but beautiful lover: sensuous and narcissistic; easy to
entrust, however foolishly, with one's heart.

Like a Plateau bumpkin, I craned my neck to see
the parrots on the balconies, the carved demons on the
roofs, the tame fish as long as my arm, circling gracefully in the sparkling water of a fountain. I heard music: the sweet, delicate tones of a tiny flute, the hollow
twanging of a *dishtar,* the whining call of a rag man
coming down the side street.

Ashami, I once heard a drunken lout say, is a Par-
adise full of leeches. I tucked my pouch securely into
the front of my tunic, where a purse snatcher's razor

could not cut its strings and steal my last few coppers. The thieves in Ashami look like everyone else. They can steal you blind in the middle of the street, and no one, including you, will be the wiser. But the racketeers are worse. With their extortions and schemes they can take everything you own or hope to own, and your life as well.

I did not catch another sight of the black-robed Separated One or his cloaked companion. He would help me get through the Wisdom Gate, the last obstacle which barred my journey home, but it was not for service that I searched for him. Something still nagged at the back of my brain, a teasing voice whose words would not come clear. But I traveled the entire length of Three Bells Boulevard until the Wisdom Gate, thrice my height and tightly shut, barred my way, without seeing a black robe again. There, a scarlet uniformed woman stood guard; without a pass I would not be allowed to enter.

In a side street, I found a scribe's little shop, where I purchased a sheet of paper and the use of a pen. I wrote, "I am in the One-Eyed Dragon" and signed my name. I brought this sealed letter to the Wisdom Gate, and handed it to the guard, saying to her the string of nonsense words which identify an official courier. "Deliver this to any blackrobe," I finished.

Then I went back down the Boulevard and into the One-Eyed Dragon, to wait.

It being too early yet for the saloons to open, sightseers crowded the tea shop, early arrivals for the Concourse Festival, alongside businessfolk sealing deals with tea and cakes. I sat in a corner and ordered a bowl of noodles in broth, which the serving boy sprinkled with a few bits of sliced green onion. When my noodles were finished, I ordered green tea. I paid with the last of my coin. The customers, speaking a dozen different dialects, filled the shop with the din of their voices, as they made deals, cast bets, played Shi-Sho, and argued about who would win the coming race. Adline was no longer a favorite to win, though I could not determine from the overheard conversations whether she was still ill or whether she was dead.

I had drunk half the pot of tea when the door suddenly opened and a startled hush filled the shop. The serving boy scuttled forward, bowing so deeply his nose rubbed his knees, but the Separated One shoved past him without speaking, a blur of black, with black-gloved hands, and a whip coiled upon the hip. As the masked, hooded figure approached me, I studied the mirror lying on the breast of the black robe. The engraved back of the mirror, with its curliques of vine encircling an official seal, told me the identity of the person behind the mask. It was Kathe. I stood up, as if startled.

"Come with me," he said, his voice cold as ice upon stone.

"But—sir—"

"Put this on." He handed me a black prisoner's hood, which I hesitantly pulled over my head with shaking hands. I could hear the silence of the tea shop as if it were a tomb, but I could see nothing. Kathe took my hands and bound them at my back.

I had not thought it would be this hard. The fear of the people crowded in that small room infected me, and I found, when Kathe shoved at my shoulder, that I could scarcely take a step.

"Walk!"

I walked blindly, guided only by his iron grip upon my shoulder. As I scraped past the doorposts of the tea shop, I thought I heard a whisper, but it was only a voice speaking in my memory.

"They will have to kill you," the voice said. "They will have no choice. They will have to kill you."

Chapter 18

So I reached my goal at last: Hooded and bound like a criminal, stumbling blindly as my captor propelled me through the Wisdom Gate. The gates clashed shut. As if we had briskly stepped from the cacaphony of a midday market into the hush of a dawn garden, silence enveloped us. The cries of vendors, ringing of cart-bells, shouts of children, and tootling of street musicians' flutes faded into stillness. Now I could hear my uncertain footsteps rasping faintly upon cobblestones. I heard the muffled sound of a bird singing.

To calm myself, I imagined the serene street, for I had passed this way many times. Behind me, at either side of Wisdom Gate, the inner guards, uniformed in scarlet and framed by lintels of rose marble, stood stiffly at attention, gazing judiciously across the road into each other's eyes. Kathe, identified by his robes and mirror, needed no pass before he would be allowed to enter. But he would have signaled the inner guards as we crossed before them, an additional assurance that he was indeed who his uniform proclaimed him to be.

Now, we walked past ornate porches and plazas, which flanked the two-story, wing-roofed buildings on either side of the road. Here, a bustle of business was normally carried out, though today it sounded empty and silent as a sepulcher after the grave robbers have visited. I heard, faintly, a musical chiming, piercingly sweet. We were passing the Avenue of Bells, where the overhanging branches of the ancient trees are hung with a thousand wind chimes. Few are the people who journey down this musical road, for it ends at the Imperial Gate. There, beside a pristine reflecting pond, stands the Emperor's palace. Fantastically made of white marble, defying gravity with every sweep of its delicate archways, from a distance it resembles nothing so much as a confection of spun sugar.

I felt a breeze wash across the city, startling the chimes into a sweet chorus of sound. Hard upon the breeze came the rain: large, cool drops of water which made my feet slip on the soles of my sandals. Kathe grunted, picking up the pace. I counted another hundred strides, and then the rain abruptly stopped. Had we entered the Abundance Gate archway? I heard a guard's challenge.

"Emperor's business," said Kathe.

"Pass."

A gate clanged shut behind us once again. My heart thundered frantically in my ears. No blackrobe could pass the Wisdom Gate unmasked, but beyond Abundance Gate such discretion needed not be practiced. Would Kathe release me from my disguise, or was I truly his prisoner?

For another twenty steps, the rain fell once again upon my hood, rousing the faint scent of wet wool. Then the rainfall stopped, and I let out a relieved sigh as Kathe gave a sharp tug to the slip knot which bound my hands. With my freed hands I pulled the hood from my face, blinking in the cloud-dimmed daylight.

We stood in an arbor, thickly hung with blooming vines. The rain had roused the sweet, heavy scent of the blossoms, which cast loose their pink and white petals to drift lazily to the graveled walkway. Kathe pushed back his hood and lifted his mask. The humid warmth of the afternoon had brought forth a slick of sweat upon his face. I looked out of the arbor. Though an everyday rainstorm such as this normally goes unnoticed, the roads and walkways were deserted.

"Is it seventh-day?"

"Yes, madam."

That explained the silence of the Wisdom District as well as the silence here. On seventh-day, the officials, stewards, and nobles of the realm seek transcen-

dence and harmony with nature through contemplation
of their gardens. This philosophy is foreign to most
denizens of Callia, who are generally content to worship whichever god has ascendance in their region, in
whatever method tradition decrees. The Ekatan philosophy, however, gives the gods little importance, and
is therefore much better suited to a man like the Emperor.

"When is the Concourse Festival?"

"In seven days."

The sun appeared suddenly in a break between the
clouds. Kathe squinted, fans of wrinkles deepening in
the corners of his eyes, which were deep-set within
the distinctive, craggy features of an Insa-Mar native.
The Insa-Marin are a laughing folk, practitioners of
the high art of the practical joke. However, though I
have known Kathe since childhood, I have never
known him to smile.

He coiled the rope and clipped it at his belt, and
took the hood from my hands to fold it neatly. He lives
alone, and has no servants, for he cannot find any who
are quick, clean, or predictable enough to suit him. In
fact, there are few even among the Separated Ones
who can endure his company for long; for he must
always be lining things up and putting them in order,
as if the future of the Universe depended upon keeping
things perfectly neat. A deadlier assassin does not walk
upon the face of Callia, and he has raised the use of
the blowpipe to a fine art. Death, to him, is a very
orderly business.

His alter-self, Patsin, must be a trial to him, for he
rushes like an untamed cataract through the orderly
architecture of Kathe's life. Patsin is profoundly intelligent, intuitive, highly creative, completely undisci-
plined, and as moody and changeable as the weather
of Iska Terminus. He and Alasil have been lovers for
years, a relationship which has been the cause of some
embarrassment for Kathe and myself.

I do not like Kathe; I doubt that anyone does. But
his extraordinary obsessiveness guarantees that his in-

formation is accurate and his conclusions absolutely dependable.

"Tell me all that has happened," I said. "Have I been given up for dead?"

Kathe said, "When you failed to appear at the proper time, I was a member of the party that went out to seek word of you. The innkeeper in Akava had turned your horse and goods over to the local officials when you failed to return for them. He told us that your last visitor had been a boy, Agamin Oman's leman. Agamin's boy was seen leaving the city on foot, in the company of a stranger . . . by the description, we knew it to be you. There was no indication that you accompanied the boy unwillingly.

"We had been in the area for four or five days when Oman's boy showed up and began talking in the streets about how he had traveled with you at your request, deep into the mountains, where you fell into a ravine. He claimed to have gone for help, but when he returned, you were gone. He said you had told him your name was Ishamil."

That name again. Baffled, I swung my empty pack from one hand, up and down. Across the azure sky, a flock of parrots winged.

"After we had taken them prisoner, Agamin Oman immediately volunteered that he and the boy had conspired to murder you. But the boy denied it, continuing to claim that you had begged him to travel into the mountains with you, and he had never done you any harm. He could not be compelled to tell the truth."

"Well, that's impressive," I murmured. Normally, under the torturer's knife a person will confess to anything. That Duhan had stuck to his tale, when altering it would have give him the relief of death, only demonstrated more clearly what a fool the boy had been. "I assume he finally died." Kathe walked down the road with terrible precision, stepping on every fifth cobblestone with the ball of his foot, never stepping on the gaps between stones. I said, "Ishamil. Have you ever heard that name before?"

Kathe did not speak immediately. On the rooftop of

a petty noble's city house, a spectacular macaw squawked at a battered roof demon and lunged for its splintered nose. Kathe glanced up and hastily looked down again, lest the placement of his feet go awry. "I thought—Patsin might have a clue of what happened to you. Because of—"

I waved a hand, excusing him from mentioning a subject which only embarrassed us both. "And?"

"He has heard the name before. From Alasil."

"Ah," I said, and nodded once, gravely, as though my heart had not stopped, dead and cold as a stone, within my breast.

"He refused to tell me any more than that."

"Well, our alters have their secrets." I casually slung my pack onto my shoulder, trying to appear the very picture of unconcern. But, within my head, I heard a peculiar, anguished screaming.

Kathe glanced at me. The silence had gone on too long. It was time for me to share information in return for what he had told me. But what could I afford to say to him, without putting at risk everything I worked and lived for?

I said, "Tell me about Adline Asakeiri. Her name seems to be on everyone's tongue. Daily, I expected to hear that she was dead, but as far as I know, she still lives."

"She is alive, but paralyzed. We bribed her cook to poison her food with *kilpth*."

"Why was she not killed?"

Kathe shrugged. "She is too popular. With every race she fails to run, her popularity wanes. I doubt she will return home alive."

Aman Abad's front gate is guarded by stone dogs perched atop marble columns, and, even on seventh-day, patrolled by a uniformed guardsman. The iron bars of the gate and fence are tipped with stylized spearpoints. The house itself is huge, built in the old style, with ornate, sway-backed roof lines, and the various wings jumbled one next to the other like spilled building blocks.

His household, as well, is enormous, with a hun-

dred or more servants, retainers, assistants, and armed
guards in residence. But Abad himself has neither wife
nor children nor even a leman, and has never demonstrated any inclination to acquire them. He often says
that the Separated Ones are his children. It would be
more accurate, however, to say that we are his fortune,
and the source of all his power. I have heard that he
began life as the son of an obscure clockmaker. How
he became the feared molder, manipulator, and manager of the Corps of Separated Ones is a tale that will
never be told, I wager.

The guard snapped to attention at the sight of Kathe's
black robe. "I regret that his lordship is not to be
disturbed."

"He will change his mind when you tell him that
Jamil is here."

The guardsman hurried stiffly away to consult with
someone, for only a guard of most junior rank would
draw duty on seventh-day. I offered Kathe my hand,
which he took uncertainly. "Well, it will take some
time for them to let me in, I think."

Kathe's hand was warm, the skin of his palm horned
by fighter's calluses. He gazed into my face distractedly, perplexed by the sloppiness of my situation. Perhaps all those unanswered questions would keep him
awake at night, the poor fool. I said, "I will explain
everything to you as soon as I can. Thank you for your
help."

He blinked, startled by my expression of gratitude.
As he walked away, I myself wondered at my behavior. We Separated Ones do not thank each other. We
do not grasp hands. Our loyalty to each other is like
the loyalty of comrades in arms: little more than a self-
serving ritual which happens to be necessary to keep
us alive.

I whiled my time at Abad's front gate, thinking about
Duhan and Agamin Oman, those Akavan fools, and
very carefully avoiding all thoughts of Alasil, and what
would happen to both of us if she had betrayed me.

The gate guard returned with a fat little woman who
carried a highly ornamented pair of garden shears in

one hand. She examined me through the elegantly
wrought iron of the gate. Abruptly, she cuffed the
guard. "Of course it is Jamil, you fool. Unlock the
gate."

I could not remember the woman's name. A second
or third level underling, today she would be making
Abad's garden look as if he spent one day out of each
seven perfecting it to reflect his own internal vision of
the universe, when in fact he never set foot in it.

"I know my lord will want to see you right away,"
she said, leading me briskly through the ornate front
garden. The meditative silence of seventh-day wrapped
Abad's small palace like a muffling fog. Even the caged
nightingales hanging in the ornamental trees uttered
not a chirp, sitting ruffled and sullen on the perches
of their gilded cages, which the rain had further decorated with droplets of water. Blooming jasmine
shaded the ornately carved ebony lintel of the front
door. The woman took me around to a side entrance,
and up a narrow spiral staircase, paneled in mahogany, and dimly lit by cunning little oil lamps, with
reflectors of highly polished brass. This staircase
opened into the far end of a hall, where a priceless
carpet spread beneath a cloud-painted ceiling, and upholstered benches with arms upswept like the handles
of serving trays stood in front of intricate murals of
idealized scenery.

In my youth I had whiled away many hours in this
hall, awaiting Abad's pleasure. Nowadays, others
waited while he gave me a prompt audience.

My guide asked me to take a seat, but I paced the
hall. She reappeared quickly and beckoned me through
the huge double door which leads to Abad's study.

Aman Abad is nearly seventy years old now, his
flesh shrinking upon his bones, his hair white and
sparse. But I remember him as a man in his prime:
vigorous and sometimes arrogant, with eyes that turned
hard and cold as stones when I dared talk back to him.
He had been my first teacher; the first adult of whom
I have any clear memories. He treated the children of
my group like prize racehorses, giving us every phys-

ical comfort a child could want, sending in his doctors to fret over our ailments, and prescribing for us every hour we spent in study or recreation. We were the first of his great experiment, and he watched over our progress personally. Now I am the last survivor of that first group of children, the only one who remembers.

I bowed, neatly and correctly, and he came out from behind his cluttered desk, holding out his hand to grasp mine. He smiled with only his mouth.

"Jamil! I can scarce believe my eyes! We gave you up for dead three months ago!"

"Yes, my lord." I let him take my hand and draw me over to some easy chairs, where the brocade curtains had been pulled back to reveal the view. Minarets pierced skyward, cloaked in delicate foliage, already flying the scarlet and silver flags of the Concourse festival. Dark rooftops rose above manicured gardens. Here and there, light glimmered from the surface of an artificial pond.

I said, "Pardon me for coming here unwashed."

He waved a hand. "There is always time for the bathhouse later. I asked Mina to bring us some food—she said you look half starved. Tell me what happened to you."

I gave him a lengthy and reasonably accurate account of my misadventures. It was a fool's tale, and I hated having to tell it to anyone, but most especially to Abad. In the midst of my account, Mina reappeared, bearing delicate morsels of meat and pastry, cakes, tea, and wine. In the absence of servants, Abad served me.

He interrupted me from time to time with questions that I could not answer. I could not tell him what Agamin Oman had hoped to accomplish by having me kidnapped, or exactly by what means the sorceress Clar had gained such control of me, and over such a distance. I could not tell him why my captors had sacrificed me so lightly, after having gone through such trouble to kidnap and capture me, nor could I tell him why the Asakeiri had allowed me to live and even helped me to escape the mountains. I could not tell him what had happened that night Ata'al had me drugged.

"Well, this is a very queer adventure you have had," Abad finally said.

I have never killed in anger, but I could have done so in reaction to that dubious, patronizing comment. Instead, I took another cake from the tray and walked over to the gracefully curtained window. I stared out, at the walls, the swooping rooflines, and the drooping willow trees, and felt a restlessness deep in my bones. Like an old horse, I had been eager for the comfort of the stable. But now the walls closed in around me, and I remembered how, for just a little while, I had walked the roads of the land without a mask and looked into a face now and then which was innocent of fear.

"I have never been wrong," I said to him at last. "I am the one you always turn to, when you need a conclusion drawn on scanty evidence. You come to me because you know I am never wrong. Why do you doubt me now, Aman Abad?"

"Because it isn't like you, to turn your back on so many unanswered questions."

I did not tell him that I had found it nearly impossible to accomplish anything of value without the invisible authority of the Emperor's hand backing me up. I did not mention how overwhelmed I had been by simple problems of finance. My image was already tarnished enough. "I was concerned for the safety of the Emperor," I said.

"The safety of the Emperor?"

"Adline Asakeiri was not merely using the race to embarrass him, but to get physically close enough so she can assassinate him."

I looked again out the window. A panting horse now stood at the gate. I heard a faint commotion downstairs and glanced at Abad to see if he had heard it. But he still considered my last words, turning them over like a mouthful of sour wine that he could not swallow and dared not spit out.

"Even the Asakeiri would not be such fools," he said at last.

"You don't know them as I do."

He gave a little bow in my direction. Certainly, I had lived longer with the Asakeiri than had any other outsider, and my knowledge would prove valuable. But I detected a trace of irony in Abad's attitude, as if he were secretly laughing at me.

"Well, you need not have concerned yourself as she has been poisoned by *kilpth*. . . ." At a knock on the door, Abad turned, frowning. "Open!" Mina appeared and bowed, deeply and awkwardly. "I beg your pardon, my lord, but an incident has occurred at Wisdom Gate and the guard captain requests your presence."

Even on seventh-day, the Emperor's Secretary could scarcely be expected to walk the short distance to Wisdom Gate on his own two feet. With the stableboys visiting friends or family outside the gate on this seventh-day, I hitched the Secretary's horses and drove the carriage myself. If I had not been there, I suppose Mina would have done it.

At Wisdom Gate, only one of the two scarlet-dressed guards kept his rigid vigil. Several others, out of uniform but well armed, stood in a circle around a huddled, crumpled figure. As I drew the horses up, I heard a strange, eerie sound: a keening cry that rose as if from the depth of the earth, growing to an earsplitting screech and then fading back into silence. The guard captain, elegantly dressed in a blue silk shirt and skintight trousers, stepped forward to greet us as I leapt down to open the carriage door for the Secretary.

The captain gave me the blank look that many people reserve for their servants, and then blinked as he recognized my face. I tapped my fingers ironically to my forehead, parodying a servant's salute.

"Good. This will interest you greatly," the captain said. A professional, he evinced no surprise or curiosity at my presence. "My lord, my apologies for in-

terrupting your seventh-day—'' began the captain, as
Abad dismounted from the carriage.

The ear-splitting screech began again, an eerie, anguished keening. The captain raised his voice to be
heard over the sound. "This pair was given entry, but
they failed to offer the proper signals to the inner
guard, and then they tried to flee when he ordered
them to halt for questioning. The guard killed one of
them, the one who wore the black robe. I am sure it
must be an imposter, but just to be certain, I thought
it would be better to send for you."

The circle of armed men parted before the three of
us, revealing a black-robed figure, bloodily skewered
with a spear. Over the robed body crouched a bulky
figure, cloaked in brown. She shook the fallen person's shoulder impatiently as if to awaken him, all the
while keening like a wild animal. I had glimpsed her
before, at the train station, and no wonder the sight of
that cloaked figure had plucked so insistently at my
memory. It was Clar, the crude sorceress who had first
abused me, and then abandoned me to die in the snowstorm.

Abad strode forward, demanding that the guards pull
the woman away and turn the other person over so the
fact might be seen, but I hung back. Four men it took
to drag Clar aside, as she struggled, screamed, and
spat like a wild thing. Blood had stained her knees
and her hands and the edges of her cloak. Abruptly,
she began to weep hysterically.

The men turned the black-robed figure onto his side,
and stripped away the hood and mask. The revealed
face gazed peacefully at me. His lips were parted as
if he wanted to speak, but I could see that he was
dead. Hastily and eagerly his spirit had departed, like
a horse leaping the corral gate and heading for the
hills. Poor, weak, kindly man; what had he been
thinking of, to impersonate a Separated One? Only
Clar could have put him up to such an act of idiocy.

Abad lifted and studied the silver mirror hanging
around Moy's neck. He would recognize it to be mine.
I pushed through the guards to Clar. As soon as I

blocked her view of Moy, she began to struggle in the grip of her captors, screaming once again.

I slapped her, harder than I meant to, shocking her and myself with the vehemence of my anger. Her startled glare changed to a gape of disbelief as she recognized me.

I said mildly, as if we were neighbors having a friendly conversation, "What did you hope to accomplish, Clar? What did you come here for?"

She hunched her head down against her shoulders.

"You came here to steal?"

"Who would begrudge an old woman her retirement, eh?" She glared at me defiantly, then her face collapsed. She looked gray, and old, and numbed by despair. I saw no trace of the sinister sorceress, just a cruel and greedy old woman, destroyed by her own foolishness. She said, with genuine desperation, "Moy was good to you. You'll help him, won't you?"

"Moy is dead."

"He's just hurt! He'll recover—he's recovered from worse."

"How much did Agamin Oman pay you?" I asked.

"What?"

"Agamin Oman! The one who hired you to kidnap me! What did he pay you?"

She drew herself up in the grasp of the guards, affronted. "Kidnap! You saying I'm some kind of criminal? I never did anything like that for money! And I never heard of this Agamin."

I gazed at her for a long, speechless moment. Then I turned away, to find that Abad had drawn up behind me.

"Is this your powerful sorceress?" he asked.

I walked away from him without answering. Under the torturer's knife Clar would tell him everything he wanted to know: how she and Moy had stumbled across me by accident and stolen all my goods. How they had planned to sell me to the mines but abandoned me when I became too ill to walk. How she thought she dreamed up a way to profit from the stolen

robe and mirror, and talked Moy into impersonating
a Separated One.

She would tell Abad that I had been a fool, willing
to believe any tale I could dream up for myself, rather
than believe the truth: That my own self, Alasil, had
betrayed me.

I leaned against Abad's carriage as the guards carried away Moy's body, hustled Clar into lockup, and
began cleaning up the mess of blood which stained the
roadway's white stones. One of them presented me
with my mirror, which she had washed clean of blood
and carefully wrapped in a white cloth. I accepted it
in silence. At last Abad climbed into his carriage, and
I drove him home.

After a brief winter twilight, darkness fell, sudden
as a blanket dropping to smother a lamp. I followed
the dim light of a bobbing candle, paying no heed to
the fussing of my old steward, who had been fetched
by a runner to accompany me to my old rooms. Now
within the familiar walls of the private compound of
the Separated District, walking down the familiar narrow walkways, an illusory sense of safety mocked me.

My life here had always been as predictable as the
seasons. My meals were prepared and served to me in
the Common Hall. The mornings belonged to me as I
taught classes, wrote reports, corrected maps, and attended such meetings and events as Abad might request of me. The afternoons were Alasil's. She honed
her fighting skills in the practice ring, or perfected her
extensive knowledge of poisons. The evenings I spent
in precious solitude, unless I had agreed to let Alasil
visit one or another of her lovers. My life here had
been so predictable that I felt as if, simply by walking
through the Separated Gate, it had become predictable
once again.

Shaking my head at my own illogic, I followed my
steward into my own house, where, since my youth, I
had shared servants and a receiving hall with three
others. All three of my original housemates had died,
disappeared, or gone mad. Others replaced them, and

still others replaced those. It made little difference since I rarely saw them.

The steward mounted the stairs, talking more nervously now, since I had not said a word to her throughout our little journey. The lamps had been lit, illuminating the plain, clean furniture, the simple architecture, the primitive weavings and baskets which I and my fellows had collected on our early journeys. The land had still been full of wild places then: untamed peoples, unexplored territories. I and my kind had discovered, categorized, subverted, and conquered the land, delivering it to the young Emperor like sweetmeats on a platter.

"Here you are," said the steward, as if I were a visitor who did not know my own way to my rooms. She opened the door. "Now, like I was saying, we haven't been cleaning in here, so it'll be a bit of a mess. If it wasn't seventh-day. . . ."

"I have been sleeping on the bare ground for nearly a month. I can live with a little dust."

She lit a couple of lamps and left me.

I would take some clothes out of the wardrobe, I thought, and go to the bathhouse, and then eat a late supper in the common hall. I lifted a lamp and went wandering through the sitting room, past the comfortable, worn-out furniture; the dusty desk. The bookshelves were empty; my servants had returned all the books to the library where they belonged. Spider webs garlanded the corners of a doorway. The rooms smelled of stale air, dust, and mildew. I unshuttered and opened the windows, to let the fresh, cool air wash into the room.

I knew what I would find in my own room: a narrow monk's bed, a wardrobe full of plain, somber clothing, a washstand with an ivory comb in one drawer. The window looked out onto the green below, where once a day solemn children took their exercise, marching in a neat line behind a grim adult.

But what lay behind this other door? Knowing that I never violated Alasil's privacy, had she kept any secrets here? I opened the door and entered, holding high the lamp.

I don't know what I had expected: A fanciful room, perhaps, childishly ornate, filled with the clutter that I denied Alasil everywhere else. And no, there was none of my own self-denial here: she had a large bed, large enough for two, or even three. A few dusty liquor bottles sat atop one cabinet. But no cosmetics mounded her dressing table; her furniture was beautiful but not garish, and several delicate watercolor sketches hung on the wall. Her fighting leathers hung in one wardrobe, and in the other hung clothing of a quality that I myself might wear: quietly dyed fine linens and woolens, with a couple of formal outfits in silk, sandals and good walking shoes. Most surprising, she had a shelf of books, as worn and dog-eared as those in any used bookseller's stall. I opened one, and found it to be a book of melancholy poetry by one of the great Ashami-Sha masters of a hundred years ago.

It was the bedroom of a stranger.

The lamp flame began to dim. I walked over to her dressing table and absentmindedly opened a drawer. A pair of scissors. She had always been the one who kept our hair trimmed.

The pain surprised me: alien and strange, a ghost ship slipping through the fog of a still night. I examined the pain remotely, but did not know what to call it. Betrayal? Loneliness? Despair? I shut the drawer firmly upon the scissors, but stared at its filligreed handle for some moments, as if I expected the drawer to open again on its own.

I raised my head at last and looked into the drawn face of an Asakeiri woman. She seemed tired and bewildered, sitting alone in the dim light of the lamp. Her life had drained her; her face seemed brittle and empty as a dried leaf blowing on a winter wind. She stared at me bleakly. Her short black hair frayed away into the twilight. Had someone cut away her life and fed it to the dragon? And what was an Asakeiri woman doing here within the walls of the Separated District?

I reached out to touch her, and smeared my fingers across the dusty, cold surface of a mirror.

The servants found me in the morning, unconscious, with an empty brandy bottle on the floor.

Chapter 19

The servants threw open the windows; evicted the dust motes and spider silk; changed the linens; washed, polished, mended, and even painted every surface; piled the furniture; rolled the carpets and carried them briskly outdoors to be beaten under the sun; and scrubbed the floors with brushes and stones. For two days they occupied my territory. I heard them singing and laughing as I came up the stairs, but they fell silent when they heard my hand turning the doorknob.

I envied them.

"Jamil? I hear you have been ill," Alris said politely to me, one morning in the Common Hall. Solitary at my own table, booted feet sinking in layers of carpet, I sipped weak tea and nibbled at a piece of soft, white bread. I examined her distantly from behind my tea pot. She is a strange hybrid of a person: rich brown skin, short yellow hair as straight as straw, eyes the color of an old blue dress that has been washed and left to dry in the sun too many times. Her memory is like an old miser's money chest: every event of her life, every piece of information she ever collected, every story she ever heard, no matter how trivial, is packed away like treasure, as clean and complete as if it had happened yesterday.

"They tell me I'll live." No one ever died of crapulence, though more than a few must have wished for death. Two days had passed, and I still doubted my ability to stomach anything more substantial than the bread and tea over which I lingered this bright morning, having nothing better to do. I waved a hand, inviting her to sit. I had been avoiding company but could scarcely continue my isolation forever.

"What about Alasil? As soon as I heard you were back, I expected to see her at the ring."

"She's been ill, too."

"Her health is usually so good—"

I asked suddenly, "What race are you?"

"Oh, probably a mix of northern desert folk and some outland yellow-haired breed." She laid her long, thick, knife-scarred fingers across the tabletop. If my question surprised her, she kept that surprise well hidden behind her mask. She is dry and empty as a fallen leaf, I thought, looking at her pale eyes. She told a hovering servant to bring fruit and bread and a pot of green tea.

In the dining room, a dozen Separated Ones lingered over late breakfasts. In one corner, two men and a woman engaged in lively debate. I could hear scraps of their argument, which seemed to be philosophical in nature. Other diners sat in relative stillness, talking quietly to companions, reading the daily broadsheet which we publish for ourselves, or simply sitting alone, like myself, staring blankly into space. Overall, a stranger visiting the Common Hall would rightly conclude that the Separated Ones tend to be a grim and solitary people.

"You don't remember your native people?" I said to Alris.

"No. Should I?" Her mask face gazed at me, her eyes bleak and blank with unspoken secrets.

"Don't you remember everything?"

"You bet I do. Ask me a question—any question."

"What is your mother's name?"

"Gods, Jamil, was it something you ate?" Thoroughly irritated with me now, she leaned threateningly across the table. I recognized the method; after all we had learned the art of intimidation from the same masters.

I put another little piece of bread, slightly more substantial than air, into my mouth. "Aren't you even curious?"

"No."

Her lie did not surprise me. We lie to our enemies and to our friends; we lie to our betters; to each other; and to our alter-selves. As I had painfully learned, we even can lie, profusely and glibly, to ourselves. Alris ate hastily and bid me a cool farewell. I remained at my solitary table for a long time after she left, watching the Separated Ones come and go. Tall and short, thin and heavy, dark and pale, male and female, each of them wore the same mask. Each of them lived like a prisoner within their own skin.

In a rancid, ugly mood, I went to the hairdresser. A mass of hair fell to his polished floor that morning, stiff, wiry, curly stuff as black as a dragon's mouth. When the man had finished his work, he offered me a mirror, but I would not look at my face. I did not want to see that aging Asakeiri woman again.

"Madam," he called after me, as I turned to go. He held out his hand. Two beads rested in his palm; one blue, one black. "I hear some people wear them in their hair as a sign of their sympathy for Adline, the Concourse Runner," he said, smirking to conceal his curiosity.

I took the beads and put them in the pouch I wore at my belt. "Have my steward send fresh clothing to the bathhouse."

"Madam." He gave a crisp little bow as I left his shop. Thirty years he has been cutting and dressing the hair of Separated Ones. To this day, I do not know his name.

I had accumulated an extraordinary amount of road grime since my last bath, at River's End. Standing in a shallow basin, I scrubbed myself with scented soap and a bristle brush until my skin tingled. The muscular bath attendant doused me with a bucket of warm water, which turned more black than gray by the time it trickled down the drain. I sat on a damp stool as she shampooed my cropped hair, groaning with pleasure as a little of the pain from my two-day headache seeped away. More dousings, and at last the water ran clear.

The baths, with their endless supply of hot water

continually replaced by steam-operated pumps, are the technical marvel of Ashami-Sha. This was not the thick, sulfurous water of a hot spring, but clean, fresh water, heated over coals. No glowing mosses grew here in the half-darkness. Skylights let in the sun which glimmered on turquoise tiles grouted with gold.

As I lay soaking, alone in a hot pool at a time of day when most of my kind have business, studies, or other work to attend to, one of my servants arrived with an armload of clothing. She laid it carefully on a dry shelf, then sat on a low stool to await my pleasure.

When I spoke, echoes distorted my voice, giving it a hollow, formless sound in which the words could scarcely be distinguished. "What is your name?"

The servant, startled out of her daydream, gaped for a moment. "Begging your pardon—was it to me you spoke, madam?"

"You're the only one here."

"It's Mari. Three years I have served you."

"Yes, I know your face. Tell me the day's news. What do you know of the world?"

"Well . . . they say old man Amin-Car is not expected to live out the winter. The Montre family arrived last night for the Concourse. Naia Montre is pregnant. More of the Concourse contestants are expected to arrive today. Adline Asakeiri is still ill, I hear, but will be taking up residence in the Champion's House anyway. They were out cleaning the rugs this morning. . . ."

She prattled nervously on, telling me what fashions were in style this season, and what new fruits and vegetables could be had in the market, and describing for me the antics of a new acrobatic troupe. I pondered an old story in which an ant struggles to climb an enormous obstacle, the same piece of grass which an elephant then plucks casually out of the ground and eats. So it was with myself and the servant girl: we trod exactly the same piece of ground and slept under the same roof, but we might as well have lived in different countries.

She rushed forward with a towel as I dragged myself

out of the water. "If you'll pardon me, madam, your color isn't so good—" She guided me over to the stool where she had been sitting and hurried away, returning quickly with the bath attendant, who carried a glass of fruit wine and some biscuits on a tray. I rested my cheek against the cool tile wall until the dizziness passed. The two women hovered over me anxiously, urging me to take another sip of the sweet wine and try one of the biscuits. If something happened to me in their presence, they would be held responsible for it.

"Is the water too hot?" the bath attendant asked worriedly.

"She hasn't eaten in two days," Mari murmured, thinking I couldn't hear. "And look at how thin she is! She's been on a hard journey, and it's worn her down to the bone. What she wants is a little rest and a square meal or two."

Mari was the one who had found me, unconscious in my own vomit on the floor. It was circumspect of her not to mention the source of my current malaise, and I smiled at her faintly as I got carefully to my feet. "We'll get you dressed," she said, "and get you home, and we'll have Dali cook you some good plain food, not like that fancy stuff they give you at the Hole. Good brown bread he makes, and fish stew."

Usually, the servants call the Common Hall "the Hole" only among themselves. It felt very strange, to be treated by my own servant as if I were a human being.

By evening, the frenzied war against decay had been won in my quarters for another season. Solitary again in my echoing sitting room, I sat at the desk, writing by lamplight, as the voices of winter cicadas buzzed in the trimmed bushes below. Dali's good plain food, delivered by runner from the servants' kitchen, had been good indeed; though after my long and slow starvation I found I simply could not eat much of it. Mari had given me a folded note out of her pocket before she left, and now it lay near me on the desk top. Alasil's name was written on the outside, and I had not opened it, but I recognized the soft rag paper preferred by Patsin. It appeared that Kathe had let his alter-self out of his cage for the evening, and he wanted to see his old friend Alasil once again.

I wrote steadily, composing a dry, emotionless account of my activities since spring. Every year, in this final report, I laid out the pattern of my activities, as intricate and strategic as a Shi-Sho game, with each move developing naturally from the long history of moves which went before and leading naturally toward all that would follow. This written account would be archived in the library, beside seventeen others which, taken together, constitute my autobiography. The sum effect which I have had upon the world is written upon those pages: The people I have killed, the governments I have toppled, the small lives that I have altered and destroyed, the economies that I have created, the markets that I have exploited, the sources of wealth that I have uncovered, the native tribes that I have disemboweled.

Weary, I sat back from my labor, rubbing my eyes with ink-stained fingers. Tonight the writing was not going well. I missed an element vital to successful completion of the report: the element of blind self-satisfaction. I dropped my pen onto the desktop and paced restlessly across the sitting room and back again. My head felt light and unfamiliar; absently I raised a hand to touch my cropped hair. My clothes hung loose on my bony frame, and my feet still ached, remembering the long, lonely road I had traveled. And for what? I asked myself. And where now? And why?

Still wrapped in its white cloth, my silver mirror lay upon a tabletop. I unwrapped it, noticing absently that some dried blood still remained, caught in the etched design that formed my official seal. Without my mirror, I had become no one: a friendless stranger, a penniless wanderer. Now, though the mirror had been recovered, the stranger remained. I still called myself Jamil, but I felt as if the very shape of my personality had been drastically altered.

I sat in the corner of a divan, old-fashioned now and still dusty despite the servants' administrations. For a long time I stared at the wall. My thoughts were deep, secret things. I felt them moving deep within my belly, as stately and powerful as whales swimming far beneath the surface of the sea. At last, I lifted the mirror and looked into its polished surface. There I saw myself, ghostlike in the twilight, an Asakeiri woman in her prime, her head shorn, her life lost. "Alasil," I said quietly.

Dressed and hooded in black, she emerged from the twilight: my partner, my enemy, my only friend, my self. I looked into her face without speaking, and she gazed as somberly into mine. She, too, seemed thinner, older, wary and tired, as if my strange and pointless journey had infected her dreams during her long and uninterrupted sleep. A lamp flame that burned only in her world illuminated her face. My silence did not seem to surprise her; my long regard did not make her restless. Had she no curiosity, or was this merely a knife fighter's alert stillness as she goes into battle?

Still, the silence; a strange notion formed in my thoughts as I studied her countenance. She owed me nothing. I gave her nothing. By what right did I expect her loyalty?

"Alasil," I said again, but I could not think of anything else to say.

"Well, you have come home."

I rubbed a damp palm across the soft linen of my leggings.

"A hard journey?" she prompted. I heard the mockery in her voice, and the rage which lay behind it, and beyond that rage I heard something else.

"Alasil, do you love me?"

She turned her face away, then turned it back again. "Why should anyone love you, Jamil? You command the world, but you walk through it like a stranger. You mold it like clay, but you are never changed by it. You expect obedience, but you trust no one. You have never lost anything. You have nothing to lose."

"Is that all I am—an empty mask?"

"Yes."

"Yet you love me."

"Yes."

I wanted to touch her then. But her face was only a vision, captured in cold, polished silver. She looked strange, and sad, and oddly intent.

"Listen, if you would," I said, as if she had a choice. "Things have not gone well for me—for us. I've lost my status. Probably, Abad thinks I'm losing my mind. Maybe he's right."

"What has happened?"

"I—was wrong."

Her laughter startled me. Rich and throaty, lazy and luxurious, lush with gentle mockery, she laughed at me so kindly that I had to smile. "My whole reputation—" I tried to say, "And I wasn't just wrong; I was drastically, radically—" Still, she laughed, until I began to laugh too, then stopped suddenly, with tears on my hands.

"And you betrayed me," I said.

"Oh, it is so simple to you! Am I not also betraying you if I betray myself?" She paused, taken aback, I think, by sudden awareness of my tears. No more so than I. "Jamil," she said gently, "you are such a fool."

I said nothing. This alien pain, it incapacitated me.

"You still don't know. After all these months, you still don't know."

"What? What don't I know?" I shook the mirror, as if I could hurt her. But I could only hurt her by hurting myself.

"By telling you the truth, I will only take it away from you. But I will give you a clue, a riddle. Does a broken bowl hold water?"

"That's no riddle," I said angrily.

"That's right. The answer is simple and obvious. You can't see it only because you can't bring yourself to look."

The cicadas buzzed feverishly outside the window. A cool wind washed suddenly into the room, and I got up to close the sash. The winter days in Ashami could be sweltering, but at night one could sometimes remember that elsewhere in the country snow might be falling.

I picked up the mirror from the cushion. Alasil still waited there. "How is it that you know me so much better than I know you?"

"I have the advantage," she said. "I have been standing at the doorway watching you for some time now. I saw much to admire and much to regret."

"Standing at the doorway? What do you mean?"

She took a deep breath, as if steeling herself to a difficult task. "Do you remember when you were ill, after Ata'al found you in the snow and took you to the village?"

I found, for a moment, that I could not speak. Perhaps I still hoped to learn that Alasil had not betrayed me. But if she had indeed been unconscious during the several months since I lost the mirror, then how did she know that I had been ill? How did she know that I had been taken to Asakeiri Home? Speaking hoarsely, because that ghostly, haunting pain had taken hold of me by the throat, I said, "I have no memories of that time."

"But you do," she said, so gently that the unheard of contradiction slipped past me, all but unnoticed. "There are images that haunt you still, which are memories from that time. The snow falling in the darkness, do you remember that? And a door, hanging ajar, banging in the wind. And a child, lost in the snow."

"She played with stones." The memory lay before me, startling in its clarity. A child squatted in a corridor, playing with stones that she took out of a pouch, an Asakeiri child, with beads in her hair. But what corridor was this, and how had I come here? Wraithlike, it seemed, I wandered a maze of such barren corridors, following narrow walkways between walls of coarse gray stone. The corridors took me nowhere, doubling back upon themselves, twisting and turning, with never a door that led anywhere except to another corridor. It might have been an age that I wandered there like a forgotten ghost, lost in a labyrinth that seemed horrible to me even in memory. Horrible not because of the monsters it contained, but because of its wintry, echoing emptiness.

At one place in this labyrinth, the snow always fell. As I approached it, in one of the hundreds of times I wandered past that place, I saw that the child I encountered from time to time had been buried beneath the falling snow.

I could still make her out, a humped shape beneath the pristine white blanket. I glanced upward into the darkness, wondering where the snow might be coming from. I could see neither sky nor ceiling, only the steep stone walls disappearing into gloom.

I walked down the corridor toward the falling snow. I heard it crunch underfoot, though when I looked back, I saw no footprints. The child had seemed close by, yet I walked a long way before I could bend over and touch the huddle of snow that covered her. I brushed at the snow with an ephemeral hand, succeeding in dislodging a few flakes. My efforts were all but ineffectual, yet, slowly, I made headway, removing the snow slightly faster than it was replaced as it fell from the gloom overhead.

Flake by flake I revealed the child's face: Parted white lips, skin like bleached sand, nostrils caked with ice, eyes blocked by snow. Carefully, to avoid packing the snow any further, I scratched at it with my fingers, slowly uncovering the black eyebrows, black eyelashes. Then suddenly the girl's eyes opened, and she looked at me.

"I wanted to sleep," she said.

"You're too young to die." A foolish comment, indeed.

"*Die?* How could I die? I would have to be alive first, wouldn't I?"

"You don't talk like a child," I said, taken aback.

"I am a very old child." Hooded in snow, she examined me. She had that haunted look in the eyes that children sometimes get, the look from having seen things a child should never see. "Do you know who I am?" she asked curiously.

"Of course not."

"I know who you are. Jamil, the Watcher."

"Who are you?"

"You don't know me." She said these words sadly.

"You have some stones in a bag."

"Dragonstones. I took them with me from home. But that was a long time ago."

"Why are you here?"

"Why?" The child suddenly shook herself free from the snow, like a dog shaking water out of its fur. I flinched back, for she had more substance than I and could easily have hurt me. But she did not. Suddenly, her tears fell again, and she turned her face away. "You don't even know who I am!"

Her tears and words struck at me like blows. In terror, I backed away from her. "What do you mean?"

"Jamil, the Watcher, the keeper of the keys!" She cried these words like an indictment. I continued to back away from her, rubbing my ghostly hands anxiously on my ghostly trousers.

"Why don't you unlock the door?" she said. "Why don't you unlock the door and let me out?"

"I don't know what you mean." But when I turned my head, I saw the door in the wall, where no door had been before. And I held in my hand a key, though only a moment before my hand had been empty. I dropped the key as though it were a burning coal, and I fled, like a wild animal does from the things it cannot understand. I fled down that passageway, until the snow no longer crackled under my feet. Then I stopped, and turned, though terror thundered like a drum in my small, ghostly heart.

The little girl had picked up the key. She gazed down at it, then she turned and gazed at me. Though a great stretch of hallway separated us now, her voice rang in my ears. "This door will never be locked again."

"It has to be locked!"

"You gave me the key. I can do anything I want to now." She approached the door, and turned the key

in the lock. I screamed as the door hinges creaked, for I
knew that something horrible lay on the other side. But
the open door revealed only a small, square room.
Heavy beams supported a low ceiling of ancient wood.
Lamps burned, clustered on a simple low table. A
hunched shape huddled on a stool near the lamps,
sewing something by the uncertain light. On the straw
bed lay an emaciated, oddly familiar figure, her chest
rattling with every breath she took.

The child paused in the doorway and looked back
at me. "I could lock you in," she said thoughtfully.

Then she stepped into the small room. But she did
not close the door behind her. I watched from the dark
passageway. Watched as the old woman sewing turned
her head, as the little girl in the bed sat up slowly,
rubbing her eyes as if she had just awakened from
sleep. "Mama!" She leapt out of the bed, and into
the old woman's arms.

I had been silent for a long time. Within the mirror,
Alasil gazed up at me. She had deep brown eyes, almost black, with sparks of light in their centers, reflecting from the unseen lamp. "Well, you are right,"
I said briskly, "I do remember something from that
time. A kind of dream. . . ." My voice betrayed me
then, wavering uncertainly into silence.

"You know perfectly well that it was no dream."

"I looked through the door, and saw myself lying
ill upon the bed. I saw Ata'al, sitting beside me, sewing. Is that what you are telling me, that you also stood
at the doorway and watched . . . as if you were dreaming my life?"

"Sometimes it was like a dream. Sometimes I
walked inside your body like a ghost. I felt your words
in my throat. I tasted the food in your mouth. Sometimes it was almost like being alive."

No wonder she had gotten so thin, I thought. Slim
fare it had been, more often than not. And that food
at River's End, how she must have enjoyed every sensuous bite of it. Was it she who tempted me into the

cup of chocolate? This is madness, I thought. Madness—and yet I did not fear it.

"I fit myself into you," she said, "like putting on a pair of old clothes. And I talked to you all the time, though you did not seem to hear me. But it was better, much better, than waiting for you to awaken me from sleep."

Madness, I thought. Madness. Wholeness. Madness. Does a broken bowl hold water?

I said, "What is it like, to make love?"

I felt her leaning forward, as if somehow she could come through the mirror and sit down beside me on the divan. "Do you really want to know? I cannot tell you, but I can show you."

"You can what?"

"You needn't sound so shocked. You're the one who brought it up."

"It was just a hypothetical question!"

"Gods, Jamil, all day you've been in a state because you finally recognized your talent for deceiving yourself. Wouldn't this be a good time to stop the deception?"

Looking at her in the mirror, I spotted a peculiar thing. Her hair, too, had been cropped short this day, all except for a single lock of hair. And there hung the two Asakeiri life beads, the blue and the black. Alasil had not been able to prevent me from cutting them out of my hair, but somehow she had kept me from cutting them out of hers.

If she had told me they were so important to her . . . I thought. But she probably had told me, and I simply had been unable to hear. *Maybe this is another door to which I have the key.*

In a day so infected by strangeness, this peculiar idea scarcely gave me pause. "I would like to know what it's like," I said. "Is there some way, do you think?"

"I've been walking inside your skin for so long. If only you could feel me, and hear me—"

"—It would be as if I were you—"

"—And I were you."

I turned the mirror, so it lay facedown upon the divan. My hands were trembling. I took a deep breath. "Alasil," I said, "I want to be you."

And I felt her come pouring into me, like wine into an empty glass.

Patsin waited in the dining room, with a bottle of wine open before him, and a glass half empty at his elbow. He turned impatiently as we entered, then leapt to his feet to envelope me in a fierce embrace. "Alasil, where have you been? Why is she keeping you prisoner?"

We laughed, a deep and rich laugh, clasping his hand between mine. "Gods, I missed you!" I kissed his fingers, one by one.

The food came. I closed my eyes to better taste the complex flavors of the sauce. My skin quivered as Patsin bent close to me, stroking my arm with a fingertip.

"And what with Jamil? Has she gone soft in the head, like they say? Or even become a drunkard? I've heard rumors—she's been in town for two days, and Abad hasn't even sent for her. She's not going to land you in the bin, is she?"

I bent forward and kissed him. "There's more to her than you know." His lips opened under mine, soft and wet and heady as red wine. "There's more to her," I murmured, "than you could possibly imagine."

Madness, I thought later, as his strong hands stroked me, and the breath came sharp and harsh in my throat. Madness, I thought. If this is madness, let me never be sane again.

Chapter 20

I awoke amid tangled sheets, to the strange sound of another person snoring softly beside me. The air of the small, cluttered bedroom had been scented by the passion of my encounter with Patsin, but now the night breeze washing in through the open window replaced that heated musk with the cool salt scent of the nearby sea. My body felt slack and loose and well and thoroughly aired out. If Patsin's lovemaking left Alasil feeling this good, night after night, I could understand why she kept coming back to him. There must be few enough people in the world who could so unhurriedly and thoroughly make love to a trained and skilled assassin.

I slipped off the pallet as quietly as I could, dropping to my knees on the floor mat, where I felt about for my discarded clothing. Starlight filtering in through the open window outlined the shape of Patsin's shoulder, turned gracefully to tuck an arm beneath the pillow. I pulled my tunic over my head, picked up my sandals, and slipped out the room.

Outside, the swelling moon lay upon the horizon, and the cicadas had fallen silent. The hour was midway between midnight and sunrise, I guessed, a cold, silent time of night, reigned over by winter stars. I studied them as I walked, imagining, as I had learned to do as a child, that a compass rose lay spread across the sky. South, just beyond the long-toed boot of Aela Peninsula, lay the open sea, where galleys and frigates follow the trade winds westward. East, the Ipsenum Delta, where a tiny, insolent people once guarded their precious Alivum nuts against theft. The people are gone now, of course, and the Alivum nuts, having been over-harvested to the point of extinction, are now protected by Emperor's Law. West lies the rail route I have taken before, going widdershins around Callia's perimeter. And to the north lay the empire, once a patchwork land of isolated peoples, separated by obstacles of land and culture, now united by imperial decree into one strong, potentially rich country.

The Separated Ones may have been slaves to the Emperor's vision, but did that mean that we served an unsound purpose? With Callia's existence having been discovered by those tyrannical and land-hungry monarchies just a short ship's journey across the sea, our choices had been to unite or be conquered. Yes, the cost of unity had been high, but what would the cost have been had we not done it?

By the time I reached my own lodgings, I had talked myself firmly back into the Emperor's camp, and had decided, quite coldly, that I needed to rein Alasil in. Oh, she had been clever, and I admired her for it. But my dominance over her had been no accident—it was I who could guarantee our survival. To give way now before her, voluntarily, tempted by those old bribes of sensuality and passion . . . I snorted. These were an old man's weaknesses. And what, was I willing now to cease to exist, to let my self be somehow incorporated into a unified person such as Ata'al claimed to be? What had I to gain from my own destruction?

My lodgings echoed with silence. In the sitting room below, a single lampflame guttered. My fellow lodgers slept their righteous sleep so that they would be fresh for tomorrow's business. Tomorrow I would have business as well: I would arrange my teaching schedule, and visit the library. Within days I would be able to say that this peculiar period of my life was over.

My steward had left a lamp burning in my private sitting room. Like the lamp downstairs, it had burned down its wick and soon its last glow of light would flicker out. I latched the door behind myself and crossed toward my bedroom, preoccupied with my plans. The windows had been left open, and now a flickering shadow winged across the faint light of the glowing lampwick. Could it be a moon moth? They were rare at this time of year, but if the weather had been warm. . . . I paused, hoping for a sight of this beautiful insect, with its glowing eye spots and pale green wings.

I heard a sigh like the sighing of the wind. Startled, I froze with my hand upon the doorlatch. The frigid cold of a high mountain snowstorm washed over me. "Who's there?" Shivering, I crossed the room to turn up the lamp.

The room was empty. No moth wings flickered confusedly in the lamplight. The papers lay on my desk as I had left them in the evening, with my pen carelessly tossed aside. I put it in its holder, an ordinary act. "Alasil, don't play your games with me," I said softly.

The room sighed once again, and a ragged, insubstantial presence shifted across my field of vision: a nothing, a disturbance of the air, a ghost. She wandered restlessly in the brightness of the lampflame, neither visible nor invisible. I bent over the lamp, turning down the wick until I could see a spidersilk tracing of floating hair, slender hips, restless, hollow eyes. "Vicci, did Ata'al send you?"

If silence had an echo, that echo would be her voice: a lack of sound, an emptiness around which the wind could form, like clay around a mold. *Where is Ashami?*

"This is Ashami. You are here."

The Ashami of my dreams!

What was to be gained by lying to a formless ghost? "In your dreams you will find it."

This is only a hollow place.

"Then go home," I said gently. "Go home, and remember next time that hollow people have hollow dreams."

That blurred motion, like the fluttering of wings. Was she gone? No, there she stood once again, the outlined memory of a young woman, the shreds of her face, the empty places which had once been her eyes, the lonely misery which had outlasted by far the bitterness and the anger.

You promised to show me the city.

"I promised you nothing! Why have you come here?"

To decide. . . .

Had Ata'al, determined not to saddle the Asakeiri once again with so sullen and unmanageable a child, commanded this dislocated soul to acquaint herself with the world?

"Well, it matters not to me what you do," I said indifferently. "Just do not haunt this place, for I can easily have you exorcised. But if you do go back home, tell Ata'al something for me. Tell her that her plan didn't work."

The ghost shifted slowly across the room. At last she sat upon the couch, making no dent in the cushions, and gazed blankly up at me. *Which plan?*

"The plan to make me feel compelled to help Adline. The plan to turn my own self against me. It was clever, to give me the clues and then wait for me to realize on my own that I am her lost daughter. I suppose she thought the realization would change me somehow . . . make me ally myself with the Asakeiri, perhaps. But I care nothing for the past; it is irrelevant to me."

The ghost continued to gaze at me blankly, unmoving.

"Just tell her that, when you go."

Why should I tell the old crow your lies?

A ghost's disdain is cold indeed. I shivered with the chill in that hollow voice, and I asked myself if indeed such a miserable shade could be so easily extricated from my house by those charlatans who call themselves magicians. For all her insubstantiality, Vicci's ghost still bore at the center a hard and obstinate core that might prove difficult to dislodge.

The ghost said, *You would have me think that you are free. But I see your shackles.*

"How can you see anything? You have no eyes."

I see better without them. Vicci's ghost gestured lazily, a movement reminiscent of her stylized gestures of long ago, as she waited for me in the hot pool at the heart of Asakeiri Home. For a moment, I felt my own guilt. But I also remembered the courage and despair of that terrible time, after the dragon had all but obliterated the Asakeiri people from the face of the earth, and we struggled to establish a defensible position against the invading winter.

"Tell me," I said. "How are they doing, the Asakeiri?"

What do I know? I am dead.

I paced to the open window, and looked out into the starlit night. The fronds of the palm tree which grew against the wall rattled in the wind. Far away and faint, a night bell rang, telling the time for those few who sat awake. "What should I regret? That I could not spend my lifetime chasing half-wild goats up the mountainside? That I could not shiver away the winter in that crowded stone village, terrified every time the earth moved, with nothing to feed my intellect but superstition and folk magic? What is there to regret?"

The ghost said nothing. I doubted she even heard me, really.

"Ata'al wants me to believe that I would have been a wisewoman among the Asakeiri. She wants me to believe that my extra soul was deliberately induced to take up residence here in this body, because many souls give many powers. That's what she wants me to believe. But why should I believe a tale which is so blatantly self-serving? The Asakeiri are a dying people—" But even as I said these words I had to pause, remembering that they had not been dying at all, when I first arrived at Asakeiri Home. They lived in a fine village, well-maintained and well-designed, its storerooms filled, its people reasonably healthy and well-fed, its hallways vital with the movement of active young children. "They feared only the dragon," I said out loud, contradicting myself.

The ghost's reply startled me. *The Asakeiri never feared the dragon. Only his restlessness.*

"Well, they fear the Emperor, then, and needed

someone to shield them from his wrath—'' But once again, I had to stop, because I knew by direct experience that the Emperor's blockade of the Asakeiri people had long since lost its effectiveness, and that in any case the Asakeiri could continue to hide from his troops until time curled in upon itself and the sun fell into the sea.

"Her lies were blatantly self-serving," I said again, weakly. The faded ghost shivered faintly in the lanternlight, as if she were laughing at me. "Ata'al expects me to help Adline assassinate. . . ."

Adline has the heart of an eagle. She does not need the help of a hollow woman.

"No? Well, she'll never run again. That poison they've given her—the damage to her nervous system is permanent. She will never recover. Never walk again, much less run. Eagle heart or no eagle heart."

The ghost shivered again, and I heard her laughter, like air puffing out of a bellows.

"You tell me why, then," I said. "Tell me why Ata'al lied to me." My voice had that knife's edge sound to it, but that would amuse Vicci's ghost even further, no doubt. All my threats and intimidation were just bluster, when the worst that I could do to her had already been done.

The ghost said, *She told you the truth. Why should she lie to the daughter she had loved, and lost—and found again?*

"Ata'al is no soft-hearted fool, to treat an enemy like a friend just because—she happened to give birth to me. Do you expect me to believe instead that the Emperor and Abad have been lying to me since childhood? That I was in fact a beloved child, stolen out of my mother's arms? Why would they do such a thing? No, we were taken for our own safety, and taught us how to overcome our madness, and educated, and given a role in the world. That is the truth of the matter."

And why would the Emperor do such a thing? asked the ghost mockingly.

"Why—out of charity."

At this, Vicci's ghost literally dissolved with laughter. The frail filaments of her being shook so violently that they disappeared entirely, and only slowly reappeared, in bits and pieces that seemed oddly disarranged, like the pieces of a puzzle that did not quite match anymore.

I knew what it felt like. I turned away, as if that simple act could keep the truth of my own dismay hidden from a ghost. Since when had the Emperor, or Aman Abad, made any decisions on the basis of anything besides expediency? No one knows better than I that the people of the land are mere playing pieces to the Emperor, to be used or thrown away as he sees fit. We Separated Ones are useful to the Emperor; and so he keeps us. Charity? Since when did the Emperor know the meaning of the word?

You think you are free. But I see your shackles, whispered the ghost, in her voice like the aching hollow of silence after the wind had passed. Then I heard that sound, like the fluttering of wings, and something passed across the lampflame like shaken gauze.

When I turned to look, she was gone. Hastily, lest she return again, I closed and barred the window.

I walked the length of the room and back again. When I looked down, I saw that I had picked up my silver mirror. I set it down again, and walked over to my bedroom. The hour was late, and tomorrow, I had promised myself, my life would return to normal. I needed to get up early, and visit Aman Abad. I found myself once again standing at the desk, with the mirror in my hand. I set it down.

I sat down on the divan. Somehow, the mirror had come into my hand again. I looked into it, and saw my own face. Then I saw Alasil's face, but it was the same as mine. I said, "Do you know why the Emperor chose us, the many-souled children, to be his Separated Ones? He could have had any pick of children— a hundred desperate mothers would have gladly brought their starving infants to his door. Why choose us, unhealthy and half-mad, expensive and time-consuming to keep? Why us?"

Alasil stared at me as blankly as Vicci's ghost.

"Do you know?" I said impatiently. "What is wrong with you?"

"I am not a lamp, to be blown out and lit and blown out once again. I am tired of you, Jamil. I am tired of helping you. Find your own answers. Fight your own battles. If you won't let me live, then leave me alone."

"What?"

"We work together," she said, "or we don't work at all."

A long, cold time we stared at each other. My choices laid themselves out, neatly as bottles lined up on a windowsill, and I asked myself a strange question. I asked myself how I wanted to live my life.

As a hollow woman, a mask that does the Emperor's will and speaks the Emperor's words? With my powers of analysis forever shut down, for fear that I might accidentally ask the wrong question, dig up a buried secret, remember again that for a little while I had tested, however cautiously, the extent of my shackles? Is that how I wanted to live?

Alasil stared at me, waiting. My passionate, self-indulgent executioner had been all but extinguished by this strange journey we had taken together, if she had ever existed at all except in my own mind. Here before me sat the stranger, the sullen slave, the reader of poetry, the keeper of secrets. How much was I willing to sacrifice for that sake of knowing her? My freedom, my very self? Strangely, these seemed small prices to pay.

I said, "I know I shut you out earlier, when I awoke in Patsin's bed. I'm afraid it will take more than a day for me to change the habits of twenty years."

Perhaps the harsh line of her mouth softened a little but that was all. She said nothing.

"What you're offering me—you call it life, but to me it feels like death. Do you expect me to wholeheartedly embrace it, all in a moment, like a lover rushing out to meet her beloved at the gate? When have I ever been so incautious?"

Alasil smiled faintly. "Not often. But I always hope."

I stood up, suddenly restless. "I want you to go somewhere with me."

"What, tonight? It's only the third hour of morning."

"What better time to look for the things that people don't want us to see?"

"We'll want to bring some weapons, then; at least a knife and a blowpipe."

I started to get up, but her voice stopped me. "Where are we going?"

Her eyes were bright and eager, but I saw some of my own caution there as well. It occurred to me suddenly that this might be the last time I looked into Alasil's face without also seeing my own. Not death, I reminded myself, but life. "We're going to the Childrens' Compound," I said.

Chapter 21

In the orderly darkness, I dressed in assassin's clothing. The exotic drug of Alasil's vitality and energy pumped through my veins, erasing the aches which lingered after my long, plodding journey home. Though I quivered with eagerness and curiosity, I checked my weapons carefully as I slipped them into my boots, and I spent no small amount of time arranging the knitted hood over my head, so that no part of my vision was obscured. I looked a fearsome sight in the mirror, dressed from head to foot in dull black, with three vials of poison hanging from my belt.

Even as I dug a grappling hook and a coil of rope from under the bed, I watched my own preparations as if from a great distance. Over this watching self panic washed like the waves of a stormy sea, but between those waves lay troughs of peace. So this is madness, I thought, quivering with joy, shivering with horror, turning my cool, objective gaze to evaluate the steadiness of my hands. So this is the awful fate I had wasted my life avoiding.

The panic rose and washed over me. The first time Alasil and I joined souls, I could pretend it was just a daring erotic experiment, a way to escape for a few hours the cold wasteland of intellect in which I had lived my life. I put on my alter-self's face as if it were a mummer's mask, thinking that I could just as lightly lay her personality aside again. But this time, I had promised that the joining would be irrevocable. And I had made this promise with little apparent consideration and even less analysis. What idiocy was this?

The wave of panic passed. What did I think needed

to be considered and analyzed? From either side of a chasm, a bridge had been built. Now, the boards had been laid across the last remaining gap, and the two sides of the gulf, once hopelessly separated, were now forever joined. So the entire fragmented country of Callia had been joined together, one bridge at a time. "It's just simple engineering," I said to myself.

Then the panic began again.

I blew out the lamp and stood still, waiting for my eyes to adjust to the darkness. Gradually, the familiar shapes of my sitting room's furnishings emerged from the shadows. Wending my way among these obstacles, I crossed to the door and slipped out. The hallway led me to the top of the stairway which swooped gracefully down into the darkness like a stylized waterfall outlined in starlight. At the bottom of the stairs, the sitting room now lay in darkness, the lamp having finally burned itself out.

Outside, wind stalked the narrow walkways. Light-footed, I followed the same paths, finding my way by starlight. The palm trees rattled their leaves, like the pages of a book ruffling beside an open window. On my left rose the archways and columns of the library, like bleached bones of a magnificent monster. On my right, the walled Children's Compound slouched out of the shadows. By daylight, its stone arches and draping greenery gave the compound the appearance of beauty: an architectural marvel, with many towers and multileveled buildings, all straining eagerly skyward. In the darkness, with its disguise stripped away, I saw only a prison wall.

Ten years I had lived behind that wall, sharing the imprisonment with an ever-shifting population of children. Newly arrived, they all looked the same: lost, shocked, with eyes like dried bones. They wept in the dormitory or awoke from their sleep, crying out with terror. Their screaming panics could be sparked by the smallest thing: a touch, a word, an insignificant interchange. Many of the newcomers disappeared and never reappeared again. We children who survived believed that they had not been able to establish a dominant self, and had gone mad.

At age sixteen, I and ten others, the only survivors of a group which had originally numbered thirty or more, walked somberly out of the front gate and were taken to meet the Emperor. I never returned. I never asked what had happened to the others, those who did not make it. I had survived; I had excelled. The Emperor was pleased with me. Nothing else mattered.

The grappling hook tugged impatiently at its tether, glimmering with starlight as I swung it on the axis of my arm. I fed my vitality into that twirling hook, and it sprang eagerly out of my grasp, flying lightly over the wall and landing silently in the plush grass which grew on the other side. The sound of metal grating on stone as I dragged the hook up the side of the wall attracted no attention.

The hook caught in the carved arch and I leaned my weight on it, testing its hold. Good enough. Wrapping my gloved hands in the slender rope, I began to climb and reached the top easily. My hook rang once against stone as I released it. I huddled atop the wall, listening. But the keepers of the children—the doctors and teachers and trainers and chaperones—all of them slept quietly in their beds. The locked doors would keep even the most adventurous of the children safely restrained. I doubted that the children's keepers planned for or expected an invader from outside.

With my rope and hook once again over my shoulder, I jumped to the ground, landing in an easy roll on the soft grass. They had taught me how to do this, how to climb walls and slip silently through the darkness. "Watch the cat," they had instructed me. Like a cat, I moved from shadow to shadow. I had landed in the large yard where the young children were set loose in good weather, to play with balls and threaten one another with stick swords. The side door was locked, of course, but I had a lock pick in the seam of my boot. The door soon sagged open upon well oiled hinges, and I slipped through.

Here in the kitchen, my Alasil self had sometimes

lingered after arms practice, hoping for a piece of hot bread from one of the cooks. They taught me a little cooking, and I learned more on my own. They taught me about wines, too, when I had grown older. Now the kitchen was empty, the cooking fire banked in the huge fireplace, the dishes and pans all tidied away in their cupboards, the work table scraped clean, ready for the new day. Sand grated underfoot as I crossed toward the scullery and paused there.

Where did I want to go? To the living quarters, to look into the faces of the children as they slept? Would all my questions somehow be answered then? Or I could follow the main hallway through the house, visiting the empty school rooms, the study rooms, the library. I could climb the stairs, higher and higher, passing from wing to wing, where the older children moved as they grew older, farther and farther from the watchful eyes of their caretakers. I could climb a tower and look out upon the buildings and walkways and tiny, delicate gardens of the Separated District as I had used to do.

But I would find no answers there, just old and insignificant memories.

I walked through the scullery and into a vast, irregularly shaped storeroom, its shelves cluttered with dusty household items that could have lain untouched for thirty years. But a track glimmered across the dusty floor, where scuffling feet had buffed the old wood to a dull polish which reflected the faint light coming through a single small window. My nostrils itching with the stale scents of dust and mold, I trod lightly down that track and felt a strange thundering begin within my body.

Not panic, but terror.

The track led to a cellar doorway wide enough to allow easy passage for a keg of beer or barrel of apples. But the steel clad door, triple bolted with heavy iron locks, told me that something more precious than carrots and wine was stored there. I set to work with my lock pick, but this door proved resistant to my careful seduction. I closed my eyes to better sense the pattern of the lock but could see only the shape of my own desperate fear.

Something was down there. Ringing faintly, my pick fell to the stone floor.

Breathing heavily, I got up and paced the length of the storeroom and back again. My selves argued with each other, the watcher standing in her remote tower and the assassin pacing that polished floor. They each insisted that there was nothing to fear, and both insisted that the terror did not originate with them. But the immobilizing horror remained. Though I could force myself back to the cellar door and fumble for the lock pick, my trembling hands were useless for such delicate work. I began heedlessly to search the storeroom for anything with which I could break the door down.

A door banged. I froze in the darkness, my hands full of rotten oilcloth. Had the door through which I entered the building opened again, and begun banging in the wind? No, the sound had been closer, hollow, the sound of a hall door being shoved carelessly open. Hastily, I shoved the oilcloth into the window, blocking the starlight and leaving the storeroom in utter darkness. I crouched near the storeroom door, where the light of an approaching lantern would not illuminate me.

I heard boots scrape across the sand-scattered tiles of the kitchen. A man grunted, and then sighed, as if he had set down a heavy burden. Now light flared as he lit a lamp, and I shrank back into the dim shadows. Keys jangled, and the grating footsteps came into the scullery. Light fanned across the storeroom floor, illuminating the footprints, which I had scuffed clearly in the accumulated dust.

If he noticed the footprints and cried a warning— but he trudged right past me. I pressed the blowpipe to my lips. His hands lifted involuntarily to slap at the little stinger that pierced through the cloth of his shirt and into his arm. One more step he took, and then he fell, boneless and limp as a bag of potatoes.

I leaned over him to snatch up the fallen lamp. The

chimney had broken, but the flame had not gone out.
By its light, I plucked the little barb out of his arm.
Cautiously, lest I be stung as well, I dipped its tip into
one of the vials of poison that hung from my belt like
tiny decorative bells, and slipped it back into the
blowpipe, where I could not accidentally stab myself
with it. My victim would sleep for a few hours, and
awaken with a headache. Anyone who knew blowpipes
would guess what had happened, but, with luck, he
might think that he had suffered a shameful fit, and
mention it to no one.

He had fallen on the ring of keys, and since he was
a large, muscular man, it took some doing for me to
extricate them. With the keys in my hand, I approached the cellar door once again. Now, I thought
grimly, this door will be opened.

Beyond the cellar door, the solid stone staircase had
a sturdy banister such as a workman carrying a heavy
burden might lean upon for balance. At the bottom lay
a room, empty except for a few bits of scattered debris: a rag of clothing, a moldering bit of carved wood
that might have once been a child's toy. I held the lamp
high over my head, and the shadows beyond the reach
of its light shivered with the trembling of my hands.

The basement, if I could call it that, smelled of damp
and decay, and of a faint, sickening scent that I had
before smelled only in slaughteryards and charnel
houses. A faint, chittering murmur came to my ears,
the sound of worms and termites, gnawing away at the
collapsing timbers. I took my knife out of my boot,
but holding its cold metal gave me little comfort. Unsteadily, forcing myself forward, step by step, I exited
the barren little room, and entered a narrow, dripping
corridor, as harsh and dank as any dungeon. The rough
stone walls sagged with age; the floorstones were green
with mold. Ancient torch holders had been cemented
into the walls, but over the years their metal had rusted
into shapeless ruin. At a door which had rotted loose
from its hinges and fallen inward, I held up my lan-

tern, but saw only a dark and decaying hole, and the scurrying shadow of a rat.

It was an old place, much older than the compound built on top of it. Fifty or so years before I was born, Ashami-Sha had been invaded by a small army which bravely traveled by boat across the calm summer sea. For a year or two the foreigners had ruled the southern shore, building their alien wooden palaces out of the native wood they found here, and burrowing deep into the ground as well. They called the native people barbarians because they built out of stone, but within a year their wooden houses had begun to collapse, destroyed by insects almost as soon as they were built. The invaders mostly died as well, killed by Summer Fever; a child's disease.

One of those wooden testaments to the dangers of arrogance and ignorance must have once stood in this very spot. The basement, built primarily of stone, had outlasted the palace, but as it was now on the verge of complete collapse, surely it was unused. Then why had the man I encountered upstairs been carrying a set of keys?

Arguing with myself once again, keeping a firm grip on the struggling form of my unreasonable fear, I continued down the hallway. Its ruin reminded me vaguely of the ruin of Asakeiri Home, and I caught myself listening intently for the faint rumbling of the dragon.

I encountered a series of rotting doors sagging on their hinges, and a cold pool of water through which I waded cautiously, having probed its depth first with a length of rotten wood crawling with worms. The carrion smell grew stronger. I came upon a length of hallway where the doors remained intact. Big, rusting padlocks latched them shut on the outside, but I could lift my lantern to the barred grate and look in at the shadow-striped floor of a barren cell. A crumpled blanket lay in one corner, as if this awful room had been recently occupied.

I lifted my lantern to each cell as I passed. All were empty, but several still stank from recent occupation. In one, I could count the mounds of excrement in a corner. For fifteen or twenty days someone had been held prisoner in this place—a small person, a young child.

Lying in the damp wrapped in a single blanket, listening to the rats scrabble—

Screaming when the key turned in the lock, screaming and screaming— Because I knew what they would do to me—

A moan escaped my lips. I opened my eyes to find myself huddled on the mucky floor. My limbs felt paralyzed and numb; my thundering heart set my bones to trembling. With difficulty I raised my head. The lantern lay on its side, but, miraculously, its flame flared to life again as I righted it with a shaking hand. I raised myself to my knees. My thoughts were as incoherent and chaotic as if I had just come out of a faint. Even as I got carefully to my feet and checked the precious contents of my boot, I heard in my inner ear the panicky screaming of a child.

It was a familiar sound. Perhaps I had been listening to it for my entire life.

"I'll take care of you," I said out loud. "It's all right; I'll protect you. Just a little farther now; a few more steps. . . ."

I walked farther down the nightmare hallway. I knew now what I would find there, but I needed to see it with my own eyes. I needed to prove that it was not just a child's half-forgotten nightmare.

I found the torture chamber. Its gruesome machines could not have accommodated even the smallest of adults. Those machines could only clasp around a wrist the size of a child's.

Behind a closed door, I found the bodies of the children. They had been thrown into a sunken pit and sprinkled with lime. The white powder lay upon their moldering bodies like snow. Hundreds of children, lost in the snow. I felt very far away from myself as I stood at the edge of the pit, remotely examining those pathetic corpses by the uncertain light of my lantern. One who had died very recently had been flung atop the pile, arms askew, head unnaturally twisted. Some others lay in gruesome decay, and of others little remained but shattered skeletons, half buried in the muck.

The open door banged in the wind. I saw her standing there in the doorway, an Asakeiri child, hunger-thin, her head raggedly shorn of its precious beads. I wanted to draw her to me, and cover her eyes against the sight of those dead children. But oh, those eyes have seen worse sights than this, haven't they, my sacrificed child, my keeper of memories, my lost self? We three were born clasped in each other's arms, and it had taken this—this nightmare—to shatter us apart. Despite that shattering, we three had survived, though our peers died around us. How strong we could have been, had we been left whole! Patterner and decision-maker, charismatic leader, beloved friend, brave fighter, risk-taker and journeyer, we could have become all these things. But instead, shattered and crippled, we became the Emperor's Knackers.

Oh, Abad was a genius, to have had such a vision. All the great leaders who might have challenged the Emperor's rule lay moldering in that pit of corpses. The visionaries and magicians, the poets and prophets, there we lay, thirty years dead.

My victim groaned a little as I hung the ring of keys once again at his belt. In the kitchen, dumped on the floor, I found the burden he had been carrying: a little boy, still warm to the touch, his skin purple from the swift poison with which he must have been dosed at bed time. Just a sleeping draught, my dear, to keep those nasty nightmares away.

Those of us who survived, we survived by forgetting. If we remembered, even in our nightmares, they killed us.

I climbed the prison wall once again. The cold stars still blinked overhead, remote observers. I saluted them as I crouched atop the wall, checking the horizon for signs of dawn. All was well; even the servants would not be out of their beds yet. I jumped off the wall and hurried home.

Safely in my lodgings, I wrapped my stinking clothing in oilcloth, and buried it amid the gear beneath Alasil's bed. Still, my very skin smelled like death. I could not bathe so early in the day without arousing suspicion, so I splashed myself with a little scent from the dressing table, wrapped myself in a robe, and waited until I heard voices in the hallway. Then I emerged, yawning, and called for the circumspect Mari to accompany me to the baths.

"Bring my dress clothes," I instructed her. "I am going to Abad's house this morning. It's time I took up teaching again. If anyone calls for me later, I'll be in the library and won't return until late afternoon."

It was high noon before I rang the gate bell at the Champion's House, standing bare-faced beneath the flapping edge of a Concourse flag. A taut, grim man answered my summons and said, before I could open my mouth, "Adline is still ill and cannot see anyone. It's no good offering me a bribe; she pays me well enough." He turned away, clearly expecting no argument.

I rattled the bars of the gate. "She will see me."

He snorted, and continued to walk away.

"Listen," I called. "Tell her I am here: her sister, Ishamil."

Chapter 22

The Runner's Court, a neat square of houses facing inward upon a well-groomed grassy yard, stands empty most of the year, the wide windows shuttered, the balconies collecting debris, the doors locked and barred. Once a year, as mid-winter moon approaches, servants converge upon this place like a conquering army, and challenge the debris and decay to battle. Close upon the heels of these foot soldiers come the Runner's Contingents: the advisors, caretakers, and hangers-on that a good runner attracts throughout the Concourse, and, of course, the runners themselves. In a matter of days the vacant wasteland is transformed into a carnival.

I watched the activity disinterestedly as I cooled my heels at the Champion's Gate. The runners' colors, displayed proudly at the gates along with their ornate prize ribbons, flapped and snapped in the strong afternoon wind. Servants scurried in and out of doors, bearing laundry, baskets of food, buckets of water. Steady streams of visitors and well-wishers rang the gate bells. Out on the green, several runners, with their bodyguards and advisors standing by, stretched and pranced upon the grass. Others ran mock races in the road that circled the court, which by no accident was exactly the same length and configuration as the racecourse of the Ashami Arena. Race enthusiasts, dressed in the colors of their chosen champion, hung about in small groups, watching their idol prance on the green, or gazing longingly at their lodging.

At the Champion's House, a few devotees, dressed in green and white, gathered along the fence. The many prize ribbons hanging above the gate streamed their bright colors in the wind, but the faces of Adline's devotees were somber. As I wore only expensive, buff-colored linen, and carried over my shoulder a wrapped bundle as if I had recently been to market, my arrival had excited little interest. But at least one of the Green-and-Whites had overheard my conversation with the gatekeeper, and now they whispered among themselves, turning their heads one by one to stare at me.

At last, one approached. "Your pardon, but did I hear you say you are Adline Asakeiri's sister?"

I gazed at the young man, unimpressed by his fawning attitude and absurd dress. He had twisted his hair into Asakeiri style locks, decorated with garishly colored artificial life beads. His shirt was white, his leggings green, and he even wore a green sandal on one foot and a white one on the other.

Undeterred by my silence, he held out a decorated basket, in which a little ceramic pot nestled in a bed of straw, its cork sealed many times with various cryptic symbols of the sort used by magical charlatans to impress the willing dupes who come to them in the marketplace. "We consulted with De'wa the Magnificent, on Adline's behalf. Her magic has saved many lives—"

"—A hundred, at least," piped in a younger girl, who had remained shyly at a distance.

"—She gazed into her Bowl of Truth, and saw there that Adline is under a witch's curse. All she needs to do is drink the contents of this bottle at midnight, and say the words of this spell . . ." The young man pointed delicately with a fingertip at the spool of brown paper nestled in beside the bottle. ". . . And she will be made whole!"

I continued to gaze at him without speaking, unable to think of any words adequate to the situation. He took my silence for speechless wonder, or awe perhaps, and after a moment said reassuringly, "It won't hurt her—it will help her. She must get well for the great race; it is only two days away!"

I nodded gravely. "How much did you pay this—
De'wa—for her services?"

"It doesn't matter," the lad said earnestly. "We all
shared the cost. Will you bring this to Adline?"

"Why don't you just give it to the gatekeeper?"

The lad lowered his voice. "Well, we suspect that
he doesn't bring her everything—"

With a sigh, I took the basket. "Now you're certain
this is from no charlatan? It will not make her more
ill?"

The entire group of green and white dressed devotees shook their heads earnestly. "Well, I will do it.
Now leave me alone; I have had a hard journey." I set
down my bundle with a sigh, and leaned against one
of the gateposts, holding the basket carefully in my
hand.

The gatekeeper returned, looking vaguely surprised. "Your name again?"

I said formally, "Ishamil *isa* Ata'al *isa* Asakeiri."
The gatekeeper repeated the name twice, and left once
again. I thought I detected rather more speed in his
gait. I turned back to my review of the strutting runners and their admirers. Normally, the sight would
arouse my cynicism, but today I welcomed any dis-
traction.

The gate lock squawled. "Ishamil? Come this way."

The devotees crowded close, crying messages of
good will. "Tell her to get well! Tell her to take the
draught! At midnight, hear? Tell her we love her!"

I stumbled on the cobblestones of the small courtyard within the gate. The gatekeeper paused solicitously, catching me lightly by the elbow. "Madam?"

"I'm just tired." I examined distantly the smear of
tears on the back of my hand, and concentrated on
breathing deeply.

My earlier interview with Abad had been as brilliant
a piece of play-acting as I ever concocted. Judiciously
and cleverly I had mixed my emotions: just enough
dignity, just enough disguised humiliation, slightly too
much tractability, (to let him know that I meant not
only to be obedient, but to be overly obedient). Alasil

had played me for a fool, I told him. But I had well and thoroughly chastised her, and such an incident would never happen again. I was still valuable to him, I told Abad. If anything, I was more valuable than before because I had learned so much from this experience.

Only once, at the very beginning of the interview, had I been disconcerted. As a footman opened the door to his sitting room to let me in, Abad had looked up from his desk and hesitated, confused. "Jamil, is it?" he finally said. Never before had he been unable to distinguish my selves from each other.

I strode firmly into the room, as crisp and contained as any well-trained soldier, holding Alasil's fierce rage firmly in check. "Yes, it is I, Jamil." Incredibly, he had believed me.

Astonishingly, he had accepted my tale. He stated that he would keep a close watch on me but welcomed my return to sanity with relief. He liked me no more than I liked him, but my experience and unswerving obedience meant that I remained, in his eyes, irreplaceable.

But now I felt weary to the marrow. I saw with a peculiar double vision: I saw the pristine courtyard, lush with winter flowers, with a self-important litter resting near a fountain where fishes swirled, like animated pieces of gold jewelry. And I saw the rotting dungeon, and the carcasses of a hundred children, piled like garbage in the mucky pit. Grimly following the gateman, I set one foot in front of the other, and wondered what I would have to say to Adline, or she to me.

A graceful balustrade swept up the front stairway, which spread like a pleated apron at the foot of the pretentious doorway. There, at a double door inlaid with half a dozen precious woods, in deep, rich colors ranging from pale gold to deep mahogany, waited a broad, fierce woman, with her fisted hands resting on her hips. I knew at once that she was the true gatekeeper, the guardian of the household, the type who would secretly welcome Adline's disability; since the greater her helplessness the more thoroughly she could be watched after. Perhaps she was even the one who had been bribed to poison Adline. I approached warily.

"You won't be giving that to Herself, will you?" She pointed an accusing finger at the ornate little basket in my hand.

I continue to climb the stairs, unspeaking. A second time she challenged me from above. "I'll have no charlatan's wares in this house!"

Grimly, I climbed, mounting the last step as she opened her mouth to speak a third time. I stood over her now, a full hand taller than she. "If you would step aside," I said.

"I'll not allow—"

"Adline has agreed to see me. Step aside." I stepped forward, giving her the choice of giving way or being pushed out of the way. She opted to stumble back gracelessly.

In the receiving room beyond, three lounging people, two women and a man, all in plain dress, rose hastily to their feet as I entered, turning their heads to conceal their smiles of amusement at the discomfiture of the guardian. They introduced themselves by name. I had heard that Adline kept few retainers; this could be her entire household.

"You are beyond any doubt her sister," a compact little woman named Rusalii commented dryly, remarking more on my behavior than my appearance, I guessed.

"Where is she?"

"In her bed, of course. Pay no mind to Iyala—not that you would." She gestured mockingly at the huffing guardian, who looked ready to rip me limb from limb.

"If you would take me to her."

"Of course." Rusalii bowed neatly, as if to a visiting noble. "Follow me. Ishamil, you said your name was?"

"Madam will do."

"Oh, pardon me . . . madam." Rusalii started up the central staircase, chortling to herself.

I followed her in grim silence, little inclined to share her amusement.

A second double door, nearly as ornate as the first, gave entry to a plush sitting room. Here, the unseemly clutter of uncleared wine cups and the disarray of crushed pillows demonstrated once again the lack of proper servants. We did not pause here, but continued through a second door into a bright bedroom where open windows allowed the afternoon breeze to wash through, setting the gauze curtains to billowing. If the rest of the house seemed neglected, the invalid was certainly well cared for. Never had a sickroom smelled more fresh. Rusalii gestured me into a plush armchair, and bent solicitously over the pallid, wan figure in the bed. Amid the overwhelming quantity of pillows, the invalid all but disappeared.

"Adline . . . Adline, your sister is here."

The champion stirred and murmured.

"Here, I will help you to sit up."

Rusalii may have been a small woman, but her arm muscles bulged like an ox-driver's as she lifted the nerveless athlete, grabbing pillows to support her back, inquiring gently if she were comfortable. At last she stood back, and I could see Adline.

Slack-faced, dull-eyed, she gazed at me. She had cut off all her hair.

I said, "I bring greetings from your mother and husband. I have come only recently from Asakeiri Home. Ata'al gave me a token to bring to you—" Out of my bundle I extricated the little waxed leather box, which I had carried so uncaringly home with me, letting it travel unforgotten in the bottom of my pack among the crumbs and lint and bits of thread. It had fared well enough, for all that; a quick polish with a soft cloth and it looked better than the day Ata'al first gave it to me.

I laid the box onto the edge of mattress, purposely out of the line of Adline's vision. I watched her eyes, as they tracked the little box in my hand, until she could see it no longer without moving her head. This she apparently could not do.

Rusalii murmured that I would have to open the box for her. Adline had lost her power of speech as well, she added.

Smiling sympathetically, I leaned forward to pat Adline's warm hand. I spoke in the language of the mountains: "Never mind, little sister. I'm certain that you will soon have a remarkable recovery," The subtle inflections I used would imply, only to a native speaker, a second, hidden message. "Just for sport, I'll pretend that I don't know," I had said to her, "but you're playing a game with me."

Adline's slack mouth tightened into a thin line. "Rusalii, did you think to search this woman for weapons?"

Hissing like a cat, Rusalii leapt forward, every bit as protective as, but probably far more dangerous than, the guardian downstairs. I raised my hands, and peacefully allowed myself to be searched, as Adline extricated herself from the bedding, the little box in her hand. Keeping a sharp eye on me, Rusalii untied the protective covering of my rolled bundle. She hissed again, jerking her hands away from the revealed black cloth of my robe and mask, as if it could infect her. "A Knacker! Gods above and below . . ." Her voice throbbed with despair. "And we came so close—"

Adline bent grimly over the little box, carefully picking the lacing loose. The pallor of her skin ended at her neck and elbows. Had she bleached it, I wondered, or put on makeup? The latter would be easier to discover, but her impressive corps of protective assistants had probably been able to keep most unwanted visitors away. The lacing gave way. Adline peeled back one waxed side of the little box, then turned to look at me, and at Rusalii, rocking and moaning at my feet.

"She is indeed my sister, Rusalii," she said. "She was kidnapped years ago; you can't guess how often I have heard the tale."

She had spoken in Asakeiri, but Rusalii responded in the Common tongue. "If you think it will make any difference to her—"

I said nothing in protest or defense. I was tired;

tired of being who I was, tired of being blamed for choosing to survive in the only way I could. I rested my face in my hand and waited.

"I do not think she is our enemy."

"You are an innocent; you cannot know—The Separated Ones, they have no loyalty."

"Well, then, if all is lost, what harm in hearing what she has to say?"

I raised my head at this. "What did Ata'al send to you?"

She showed me, nestled within its clever box, a small figure, made of straw. A dragon.

A dragon, made of staw, held high in Ata'al's hands. Chanting, dancing, the Asakeiri circle her: men and women, old and young, shouting and dancing—

It was Ishamil's memory: she attended that night's secret gathering, after Jamil had been drugged into sleep. I could force her to give the complete memory to me, if I wanted to, just as I could force the memory of that first, childishly foolish journey I took in Duhan's company, or of the time that Jamil had lain, supposedly stricken with pneumonia, while the child had the run of the village, reveling in her homecoming. I could force her to give me these memories, and then all my questions could be answered. But that was no way to win the trust of a frightened child.

"You are not really Ishamil, are you?" Adline said.

"I am still separated from her. Jamil and Alasil are my two selves. Jamil will give you a reasoned response; Alasil an impassioned one. Or you can talk with Ishamil if you want: I think she will hear you. She is still just a child, though. A brave child, a risk-taker. But a child."

This peculiar response to a peculiar question did not seem to cause Adline much confusion. She should understand, I thought, gazing into the rich complexity of personality reflected in her face. Ata'al had borne not one, but two many-souled daughters. The second she had managed to keep out of the Emperor's hands . . . until now.

"How long did you remain with the Asakeiri?" Adline asked.

"A few months, from first snowfall until the most recent full moon."

One of Adline's other companions, the man named Cherin, who seemed by his appearance to be a native of the Ansilin Valley, entered the room bearing a tea tray. He froze, startled at the sight of Adline perched on the edge of the bed, and my black robes spread out on the floor, and Rusalii huddled there, gradually being drawn by curiosity out of her black despair. Adline waved him in, and he began rather distractedly to pour cups of green tea.

"Tell me," she said longingly, "how fare my people and my mountains?"

I sat back in the chair and studied her face, pondering whether I should spare her the truth. But she would recognized the lie, even from so accomplished a liar as myself. She had the second sight, a vision which enabled her to see not just ghosts, but any secret and hidden thing. I, too, had this talent; many times it had saved my life, just as Adline's had saved hers. "There was a terrible earthquake," I said. "Many survived, but many did not."

For a long time, as the tea cooled in the cups, and Cherin sat companionably on the bed beside Adline, and Rusalii stood up to pace the room restlessly, Adline and I talked about the earthquake, and about the problems her people faced, and about how likely they were to survive the bitter winter that still lay mostly ahead of them. For those few moments, both of us were able to forget the divisions which separated us, and we talked as if we were indeed both inheritors of our mother's power, Asakeiri wisewomen, struggling together to formulate a solution to the Asakeiri predicament.

At last Adline stood up, the straw dragon still clasped in her hand, her face grim. "Our people have survived some terrible winters. I am glad to hear that you think they will survive this one as well. But for the sake of the rest of Callia—I must still run my last race.''

I said quietly, ''You must understand that my loyalties are divided. Take care what you say to me, for what I do not know I cannot reveal.''

''Do you think that I do not know, or cannot guess, what they had to do to you, to make you what you are? That knowledge lies fresh upon you, like the scars of a beating. And yet you remain loyal to them?''

I felt my face twist painfully. ''Yes. Though it is Jamil's kind of loyalty, a loyalty which weighs only benefits against costs. Therefore I am divided, as should be no great surprise to anyone. . . .'' Those traitor tears again, the tears of my third self, the only one who remembered how to cry.

I continued to speak steadily, wiping away the tears as they fell. I suppose most of my observers thought me a little mad. ''There are few people alive who know more about the political state of the country than I. If the Emperor were to be killed, the dragon would not sleep more peacefully because of it. The Emperor's hold on Callia is not so certain that his twelve-year-old daughter would be able to maintain it. The great leaders of our time, who might avert disaster with their own visions of the future, lie moldering in a shameful grave. Therefore, the generation that follows the death of the Emperor would be plagued by wars and chaos, and the outcome could be a situation only worse than that in which we now find ourselves. I cannot participate in such a plan, not even for the sake of well-earned vengeance.''

Adline stilled Rusalii's restless pacing with a touch, and came back to stand before me. ''If not to kill me and not to help me, then why did you come to me?''

''To meet you. To free myself of an obligation.'' I gestured toward the straw dragon in Adline's hand. ''And for the child, I think. It was seeing you run your first race in Akava that awoke her from her long sleep, and started me on the strange journey which has ended here. Perhaps it will give her some peace, later, to have met you face-to-face.''

"Later when I am dead, you mean?"

I said, "You can still choose to quietly go back home."

Adline uttered a dry snort, a sound too anguished to be laughter. "Cold choices, Jamil. It *is* Jamil I am talking to?"

I let my silence be my confirmation. Ishamil's tears had ceased to fall; perhaps she had gone beyond grief and back into despair.

I heard a rustle of cloth. Adline had opened her tunic, and held the cloth apart, to reveal to me a strange and terrible sight: a deep scar ran the length of her chest, from just below her breastbone to the bottom of her rib cage. Whether or not an eagle's heart actually beat within her breast, what a grim and terrible ritual she had endured!

I nodded once, to let her know that I understood. Neither could I have turned back, after having survived so much.

Adline said, "I will say this little, though I do not know how to make you believe me. Ata'al knows that to kill the Emperor would serve no good purpose. We are the Asakeiri, the people who sing the dragon to sleep. We live for peace, not for war. My hands have never held a weapon. I will not harm the Emperor, I don't even know how to do it."

"Then why else could this race be so important?"

"If Ata'al did not choose to tell you, then neither may I. Ask your child, your Ishamil. Perhaps she can give you the answer."

"She has no reason to trust me, Adline." I sat for a long moment, my head resting like a heavy stone in my hands. At last I raised it wearily. "Well, I must go, before someone starts to wonder where I am. A madwoman's execution faces me, if I cannot keep a semblance of normalcy."

Adline picked up the little basket I had set on the floor. "What is this?"

I laughed humorlessly. "Some of your devotees begged me to deliver it to you: a magic potion. They said to tell you they love you."

Adline shook her head, bemused. "I do not even know these people."

"Send someone out to give them green and white ribbons as tokens of your gratitude, and they will worship you forever." I bent to pick up my black robe, and paused. "You have a back door? I cannot enter Wisdom Gate unless I am wearing my robes."

"Rusalii will show you."

"Will you tell me one thing? Why are you pretending to be ill?"

"If the blackrobes knew they had failed to execute me, they would have tried again, yes? I have been running at night, or exercising indoors, to keep my edge."

"And when you arrive unlooked-for at the Ashami Arena in two day's time . . . you believe the assassins will not be waiting for you?"

"That was the hope." She looked at me cautiously, wanting to ask me if I planned to spoil her secret.

"Have you had no other guests since your arrival in Ashami?"

"There have been a few that we could not tactfully turn away . . . the Emperor sent his personal doctor yesterday. Why?"

"Did this 'doctor' take an object, as I did earlier, and test to see how far your eyes can follow it? It might not have seemed a test at all, just a casual motion."

Adline glanced at Rusalii, frowning.

Rusalii said, "When he took your blood, to see its color, he said, your eyes followed the little knife. Whose would not?"

I said, "Then no one who matters will be surprised to see you at the Ashami Arena on Race Day. *Kilpth* affects the nerves in all your muscles, including your eyes. And this room smells much too sweet. You should not be able to control your bodily eliminations, either. So you need not worry that I will betray your secret. It has already been betrayed."

The inhabitants of the room watched, fascinated, as I pulled on the robes and lifted the hood to cover my cropped hair. But I did not put on the mask yet. "The assassins will be waiting for you, Adline. They will use blowpipes, I guess, before the race actually begins: During the parade, or on your way into the arena."

With Rusalii trailing me reluctantly, I paused once again at the door. "Your mother is old. Go home, little sister, they need you there. Go home to your people."

Chapter 23

Morning dawned in a flush of soft color, washing the plastered walls of Alasil's bedroom with gentle shades of rose and gold. For comfort, I had slept there, amid the luxury of soft pillows and thick mattresses, but through most of the night I had endured a torment of nightmares, interspersed with periods of equally agonizing sleeplessness. During waking hours, I seemed able to hold my horror at bay, using Jamil's still effective tools of objectivity. But at night, anguish and terror hemorrhaged out of the wounds of my child, Ishamil. I could only endure, waiting for daylight.

"You don't look well," Mari said, as she helped me dress in my black formals. I would be miserably hot in the heavy-weight, closely tailored clothing, but today I needed every tool I could summon to make my first impression on the young apprentices assigned to my care for the winter.

Mari pinned four stars of rank across my right shoulder, and, beneath them, my three scarlet Ribbons of Eminence, awarded to me by the Emperor himself. I sat still, dull and patient as an old horse, as she fussed over the alignment of these decorations. She said, "You haven't been drinking again, have you?"

I roused myself enough to raise an eyebrow at this impertinence. "I doubt I will be so unwise again. Pour me some tea, please, and tell me the news."

Mari brought me a cup of pale green tea, and at a gesture from me poured herself a cup as well. Ever since she walked through the door bearing the tea tray, I had sensed her excitement, simmering just below the correctly neutral surface expression of her face. Now she said, with great drama, "There's been a miracle at Runner's Court!"

I looked down at the tea leaves floating in the pale green tea, and noted with weary cynicism how carefully and correctly I held the tea cup, using a finger and thumb of each hand, with the other fingers held up like the wings of a butterfly. I looked up at Mari only when I knew I had my expression rigidly under control. "You must tell me more."

"I heard it in the kitchen this morning, shortly after sunrise. Some of Adline Asakeiri's devotees bought a potion for her from a market wizard. All night they waited at her gate, and then, at first hour, Adline herself came down to speak with them. They had saved her life, she said, and she gave them beads from her own hair. She promised them she would run the Ashami Race . . . Madam, are you unwell?"

"Oh, no, please go on. This is a fascinating tale."

"Well, there isn't much more to tell," said Mari, clearly disappointed by my reaction. "You will be going to the race, won't you, madam? To see Adline run?"

Of course, Adline would never run the Ashami Race. With this morning's dramatic announcement, she had signed her own death warrant. Oh, she would be mourned, by everyone for whom she had become something more than just a talented human being. But only I would be mourning the loss of an arrogant, foolhardy, clever, and profoundly courageous sister.

"Of course I am going," I said. "It will be the event of the season."

Throughout the two agonizing days which followed, I dueled with myself, raising arms of intellect to challenge the weapons of passion. Long and dreary were the days, as I taught a class of shattered young people how, in turn, they could shatter others' lives; or studied old truths in the library, truths which tended to turn upon me like venomous snakes; or practiced in the ring the techniques of death. Longer and even more dreary were the nights, when I lay awake, engaged in angry, miserable debate with myself, haunted by the probability that as I lay there, another child's body was being added to the heap in that moldering dungeon.

But for all my anguish and distress, the sun continued to rise and set, and so on Race Day the sun first blazed upon the horizon, finding me as usual already awake. But this time, rather than having been awakened by a horrendous nightmare, I had awakened out of a wonderful, lyrical dream. In my dream, three sisters joined hands and danced. As I awakened slowly out of the dream, I pondered the mystery of my selves, and came to understand a simple thing, a thing almost too simple to put into words. Each in their own way, my selves had been pitting themselves against each other. This was no dance, but an immobilizing war.

No doubt, Mari came for me that bright morning, planning to deliver all the Race Day gossip along with the tea tray. But I had left my lodging long before I heard the servants' steps on the stairs. The sun had not finished climbing the barrier of the horizon when the guards let me through Wisdom Gate, and I stepped out into the streets of Ashami.

There, a carnival had evolved over the last few days, spreading from the overcrowded doorways of the taverns and tea shops onto the walkways and into the boulevards. Hawkers and dancers, vendors and bookmakers, musicians and horse-dealers, all rubbed elbows in a shouting, good-tempered competition for the attention of the brightly-dressed passersby. Festival banners festooned the balconies, and even at this early hour the scent of delicious food wafted from nearly every open window. Many of the festival goers, having spent wild nights in the taverns, seemed the worse for wear: their good clothing crumpled and stained, their gazes dull and bleary. Many bore the marks of one memorable encounter or another: love marks on necks, black eyes, torn clothing.

I passed among them, my black robes casting a pall over the merrymaking, like a stormcloud passing over the sun.

As I drew near the Ashami Arena, the crowds thickened into impassibility. Entire families bearing blankets, paper parasols, and baskets of food already waited patiently for the gates to open. Skirting the crowd, I made my way to the Boulevard of Champions, which uniformed guards had kept cleared throughout the night, so that the nobles and those sitting in the Emperor's box would not have to rub elbows with the unwashed multitude. Through the gate reserved for these privileged few I entered unchallenged, and mounted the steep stone steps to the top of the arena embankment.

The nobles, who did not need to rise early to compete for a good view, probably still lay abed, recovering from the balls and soirees of the previous evening. The stairway was deserted. As I reached the top of the embankment and could view the long slope down to the depressed arena, I saw that the nobles' servants had arrived the day before, bearing expensive carpets, upholstered armchairs and fine side tables, which they had set up in the groomed grass of the terraced hillside. Unlike the commonfolk, who would sit on blankets on the ground, the nobles would view the coming spectacle in luxury.

To my left stood the marble colonnade which supported the various levels of the Emperor's viewing stand. At the highest level, shaded by a marble canopy, busy servants already had arrived, to brush away the few specks of dust which might have settled there during the night, and arrange the satin pillows onto the marble throne. Below, between the pillars of the colonnade, through a tunnel which pierced completely the great embankment, the various competitors and entertainers would enter and exit the walled arena. Then, at high noon, with great fanfare, the participants in the main event, the Championship Race of the Emperor's Concourse, would march solemnly out to the starting line.

I walked along the crest of the embankment, feeling empty and passive as a bowl waiting to be filled. A hundred festival flags snapped and flapped in a fey breeze. The faint sound of voices came to my ears, the voices of a few scattered workers shouting to each other as they raked and smoothed the racecourse. Already, armed guards were posted along the edge of the track, to guarantee that no one set foot there once the workers had finished their final check. In past years, devotees or the runners themselves had attempted to sabotage the race with broken glass, stones, smoke bombs, or other obstacles. The breeze also carried up to me bits and pieces of tattered sound from the streets below: a few notes of music, an angry shout, raucous laughter.

When the outer wall of the Emperor's box blocked my further progress, I followed the flight of stairs down to the arena wall. Here an armed guard let me through the gate onto the field. At the time of the race, even the armed guards would leave the racecourse. No obstacles or barriers, behind which an assailant might hide, cluttered the field. The runners would be alone on the track.

I walked between the columns, into the tunnel, the walls of which had been built two generations ago by the finest stoneworkers in the world. Here, so the competitors would not be disadvantaged by the transition from the dim tunnel to the bright racecourse, dozens of oil lamps hanging from the ceiling would be lit to chase away the gloom. They had not been lit yet, and I slipped comfortably into its shadows.

Along one side of the tunnel, a chest-high causeway had been built, to enable foot traffic to walk separately from the spirited racehorses which frequently made the journey through the tunnel. I climbed the causeway steps, and stood still for a moment, studying the placement of the lamps. Their light would dazzle the vision of anyone walking down the main corridor, rendering the people on the shadowed causeway all but invisible.

The runners, at this point unescorted and keeping their distance from each other because of the chance of foul play, would be completely vulnerable to attack from the causeway. Even if someone expecting attack were to hug the far wall, a blowpipe's dart could cross the distance accurately. And if the assassin were to miss; well, they would have plenty of opportunity to try again. Certainly, there would be only one assassin; more would surely attract someone's notice. The Emperor would certainly have given Abad strict instructions on this subject. No one was to be able to offer proof that Adline had been murdered by Separated Ones. No one was to know that the Emperor had been so threatened by a poor tribal woman that he ordered her killed.

I walked the entire length of the causeway, and found it empty. Well, I had arrived overly early. I squatted down in the shadows to wait. I thought about Ata'al, waiting in the mountains, perhaps sitting in her place of visions and watching me across the length of half the country. I thought of my sister Adline, pacing in her airy bedroom, peering through the windows at the green and white army gathering below, to escort her in a triumphant parade down Champion Boulevard, as was traditional before the race. But Adline, if she had any self-preservation remaining, would slip out the back door into a covered carriage, and make the journey in secret.

I rose to my feet as another hooded and robed shadow walking along the causeway emerged from the darkness. "Greetings, in the name of the Emperor."

The approaching Separated One paused, his expressionless half mask examining me, then he said in a low voice, "I was told I would be alone. No one else would even know."

"Is that Kathe? Alasil." In twenty years, Kathe had never missed a target; in Abad's place I would also have chosen him to be the assassin.

"What is your business here, Alasil?"

"Jamil sent me to wait all night. I will leave the tunnel now by the way you came in, and the guards will think that you have left again."

Deeply troubled by this irregularity in planned procedure, Kathe said, "No one told me about this."

"Jamil suggested it to Abad, late last night. As you know Jamil has lost some status with him. She wants to gain it back, though this seems to me a trivial way

to go about it.'' I held out my hand. "I'm off to watch
the races. Gods' luck to you.''

As he had seven days ago, when he first brought me
into the Separated City, Kathe took my proferred hand
with an air of strained bewilderment. My fabricated
tale troubled him, but he dared not challenge me;
Kathe's only weakness is that his rigid nature does not
allow him to question anyone who outranks him. His
hand was cool. He wore no gloves today, as I had
known he would not, needing all his dexterity to load
the poison barbs into his blowpipe. To accidentally
pierce himself, now that would be a disaster.

I brought my other hand up, as if to clasp his in
both of mine, and drove the little thorn hidden between my fingers deep into the flesh of the back of his
hand.

Shocked, he stared up at me, his eyes blank and
hidden in the shadow of his mask. Then his knees gave
way, and I caught him as he fell.

Soon, the lamplighters came through the tunnel,
spreading behind them a blaze of light. Neither I, huddled in a convenient shadow, nor Kathe, crammed into
a corner with his robe draped over him, were spotted
by the workers. Now the parade of performers began:
brightly dressed dancers, pasty-faced clowns, acrobats
and trained horses, a series of heavily muscled men
and women who chatted companionably out to the field
of combat, and returned, broken and bleeding, some
carried on stretchers. I heard the shouts and horns as
the runners' parades arrived at the Champion's Boulevard, and still I waited, standing at the side of my
unconscious companion. Out in the arena, a restive
chanting began, a swell of sound that rose and fell like
waves upon a sandy shoal.

The runners came at last, eyeing each other cautiously as they strode down the narrow tunnel. Dressed
in brightly colored, loose-fitting silks, shod in lightweight boots custom made for them by the finest boot-
makers in the empire, their eyes bright and shining
with apprehension and anticipation, they walked like

yearling colts toward that last starting line. Their muscles bunched and sprang in their powerful thighs. Their hands hung loosely at their sides, fingers slightly curled. They held their chins at arrogant tilts. Among them marched Adline, with the straw dragon hanging by a green ribbon around her neck, gazing straight ahead of her, walking strongly down the center of the tunnel. Though she had to know that an assassin waited for her here, I saw no sign of anxiety or fear.

She passed without seeing me, and I heard the thunder of acclaim as she stepped out into the arena.

Alone again, I pondered the dilemma lying at my feet in the form of Kathe. If I killed him, I might still emerge from this day with the shape of my life essentially unchanged. But Jamil's logic of cost and benefit no longer held reign over me, and when I squatted over Kathe at last, it was only to ensure that he would remain unconscious until Abad sent someone to look for him.

I walked down the tunnel to the Champion's Gate. Through the grate, I saw a noisy, struggling crowd of devotees, all dressed in one or another runner's colors, fighting each other to get into the arena before the race began. But in the guarded Champion's Courtyard, only a few people remained, those in the runners' contingents who had been designated to wait here, and never know the outcome of the race until someone told them. The guide opened the gate to let me into the courtyard, and an ugly murmur rose up among those waiting, as they realized that a Separated One had been in the tunnel with the contenders. Rusalii stood alone, grasping the fence with one hand, shoulders slumped wearily. Of all of them, she alone waited to hear, not that her runner was the champion, but that her runner had survived. She did not notice my presence until I stood at her elbow, and she flinched away, angry and frightened to find my awful visage so near.

I said, "I will not say my name out loud in this place, but you know who I am. Adline has safely reached the arena, and they will not be able to kill her now." Rusalii opened her mouth to speak, but I cut her off. "Go back to the Runner's Court and pack a few things for a foot journey. Be sure to bring all the money Adline has and the beads from her hair."

"So you think we are fools? The carriage is already packed and waiting at the end of the Boulevard."

"Then take it to the north gate, for later the crowds will be too thick for you to get through."

"And how will Adline get there? She'd be mobbed if she tried to walk—"

"I will get her there."

I waited until Rusalii had reluctantly left the court, then I went back through the Champion's Gate and hurried down the tunnel. I hated to enter the arena so publicly, but contending with the crowds would have slowed my progress more than I could afford. As I drew near the tunnel opening, the first blare of trumpets echoed hollowly from above, and the high, thin shout of a herald began announcing the names of the runners. With everyone's attention on the field, I slipped all but unnoticed out of the tunnel and through the gates in the arena wall, which I had used earlier that morning.

The noblefolk, many of them wearing broad-brimmed hats, had gathered in their temporary outdoor sitting rooms to view the race in appropriate comfort and splendor. Their servants kept them well-supplied with sweetmeats and fine wines. The bright and varied colors of their embroidered silk robes reminded me of a gathering of spring butterflies, especially when the breeze picked up and set everyone's clothing to fluttering. None of them paid any attention to me as I climbed the stairs.

At the door which gives access to the lowest level of the Emperor's box, I held up my silver mirror so the guards could see the seal. Even this symbol would not get me past this last barrier, so I said, "I need to see Abad."

The trumpets blared a second time. The runners' names had been announced, and now they moved into position. "Hurry!" I cried.

One of the guards slipped in through the door, returning in a few moments with a flustered Aman Abad, whose face shone with sweat in the heat of the afternoon. "Jamil?" he said, after glancing at my mirror.

"Yes, it is I. I thought we would have stopped Adline by now—has something gone wrong?"

"Apparently it has."

"Perhaps you should take me up to the Emperor's box. If she does win the race, Alasil can prevent Adline from attacking the Emperor when he gives her the prize. If she never attacks him or does not win, well, what have we lost?"

One of the runners had complained regarding the status of the track, causing a delay. On the far side of the arena, a lavender and gold crowd started booing vigorously to protest this blatant attempt to subvert the other runners' concentration.

Abad did not consider long. He, too, did not want to miss the race. "I assure you, she cannot win the race. But come watch with me."

Murmuring apologies, he led me among the select few, who fluttered their fans irritably, or lifted wineglasses of fine crystal in a polite toast as we passed. As he settled into his own seat, I found a space against the wall, where I could stand without blocking anyone's view.

The trumpets sounded once again. The runners gathered on the starting line, their silks flapping in the breeze. Adline's draw had left her in a mediocre position, midway between the inner and outer edges of the track. As the herald raised his kerchief, she crouched, her attention as intent upon the track before her as an eagle's upon her prey.

Never had I had such a good view of the Ashami Race. I held my breath as the handkerchief fell.

Chapter 24

All the runners seemed to hesitate, like lunatics who suddenly regain their sanity just as they are about to plunge over a cliff. Then the whole pack shot forward, and within three strides, Lavender-and-Gold had taken the lead. "There goes Filelo!" cried someone in the Box.

"Filelo! All flash and no stamina," another responded.

Blue-and-White pulled quickly into second place. The remaining runners jockeyed for position, so tightly bunched that it seemed incredible they did not all trip on each other's feet. I picked out Adline in the midst of the pack, boxed in on all sides, poorly positioned for any kind of a break. The leading runners pulled ahead, with the rest of the pack trailing behind them. By the time the runners reached the first quarter-pole, the first two runners and the remaining eight were separated by three strides.

By the time they reached the half-mark, it was obvious to me that four of the runners had joined forces to keep Adline from winning the race. Still blocked both on the inside and on the outside, she was being forced to run a longer race, positioned far from the inside rail. The runners packed tightly around her like bodyguards. All across the arena, the groups of Green-and-White booed vigorously, throwing handfuls of torn paper into the air to demonstrate their displeasure.

I stood behind Abad's chair like a black stone. Abad would have picked his runners carefully and paid them well, for by denying Adline her chance to win the race, they were also giving up their own. With the race half run, the blistering pace began to slow imperceptibly; rare indeed was the runner who could finish the second half of a race as quickly as the first. As the runners tired, the pack began to string out and hug more closely to the inner rail.

They neared the fourth quarter-pole. Lavender-and-Gold and Blue-and-White now raced shoulder to shoulder, beginning the final sprint for the finish. Adline's bodyguards, apparently feeling the effects of the grueling run they had forced upon her, began to drop away. Painstakingly slowly, she emerged from their influence.

Then she stretched out her legs and began to run.

She ran as if the race were just beginning. Lightly, effortlessly, she pulled abreast of the three runners ahead of her, and then she passed them. Two strides separated her from the front runners, and then one. Everyone in the arena came to their feet, regardless of the colors they wore, and began screaming. But within the marble box, everyone sat in paralyzed, voiceless horror. I glanced over at Abad. He, too, remained seated and silent, his face rigid and grim. How emphatically had he promised the Emperor that the Asakeiri woman would never earn the Champion's Ribbon?

Adline Asakeiri was making a fool of him.

The two front runners hugged the rail, neither one giving way to the other. The finish line looming, Adline swerved around and past them, and crossed the line a full stride ahead of them.

Abad got quietly to his feet and started for the wide stairway which led to the Emperor's box. Unbidden, I fell in behind him. He spoke to me without turning his head, his words all but lost in the overwhelming roar of screams, shouts, and blaring horns. "Kill her," he said. "Make it look like something else."

"It will be done."

I followed him up the stairs, to the broad, airy porch where the Emperor sat amid his silken pillows, glaring down at the scene below. A group of the highest nobles, wrapped in flowing layers of multicolored silk like caterpillars in their cocoons, clustered near the throne, also staring in disbelief at the racecourse, where runners now walked in slow circles, huffing air desperately into their lungs. All eyes turned toward Abad and myself as we topped the stairs, but no one dared speak.

The Emperor turned his head, and instantly a solicitous servant stood at his elbow. "Fetch Abad."

"Your Eminence," murmured Abad, "I am here." He stepped forward, then dropped to his knees and pressed his forehead to the carpeted marble. I remained where I stood; the Separated Ones are not expected to abase ourselves, even to the Emperor.

"So," roared the Emperor, "Adline Asakeiri will never run again!"

"I take full responsibility, your Eminence." With astonishing dignity, considering the position in which he crouched, Abad spoke at length, describing for the Emperor the measures which had been taken against Adline, and the extraordinary facility with which she had foreseen and evaded ruin. "She is an amazing, clever woman," Abad concluded. "She has out-tricked us at every turn. I still do not know what happened to the assassin who awaited her in the tunnel. And the fact that she could win the race despite the obstacles— In the last day I have spoken with three different experts, and they all assured me that she could not possibly overcome such a handicap. It is clear now that we could only have stopped her by killing her outright. But at every turn the need for discretion has hampered us."

Somewhat mollified, the Emperor cast me a curious glance. Except for ceremonial occasions, the Separated Ones rarely come into the Emperor's presence. It is strange to think of so powerful and expedient a man as squeamish, but I have long suspected that he avoids close contact with us because he cannot stomach the work we perform, though it is done at his behest. The Emperor said, "This Adline did run a courageous race. But we will not countenance being embarrassed before our own people like this! What shall we do now; refuse her the Champion's ribbon?''

''The Emperor can refuse to award it because the race obviously had been fixed,'' suggested one of the clustered advisors.

''It was fixed against her! Yet she won the gods-cursed race! How can we refuse her the ribbon now, without looking the fool?''

The disorganized cheering of the spectators had evolved into a rhythmic chanting of Adline's name. But Adline remained modestly among the other runners, accepting their congratulations and continuing the pace slowly up and down in front of the Emperor's viewing stand.

''Get up, man!''

Abad rose to his knees. ''If the Emperor will allow me to make a suggestion. . . .''

''Speak!''

''Your eminence, I have taken the liberty of bringing with me Jamil, whose reputation precedes her. As you recall, she is known for her gift of predicting how current events will play out in the future. She has believed for some time that Adline Asakeiri intends to try to assassinate you even as you give her the Champion's Ribbon. Of course, Adline will be thoroughly searched before she is allowed to approach you, and we can guarantee that she will have no weapons. But we could turn this situation to our advantage, by using it as an excuse to finally rid ourselves of Adline Asakeiri. If the Emperor would allow her to approach you, Jamil will kill her—in a manner which will cause no great disgust to those gathered here. Then we can claim that Adline was killed because she moved to attack the Emperor. No one except those present will be able to disprove this tale, for the distance is such that no one will see clearly what happens.''

The advisors around the Emperor drew back in shock, but he, after a moment's consideration, said speculatively, ''A daring plan.''

Abad rose to his feet. In the arena below, the heralds shouted the names of the winners. One by one, the third and then the second place winners mounted small open carriages to travel the circuit of the arena, and be pelted by paper, flowers, and a few coins from their disappointed supporters.

The Emperor said, "What do you say to this plan, Jamil?"

"As the Emperor wills," I said. My voice sounded as if it came from the depth of a cavern.

Abad gestured toward a curtained alcove, where I could retire to shift selves from Watcher to Executioner. Behind the curtains, a lounging chair and an ewer of cool water lay ready, should one or another of the noble visitors be taken ill, or be overcome by the heat. I sat on the edge of this chair and listened indifferently to the sounds coming from the arena. Had Abad been privy to my every move in the last seven days, he could not have more effectively planned my downfall. But no, this terrible turn of events seemed to be just a continuation of my appallingly bad luck.

This time, I could not even imagine how I would extricate myself and Adline out of this disaster. I could use an unpoisoned dart on her, but how could I guarantee that my strong willed sister would promptly lie down and play dead? Even if she did so, it would not take long for the artifice to be discovered. I could use the nonlethal poison, and render her unconscious, but I feared that taking this option would only delay her inevitable death, rather than preventing it. Even if I were able to extricate her from the custody of the Emperor's Guard, I could not easily spirit an unconscious woman out of the city, and I knew of nowhere nearby where I could hide her until she awakened. Still, of my few options this seemed to offer the most hope, so I loaded my blowpipe accordingly and left the alcove.

Adline had nearly completed her circuit of the arena. Coins fell like rain in the sunshine; a victor's fortune, enough to live the rest of her life in modest luxury. More than anything else, it was for this shower of coins that the runners in the Emperor's Concourse endured the grueling contest. The arena workers would spend the rest of the afternoon picking up the wealth, under the watchful gaze of the Champion's manager.

I took a position near the Emperor's throne, out of direct view from the watchers below. The other nobles in the box glanced at me from the corners of their eyes, pretending mild interest. Like the Emperor, they preferred not to witness under such close quarters the repressive work of their regime. But now that they had quelled their initial shock, the neatness, the sheer genius of Abad's solution appealed to them. How much more appealing would it be, if they could see the Asakeiri face behind my mask and perhaps realize the incredible irony inherent in Abad's choice of assassins.

A herald helped Adline out of the carriage, and preceded her to the Champion's Stairs, where with a fanfare of trumpets the gate was opened. We could see her no longer, but the fanfare measured her progress from landing to landing. A lengthy delay followed, as on the level below the Emperor's box Adline submitted to a thorough search. Then she appeared at last, somber, sweat-stained, seeking with strange and unexpected hunger her first sight of the Emperor. For a member of a rebellious and hard-headed clan, she knelt willingly enough, and at such a respectful distance from the Emperor's throne that Abad turned to me with an accusing scowl. "Since when do assassins keep such a distance from their target?" he seemed to ask.

I focused my attention on Adline. What would she do? The Emperor bid her approach to receive her prize, but she bowed her head in exaggerated humility and would not draw closer to the throne. She spoke carefully and awkwardly, a rehearsed speech in a language she did not know. "Lord Emperor, for over thirty years the Asakeiri people have lived like exiles in the heart of this land Callia, the back of the dragon. There has been war between my people and yours, and we have not been able to visit other lands, or bring home husbands or wives from other tribes. Therefore the Asakeiri named me their messenger, to speak to you of their desires. The people of the high mountains are a peaceful people. Therefore, we ask you to accept the gift of Asakeiri land and people. We will become willing subjects of the Empire.''

She took the straw dragon from around her neck, and held it out to me. "Sister, give this to the Emperor," she said in the Asakeiri tongue.

How she recognized me in my robe and mask I cannot guess. I took the straw dragon in my left hand— light as a feather it was, and yet it lay in my hand with an inexplicable weightiness. Puzzled, I stepped forward to give the harmless thing to the Emperor who examined it dubiously.

Once again speaking in Trade, Adline continued, "The dragon, to the Asakeiri people, is the symbol of rank and responsibility. Therefore we ask you to wear this dragon around your neck, as evidence of your willingness to rule the people fairly and thoughtfully. So long as you wear the dragon, the Asakeiri people will willingly obey your edicts, allow your servants to enter our lands, and pay tribute. This is the decision of the Asakeiri people.''

As suspicious and startled as a child who expected to be punished and was instead given a present, the Emperor cleared his throat several times before speaking. "Well, Adline Asakeiri, we are certainly pleased by this unexpected message from the Asakeiri people.'' He looked doubtfully down at the little toy made of straw, as if he thought it might come to life and bite him. A faint breeze made it rock slightly in the palm of his hand. "Gladly we accept this dragon," he finally said.

Without speaking, Adline gazed solemnly and expectantly up at the Emperor's face. The contrast between their faces was arresting: hers was narrow, ascetic, and suffused with extraordinary, almost predatory intensity. His was puffy with self-indulgence, gray with too little exposure to the sun, and his intelligent, piercing gaze had long since begun to be dulled by dissolution. With a polite nod, the Emperor took the dragon and placed the ribbon around his thick neck.

I started forward a step, with an unvoiced cry in my throat. But I checked myself, and only watched, helpless and oddly exalted, as the little straw figure settled incongruously among the jewels and embroidery which crusted the Emperor's chest. The Dragon. The Emperor had hung the Dragon Callia around his own neck. Never again would the Asakeiri people sing their desperate lullaby. They had given the Dragon to the Emperor. Let him sing the dragon to sleep, if he could.

Aman Abad, his eye no less sharp than mine, leaned anxiously forward. Had the Emperor's face paled, and his breathing quickened? Abad gestured frantically at me, as the Emperor rose rather more heavily to his feet than usual, and offered Adline his hand. Abad did not understand what had happened, but he knew he did not like it, not at all. Was it out of vengeance that he still wanted me to kill Adline, or did he simply not yet realize that to kill her would change nothing?

The Emperor stood with Adline by his side, and in the sight of everyone in the arena hung the Champion's Ribbon around her neck. She knelt prettily and kissed his hand, then waved triumphantly to the cheering throng. But she took her leave early, long before the crescendo of acclaim had begun to fade, and started down the flight of stairs. This time, I acknowledged Abad's signals with a nod, and turned to follow her.

The marble stairway echoed the faint whisper of my footstep, but I could not hear hers over the continued raucous acclaim from the arena. At the first turn of the stairs, I found her waiting for me, with her back against the wall for support. I paused there, breathing heavily, and pushed back my hood and removed my mask. I would not be needing them anymore. "Your death warrant has not been countermanded, and Abad is a vengeful man. You had better put these on."

Without an objection, Adline dressed in my robes. I hung my mirror around her neck, and she fingered it speculatively. "It's heavy."

"It's gotten heavier."

She grinned triumphantly, her eyes bright despite the knee-trembling exhaustion which had overtaken her.

"Our mother is a clever woman. But you—" I shook my head, speechless, and reached out to adjust the mask over Adline's face and pull the hood over her head. "I told Rusalii to wait for you at the north gate. I hope you can walk that far."

She shrugged, seeming too tired to reply.

"How did you know I would help you?" I said.

The mask had hidden her face from me, but I saw pained laughter briefly contort her body. "What kind of fool would expect someone like you to help them?"

"What kind of fool indeed?" I repeated sternly.

"You said you were divided against yourself, and certainly it was true. So I forced you to make a choice."

"But how did you know I would choose you?"

Another contortion. Laughter again, or just a spasm of exhaustion? "I didn't know you would," she said. "I didn't know at all. Even when I saw you standing at the Emperor's side, I thought you might be there to kill me."

"Well, it wasn't your only narrow escape this day. We had better go."

As I followed Adline down the stairs, I instructed her in how to behave like a Separated One. But I need not have worried. The gate guards saw only a silver mirror and a black robe, and no one asked any questions.

The happy, drunken crowd also parted easily to let us pass. With me walking two or three paces behind her, drawing closer from time to time to tell her which turns to take, we briskly outwalked the slow-moving holiday makers. The rest of the city was deserted except for the watchmen left behind to protect the stores against theft. We reached the north gate unmolested.

There, the closed carriage, piled with baggage, waited by the side of the cobbled road. Rusalii paced up and down beside it, lifting her head sharply as an occasional faint sound carried this far across the rooftops of Ashami. An elegant peacock stalked along the top of the wall, looking at her curiously. No city guards were in sight; probably they were all still at the arena.

Just outside the gate, Adline stopped to strip off my robes and give them back to me. I folded them absentmindedly, as Rusalii rushed forward to grasp Adline by the shoulders. "What's this?" she cried, touching the Champion's Ribbon that Adline still wore. "Names of the gods, you not only survived, but you won?"

"Yes." Adline grasped her friend briefly by the arms, and then let go of her.

"Well, you are somber for a champion," said Rusalii, clearly puzzled.

"Much more has happened today than that! Did you truly think that I would have taken this perilous journey just to win a race?"

"It's a perilous journey for all who compete."

Adline smiled then, briefly and ironically. Perhaps there had indeed been a time that the joy of running and the challenge of competition had been all she cared for. But that had been a long time ago. She turned to me. "It will be a long journey home. Best get started."

"She's coming with us?" cried Rusalii, in outright astonishment.

Adline looked at me, waiting. I glanced down at the black robe in my hands, wondering if I should just drop it on the ground. But no—it might still be useful, for a little while longer. "Yes, I am coming with you," I said, and stepped forward, with my robe, mask, and mirror under my arm.

* * *

The memory of the days I traveled with them I will hold close in my heart for the rest of my life. Rusalii and I took turns at the reins, but often Adline, unwilling to end the conversation we had been having in the carriage, would climb up to sit beside me. Through sunshine and rainfall, past jungle and village, over pie and tea in a roadside eating house, we talked. Through hearing her life story, I was able to reclaim part of my own. I began to wonder if I might indeed be able to go home, take a husband or a lover, get some goats and start my own herd, and learn to live as my people live.

But at night I lay awake studying the stars, and asking myself a strange question. I had been born to be a wisewoman—but a wisewoman of which tribe?

On the fourth day of the journey, with the Vine in sight, I kissed my sister on her cheek and grasped Rusalii's hand, then I left them. Alone and on foot, I returned to Ashami.

We all have our own kind of madness. Ata'al, having never ceased to grieve the loss of her first wise daughter, sent her second on an impossible quest. That is one kind of madness. Adline traded her heart for the heart of an eagle, and won a race in which the future of Callia was at stake. This, too, is a kind of madness. I, having broken through the barriers that made me a prisoner within my own skin, turned my back on the journey home, and instead walked back to my tribe of lost children, and certain execution. Clearly, I was mad, too. But the third kind of madness, the strangest kind of all, was the madness of the Emperor. His personal servant met me at the north gate of Ashami and conducted me to the palace's private meditation garden, where the Emperor himself begged me to accept a commission as the new Commander of the Separated Ones. Aman Abad had suddenly decided to retire.

The straw dragon still hung around the Emperor's neck, but it looked less incongruous now that he had taken to dressing as plainly as an ascetic monk. "There will be changes," I warned him.

He would not let me kneel as he pinned a jeweled sun to the road-grimy cloth of my tunic. "I would hope so," he said.

It does not surprise me to discover that the weight which hangs from the Emperor's neck also hangs from my own. I went directly to the Children's Compound to oversee the immediate release of its prisoners. That was the easiest decision; the others which now face me are not so simple. Is it reasonable to believe that half a hundred hardened killers can be reclaimed and returned to their people? Is it sensible to envision a day that the Separated Ones are separated no longer? Am I insane to think I can show the way when I myself am stumbling in the darkness?

Yes. Yes. And yes. No group in known history has changed the world as effectively and cleverly as the Order of Separated Ones. We can change it back again.

Sleep, dragon. Sleep.

DAW

Laurie J. Marks

THE CHILDREN OF TRIAD

☐ **DELAN THE MISLAID: Book 1**   UE2325—$3.95

A misfit among a people not its own, Delan willingly goes away with the Walker Teksan to the Lowlands. But there, the Walker turns out to be a cruel master, a sorcerer who practices dark magic to keep Delan his slave—and who has diabolical plans to enslave Delan's people, the winged Aeyrie. And unless Delan can free itself from Teksan's spell, it may become the key to the ruin of its entire race.

☐ **THE MOONBANE MAGE: Book 2**   UE2415—$3.95

Here is the story of Delan's child Laril, heir to the leadership of the winged Aeyrie race, but exiled because of an illegal duel. Falling under the power of an evil Mage, Laril must tap reserves both personal and magical to save the Aeyrie people from the Mage's deadly plans for conquest—plans which if successful, would set race against race in a devastating war of destruction.

☐ **ARA'S FIELD: Book 3**   UE2479—$4.50

For many years, members of the Community of Triad have been striving to make it possible for the four primary species of their world to coexist. Now, the sudden, ugly murders of many high-ranked Walker and Aeyrie officials have shattered all hope of peace. Caught in the chaos of imminent war, the children of Triad must discover who is playing this deadly game of death and somehow force them to stop—before their world erupts in a genocidal war of species against species.

DAW

New Dimensions in Fantasy

Sean Russell

☐ **THE INITIATE BROTHER (Book 1)**   UE2466—$4.99
In this powerful debut novel rich with the magic and majesty of
the ancient Orient, one of the most influential lords of the Great
Houses is marked for destruction by the new Emperor and
must use every weapon at his command to survive—including
a young Botahist monk gifted with powers not seen in the world
for nearly a thousand years.

☐ **GATHERER OF CLOUDS (Book 2)**   UE2536—$5.50
Initiate Brother Shuyun, spiritual adviser to Lord Shonto, re-
ceives a shocking message: the massive army of the Golden
Khan is poised at the border, and Lord Shonto is caught
between it and his own hostile Emperor's Imperial Army. Yet
even as this trap closes, Brother Shuyun faces another crisis.
For in the same scroll that warned of the invasion was a sacred
Udumbara blossom—a sign his order has awaited for a mil-
lennium. . . .

Elizabeth Forrest

☐ **PHOENIX FIRE**   UE2515—$4.99
As the legendary Phoenix awoke, so, too, did an ancient Chi-
nese demon—and Los Angeles was destined to become the
final battleground in their millennia-old war. Now, the very earth
begins to dance as these two creatures of legend fight to break
free. And as earthquake and fire start to take their toll on the
mortal world, four desperate people begin to suspect the terror
that is about to engulf mankind.
